The Ghosts of Pemberley

A Paranormal Pride & Prejudice Variation

Catherine Bilson

SHENANIGANS PRESS

Contents

Chapter One

Elizabeth Bennet woke for the last time in the bed she had slept in since childhood and lay still, listening. The crack in the plaster above the wardrobe had been there since she was nine. The faded roses on the wallpaper had not changed since long before that. Everything was exactly as it had always been, except that after today, none of it would be hers.

From the corridor came the muffled sounds of a household in controlled upheaval. Mrs Hill's voice issued instructions to the maids. Somewhere below, her mother's higher register rose in what was either delight or despair; with Mrs Bennet, the two were often indistinguishable.

The clatter of crockery suggested that breakfast was being laid with considerably more fuss than a Tuesday in late September would ordinarily warrant.

Elizabeth closed her eyes. One more breath of this air, which smelled of dried lavender and old linen and the faintest trace of woodsmoke from the chimneys below. Then she sat up, pushed back the covers, and planted her feet on the cold floorboards.

"You might have put your slippers on first," said Aunt Irene, from the chair by the fireplace. "You will catch your death, and then what a waste of a wedding this will be."

Elizabeth did not startle. She had not startled at the unexpected dead since she was four years old, when the ghost of her grandfather's spaniel had walked through the nursery wall and she had shrieked so loudly that Jane had fallen out of bed. One learnt, over the years, to moderate one's reactions.

"I shall not catch my death from cold feet, Aunt Irene," Elizabeth replied, reaching for her dressing gown. "And even if I did, I trust you would inform me promptly of the fact."

Aunt Irene sniffed. She was, in truth, a great-great-great aunt, or possibly one more great than that; Elizabeth had long since given up counting and settled on the simpler address. She had been sniffing in genteel disapproval for the better part of a hundred years after her death, and had, if anything, grown more proficient at it. She was a spare, upright figure in the chair, a Bennet born and bred. She had never married, never left Longbourn, and was thoroughly disinclined to leave it now merely because she happened to be deceased. Her gown was the style of the previous century, her cap pinned rigidly in place, and her expression that of a woman who had seen every folly the Bennet family had to offer and was not yet finished tallying them.

"You are remarkably composed," Irene observed, "for a girl about to leave everything she has ever known."

"I am remarkably composed," Elizabeth corrected gently, "for a woman about to marry the man she loves. There is a difference."

"Hmph." Irene folded her translucent hands in her lap. "Love. Your grandfather said the same thing about your grandmother, and she rearranged all the furniture within a fortnight of the wedding. Nearly gave me an apoplexy. That escritoire had been in the same position since Queen Anne's time."

"You had already been dead for twenty years when Grandmama rearranged the furniture."

"That does not mean I did not have feelings about it."

Elizabeth smiled, tender and affectionate. She was going to miss Great-Aunt Irene almost as much as any of her living family. She crossed the room and stood before Irene's chair, looking down at the sharp, familiar face that no one else in this house could see.

"I need you to look after them," Elizabeth said quietly. "Papa especially. He will pretend he does not miss me, and everyone will believe him, because he is very good at pretending. But you will know."

Irene's expression shifted, a softening so slight she would have denied it furiously if accused. "I have looked after this family since before your grandfather was born, Elizabeth. I do not require instruction."

"I know. But I require the comfort of giving it."

A pause. Then Irene inclined her head, the gesture carrying more dignity than many a living woman could manage with a full curtsey. "Very well. I shall keep watch. Your father will not want for company, whether he knows it or not." She hesitated, then added, her tartness not quite concealing her feeling: "And I shall keep an eye on that Collins creature when he comes sniffing about. We do not want that inheriting any sooner than strictly necessary."

Elizabeth laughed despite herself. "No, indeed. Though I think Papa is likely to outlive us all from sheer contrariness."

"He does bear a strong resemblance to your grandfather in that respect." Irene settled back in her chair, taking up her permanent post. "Now go and dress, child. You have a wedding to attend, and I will not have it said that a Bennet bride was late to her own nuptials."

The morning passed in a blur of muslin, ribbons, and her mother's voice, which seemed to fill every room of the house simultaneously, as though Mrs Bennet had somehow acquired the ability to be in five places at once through the sheer force of maternal agitation.

"The lace, Hill; no, not that lace, the good lace. Oh, where has Mary put the prayer books? Mary! Mary! And for heaven's sake, somebody find Kitty, she was supposed to be pressing the ribbons."

Elizabeth stood in her mother's dressing room while Sarah, their most capable maid, arranged her hair, her steady hands untroubled by the ambient chaos of the Bennet household.

"There," Sarah said, setting the final pin. "You look beautiful, miss. Ma'am, I should say."

"Not yet," Elizabeth said, smiling at the thought. "Not for another two hours, at least."

In the reflection, she could see her mother hovering in the doorway, one hand pressed to her bosom and the other clutching a handkerchief that had already seen considerable use that morning. Mrs Bennet's eyes were bright, too bright, and her chin had the particular wobble that preceded either a great outpouring of emotion or an extensive commentary on the inadequacy of the neighbours' curtains.

"Oh, Lizzy," her mother said, and her voice cracked on the name. Sarah made a tactful and swift departure, leaving mother and daughter alone.

Elizabeth turned. She had braced herself for raptures about lace, carriages, and ten thousand a year, and was therefore entirely unprepared for the look on her mother's face, which was not triumph but fear.

"Mama?"

"You will be careful," Mrs Bennet whispered, and Elizabeth understood at once that they were not speaking about lace.

She crossed the room and took her mother's hands. They were trembling. Mrs Bennet had known about Elizabeth's gift since Elizabeth was five years old and had greeted a woman at the market who had been dead for a fortnight. The screaming, Mrs Bennet's, had lasted the better part of an afternoon. In the years since, her mother had dealt with the knowledge in the only way she knew how: by refusing to discuss it, by pretending it did not exist, by building a wall of noise, nerves, and relentless chatter so high and so thick that the terrifying truth about her second daughter could not possibly be seen over it.

It had not been courage, but it had been, in its own frantic, fluttering way, a kind of love.

"I will be careful, Mama," Elizabeth said steadily. "I always am."

Mrs Bennet nodded, rapid and jerky, and then pulled her hands free to dab at her eyes. "Well! That is settled, then. Now, the flowers, Hill, I expressly said white roses, not; oh, never mind, they will do, they will do." And she was gone, her voice trailing behind her, already onto another grievance, haranguing someone about the arrangement of the carriages.

Elizabeth let out a breath. In the mirror, she saw herself: dark hair pinned and curled, the new cream silk gown her mother had insisted on with Brussels lace at the collar and cuffs, pearl earrings her mother had loaned her. Great-Aunt Irene said they had been in the Bennet family since before even her time. Her own clear, watchful eyes looked back at her.

She was leaving Longbourn. She was leaving her parents and the ghosts who had been her companions, part of her extended family, since childhood. She was going to a house she had visited only briefly, to a life she could barely imagine, with a man she loved and had not told the truth.

The thought sat in her chest like a stone, familiar and heavy. She had carried it through the engagement, through the preparations, through every tender moment with Darcy when the words had risen to her lips and she had swallowed them back down. I see dead people. I have always seen them. They are as real to me as you are, and I have never told a living soul outside my family. Even Charlotte, the closest friend I have ever had, does not know.

Not today. Today was for joy, for the beginning of things. She would tell him. She would. Just not today.

Her father appeared in the doorway, his expression carefully arranged into mild amusement, as though escorting a daughter to her wedding were a task of no more consequence than selecting a book from the library shelf.

"Well, Lizzy," he said. "Are you ready to make a very proud man even more insufferably pleased with himself?"

"Papa." She took his arm, and felt the faintest tremor in it. "Shall we?"

Mr Bennet patted her hand where it rested on his sleeve. "We shall." He paused for a beat. "Though I reserve the right to claim you back if he proves unsatisfactory. I have it on good authority that Longbourn cannot function without at least one sensible person in residence, and your mother has already informed me that I do not qualify."

Elizabeth laughed, and the sound was bright enough almost to dislodge the stone in her chest. Almost.

The church at Longbourn was small, plain, and old, its stone walls steeped in centuries of prayer, gossip, and the slight feeling of damp that afflicted every building in Hertfordshire between September and May. The Bennets had been christened, married, and buried here for as long as anyone could remember, and a good deal longer than that, as Elizabeth well knew.

She knew because they had told her.

The resident church ghosts were among her oldest acquaintances. Old Reverend Hackett, who had presided over the parish in the reign of King George the Second and still considered the current incumbent a dangerous radical for having once preached a sermon on charity. Mrs Turnbull, a farmer's wife who had died in the pew during a particularly tedious Easter sermon in 1742 and had simply never got up. Young Thomas Briggs, dead at fourteen of a fever, who had been sweet on Elizabeth since she was twelve and still blushed, or performed whatever ghostly equivalent of blushing was available to him, whenever she walked in.

They were all present this morning. None of them could leave, of course, but Elizabeth knew they would not have missed her wedding even if they could have been elsewhere. Like the ghosts of Longbourn, they loved her, and they had been talking about little else for weeks.

Elizabeth entered the church on her father's arm, Jane on his other side, and immediately felt the familiar press of spectral attention; a prickling along her skin, a subtle shift in the air, as though the room held more people than the eye could count. Which, of course, it did, though only she could see them.

Jane glanced across at her, serene and radiant in a way that only Jane could manage, and squeezed their father's arm. Mr Bennet, escorting two daughters at once, looked as though he could not decide whether to be proud or upset, that he was losing the only two daughters with whom he considered he could have sensible conversation.

The living congregation was impressive enough. The pews were full: the Lucases, the Phillipses, the Longs, the Gouldings, the Hursts, and many other locals Elizabeth had known her whole life, all beaming proudly at her. Lady Matlock sat in the front pew beside Lord Matlock, her posture flawless, her expression gracious, her hat architectural. Elizabeth had been nervous about meeting them, but the earl and countess had proved so warm, so genuinely kind, that her anxiety had melted within a quarter of an hour. Georgiana was with them, her expression one of pure delight.

Caroline Bingley sat with the Hursts in the row behind; her gown was of such aggressive elegance that it seemed designed less to celebrate the occasion than to register a formal protest against it. Her smile was fixed, brittle, and did not reach her eyes. Kitty and Mary sat together with Mrs Bennet, Kitty's eyes drifting rather more often than was strictly necessary toward Colonel Fitzwilliam, handsome in his red coat.

At the altar, two grooms waited. Bingley was beaming so broadly that he looked in danger of levitating from sheer happiness, bouncing slightly on his heels as though the effort of standing still were almost more than his good nature could bear.

And there was Darcy.

Elizabeth's breath caught. Not dramatically, not visibly, but in the small, private way that had become habitual whenever she saw him unexpectedly. He stood straight, his dark coat immaculate, his hands clasped behind his back. He was watching the door, and the look on his face was so openly, unguardedly hopeful that Elizabeth felt her heart turn over. He looked like a man who was not entirely certain this was really happening, and was bracing himself against the possibility that it might not.

Then he saw her, and his whole face changed.

She had seen Darcy smile before; rare, swift smiles that transformed his features and vanished before anyone could properly appreciate them. But this was something else. This was joy, unmasked and undefended, directed entirely at her. For a moment Elizabeth forgot about ghosts, secrets, the stone in her chest, and simply walked toward him.

"Took your time," murmured Old Reverend Hackett from his customary position near the baptismal font. "The tall one's been sweating like a sinner at Judgement Day. The ginger one's been grinning like a fool since he arrived."

Elizabeth pressed her lips together hard.

"Ooh, but he is handsome," sighed Mrs Turnbull, drifting closer for a better look at Darcy. "Those shoulders! That jawline! I had a cousin who had a jawline like that, though he was considerably shorter and had a terrible squint."

Elizabeth fixed her gaze on Darcy's cravat and thought desperately about arithmetic.

"Ten thousand a year," young Thomas said mournfully from somewhere near the organ. "I haven't got ten shillings."

"You haven't got a pulse, Thomas," Reverend Hackett pointed out. "Priorities, boy."

Elizabeth bit the inside of her cheek so hard she tasted copper. Her father glanced down at her, and she arranged her features into what she hoped was bridal serenity rather than the suppressed hysteria of a woman receiving unsolicited commentary from three dead parishioners during her own wedding ceremony.

Mr Bennet placed Jane's hand in Bingley's first, and Bingley received it as though he had been handed a holy relic, his face shining. Then her father turned to Elizabeth, and placed her hand in Darcy's. His fingers closed around hers, warm and steady, and he squeezed once; a private communication that said more than any words the vicar was about to pronounce.

"Dearly beloved," the vicar began, and Elizabeth gave herself over to the ancient words, to the cool stone, to the warmth of the hand holding hers.

Behind her, the ghosts settled. They were quiet now, even Mrs Turnbull, even Thomas, watching as people do who understand, perhaps better than most, that some moments are sacred. They had watched Elizabeth grow from a startled child who could see them into the woman standing here today, and whatever she was walking toward, they would not follow. Longbourn's dead belonged to Longbourn.

The vows were spoken twice over. Jane's voice was soft and sure. Bingley's cracked on "I will"; he laughed at himself, half the congregation laughed with him, and even Darcy's mouth twitched. Elizabeth heard her own voice, steady and clear, making promises she meant entirely, all except one that snagged, just slightly, in her throat. Forsaking all others. She had not forsaken the dead. She had never been able to, and she did not know if that counted. It was not the sort of question one could put to a vicar without inviting an uncomfortable conversation.

Darcy's voice was low, sure, and carried a note of wonder that he did not seem to know was audible. When he said "I will," there was something in it that went beyond the words; not rehearsed, not composed, but raw and grateful and entirely his.

The ring slid onto her finger. Cool metal, a perfect fit. His thumb brushed over her knuckle as he settled it, and warmth flooded up her arm and into her chest, displacing, for a moment at least, the weight she carried there.

"Those whom God hath joined together, let no man put asunder."

From the congregation, Mrs Bennet produced a sob of such magnificent volume that it startled a pigeon from the rafters. Lady Matlock, to her eternal credit, did not flinch. Caroline Bingley's smile had calcified into something that could have been chipped off her face with a chisel. Georgiana Darcy was crying, though Elizabeth was sure they were tears of happiness; Colonel Fitzwilliam put his arm about her shoulders and gave her his handkerchief.

Two couples, newly wed, turned to face the congregation. Jane was crying too, beautifully as only Jane could, and Bingley was looking at her as though the sun rose and set in her face. Elizabeth caught Darcy's eye and found him watching her, not the congregation; watching her as though he intended to memorise this moment down to its smallest particular.

Elizabeth Darcy, the name strange and new, stepped out of the church into the pale September sunshine, her husband's arm beneath her hand, and did not look back. She did not need to. She could feel them watching; Reverend Hackett standing straight, Mrs Turnbull dabbing at eyes that could not actually produce tears, Thomas raising his hand in a shy, hopeless wave.

And in the house beyond the lane, Aunt Irene sat in her chair by the cold fireplace, watching over a family that could not see her, and would not leave her post until the walls of Longbourn themselves came down.

Chapter Two

THE WEDDING BREAKFAST AT Netherfield was a grander affair than Elizabeth had expected, though she supposed she ought to have anticipated it. Bingley had thrown himself into the preparations as enthusiastically as he did everything, thoroughly encouraged by Mrs Bennet. The result was a dining room transformed: hothouse flowers in towering arrangements, silver, crystal and china which would not have disgraced a palace, enough food to sustain a small army through a siege.

Elizabeth sat beside Darcy at the head of the table, acutely aware of the ring on her finger and the strange new weight of her married name every time someone used it.

Mrs Darcy. She caught Jane's eye across the table and saw her own bewildered happiness reflected back. Jane, seated beside Bingley, looked as though she had been gently placed inside a dream and was in no particular hurry to wake from it. Bingley kept touching her hand as though to reassure himself she was really there, and Jane kept letting him.

"You are very quiet," Darcy murmured, leaning toward her under cover of the general conversation.

"I am absorbing," Elizabeth replied. "There is a great deal to absorb."

"Is it too much?"

She looked at him. He was watching her the way he had at the altar, as though she was the only person in the room. Something in her chest, the familiar stone, shifted and settled. "No," she said. "It is exactly enough."

His mouth curved; not the guarded half-smile she had grown accustomed to, but something softer. He lifted his glass to her, slightly, and she lifted hers in return.

From the far end of the table, Caroline Bingley's voice rose above the chatter, bright and brittle as spun glass. "Such a charming little ceremony! So quaint. One does admire the simplicity of a country church, does one not, Louisa?"

Mrs Hurst murmured something vaguely affirmative.

"I do hope," Caroline continued, her gaze skating toward Elizabeth, "that you will not find the transition to grander surroundings too overwhelming, Mrs Darcy. Pemberley is, after all, quite a different prospect from Hertfordshire."

"I am sure I shall manage," Elizabeth said pleasantly. "Though I thank you for your concern, Miss Bingley. It must be a great comfort to Mr Bingley, having a sister so attentive to the domestic anxieties of others."

Caroline's smile thinned. Lady Matlock, from further down the table, caught Elizabeth's eye and gave her a look of undisguised approval. Elizabeth smiled into her wineglass.

The breakfast stretched on through toasts, speeches, and Mrs Bennet's increasingly tearful predictions about grandchildren. Mr Bennet endured it all from behind his wine glass, offering the occasional dry remark that Elizabeth was pleased to note seemed to find an appreciative audience in Lord Matlock. Colonel Fitzwilliam told a story about Darcy as a boy that made Georgiana giggle and Darcy look as though he wished the floor would open beneath his chair. Kitty laughed so hard she spilled her lemonade, and Mary said something earnest about the sanctity of marriage that everyone politely pretended to find interesting.

It was, Elizabeth thought, a good wedding breakfast. She looked around, absorbing it all carefully, the way one presses a flower between the pages of a book, to be taken out and looked at later when one was in need of something lovely as a distraction.

The house grew quiet by degrees. The guests departed in a stream of carriages and well-wishes; the Bennets were among the last to leave, Mrs Bennet alternating between sobs and raptures until Mr Bennet steered her firmly toward the door. Mary shook her hand solemnly. Her father kissed her forehead and did not trust himself to speak.

Jane and Bingley had vanished upstairs some time ago. Caroline had retired to her room, claiming a headache brought on by the champagne; Elizabeth suspected the headache owed more to the sight of her brother married to a Bennet than to anything in a bottle. The Matlocks and Colonel Fitzwilliam had discreetly retired, and Georgiana had disappeared with Kitty, who would accompany them to Pemberley on the morrow. Kitty and Georgiana appeared to be becoming fast friends already, to Elizabeth's relief.

Elizabeth stood in the corridor outside the room she would share with Darcy tonight, their first night as husband and wife, and tried to steady the rapid beating of her heart. He was inside, she knew, waiting for her. She should go in. She wanted to go in.

But first, she had a promise to keep.

She slipped down the back stairs, shoes in hand. A lifetime of navigating around the unseen had taught her how to move through dark corridors without a sound. The house was different at night; the daytime bustle stripped away to reveal its bones. Old floorboards. Cold stone. The particular hush of a building that had stood for two hundred years and carried the memory of them in every wall.

The library was where they gathered. It had been their favourite room since Elizabeth's first visit, when she had come to nurse Jane through her fever and had found, to her unsurprised resignation, that Netherfield came with ghosts of its own. Most of them were only shades, wisps barely seen even by her, but some of them were more permanent. Solid enough to make out their features, and retaining enough personality and will to hold a conversation with her.

There were four of them. Sir Harold Pembury, a portly Jacobean gentleman who had built the original house and considered all subsequent alterations a personal affront. His wife, Lady Cecily, who disagreed with him about everything on principle and had been doing so for two hundred years with no sign of tiring. Old Margaret, a housekeeper from the last century who kept trying to dust surfaces she could no longer touch. And a young footman called Daniel who had died of consumption in the servants' quarters just a decade past and had the gentle, slightly bewildered air of someone who kept forgetting he was dead.

They were waiting for her. Sir Harold stood by the fire, Lady Cecily sat in her accustomed chair, Old Margaret hovered near the bookshelves, and Daniel perched on the window seat, his thin face brightening as Elizabeth came in.

"There she is," Sir Harold declared. "The bride. Allow me to offer my congratulations, madam, though I confess I had hoped you might settle here permanently. Your presence has been most enlivening."

"You are too kind, Sir Harold," Elizabeth said, settling into the chair opposite Lady Cecily. "But I fear Netherfield must do without me. I have come to say goodbye."

"Goodbye!" Old Margaret's hand flew to her chest. "Oh, but you will visit, surely? Because your sister is here?"

"Of course I shall visit. But I wanted to speak to you all before I left, because Jane will be mistress of this house, and Jane cannot see you, and I need you to promise me something."

Four spectral faces regarded her solemnly.

"You must look after her," Elizabeth said. "She is the best person I know, and she will take care of this house and everyone in it, living or otherwise. She knows you are here, even if she cannot see you. In return, I need you to behave."

She let her gaze rest meaningfully on Sir Harold. "That means no slamming doors when you disapprove of the dinner menu."

Sir Harold looked affronted. "That was once."

"It was ten times in a single night, and Cook nearly gave notice."

"The woman served boiled mutton on a Thursday. I have standards."

"And I need you to leave the other residents alone," Elizabeth continued firmly. "All of them. Even the ones who deserve otherwise."

A delicate silence fell. Lady Cecily studied her fingernails, or the memory of them.

"You are referring," she said, "to Miss Bingley."

"I am referring to Miss Bingley."

The memory was still vivid. The Netherfield ball, all those months ago, when Elizabeth had been trying to enjoy the evening and manage a building full of agitated ghosts simultaneously. Caroline had been holding court near the fireplace, making pointed remarks about the Bennet family's lack of connections, and Sir Harold had grown so incensed on Elizabeth's behalf that he had attempted to knock Caroline's wine glass out of her hand. He could not, of course, physically touch it, but the concentrated force of spectral outrage had created a draught strong enough to make the candles flicker and Caroline's carefully arranged curls come undone on one side.

That had been merely the opening salvo. Lady Cecily, not to be outdone by her husband in anything, had proceeded to whisper directly into Caroline's ear every time the woman paused for breath, which had the effect of making Caroline twitch, look over her shoulder, and eventually complain loudly that there was a draught in the ballroom, which had led Bingley to order the windows checked and the fire stoked, which had led to the room becoming unbearably hot, which had led to Mrs Bennet fanning herself so vigorously she knocked Mrs Long's turban askew.

Elizabeth had spent the better part of the evening conducting a whispered negotiation with four increasingly creative ghosts while attempting to dance with Mr Collins, who was oblivious, and Mr Darcy, who was not. She still did not know how she had managed to hold a civil conversation with Mr Darcy while Sir Harold stood directly behind him making disparaging remarks about the stiffness of his dancing.

"Miss Bingley will reside here much of the time," Elizabeth said now. "She is Mr Bingley's sister, and Jane will wish to keep peace in the family. You will leave her alone."

"She is a thoroughly disagreeable woman," Sir Harold pronounced.

"She is a woman who has been forced to accept her brother marrying into a family she considers beneath her, and she is unhappy," Elizabeth corrected. "Which does not excuse her behaviour, but should temper our response to it. Besides, if you haunt Caroline Bingley, she will make Jane's life difficult, and I will not have that."

The argument was unanswerable, and they knew it. Jane was the deciding factor. Jane, who had sat by the fire in this very room reading aloud from novels she knew Elizabeth was not listening to, because she understood that Elizabeth needed the sound of her voice as an anchor while she tended to business she could not explain. Jane, who had never once asked Elizabeth to justify what she could not see. The Netherfield ghosts might not be able to communicate with Jane as they could Elizabeth, but they like every other soul who came into Jane's presence, had recognised her innate goodness. Elizabeth was fairly sure they were already devoted to her.

"Very well," Lady Cecily said, her tone suggesting she was making a considerable personal sacrifice. "For Mrs Bingley's sake, we shall exercise restraint."

"We shall be models of propriety," Sir Harold agreed, rather less convincingly.

"Thank you." Elizabeth stood, and looked at them, this odd little household of the dead. "Take care of her. She is my best beloved, and I am trusting you with her."

Old Margaret was dabbing at her eyes. Daniel raised his hand in a half-wave, his young face solemn. Sir Harold bowed; Lady Cecily inclined her head.

Elizabeth left the library and climbed the stairs toward the room where her husband waited, carrying with her the quiet weight of another farewell.

Jane came to Elizabeth's room the next morning, after Darcy had gone down but before most of the household had properly stirred. She knocked softly and let herself in; Elizabeth, who had been sitting at the dressing table pretending to brush her hair while actually staring at the ring on her finger, trying to believe it was real, turned and felt something inside her loosen at the sight of her sister's face.

They did not need to speak. They had never needed to speak, not really; not about the things that mattered most. Jane sat on the edge of the bed and Elizabeth sat beside her, and they held hands. For a few minutes they simply sat and breathed together, two sisters on the edge of their separate futures.

"You look well," Jane said at last, her voice soft and warm, carrying just the faintest undertone of a question. Elizabeth understood what she was really asking.

"I am well," she said honestly. "He is everything I hoped."

Jane's smile bloomed, slow and luminous. "I am glad. So very glad."

"And you? Bingley?"

"He is..." Jane paused, searching for the word, and then laughed, a quiet, wondering sound. "He is exactly himself. I do not know why that surprises me, but it does. He is exactly who I thought he was, and somehow that is the most astonishing thing of all."

Elizabeth squeezed her hand. Outside, a bird sang; the September morning was clear and still, and through the window she could see the grounds of Netherfield spreading out in their gentle, rolling green. In an hour, or less, she would be in a carriage heading north. Leaving Jane behind.

"You will write to me," Jane said. It was not a question.

"Every week. Twice, probably."

"And you will tell me the truth? Not just the pretty version?"

Elizabeth looked at her. Jane's blue eyes were steady. She knew the shape of Elizabeth's fears. Pemberley was old, vast, steeped in centuries of Darcy history. If ever a house in England was going to test Elizabeth's particular burden, it would be that one.

"Pemberley will have them," Jane said gently, when Elizabeth did not answer. "You know it will."

"I know."

"And you will be managing an entirely new household of them, with no one who knows. Kitty will be there, which means you will have at least one confidant, but Lizzy..." Jane hesitated, then pressed on. "You have not told him."

"No."

"You will need to. Not today, perhaps. Not this week. But soon." Jane squeezed her hand. "He loves you. He married you. Whatever you tell him, he will not turn from you."

"You do not know that."

"I know him," Jane said simply. "Not as well as you, but well enough. He is a good man, Lizzy. He deserves the truth, and you deserve to share it."

Elizabeth's throat ached. She had heard this argument before, made it to herself a hundred times, and each time the fear had won. The fear of his face changing. Beneath that, buried deepest, was the certainty that the world she inhabited, the world of the dead, would repulse the man she had come to love with her whole heart. That she would lose him to a truth he would not believe, one she could not take back once she had spoken.

"I will tell him," she said. "When I am ready."

Jane did not press. She never did. She simply held Elizabeth's hand, and they sat together in the quiet morning, the distance that was coming settling between them like a held breath.

"Write to me," Jane said again, when the sounds of the household beginning to stir reached them through the floorboards. "And if you need me, I will come. Through mud and rain if necessary."

Elizabeth laughed, the sound catching in her throat. "I seem to recall that is my trick."

"Then I have learnt from the best." Jane kissed her cheek, stood, and smoothed her skirts. At the door she paused and looked back, and her expression was the same one Elizabeth had seen a thousand times: love, worry, and an absolute refusal to let either defeat her.

"Be brave, Lizzy," she said. "Pemberley cannot possibly be worse than Mr Collins at Christmas dinner."

Elizabeth was still laughing when the door closed behind her sister. The sound carried her all the way to the carriage, where Darcy was waiting, his hand outstretched to help her in. The road to Pemberley stretched out ahead of them, long, unknown, and full of ghosts she had not yet met.

Chapter Three

THE TRAVELLING PARTY ASSEMBLED in the Netherfield courtyard shortly after ten: Elizabeth, Darcy, Georgiana, and Kitty, with two carriages, a wagon of trunks, Darcy's valet, Elizabeth's new lady's maid, and a general air of nervous excitement that seemed to affect everyone except Darcy, who appeared to regard the organisation of a two-day journey northward as a matter requiring the same quiet authority he applied to everything else.

Kitty was trying not to bounce. She had been given a new travelling dress for the occasion, a sensible blue wool that Mrs Bennet had pronounced "not nearly fine enough" and Elizabeth had pronounced "exactly right," and Kitty understood that her world was about to become considerably larger than Meryton, and her excitement was overflowing. Georgiana, beside her in the second carriage, was already chattering about Pemberley's music room and which pieces they might learn together, and Kitty's face was bright with the particular pleasure of being wanted. Mrs Annesley, Georgiana's companion, had already withdrawn a book from her bag and appeared perfectly content to let the girls be.

Elizabeth watched them from the window of the first carriage and was grateful.

"They will be good for each other," Darcy said, following her gaze. He sat opposite her, long legs arranged carefully to avoid crushing her skirts, and there was something almost shy in the way he looked at her this morning, as though the intimacy of the previous night had made him more uncertain of her rather than less. "Georgiana has not had much experience of easy company."

"I think so too," Elizabeth agreed. "Kitty needs someone who will not treat her as Lydia's shadow, and Georgiana needs someone who will drag her away from the pianoforte and make her laugh."

"Georgiana laughs," Darcy protested mildly.

"Georgiana smiles politely and occasionally permits herself a small chuckle. Kitty will have her in stitches by this evening."

"You will ruin her," he said, but he was smiling.

"I will improve her. There is a difference."

His mouth twitched. "You may be right."

"I am frequently right. You will discover this in time."

"Oh, I already know it," he said, and the warmth in his voice made her want to lean across and kiss him, propriety and the carriage window and the coachman's proximity notwithstanding. She settled instead for reaching across and squeezing his hand. He did not let go.

The carriages pulled away. Elizabeth turned for one last look at Netherfield, its red brick warm in the morning sun, and Jane, standing of the steps with Bingley beside her, raising her hand in farewell. Elizabeth raised hers in return, and held it there until the house disappeared behind the trees.

The first day's journey was long but not unpleasant. The roads were dry, the weather held, and the countryside unfolded in gentle waves of green and gold. Darcy read for a time, then set his book aside.

"Tell me about your mother," he said.

Elizabeth blinked. "My mother?"

"I realise I have never asked you anything about her beyond the bare facts. I had instead been rather fixated on noting the errors in her conduct." He shifted slightly, an uncomfortable movement. "That was ungenerous of me."

"It was accurate," Elizabeth said. "My mother is vain and foolish and has driven half the county to distraction. But she is also generous to a fault with those she loves. She simply does not think particularly hard before she speaks."

"And yet you turned out sensible, as did Jane."

She shrugged. "I read. Everything. My father's library is not large, but I have been through it twice. Father encouraged it, not discouraging me from any book that drew my interest."

He listened while she talked, asking questions, drawing her out about the afternoons spent in her father's study, the conversations that had shaped her mind, the loneliness of being clever in a family that did not particularly value it. He absorbed it all without judgement, and by the time the carriage slowed for a posting inn near Northampton, she had begun to believe that she might, eventually, be able to confide in him the much larger secret of her gift.

Every mile northward was a mile closer to a house she knew, with the certainty of long experience, would be full of them. She had glimpsed two on her previous visits, both in the gallery, and had been careful to give no sign of noticing. They had not seemed to see her then; she had caught them unaware, transparent against the gallery windows, discussing the various prospects for Darcy's marriage.

"He will marry that Bingley woman," one of them had said, a man in old-fashioned clothes. Elizabeth had been careful not to look too closely, but she had suspected they were both of the servant class, given the quality and cut of their clothes.

"God help him," the other had replied. She was a middle-aged woman, dressed in the starkly plain clothes of a Puritan, and her tone had been withering. "That creature has the brain of a sparrow and the heart of a vulture. She would bleed him dry and smile while doing it."

Elizabeth had made a small sound of amusement before she could stop herself, but had managed to cover it with a cough when the ghosts turned in her direction. She had slipped away quickly, her heart pounding. She had not thought much about it afterwards, dismissing it as a stray incident, a moment of carelessness. But she would not be a visitor now; she was Mrs Darcy, Pemberley's new mistress. She would live there, eat there, sleep there. She could not avoid an entire household of the dead for long.

The thought produced a sensation rather like standing at the edge of a high cliff and being told to admire the view.

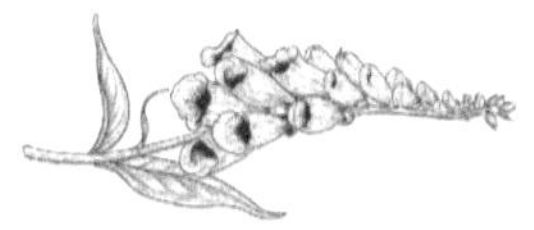

They reached the coaching inn at dusk, a sprawling, half-timbered establishment called the Red Hart that had been serving travellers on the Great North Road since the reign of Henry the Eighth, according to the sign above the door. The courtyard was crowded with coaches in various states of loading and unloading. The air smelled of horses, turned earth, and wood smoke from the kitchen.

Darcy had arranged rooms in advance, the best suite and adjoining chambers for Mrs Annesley, Georgiana and Kitty. The landlord was all bows and deference, recognising quality when he saw it, and the rooms, when they reached them, were tolerably clean and warm, with fresh linen and a fire already burning. Elizabeth could find no fault with any of it.

Except that the inn was, as she had feared, absolutely teeming with ghosts.

Not the settled kind, like Longbourn's or Netherfield's. Coaching inns attracted a different sort altogether: transient spirits, confused and disoriented, people who had died far from home and had no anchor to hold them. They drifted through the corridors, clustered in the taproom, sat in corners looking lost. The sheer density of them hit Elizabeth like a wall of cold water the moment she stepped through the door.

She froze. It was an old reflex, as automatic as breathing; when the dead pressed in, she held herself quiet and let the wave of awareness wash over her before she decided how to respond. There was a woman in Tudor dress standing by the desk, looking anxiously at the door, waiting for someone who would never walk through it. A man in a soldier's coat who kept walking from one end of the corridor to the other as though searching for something. A serving girl no older than sixteen, her face streaked with tears. Dozens of others, fading in and out of Elizabeth's awareness like clouds passing across the sun.

Most of them were harmless. Confused travellers, people who had been caught in the current of a place where hundreds had come and gone for centuries. They did not need her help. They were simply there, and they would go on being there long after she left.

But they could see her. Some of them were already turning toward her, sensing the thing that made her different, the quality she had never been able to name that drew the dead to her like moths to candlelight. The Tudor woman was watching her from the end of the corridor. A child, no more than eight, tugged at her skirt as she passed and said, "Can you see me? Can you really see me?"

Elizabeth's step faltered. Darcy, beside her, glanced down immediately.

"Are you well? You look pale."

"Merely tired from the journey," she said, and smiled, and hated herself for it.

Kitty appeared at her elbow. She slipped her arm through Elizabeth's, an easy, sisterly gesture, and said brightly, "Come, let us find our rooms; I want to show Georgiana the embroidery pattern Mama gave me before we left. Mr Darcy, would you be so kind as to have our trunks sent up? My travelling case in particular; I shall want to freshen up before supper."

It was beautifully done. In the space of a few sentences, Kitty had given Darcy a task that would occupy him for several minutes, and created a reason for Elizabeth to leave the crowded corridor full of spectral strangers. All without a flicker of anything but cheerful, slightly scatterbrained enthusiasm. Upstairs, she was equally deft, urging Georgiana and Mrs Annesley to take a few moments and use the wash-water first; she would just help Elizabeth with her outer clothing.

The moment they were alone, the door closed behind them, Kitty's expression changed.

"How bad?" she asked quietly.

"Dozens," Elizabeth said, sinking onto the bed. "Everywhere. Most of them are just passing through, I think, but there are a few who are stuck, and they can see me, and that child…" She pressed her fingers to her temples. "There is a little girl, Kitty. She cannot be more than eight. She is alone and she is frightened and she does not understand why nobody will speak to her."

Kitty sat beside her and took her hand, the same way Jane would have done. Kitty could not see the dead. She never had. But she had spent a lifetime learning the signs:

the sudden stillness, the eyes tracking something invisible, the way Elizabeth's breathing changed when the spectral world pressed too close, and she was here, now, taking the role Jane normally would. Elizabeth was unutterably grateful not to be alone in this moment.

"Can you help her?" Kitty asked.

"I do not know. I can try. But it will take time, and Darcy will notice if I disappear."

"Leave Darcy to me," Kitty said firmly. "I can ask him any number of questions about Pemberley. Tell me when you need to slip away, and I will manage it."

Elizabeth looked at her younger sister, this girl who had spent years being dismissed as silly, as Lydia's shadow, as the Bennet nobody noticed, and saw instead the person she was becoming away from Lydia's influence: steady, sharp, fiercely loyal.

"Thank you," Elizabeth said.

Kitty squeezed her hand. "Go and wash your face. You look as though you have seen a ghost." She paused. "Which I suppose you have. Several dozen of them."

Supper was a lively affair, Kitty orchestrating the conversation with a deftness that would have impressed a seasoned hostess. She asked Georgiana about the lake at Pemberley, whether one could row on it, whether there were fish, what the grounds looked like in autumn. Georgiana, delighted to have someone so interested, talked more freely than Elizabeth had ever heard her, describing the walks, the woods, the kitchen garden, and the succession houses where the gardeners grew pineapples, actual pineapples, which made Kitty gasp so theatrically that even Darcy laughed.

"You must teach Lizzy all about it," Kitty said, beaming at Georgiana. "She will want to understand every inch of the place, and you know it better than anyone."

"I should like that very much," Georgiana said softly, and there was a wistfulness in her voice that Elizabeth recognised. Georgiana had spent too much of her life in drawing rooms with chaperones. Kindly though Mrs Annesley was, the prospect of having a sister near her own age, of having company that was not supervision, was plainly something she had been longing for.

Elizabeth excused herself shortly after the meal, claiming a headache from the journey. Darcy looked concerned but did not press; Kitty immediately began asking him about the estate's tenant farms, and by the time Elizabeth slipped out of the private dining room, Darcy was deep in an explanation of crop rotation and Kitty was nodding along as though fascinated.

The corridor was quieter now, most of the living guests having retired or settled in the taproom. The spectral ones remained. Elizabeth moved through them carefully, murmuring greetings to those who seemed aware of her, offering small kindnesses where she could.

Near the kitchen stairs, a stout woman in a travelling pelisse was berating the wall with considerable force. "The chicken," she announced to no one in particular, "was not cooked through. I said so at the time. I said, 'Mr Featherstone, that chicken is pink,' and he said, 'Nonsense, my dear, it is merely moist,' and I said, 'There is a meaningful distinction between moist and raw, Mr Featherstone,' and was I listened to? I was not. And now look." She gestured at herself with magnificent indignation. Elizabeth pressed her lips together, murmured her condolences, and moved on.

The soldier on the stairs turned out to be a deserter from the war who had died of fever on his way home. He was young, not much older than Kitty. He sat with his elbows on his knees, his head hanging. He did not want help. He wanted someone to know his name. She asked for it, and he told her: William Carver, of Sunderland. She repeated it back to him, and watched something in his face ease. He did not speak again, but he lifted his head, and his eyes followed her as she passed, and she thought perhaps that was enough.

The Tudor woman was searching for her son. Elizabeth sat with her for a time, listening, but the woman's son had been dead for three hundred years, and there was nothing Elizabeth could do to ease that particular ache except to say she was sorry, and she said it, and meant it.

But it was the little girl who pulled at her most urgently.

She was sitting in the corner of the servants' passage, her arms wrapped around her knees, her chin resting on them. Her dress was from perhaps fifty years ago, practical wool, worn at the cuffs. She had red-gold hair and, when she looked up at Elizabeth, eyes the colour of April skies.

"I can see you," Elizabeth said gently, kneeling beside her. The floorboards were cold even through her skirts. "I can hear you. Can you tell me your name?"

"Nell," the girl whispered. "I'm Nell Whitmore. I was waiting for my da. He went out and he never came back."

Elizabeth settled down beside her, there in the cold corner of a servants' passage in a coaching inn on the Great North Road. "Tell me about your father," she said.

Nell's story came in fragments, pieced together from a child's understanding of events and a ghost's confused sense of time. Her father was a drover, had been a drover, had brought cattle south along the Great North Road. She had travelled with him sometimes, when her mother was ill. They had stopped at the Red Hart on this particular day, and her father had said he would go and put their horse to the cart. He had left Nell with her travelling cloak and her doll and told her to mind the innkeeper's wife.

"She was kind," Nell said. "She gave me bread and milk. But then she forgot about me. There was so much happening. People shouting. I went to the stable to find Da."

"What happened then?" Elizabeth asked, though she had begun to suspect.

"There was a cart. I did not see it. I was looking for Da. And then..." Nell's voice faded. "I was lying on the ground and the lady was crying, and Da came running, and he picked me up, and he said, 'Nell, Nell, wake up, stay with me,' but I could not. And then everything was strange and confused and I was all alone."

Elizabeth wanted to hold Nell, but that was beyond her gift. She could only sit and listen.

"I thought he would come back," Nell whispered. "He said he would come back. He said he would never leave me alone. But then so many people came, and they moved the carts, and the horses were gone, and I did not know where I was anymore. People came and went, and I saw them but they could not see me, and I have been waiting, and waiting, and he never came back."

"Oh, Nell," Elizabeth said. "I'm so sorry."

"You can see me," Nell said, and there was wonder in her voice now, and something like hope. "You are real. You are alive and you can see me."

"I can see you," Elizabeth confirmed. "And I hear you. And you are not alone."

They sat like that for a long time. Nell talked, and Elizabeth listened, and she did something she rarely did: she made a promise. She would remember Nell Whitmore's name. She would know that Nell had been loved, and wanted, and that she had mattered. It was a small thing, perhaps not even real comfort in any sense that endured. But Nell looked up at her with something like peace in her expression, and she said, quietly, "Thank you."

By the time Elizabeth climbed the stairs, her head truly was aching and her legs were heavy and she wanted nothing more than to fall into bed and sleep for days. But she had just clambered into bed and laid her head on the cool pillow when Darcy came in, trying to be quiet until he saw her eyes were open. The worry on his face was almost worse than the ghosts as he sat down on the edge of the bed and looked at her.

"Your headache," he said. "Is it very bad?"

"It is better now," she lied, and reached for him. She moved carefully, deliberately, settling herself into his arms as though she were a much more fragile thing than she actually was. He enclosed her without complaint, his lips pressing against her hair. He smelled of leather and candle wax and the particular scent that was simply Darcy.

"Three more days," he murmured. "And then you will be home."

Home. Pemberley. A house that had stood for centuries, that had seen births, deaths, wars, and plagues, that had been home to generation upon generation of the family she had married into. She had glimpsed only two ghosts on her previous brief visits, but she had not been looking. She had been careful not to look.

She would not have that luxury now.

Elizabeth closed her eyes, pressed her face against his shoulder, and said nothing. She tried not to think about what waited at the end of the road.

Chapter Four

ELIZABETH RECOGNISED THE FEELING before she recognised the road.

It had been the same on her previous visit, that summer afternoon with the Gardiners when she had come to Pemberley as a tourist and tried not to think too hard about the man who owned it until he appeared before her, much to her consternation. The house had pressed against her awareness then, a low, insistent hum at the edges of her gift, denser than anything she had felt before. She had attributed it at the time to the age of the place, to the sheer weight of centuries soaked into its stones.

Now, as the carriages turned onto the approach road and the parkland opened up around them, she felt it again. The same hum, the same pressure. Only this time there would be no leaving.

"We are close," Darcy said, and there was something in his voice she had come to recognise: pride, tempered by anxiety. She had heard it the day he asked if he could introduce Georgiana to her, and not understood it then. Despite her anxiety, she smiled to hear it now.

"I can tell," Elizabeth said in answer to his remark, and meant it in a way he could not possibly understand.

The parkland was rolling and vast, the oaks beginning to turn bronze. Deer grazed in clusters on the slopes, lifting their heads as the carriages passed, and in the second carriage Kitty leaned out of the window and said, "Oh!" in a voice that managed to be both awed and slightly terrified.

Then the trees thinned, and there it was.

Elizabeth had seen Pemberley before. She had stood on this very approach and felt the first stirring of something she had not yet been ready to name, a sense that this place and the man who owned it were altogether more than she had allowed herself to imagine. But that had been a different Elizabeth, a visitor passing through, free to admire and move on. The woman in the carriage now was mistress of the vast estate before her, and the weight of that, layered over the pressure of the house's presence, settled over her like a coat, a heavy one that was too warm for the weather, slightly suffocating.

"Well?" Darcy said.

"It is," Elizabeth replied, choosing her words carefully, "exactly as beautiful as I remembered. And considerably more terrifying."

He looked startled. "Terrifying?"

"I am about to become responsible for it. That is, I think, allowed to be terrifying."

His expression softened. "You are not alone in it. Mrs Reynolds has managed the household for many years and will continue to do so. All that is required of you is to be yourself."

"That," Elizabeth said, "is what concerns me."

He did not understand her meaning, of course. He thought she was nervous about the household, the staff, the social expectations. And she was. But beneath that was the thing she could not say: that the hum had become a roar, that the spectral presence she had merely brushed against on her tourist visit was now pressing against her from every direction, and that she was going to have to walk into that house and pretend she felt nothing at all, lest her husband think she had gone insane.

She breathed in through her nose and out through her mouth. Steady. She simply needed time, and care, and Kitty watching her back.

The carriages swept up the drive and stopped before the great front doors. Darcy stepped down first and handed Elizabeth out, and his hand was warm and steady around hers. She held onto it a moment longer than strictly necessary.

Mrs Reynolds had the staff assembled in the entrance hall, arranged in two neat lines stretching from the door to the foot of the staircase. It was a display of considerable formality: footmen in their best livery, housemaids in white caps, kitchen staff in neat dark dresses and clean white aprons, the butler standing at rigid attention, the gardeners and grooms at the far end, slightly less rigid but all wearing boots shiny with fresh polish. Every face turned toward Elizabeth as she stepped through the door, and Mrs Reynolds, standing at the head of the line, smiled with a warmth that seemed quite genuine.

"Welcome home, Mrs Darcy," she said. Here was a woman who had known Darcy since he was a child, who had served his father and his mother and this household for decades. Her investment in this moment was written plainly on her face, and Elizabeth, who had been bracing herself for judgement, found kindness instead.

"Thank you, Mrs Reynolds," she said, and meant it.

The introductions began. Mrs Reynolds walked her down the line, naming each servant, their role, how long they had been at Pemberley. Elizabeth did her best to fix each face and name in her memory, smiling, saying something personal where she could. She complimented a housemaid on the neatness of her cap, asked a youthful-looking footman how long he had been in service, told the cook she had heard wonderful things about the kitchen from Georgiana.

The problem was that not everyone in the line was alive.

She spotted the first one six servants in: a housemaid in an older style of uniform, her cap fashioned differently from the others', standing between two living girls and looking at Elizabeth with frank curiosity. Elizabeth's gaze passed over her without pause, without the smallest flicker of recognition. She could not afford to do otherwise. Not now.

Further along, a footman in a powdered white wig whose livery belonged to a previous generation, perhaps forty years past. He stood at parade rest with the correctness of long habit. A parlour maid whose cap was faded in a way that a living eye would not have noticed. A second housemaid whose feet did not quite touch the floor. Elizabeth had to concentrate, hard, not to acknowledge their bows and curtseys as she did those of their living fellows.

There were two grooms, so alike they had to be brothers, and not so long dead from the cut of their jackets. Faded, here inside the house. She suspected they would be stronger out in the stables, but they, like every other servant of Pemberley, would not miss greeting their new mistress, whether she acknowledged them or not.

At the end of the line, near the stairs, an elderly man in the clothes of a butler from a previous age. He held himself as though he still carried the entire weight of the household on his shoulders and had no intention of setting it down simply because he was dead. His eyes followed Elizabeth down the line, missing nothing, and she felt his scrutiny like a physical weight. Her composure wobbled under that spectral regard, just slightly, a tightening of her jaw that she could not quite suppress.

Seven. She had counted seven ghosts in the line, standing among the living as though they had never left their posts, and she had acknowledged none of them, but this one... she suspected this one knew she had seen them.

Kitty was at her side. Elizabeth did not know when her sister had moved there, only that she was suddenly present, asking Mrs Reynolds about the kitchens, saying something warm about the height and grandeur of the hall. The commotion was gentle, intentional, and it gave Elizabeth the space of a few heartbeats to close her eyes and breathe.

She opened her eyes and smiled at Mrs Reynolds, who was explaining the arrangements for tea, and allowed herself to be led further into the house.

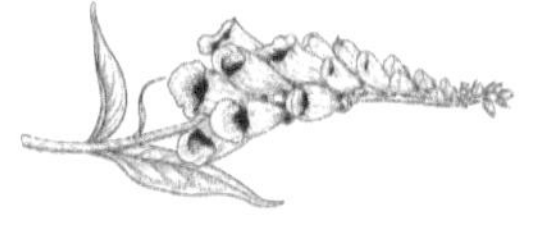

The great hall of Pemberley was grander than any room Elizabeth had stood in. The ceiling rose above them, painted and gilded, the plasterwork so intricate it seemed to contain entire dramas in miniature. The staircase swept upward in a curve of polished oak, and the walls held portraits of Darcys going back centuries: stern-faced men and elegant women and children with Darcy's own dark eyes, all looking down from their gilded frames with expressions that suggested they were reserving judgement on the new Mrs Darcy until she had proved herself.

Some of them, she suspected, were not confined to their frames.

Darcy appeared at her side, having finished speaking with his steward. "Shall I show you the house? Or would you prefer to rest first?"

"Show me," Elizabeth said, because rest was impossible and she needed to know the shape of what she was dealing with.

He took her through the principal rooms, and she tried to attend to what he was saying while simultaneously cataloguing the spectral inhabitants of each. The yellow drawing room, with its lovely gold furnishings and windows overlooking the lake, held an elderly gentleman dozing in a chair beside the window, his wig from an earlier period, his fingers steepled on his waistcoat. He did not stir as they passed.

The music room made Georgiana smile. It held nothing otherworldly that Elizabeth could sense, which came as a relief so sharp she nearly sighed aloud.

The library was another matter. The books rose from floor to ceiling; the air smelled of leather and time. In the chair by the fire sat a woman in an old-fashioned dress, reading. When Elizabeth entered, the woman looked up, assumed she had not been seen, and returned to her book with the quiet resignation of one very accustomed to invisibility.

"The library was my father's favourite room," Darcy said, walking ahead of her, oblivious. "He spent most of his evenings here. I think you will like it."

"I am sure I shall," Elizabeth managed, stepping carefully around the ghost of a maid who was kneeling beside the hearth, tending a fire that had gone out decades ago. Darcy continued talking about the library's collection, how his grandfather had acquired the majority of the volumes, and how his father had added the natural history section and the complete works of Shakespeare in folio. Elizabeth made herself listen, made herself ask questions. It was not difficult, in truth; the library was magnificent, and under any other circumstances she would have been genuinely absorbed. But the reading ghost by the fire kept glancing up at her, and the maid by the hearth had begun to hum, a low, tuneless sound that only Elizabeth could hear, and the effort of pretending she heard nothing was beginning to tell.

The dining room was mercifully empty of ghostly residents, though a chill lingered in one corner that suggested someone had been there recently. The breakfast room, small, bright, and facing east, held only the faintest whisper of presence, old and settled and untroublesome.

In the long gallery, two children chased each other between the windows, a boy and a girl in clothes from perhaps a century earlier. They were the same two she had glimpsed on her tourist visit, she was almost certain, though they had been still then, and watching. Now they were playing, and when they saw Elizabeth looking, they stopped as though struck, their round eyes widening with astonishment. She made herself look away, and after a moment the whisper of their running resumed.

She did not see the two servant ghosts from the gallery, the ones who had been discussing Darcy's marriage prospects. Perhaps they were elsewhere in the house. Perhaps they were watching from a distance, assessing the woman he had married instead of the Bingley creature, and forming their opinions. She was not sure she wanted to know what those opinions were.

"This is where I practised my dancing as a boy," Darcy said, and she could hear the faint amusement in his voice. "Rather badly, I am told."

"I cannot imagine you being bad at anything you put your mind to," Elizabeth said.

"You did not see the dancing."

"No. But I have danced with you since, and found no fault."

He looked pleased, in the quiet way that Darcy looked pleased, which was barely distinguishable from his habitual seriousness unless one knew what to look for. Elizabeth was learning.

By the time they reached the breakfast room, her temples had begun to ache with the effort of maintaining absolute composure. She excused herself, pleading fatigue from the journey, and Darcy seemed to accept this without question. He showed her to her rooms, kissed her hand, and withdrew, leaving her alone with the maid who was unpacking her trunks.

Elizabeth sat on the edge of the bed, folded her hands in her lap, and stared at the wall. Two ghosts watched her from the corners of the room, a housemaid from another era who clutched a duster she could no longer use, and a young man in a footman's coat who stood by the window as though guarding it from some threat only he could perceive. Both watched her the way servants watch a new employer: carefully, and without committing to an opinion, and Elizabeth did not acknowledge either of them. Not yet. She was not ready yet, and the living maid was placidly unpacking her trunks. This had to wait until she was alone, truly alone, because once one of Pemberley's ghosts knew she could see them, they would all know.

She thought of Jane's words at Netherfield. "Pemberley will have them. You know it will." Jane had been right, as Jane so often was about the things that mattered most. Pemberley had them. Pemberley had dozens of them. And Elizabeth, who had been managing the dead since she was old enough to understand what she was seeing, felt, for the first time in her life, genuinely outmatched.

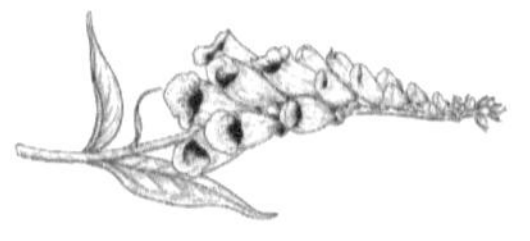

Supper that evening was a quieter affair than Elizabeth had expected, though the quality of the dishes presented told her Pemberley's cooks were eager to impress their new mistress. Just the five of them at a table that could have seated thirty. Darcy sat at the head and Elizabeth at his right, Mrs Annesley took a seat near the middle, and Georgiana and Kitty faced each other across the table. The candles threw warm light over the silver and crystal, and for a little while Elizabeth could almost pretend that she was merely a woman at supper with her family, with no second sight and no spectral weight pressing against her consciousness.

Kitty was in fine form, drawing Georgiana out about her music and her sketching. She asked about the succession houses and the gardeners who grew pineapples, and Georgiana described them with earnest enthusiasm. Mrs Annesley watched the exchange with quiet approval, contributing occasionally, and even Darcy seemed to relax by degrees, the stiffness he wore in company loosening as the evening settled into something familial.

"Mrs Reynolds tells me you charmed the entire staff," Darcy said, turning to Elizabeth. "She says you remembered every name."

"Not quite every name," Elizabeth said. "I shall need a second introduction to the under-gardeners and grooms. There appear to be rather a lot of them."

"Pemberley has extensive grounds and stables."

"Pemberley has extensive everything." She smiled, and he smiled back. For a moment the warmth and quiet domesticity of it all made the stone in her chest feel almost bearable.

"Do you ride, Elizabeth?" Georgiana asked suddenly, then coloured, as though the question had escaped before she could assess whether it was appropriate.

"I do, though not well, and I am sure Pemberley's stables will put Longbourn's to shame. My father keeps a horse that is older than I am and has strong opinions about galloping. Or trotting, if I am truly honest. I usually found my own willing feet would carry me where I wished to go faster than Nellie's reluctant ones."

"Brother has the most beautiful mare," Georgiana said, growing bolder. "Her name is Athena. She is very gentle. I am sure he would let you ride her."

"I would be delighted," Elizabeth said, and Darcy watched this exchange between his wife and his sister with an expression of cautious wonder, as though he had not dared expect it.

After supper, Georgiana offered to play for them. They retired to the music room, and she began a delicate sonata, her technique careful but growing more confident as she settled into the piece. The melody was clean and bright, and Elizabeth listened and felt something in her unclench.

She sat beside Darcy on the sofa. His hand found hers in the space between them where the candlelight did not quite reach. She held it, felt his fingers warm and solid around hers. He smelled of clean linen and the faint, woody scent she had begun to associate with Pemberley itself, something in the polish or the panelling or simply the accumulated smell of centuries of oak and stone. She leaned into him, just slightly, and felt his arm shift to accommodate her, and the simple ease of the gesture was so ordinary, so domestic, so blessedly normal that her throat ached with gratitude for it.

But the house breathed around her. She could feel it even now, even in this quiet, beautiful room, the presence of the dead pressing gently against her awareness. They were not hostile. They were curious. A new mistress at Pemberley, and they did not yet know what to make of her.

Kitty caught her eye across the room and raised one eyebrow, the tiniest fraction of movement. Elizabeth gave an almost imperceptible nod.

Later. She would deal with all of it later. But not tonight. Tonight she would sit beside her husband and listen to Georgiana play and watch Kitty becoming someone new in this grander world, and be, for a few more hours, simply Elizabeth Darcy, newly married, newly arrived, newly home.

The ghosts could wait.

Chapter Five

Elizabeth had been mistress of Pemberley for five days when she met the woman who actually ran it.

She was in her private sitting room, the small parlour adjoining the master bedroom that Darcy had said was traditionally the mistress's own. It was a pretty room, south-facing, with a view over the rose garden, and Elizabeth had been spending her mornings there, writing letters and learning the household accounts and pretending she was not being watched.

She had been careful. She had given no sign. Five days of cautiously navigating a house packed with ghosts, of stepping around the unseen, of keeping her expression neutral when a translucent figure walked through the breakfast table or a long-dead child laughed in the corridor. Kitty had been magnificent, covering for every lapse, filling every suspicious silence, steering Darcy and Georgiana away from the rooms where Elizabeth's composure was thinnest. The system they had built at Longbourn, refined over a lifetime of practice, was holding at Pemberley just as it had always held. It was simply working much, much harder, with far more ghosts and only Kitty to distract.

Elizabeth was writing to Jane. The letter had gone through two drafts already. The first had been a breezy account of her new surroundings, full of descriptions of the grounds, the library, and the kindness of Mrs Reynolds, and she had torn it up because it was a lie. The second had veered too far the other way, beginning with "Dearest Jane, there are more ghosts in this house than there are living servants, and I am not entirely certain which group is more demanding," which would have been cathartic to send but unwise to commit to paper. The third attempt struck a middle ground: domestic news interspersed with the careful code the sisters had developed over years. "The house has a great deal of character" meant "the ghosts are everywhere." "I am learning to navigate the corridors" meant "I have nearly been caught six times." "Kitty has been invaluable" meant exactly what it said.

She was composing a particularly careful sentence about the ghostly servants in the staff lineup, disguised as an observation about the interesting variety of uniforms worn at Pemberley over the years, when she became aware that someone was standing in the doorway watching her.

She looked up, expecting a housemaid or possibly Georgiana, and found instead a woman she had never seen before, alive or dead.

The ghost was old, or had been old when she died. Small, but straight-backed in a way that added inches to her bearing. She was immaculately dressed in the fashion of a century and a half ago; grey silk, cut simply but unmistakably expensive, with sleeves that fell in the style of the

Restoration and a stomacher that had been out of fashion since before Elizabeth's grandmother was born. Her white hair was pinned beneath a lace cap of considerable quality, the lace itself so fine that Elizabeth could see through it to the translucent scalp beneath. Her hands, small and dark-spotted with age, were folded at her waist. Her face was a map of determination: sharp cheekbones, a firm mouth, a chin that looked as though it had been set in that position some time in the previous century and had not budged since.

But it was her eyes that held Elizabeth. Dark, shrewd, and absolutely unblinking, they surveyed Elizabeth the way a general might survey a new recruit: thoroughly, critically, and without any particular expectation of being impressed.

She also looked entirely unsurprised that Elizabeth was looking directly at her.

Elizabeth set down her pen.

"Well," the ghost said. "So you are the one he married."

Her voice was sharp and clear and carried the unmistakable authority of a woman who had been giving orders for a long time and saw no reason to stop simply because she was dead. Her gaze moved over Elizabeth's face, her posture, her dress, her writing desk, the half-finished letter, and appeared to find all of it wanting.

"I am," Elizabeth said. "And you are?"

"I," the ghost said, drawing herself up to her full height, which was not considerable but somehow felt as though it ought to be, "am Dorothea Darcy. I was mistress of this house for seventy-seven years, which is rather longer than anyone else managed, and I have been looking after it since, which has been considerably longer still. The servants call me Nana. You may call me Mrs Darcy, until I decide whether you deserve better."

Elizabeth blinked. "I am Mrs Darcy."

"Yes. I am aware. I have been Mrs Darcy since 1684. You are something of a latecomer." A brief paused, and then a grudging "I suppose you had best call me Nana. To avoid confusion."

They regarded each other across the room. Elizabeth had spent her whole life dealing with ghosts of every temperament, from the shy to the confused to the gently melancholic. She had managed the imperious Aunt Irene, the bickering Pemburys, the bewildered dead of coaching inns. She had never met anyone quite like this.

"You married young," Elizabeth observed, recalling Mrs Reynolds' recital of the lineage of Darcys as they walked in the portrait gallery. Dorothea Darcy had been a pretty young bride, with a distinct resemblance to Georgiana, her great-great-grand-daughter, if Elizabeth was correct. Elizabeth would not have recognised that young girl in this woman, save for those shrewd dark eyes.

"I married at sixteen. I was widowed at twenty, with a son not yet walking. My husband's cousins descended like crows on a carcass, certain a girl of twenty could not hold an estate of this size. They were incorrect." Nana's chin lifted. "I held Pemberley for my son, raised him to hold it after me, and when he married a perfectly adequate woman from a family I did not approve of, I held my tongue, which was the greatest sacrifice I have made in either life. I have been here ever since, because somebody must ensure that the standards I set are maintained, and frankly the women who married into this family after me have been, on the whole, disappointing."

"On the whole," Elizabeth repeated.

"Anne was acceptable. Fitzwilliam's mother. She had no backbone to speak of, but she had taste, and she loved the boy, and she died too young for me to discover her deficiencies. Her predecessor was a disaster. Moved the blue Delft collection into the wrong room and refused to listen when I tried to tell her."

"Refused, or could not hear you?"

"Oh, refused. I was still alive then. Nobody living in this house has been able to see or hear me since the day I died.

Until, apparently, you." Nana's eyes narrowed. "Which raises a number of questions I intend to have answered."

Elizabeth leaned back in her chair, almost relieved to finally be able to tell someone the truth. "I can see the dead. I have been able to do so since I was a very young child. It is a gift, or a burden, depending on the day, and I have carried it my whole life. My family knows, but my husband does not. I would prefer to keep it that way, for the time being."

"Why?"

The question was blunt, and Elizabeth respected it. "Because I have been married for less than a week, and I suspect that telling a man that his new wife sees ghosts is not the best foundation for domestic harmony."

"Sensible, I suppose. Though I cannot approve of deception between married persons. My husband and I had no secrets."

"You were married for four years."

"Quality, Mrs Darcy, not quantity." She swept into the room and settled herself in the chair by the fire, arranging her skirts around her as though the laws of physics still applied to her. "Now. I have been watching you since you arrived, and I have a number of observations."

Elizabeth raised an eyebrow. "Do you?"

"The menus are adequate but uninspired. Mrs Reynolds does well enough with the staff, but she permits the footmen too much liberty with the silver polish; I can see the streaks from here. The rose garden has been allowed to go to ruin since old Gregson died, and his replacement has no feeling for the damask varieties. The drawing room curtains are disgracefully faded. And you," she fixed Elizabeth with a look that would have pinned a lesser woman to the wall, "have been stepping around my ghosts like a woman crossing a muddy field in new slippers."

Elizabeth was not about to be intimidated by a ghost. "Your ghosts?"

"They are residents of my house. That makes them my responsibility. I have been managing them for fifty years, and I can tell you that the servants are perfectly well-behaved as long as they are not interfered with, the children in the gallery are harmless, and the gentleman in the yellow drawing room has been asleep since before I was even born and is unlikely to stir. You need not creep about as though you expect them to leap out at you."

"I was not creeping."

"You were creeping. I have been watching. You are not bad at it, I will grant you that, but you have not yet learnt the house, and until you do, you will keep making mistakes. Yesterday you nearly acknowledged Sarah Dunn in the corridor outside the library, and Mrs Reynolds was two steps behind you."

Elizabeth felt heat rise in her cheeks. She had nearly acknowledged the spectral housemaid from the entrance-hall lineup, who must be Sarah Dunn, and it had been a close thing indeed. Sarah had stepped directly into her path, beaming, delighted, as though she had finally found a mistress worthy of the name, and Elizabeth had opened her mouth to say good morning before she remembered that Mrs Reynolds was walking immediately behind her. She had covered by pretending to cough, which had led Mrs Reynolds to offer her a tisane, which had led to a twenty-minute conversation about the housekeeper's mother's remedy for congestion of the lungs.

"I need ground rules," Elizabeth said, straightening. "If we are to share this house, you and I, there must be an agreement."

"Agreement," Nana repeated, as though the word tasted unpleasant.

"The master bedroom is off limits. To all ghosts. At all times. I will not negotiate on this."

Nana's eyebrows rose to an impressive height. "I have passed through that room freely since the day I became Mrs Darcy."

"And you will stop. I am a newly married woman, and I will not have observers in my bedchamber, dead or alive."

"I walked through that room while carrying your husband's father in my arms," Nana said. "When he was still small enough to carry. I have paced that floor and watched over that bed through fever and heartbreak and the births of four generations. You would close it to me because you are shy?"

"I would close it to you because it is mine," Elizabeth said, her voice steady. "My room. My marriage. My private life. You may have watched over that bed for more than a hundred years, and I honour the care that represents. But I am its mistress now, and I am telling you: that room is private. That is not a request."

A silence settled between them, electric and charged. Nana studied Elizabeth with an intensity that made the hair on her arms stand up. Elizabeth held her gaze and did not blink. Outside, a bird sang in the rose garden; inside, the fire shifted and popped.

"And if I refuse?" Nana said softly.

"I can see you," Elizabeth said, leaning forward. "I can hear you. I have been doing this my whole life, and in that time I have managed ghosts who were angry, ghosts who were grieving, ghosts who were confused, and ghosts who were simply stubborn. I have never yet met one I could not handle. Would you like to find out whether you are the exception?"

She was bluffing. She had no idea whether she could do anything to a ghost who refused to cooperate. She had never needed to find out; most ghosts responded to firm kindness, and the rare difficult ones had been manageable through patience and persistence. But Nana did not know that, and Elizabeth had learnt long ago that confidence was its own currency, with the living and the dead alike.

Nana stared at her. Elizabeth stared back.

Then Nana laughed.

It was not a small laugh. It was a full, rich, delighted sound that filled the room and made the candles on the mantelpiece flicker, and it transformed her face from stern authority into something warm, surprised, and genuinely pleased. The lines around her eyes deepened, her small frame shook, and for a moment Elizabeth could see the girl she had been, the sixteen-year-old bride, the twenty-year-old widow who had stared down a pack of greedy cousins and told them to get out of her house.

"Well," Nana said, settling back in her chair. "Perhaps you will do after all."

They talked for the better part of an hour, and Elizabeth discovered two things about Dorothea Darcy. The first was that she was the most opinionated person Elizabeth had ever met, living or dead, and Elizabeth had met Lady Catherine de Bourgh. The second was that she could not be managed.

Elizabeth had spent her life managing ghosts. It was what she did; she listened, she helped, she made agreements, she eased the restless toward peace and maintained companionable relationships with those who chose to stay. She was good at it. She had managed Aunt Irene's tartness, Sir Harold's pomposity, Mrs Turnbull's endless chatter. She had a system, and the system worked.

Nana dismantled the system in under twenty minutes.

It was not that she was difficult, exactly, though she was certainly that. It was that she did not operate within the normal boundaries of ghost-and-medium relations. She did not need Elizabeth's help. She did not want Elizabeth's guidance. She was not confused, or lost, or grieving, or in need of gentle management. She was, and had been for a hundred and thirty years, the self-appointed guardian of Pemberley. She had clear ideas about how the house should be run, and she intended to share every single one of them with the new Mrs Darcy.

"The east wing has damp," she informed Elizabeth. "It has had damp since 1763, and nobody has ever properly addressed it. I suggest you raise the matter with your husband at your earliest convenience."

"I have been married for five days. I am not yet raising matters of structural repair."

"Nonsense. A good wife takes an interest in the fabric of her home."

"A good wife also allows her husband to finish his breakfast before discussing rising damp."

"Mr Darcy, my Mr Darcy, would have welcomed such a discussion. He was very attentive to the fabric of the building."

"Your Mr Darcy lived in the seventeenth century and presumably had fewer breakfast options to distract him."

Nana sniffed. It was a magnificent sniff. Even Aunt Irene would have been impressed.

"Furthermore," Nana continued, quite as though Elizabeth had not spoken, "the gilt on the mirror in the morning room is tarnished. It has been tarnished for forty years. I have been staring at it every morning since 1772 and it offends me deeply."

"You are a ghost. You do not use the morning room."

"I occupy it. And the library curtains are too thin. They admit too much afternoon sun, and the spines of the older volumes are fading. My son spent a fortune on those books. One would think somebody might care enough to hang a decent pair of curtains."

Elizabeth found herself torn between exasperation and something perilously close to affection. "Is there anything about this house that meets your approval?"

Nana considered this. "The new stoves in the kitchen are most functional. I disapproved when George ordered them installed, but I will admit they are an improvement."

"How generous."

"I am not given to empty praise, Mrs Darcy. If I tell you something is satisfactory, you may rely upon it absolutely." She paused, and her voice shifted. "The rose garden, though. That is not a matter of taste. My mother-by-law planted those roses. I tended them myself, in the years after my husband died, when I had nothing but a baby and a garden and the will to keep both alive. Lady Anne loved them and nurtured them and old Gregson understood them. He knew which needed sheltering and which could bear the wind. His replacement treats them all the same, and they are dying for it."

Elizabeth looked at her and saw, beneath the imperiousness, something she recognised. Grief. Not fresh, but deep, the kind that settled into the bones over centuries and became indistinguishable from the person who carried it. The roses were not merely roses. They were Nana's hands in the earth, the thing that had kept her rooted when everything else was being torn away.

"I will look at the rose garden," Elizabeth said quietly. "I cannot promise to restore it overnight, but I will look at it."

Nana regarded her for a moment. There was the faintest shift in her expression, so small that Elizabeth might have imagined it. Then she nodded, once, as though a contract had been signed.

"Now," Nana said briskly, reverting to command, "the household schedule. Mrs Reynolds keeps the staff well enough in hand, but there is waste. The footmen spend half the morning on tasks that could be accomplished in a quarter of the time if they were properly directed. The scullery maids gossip. The second housemaid has been walking out with the under-gardener, and while I have nothing against romance so long as they conduct themselves respectably, she has been neglecting the upstairs grates, mooning over him from the windows instead of polishing the fire-irons."

"You cannot possibly expect me to raise the subject of the second housemaid's romantic entanglements with Mrs Reynolds."

"I expect you to be aware of them. A mistress who does not know the state of her own household is a mistress who will be managed by her staff rather than the other way around."

There was not much Elizabeth could say to that, because the infuriating thing was that Nana was right. Elizabeth had spent five days learning the surface of Pemberley; Nana was offering her a view beneath it, into the workings, relationships, and small dramas that made the household run. It was invaluable information. It was also being delivered in the most irritating possible manner.

By the end of the hour, Elizabeth understood that her relationship with Nana was going to be unlike anything she had experienced. This was not like any relationship Elizabeth had previously shared with a ghost, even Aunt Irene. This was something more like a partnership, or perhaps a battle of wills, between a woman who had run Pemberley for almost eighty years of life and fifty years of death, and a woman who had been officially in charge for less than a week.

"I shall visit you each morning," Nana announced, rising from her chair. "We will discuss the household, the staff, the menus, and any matters requiring your attention. You may ask me questions about the house and its history, and I shall answer them if I consider the questions worthy. In return, you will address the damp in the east wing and restore the rose garden to its proper standard."

"That is not a negotiation," Elizabeth pointed out. "That is a list of demands."

"Yes," Nana agreed serenely. "I find demands work better than requests. One saves a great deal of time." She paused at the door, turned back, and regarded Elizabeth with an expression that had softened by the smallest, most grudging degree. "You have spirit, Mrs Darcy. I did not expect to like you. I reserve the right to change my mind, but for the present, you will do."

She was gone before Elizabeth could formulate a reply, which Elizabeth suspected was entirely deliberate.

Elizabeth sat alone in her parlour, surrounded by the silence of a house that was not, and would never be, truly silent. Through the window, the rose garden spread out below her, overgrown and tangled, the damask varieties

Nana had loved choked with bindweed and neglect. She could see, now that she was looking, that it had once been beautiful. She could see, too, that it could be beautiful again.

She picked up her pen and turned to a fresh sheet of paper.

"Dearest Jane," she wrote. *"I have met the most extraordinary person. She has been dead for fifty years, she has opinions about my curtains, and I believe she may be my new closest confidante after you. I do not know whether to be delighted or appalled. I suspect I shall be both, in roughly equal measure, for the foreseeable future."*

She paused, considered the letter, and added: *"The house has a great deal of character. More than I anticipated. I am managing. Kitty sends her love."*

She sealed the letter, set it aside, and sat for a moment looking out at the rose garden. Then she permitted herself a single, incredulous laugh.

She had spent her whole life gently shepherding the dead. At Pemberley, it appeared, the dead intended to shepherd her.

Chapter Six

NANA ARRIVED AT HALF past seven the following morning, before Elizabeth had finished her chocolate.

"You are late," Nana announced, settling into the chair by the fire as though she had been using it for decades, which, Elizabeth supposed, she had. "I have been waiting since seven."

"I was not aware we had agreed on seven."

"We did not agree on anything. I told you I would visit each morning. Morning begins at seven."

"Morning begins," Elizabeth said, "when I have had my chocolate. That is not negotiable."

Nana regarded the cup in Elizabeth's hand with the expression of a woman who had died before chocolate became fashionable and was not entirely convinced it deserved to be. "In my day, we rose with the sun."

"In your day, there was no chocolate. I consider this an argument in favour of modernity."

Something that might have been amusement flickered across Nana's face, quickly suppressed. "Very well. Half past eight. But not a moment later." She produced, from somewhere about her person, what appeared to be a list of considerable length.

Elizabeth blinked. Had Nana created that list by sheer force of will? She truly was an extraordinary ghost.

"Now. The east wing," Nana began.

"We discussed the east wing yesterday."

"We discussed it inadequately. The damp has spread since last winter, and there is a crack in the plaster above the second-floor passage that would not have been tolerated in my time. I have also observed that the new gardener has been pruning the lime walk incorrectly. He cuts too close to the trunk. The trees will suffer for it within five years."

Elizabeth set down her cup. "Nana, just how long is that list? I cannot reorganise the entire estate before luncheon."

"I am not asking you to reorganise the entire estate. I am asking you to pay attention. There is a difference." She fixed Elizabeth with those dark, shrewd eyes. "Now. Shall I introduce you to the others, or do you intend to keep creeping about as though you are afraid of your own household?"

Elizabeth opened her mouth to protest that she was not creeping, recalled that she had lost this argument yesterday, and closed it again. "What do you mean, introduce me?" she said instead.

"You have been avoiding them. The servants, the older residents, everyone who has tried to catch your eye. They know you can see them, Mrs Darcy. Word travels fast among the dead. Sarah Dunn was never able to keep a confidence in her life, much less her death."

So much for discretion. Elizabeth thought of all the careful avoidance, the controlled expressions, the five days of pretending she saw nothing, and felt a surge of something between frustration and relief. "If they already know, then I suppose there is no point in pretending otherwise."

"None whatsoever. Come." Nana rose from her chair. "I shall take you on a tour. The proper tour, not the one your husband gave you, which was entirely inadequate."

Nana conducted the tour of Pemberley's dead with the same brisk authority she applied to everything else. She swept through the corridors with Elizabeth trailing behind, and the ghostly residents of the house presented themselves with a formality that suggested Nana had given them advance warning and they had better be on their best behaviour.

The servants came first. Sarah Dunn, the housemaid from the entrance-hall lineup, was so delighted to be formally acknowledged that she curtsied four times in rapid succession and had to be told by Nana to compose herself. She had been dead for twelve years, had been in service at Pemberley for twenty before that, and had, she informed Elizabeth earnestly, never once allowed a cobweb to remain in any corner under her jurisdiction.

"She was a competent maid," Nana allowed. "Her successor is not."

"My successor," Sarah said, looking wounded, "does not dust behind the clock on the second-floor landing. I have been watching."

There were others. A cook from the previous century who haunted the kitchen and agreed with Nana about the stoves being an improvement, but disapproved of the current cook's use of nutmeg. A valet who had served Darcy's grandfather and remarked with an expression of pained concern about the way the current Mr Darcy's coats were pressed.

Elizabeth greeted each of them, learned their names, asked how long they had been at Pemberley. It was the same work she had always done, the patient, practical business of acknowledging the dead. At Longbourn it had been a handful. At Netherfield, four. Here, the servants alone numbered over a dozen, and that was before Nana led her beyond the service quarters.

The most entertaining introduction was to the butler and the housekeeper, who occupied opposite ends of the servants' hall and had been bickering for as long as anyone could remember. Mr Graves, the butler from the entrance-hall lineup, was Georgian; Mrs Alcott, the housekeeper, had died during the reign of Queen Anne. They had never met in life, being separated by several decades, but in death they had developed the combative intimacy of an old married couple, disagreeing about everything from the correct temperature for serving claret to the appropriate method of storing linen.

"The claret should be brought up two hours before dinner," Mr Graves informed Elizabeth, with the air of a man laying down holy writ.

"Nonsense," Mrs Alcott retorted from across the room. "One hour is sufficient. Two hours and it goes flat."

"Claret does not go flat. You are thinking of ale."

"I am thinking of nothing of the sort. I was housekeeper here for twenty-seven years and I know perfectly well how to manage a cellar."

"You were housekeeper here in a century that had no taste," Mr Graves said, and Mrs Alcott's expression suggested she was seriously considering whether a ghost could box another ghost's ears.

In the long gallery, the two children were waiting. They stood motionless this time, holding hands, watching Elizabeth approach, round-eyed and solemn, as though they had been told to behave but were not entirely sure why. The boy was perhaps ten, the girl a year or two younger, and they wore the clothes of the late seventeenth century, well-made but plain.

"Edmund and Charlotte," Nana said. "My husband's younger brother and sister. They died of scarlet fever a few years before I came to the house. They have been chasing each other through this gallery ever since, which I permit because they are children and children must play, but I draw the line at them running through the breakfast room during meals."

"We only did that once," the boy said.

"You did it four times in a single week, and Mr Darcy, the current Mr Darcy, remarked on the draughts."

Elizabeth looked at them, these small, solemn faces, and felt the familiar ache that came with children who had died too young. They were not distressed, not confused; they had Nana, who they must have watched arrive at Pemberley as a young bride and live there for nearly eighty years after that. She must have been the most consistent person they had ever known; since her death she had accepted them as family, managing them with the same iron hand she applied to everything else. But they were so young, two children playing games that nobody else could see, and Elizabeth's chest tightened.

"I am very pleased to meet you both," she said, and meant it.

Charlotte's face split into a grin. Edmund maintained his dignity for approximately three seconds before asking, "Can you really see us? Properly? Not just shadows?"

"Properly," Elizabeth confirmed. "Every detail. Your stockings do not match, Edmund."

He looked down, alarmed. Charlotte burst into delighted laughter, and even Nana's mouth twitched.

From the gallery, Nana took her to the yellow drawing room, where the elderly gentleman in the wig was still dozing. "Sir Roderick Darcy," Nana said, lowering her voice, though Elizabeth was not entirely certain ghosts could be woken. "My husband's great-grandfather. The oldest ghost at Pemberley we can identify; there are a few of the wispier shades clearly older by their dress, but they do not speak and we do not know their names. None of us have ever spoken with Sir Roderick or seen him awake.

He simply sits, and sleeps, and does not trouble anyone. I would prefer him left undisturbed."

"I had no intention of disturbing him."

"Good. He had a reputation of being an exceptionally disagreeable man when awake."

The library held the reading woman, who turned out to be a former governess called Miss Pardoe. She had served the family in the 1740s, had loved the library above all other rooms, and had simply never left it after the influenza took her one bitter winter. She barely looked up when introduced, murmured something polite, and returned to her book with an air that seemed to indicate she had been interrupted quite enough for one century.

But it was the rose garden that stopped Elizabeth in her tracks.

They stepped out through the side door into the October morning, the air cool and sharp, the garden spread before them in all its overgrown, neglected glory. And there, sitting on the stone bench beneath the old climbing rose, was a woman Elizabeth had not seen before.

She was quite young, perhaps thirty, and she was dressed in the elaborate style of the Elizabethan period: a stiff ruff, an embroidered bodice, a farthingale so wide it occupied most of the bench. Her dark hair was pinned beneath a jewelled hood, her hands were folded in her lap, and she was smiling.

Not at Elizabeth. Not at Nana. At the roses.

"Lady Margaret Darcy," Nana said, and her voice had gone quiet, stripped of its usual command. "Sir Roderick's wife. She planted the first roses in this garden. Before my mother-by-law, before me. She laid out the beds and brought the damask varieties from the estate in Kent where she was born. She has been sitting here ever since."

"She does not speak?"

"She has never spoken. Not to me, not to any ghost I have known. She sits, and she smiles, and she tends her garden in whatever way the dead tend things. She is the oldest of us, along with Sir Roderick, and the most peaceful."

Elizabeth watched Lady Margaret for a little while. The ghost's smile was serene, untroubled, and directed entirely at the roses, which, even in their current state of neglect, were still beautiful in the way that old, established things are beautiful: the bones of the garden visible beneath the overgrowth, the structure sound even if the detail had been lost.

"I will restore it," Elizabeth said, and this time it was not a concession but a decision. "Not just for you. For her."

Nana said nothing. But she inclined her head, and the gesture carried more weight than any words she might have offered.

Breakfast that morning was a test of endurance.

Elizabeth arrived at the table having just spent an hour being introduced to the spectral population of a four-hundred-year-old estate. She was expected to sit down, eat toast, make conversation as though nothing of consequence had occurred. Darcy was already seated, reading a letter from his steward. Georgiana was buttering bread with the careful concentration she applied to everything. Mrs Annesley had the slightly glassy stare of someone who had not slept well and would rather still be in bed. Kitty was the last to arrive, slightly breathless, her hair not quite as tidy as it ought to have been; she had been exploring the grounds before breakfast, she said, and had found the most marvellous walk along the river.

"You look well this morning," Darcy said to Elizabeth, setting aside his letter. "The country air suits you."

"I have always preferred the country," Elizabeth said, accepting tea from the footman and noting, from the corner of her eye, the spectral valet hovering behind Darcy's chair and wincing at a crease in his coat. "Though I confess

Pemberley's country air is rather grander than Hertford-shire's."

"Everything about Pemberley is grander than Hertford-shire," Kitty observed cheerfully. "Even the breakfast rolls are larger. I should like to know how the cook achieves it."

"A good kitchen and a willing baker," Mrs Reynolds said, appearing in the doorway with the morning's house-hold correspondence. "Mrs Darcy, if you have a moment after breakfast, I should like to discuss the menus for the coming week."

"Of course," Elizabeth said. "I should also like to discuss the rose garden, if you have time. It seems to have been somewhat neglected."

Mrs Reynolds looked surprised, then pleased. "It has, ma'am, since old Gregson passed. I have mentioned it to the new man, but he has his own ideas."

"Then perhaps he and I should have a conversation about whose ideas ought to take precedence," Elizabeth said mildly, and caught, from the corner of her vision, a flicker of movement by the doorway that might have been Nana, nodding.

Kitty glanced at Elizabeth across the table, quick and assessing. Elizabeth returned the look with the faintest shake of her head: *I am fine.* Kitty held her gaze for half a beat longer than necessary, reading something there that satisfied her, and returned to her breakfast.

It was seamless. It had always been seamless. At Long-bourn, the system had been built among the sisters over years of practice: the silent checks, the manufactured dis-tractions, the way the other girls could sense when Eliz-abeth's attention had split between the visible world and the one only she could see. Here at Pemberley, with the stakes so much higher, the ghosts so much more numer-ous, and only Kitty to watch her back, the system was working harder than it ever had, but it was holding.

Georgiana caught Kitty's eye and smiled, a shy, tentative smile, as though she were still not entirely certain she was allowed to be happy. "Shall we walk to the lake after breakfast? I should like to show you the folly up close."

"I should like that very much," Kitty said, and the eagerness in her voice was genuine, not performed. She had been studying Georgiana with the same quiet attentiveness she brought to everything at Pemberley, and she was learning, rapidly, which subjects made Georgiana bloom and which made her retreat. London was exciting but frightening. Her brother was adored but slightly terrifying. Music was safe ground. Wickham was not, though Kitty did not yet know why. Elizabeth would not press that; Georgiana would reveal it in her own time, or not. Kitty navigated all of it with an instinct that Elizabeth found quietly remarkable.

She was also doing something else, something Elizabeth had not expected. She was learning Pemberley. Not just the geography of the house, though she was learning that too, memorising corridors and staircases with a speed Elizabeth had not quite expected from this sister she was coming to realise she had always slightly underestimated. Kitty was learning the social geography: how Mrs Reynolds ran the household, which servants could be relied upon, how Georgiana's shyness worked and how to navigate around it. She was studying the rhythms of the great house the way she had once studied the rhythms of Meryton, and she was adapting to them with a quickness that would have astonished anyone who still thought of her as silly Kitty Bennet, Lydia's shadow.

After breakfast, Elizabeth walked the grounds with Darcy. He showed her the home farm, the tenant cottages visible from the ridge, the stream where he had fished as a boy. He spoke about his plans for the estate with the quiet passion she was learning to recognise: Darcy did not enthuse exactly, he simply became more specific, his sentences growing longer and more detailed as his interest deepened. Elizabeth listened, asked questions, and found that she was genuinely interested. The management of a great estate was a subject she had never had cause to study, yet it appealed to the same part of her mind that enjoyed problems, patterns, the satisfaction of things done well.

She was also, simultaneously, aware of four ghosts watching them from various points along their walk. The spectral valet, trailing Darcy at a respectful distance. A gardener from the previous century who was tending a flower bed that no longer existed. One of the groom brothers from the staff lineup, considerably more solid out here in the grounds than he had been in the entrance hall, exercising a spectral horse. And, standing on the bridge over the stream, a man in late Tudor dress who watched them pass with an expression of profound displeasure.

"That bridge," the Tudor gentleman called after them, his voice carrying the outrage of someone who has been nursing a grievance for two hundred years, "was built in the wrong place. I said so at the time. Nobody listened then, and I do not suppose anyone will listen now."

Elizabeth kept her face admirably still. Darcy, walking beside her, pointed out a stand of oak trees his grandfather had planted and said something about timber yields.

"I shall speak with you later," Elizabeth murmured, under the cover of examining a hedgerow, and the Tudor gentleman looked so startled at being heard that he fell silent for what she suspected was the first time in two centuries.

The morning was beautiful, the grounds were beautiful, her husband was beautiful, though with Darcy it had always been less about the arrangement of his features than the earnestness of his attention. He took her hand as they walked back toward the house. She held it, and for whole stretches of time she was simply a woman walking with the man she loved through grounds that belonged to them both, the ghosts no more than a secondary awareness, a familiar hum at the edges of her perception.

But then they would pass through a doorway; a spectral servant would bow, or a translucent figure would drift across the corridor, or Nana would appear at her elbow with a reminder about the faded curtains in the drawing room. The two worlds would collide, and Elizabeth would have to smooth her expression, turn back to Darcy, say something about the weather or the wallpaper as though she had not just been addressed by a woman who had been dead for half a century.

This was her life now. This had always been her life, but the scale of it here, in this vast, ancient, ghost-crowded house, was something she had not been prepared for. She was managing. She would go on managing. But the effort of it, the relentless performance of normality, was beginning to settle into her bones like a weariness she could not shake.

Kitty found her in the parlour before luncheon, sat beside her without speaking, took her hand, and held it.

"I am all right," Elizabeth said.

"I know," Kitty said. "I am holding your hand because I want to, not because you need me to."

Elizabeth smiled, and felt the weariness ease, just slightly, and thought: *I can do this. I have Kitty, and I have Nana, and I have a husband who loves me even if he does not yet know all of me.*

She didn't have a lot of choice, after all.

Chapter Seven

IT WAS KITTY'S FAULT, which was unfair, because Kitty had not done anything wrong.

Elizabeth had summoned the dressmaker. This was an act of love; though no efforts or expense had been spared in assembling Elizabeth's trousseau and she was well equipped for her new life as Mrs Darcy, Kitty had arrived at Pemberley with a wardrobe suitable for Hertfordshire, and that would not do. If Kitty was to accompany Georgiana to London in the spring, she would need gowns that did not mark her as a country gentleman's daughter the moment she walked into a room, and the Lambton dressmaker, recommended warmly by Mrs Reynolds, had come to the house that morning with fabric samples and fashion plates quietly determined to do Mrs Darcy's sister proud.

It would be two hours at least, Elizabeth calculated. Two hours in which Kitty would be pinned, measured, and turned about, and in which Elizabeth would be, for the first time since arriving at Pemberley, entirely without her safety net.

She had not intended to go to the long gallery. She had been walking to the library, meaning to spend a quiet hour reading in the company of the spectral Miss Pardoe. But Edmund and Charlotte had found her in the corridor, breathless and insistent, tugging at her attention the way living children tug at a sleeve.

"You promised," Edmund said, planting himself in her path with the immovable certainty of a boy in the right.

Elizabeth had not, in fact, promised anything. She had said she would visit the gallery soon, which Edmund had apparently translated into a binding contract.

"Please," Charlotte added, and the word carried the devastating weight of a child who had not been able to ask for anything for a century and a half.

So Elizabeth went to the gallery. She had never been able to resist children, living or dead; Darcy was out of the house, Georgiana and Mrs Annesley were in the music room, and Sarah Dunn had promised to warn her if any of the living servants came near.

The gallery was quiet, the October light falling in long pale columns through the tall windows. Edmund and Charlotte were more solid here than anywhere else in the house, their features sharper, their clothes crisper, the details of their faces clear enough that Elizabeth could count Charlotte's freckles. They had been running through this gallery for over a century, and the place knew them, held them, gave them substance.

"Tell us about outside," Edmund demanded, settling cross-legged on the floor with the air of a boy preparing for a siege. Charlotte sat beside him, tucking her skirts around her knees in unconscious imitation of her brother.

"Outside?"

"Beyond the grounds. Beyond the park. We cannot go further than the ha-ha, and Charlotte has never been past the bridge."

"I went to the bridge once," Charlotte corrected. "But it made me feel thin."

Elizabeth lowered herself to sit on the window seat, arranging herself so that she faced the children but could also see the length of the gallery. A precaution. The door at the far end was closed, and Sarah Dunn would drift through it and gesture if anyone was coming.

Or so she believed.

"What would you like to know?" she asked.

"Everything," Edmund said.

"That is a rather large subject."

"Start with London," Charlotte said. "Nana says London is noisy and smells of horses and the streets are a disgrace to civilisation. But she has not been to London since she was alive, and that was ages ago, so she might be wrong."

"Nana is rarely wrong," Elizabeth said, smiling. "London is noisy, and it does smell of horses, and the streets are frequently a disgrace. But it is also full of wonderful things. Theatres and bookshops and parks, and the river, and more people than you could count if you spent a whole year trying."

"Are there ghosts in London?" Edmund asked.

"A great many, I should think. I have not spent enough time there to know them well; I have only been to my uncle's house there once or twice, and it is new. No ghosts at all." They looked almost disappointed at that, so she quickly added "But there are buildings in London even older than Pemberley. Some that were built even before the Normans came; we stopped briefly at a coaching inn which boasted that. I was glad not to have to go inside, to be honest."

"There would be a lot of ghosts there," Edmund said, sounding quite satisfied about it.

Boys were still boys, with an interest in the gothic and the macabre, Elizabeth thought, concealing an amused smile. Even when they were themselves dead.

"They would be different, though," she pointed out. "London's ghosts would be mostly strangers, passing through. Here, you are all family, or very nearly. That is not the same thing at all."

Charlotte beamed. "Nana says we are part of Pemberley. She says the house would not be the same without us."

"Nana is right about that too."

"She is right about most things," Edmund said, resignedly; he had tested this proposition many times and been defeated on each occasion. "She says you are acceptable, which is the best she has said about anyone who was not born a Darcy since Annie."

"That is Lady Anne," Charlotte whispered. "Your Mr Darcy's mother. Nana loved her."

"Did she?" Elizabeth filed this away. Nana had spoken of Lady Anne with approval, even warmth, but hearing it confirmed by the children gave it a different texture. Nana's approval was not given lightly; her love, Elizabeth suspected, was given even less so.

"She cried when Annie died," Edmund said. "I did not know ghosts could cry. But Nana did."

Elizabeth was about to answer when she heard, too late, the soft creak of a door. Not the one at the far end of the gallery she had been watching, where Sarah Dunn was posted to warn of intruders. The door behind her, the one that led, through an anteroom, to the music room.

She turned. Georgiana stood in the doorway, one hand still on the latch, her eyes wide.

The silence that followed was the loudest Elizabeth had ever experienced.

Georgiana's gaze moved from Elizabeth to the empty air beside her, to the place where Edmund and Charlotte sat on the floor, invisible to her, and back to Elizabeth's face. Her expression held none of the alarm Elizabeth had braced for. There was surprise, yes, and curiosity, and beneath both, a flicker of recognition, as though a question she had been carrying for a long time had just begun to find its answer.

"Elizabeth," Georgiana said carefully. "Who were you speaking to?"

A dozen lies presented themselves. The acoustics of the gallery. Rehearsing a letter aloud. Talking to herself, a bad habit, mortifying. Any of them would have served, delivered with the right laugh, the right wave of the hand. Elizabeth had been making such excuses her whole life and she was good at it.

But Georgiana's eyes were steady, and there was no fear in them, and Elizabeth found that she was bone-tired of lying to people she loved.

"Will you come and sit down?" Elizabeth said.

Georgiana crossed the gallery and sat on the window seat, her hands folded in her lap, her back rigid. She looked, Elizabeth thought, like a girl who had been preparing for something without knowing what it was.

"I can see the dead," Elizabeth said. "I have been able to do so since I was a child. There are two ghosts in this gallery, Edmund and Charlotte, distant relatives of yours, who are children. I was talking to them. I know how that sounds, and I know you have no reason to believe me, and I will understand completely if you think I have gone mad."

Georgiana was quiet. Elizabeth watched her face, looking for the flicker of doubt, the edge of withdrawal, the careful blankness that would mean she had lost her.

"I do not think you have gone mad," Georgiana said slowly. "I think you have explained something I have wondered about for years." She looked down the gallery, her gaze moving along the windows, the portraits, the long stretch of polished floor. "This room has always felt different. When I was small, I used to sit in here and feel as though someone was sitting with me. Not frightening. Just, present. As though the room were not quite empty, even when I was the only one in it. Sometimes I wanted to run, though not to run away; as though I was playing a game of chase with another child."

Elizabeth looked at Edmund and Charlotte. They were beaming and nodding happily.

"You were not the only one in it. And they were trying to play with you. You must have sensed it, in some way."

"How astonishing," Georgiana said, and a small, wondering smile touched her mouth. She paused. "Does my brother know? About... that you can see them?"

"No," Elizabeth admitted.

"Will you tell him?"

"Yes. When I am ready. I have not found the right moment, and I confess I have been afraid of finding it."

Georgiana considered this with the seriousness she brought to everything. "He will believe you," she said at last. "He believes everything you tell him. I have never known him to trust anyone the way he trusts you."

The words landed somewhere beneath Elizabeth's breastbone, in the place where guilt and gratitude had been keeping uneasy company since her wedding day. "I hope you are right."

"I am rarely right about things," Georgiana said, with a flicker of self-deprecation that reminded Elizabeth painfully of Darcy. "But I am right about my brother."

Edmund chose this moment to announce, "She is sitting on my spot."

Elizabeth pressed her lips together. "Edmund says you are sitting on his spot."

Georgiana startled, looked down at the window seat, and then laughed, a bright, surprised sound that rang through the gallery. "I beg his pardon. Where ought I to sit?"

"He is ten years old and has been dead for a hundred and fifty years, or thereabouts. He can yield a window seat."

"I heard that," Edmund said, and Charlotte laughed, a bright, tinkling sound that produced the very slightest of breezes.

Georgiana must have felt it, because she touched her cheek, her eyes widening. "Is that...?" she asked timidly.

"Charlotte is laughing at her brother," Elizabeth said warmly. "She looks quite like you, you know, though her hair is darker. The Darcy resemblance is strong."

Both Charlotte and Georgiana appeared delighted that Elizabeth thought they looked alike, and Georgiana seemed to relax, a little.

Nana appeared within the hour, drawn, Elizabeth suspected, by some instinct that told her something significant had shifted in the household.

She materialised in the doorway of Elizabeth's parlour, took one look at Georgiana sitting in the chair by the fire, still a little pale in the face, and said, "Ah."

"Georgiana knows," Elizabeth said.

"I can see that she knows. The girl is sitting in my chair." Nana swept into the room, radiating displeasure at the disruption to her routine. "Move."

"Nana," Elizabeth said. "She cannot hear you."

"Then tell her."

Elizabeth sighed. "Georgiana, you are sitting in Nana's chair. She would like you to move, and unlike Edmund, I don't think she will yield."

Georgiana stood up so quickly she nearly knocked over the fire screen. "I am sorry, I did not, how, where should I..."

"Sit anywhere else," Elizabeth said. "Nana will tell you if that is wrong too."

Georgiana chose the settee, perching on the edge of it, her eyes wide and darting about the room as though she might suddenly develop the ability to see what Elizabeth saw. "She is here? Right now? In this room?"

"She is always in this room at this hour. She has a schedule."

"I have standards," Nana corrected. "There is a difference."

"She says she has standards," Elizabeth relayed, and Georgiana made a sound that was half laugh, half gasp, and pressed both hands over her mouth.

"Nana is Mrs Dorothea Darcy," Elizabeth said, as Nana sat down and arranged her skirts. "She is your great-great-grandmother, and she lived until she was almost a hundred years old. Long enough to hold your father in her arms when he was a baby."

Georgiana looked quite awed, and made a respectful little bow of her head towards the seat she had just vacated.

"Nana," Elizabeth said, turning to the ghost. "This is Georgiana. Your great-great-granddaughter. Is there anything you would like to say to her?"

Nana looked at Georgiana closely. The sharpness in her face softened, not entirely, because Nana's face was not built for softness, but in the same way it did when she watched Edmund and Charlotte run, a way that was reserved only for those born to the house of Darcy. "Tell her that while I see the Darcy features in her, I see her mother too," Nana said quietly. "Annie's colouring, Annie's hands. She holds herself the same way, as though she is afraid of being too tall. I have been watching this child her whole life and never been able to tell her so."

"Nana says you have your mother's colouring," Elizabeth told Georgiana gently. "And her hands."

Georgiana's fingers curled in her lap. Her eyes were bright. "She knew my mother?"

"Nana has known every woman who married into this family for over a hundred years. She knew your mother very well."

Georgiana sat motionless, and then said, in a voice that was trying hard not to shake, "Is my mother here? At Pemberley?"

Nana's expression shifted. She looked at Elizabeth, and there was something in that look, a warning, a request, that Elizabeth could not quite read. Then Nana turned back to Georgiana, though Georgiana could not see her, and spoke with a tenderness Elizabeth had not heard from her before.

"Your mother was at peace," Nana said. "From the moment she died. She loved you and your brother with everything she had, and when she went, she went gently, without struggle, without regret. She did not linger. She did not need to. She knew her children were safe at Pemberley."

Elizabeth repeated this, word for word, watching Georgiana's face as each sentence landed. Tears slid down the girl's cheeks, silent and unwiped, and she did not try to stop them.

"She was the best of them," Nana added, more quietly. "The best woman who ever married into this family. I include myself in that judgement, and I do not say it lightly."

Elizabeth relayed this too, and Georgiana let out a breath that sounded as though she had been holding it for sixteen years.

"And my father?" Georgiana asked. "Is he..."

Elizabeth was watching Nana's face and saw something close over it as Georgiana asked the question, a door shutting behind the eyes. It happened in less than a heartbeat, and if Elizabeth had not been watching closely she would have missed it. But she was watching, and she did not miss it, and what she saw was not grief, or at least not only grief. It was something guarded, something deliberate.

"Your father," Nana said, her voice now brisk again, clipped, restored to its usual authority, "is a subject for another day. I have told you about your mother because you asked and because you deserve to know. But I will not discuss the whole family in a single afternoon; there are a great many Darcys."

It was a masterful deflection. The tone said: *I am an old woman and I decide the pace of these conversations.* The words said: *not now.* Georgiana, who had just been given the most extraordinary gift of her young life, accepted this without question. Of course Nana would not rush. Of course there would be more to learn.

But Elizabeth had seen the door close. She had seen the fraction of a second when Nana's composure had cracked, and something urgent and unresolved had looked out through the gap before being firmly shut away. George Darcy was not a comfortable subject. George Darcy was not a subject Nana wished to discuss at all, and the reasons for that avoidance were not the reasons she had given.

Elizabeth said nothing. She filed it away, the way she had learnt to file things away over a lifetime of listening to the dead, and turned her attention back to Georgiana, who was wiping her eyes with the back of her hand and smiling.

"Thank you," Georgiana whispered. "Thank you, Elizabeth."

"Do not thank me. Thank Nana. She is the one who remembers."

"I always remember," Nana said. "It is both my gift and my burden. Rather like yours, Mrs Darcy."

Kitty appeared at the parlour door at half past four, slightly flushed from her fitting and trailing a faint smell of new wool. She took one step into the room, looked at Georgiana's tear-streaked face, looked at Elizabeth's careful expression, and stopped.

"What happened?"

"Georgiana knows," Elizabeth said.

The colour left Kitty's face. She looked at Georgiana, then back at Elizabeth, and her mouth compressed into a thin line. She stepped inside, closed the door behind her, and turned the key.

"How?" The word was clipped.

"She came through from the music room while I was in the gallery. I was speaking to Edmund and Charlotte. She heard me."

Kitty closed her eyes for a moment. When she opened them, she crossed the room, but she did not sit beside Georgiana. She stood in front of her, and her expression was one Elizabeth had never seen on her younger sister's face: fierce, frightened, and absolutely serious.

"Georgiana," Kitty said. "Do you understand what you have learnt today?"

Georgiana nodded, her eyes wide.

"No," Kitty said. "I do not think you do. Not yet." She knelt so that she was level with Georgiana on the settee, and took both her hands. "If anyone discovers what Elizabeth can do, anyone at all, she could be destroyed. Not embarrassed. Not whispered about. Destroyed. They would call her mad. They would have her locked away in an asylum, Georgiana. Your brother's name would be disgraced, his judgement questioned, his marriage made a subject of public ridicule. And Elizabeth would lose everything. Her freedom. Her husband. Her life as she knows it."

"I would never tell anyone," Georgiana whispered.

"You must swear it. Not just to Elizabeth. To me. Because I have spent my whole life protecting this secret, and I need to know that you understand what it costs."

"I swear it," Georgiana said, and her voice was small but steady.

"Your brother cannot know." Kitty's grip on Georgiana's hands tightened. "I know that is hard to hear. He is your brother and you love him and you do not like keeping things from him. But he cannot know. Not now. Perhaps not ever."

"Kitty," Elizabeth said quietly.

"No, Lizzy. She needs to hear this." Kitty did not look away from Georgiana. "Men do not understand things like this. Even good men. Even the best of them. He would think she was ill. He would try to help, and his help would be the very thing that destroyed her. He would bring in doctors. He would tell his uncle, who is an earl and has the power to act on it. He would do it out of love, and it would ruin her, and I will not let that happen."

Georgiana looked stricken, but she did not pull away. "You truly believe he would not accept it?"

"I believe the risk is too great to find out. We have kept this secret for twenty years. Jane knows. Papa knows. Mama knows, though she pretends she does not, because that is how Mama manages things she cannot control. Mary knows. Even Lydia knows, though Papa had to threaten her into silence. Every one of us has kept it, because the alternative is unthinkable." Kitty's voice softened, but only slightly. "Some families have a cousin who drinks. We have Elizabeth. We love her, and we protect her, and we do not talk about it to anyone outside the family. You are the first person outside the Bennets to ever learn of it."

The weight of that settled over the room.

"I will tell you how we manage it," Kitty continued, releasing Georgiana's hands and sitting back on her heels. "If she goes still at dinner, I knock over a glass. If she starts to look at something nobody else can see, I ask a loud question about the weather. If she needs to leave a room, I invent a reason. I have been doing it since I was old enough to understand what was happening, and I am very good at it. You will need to learn to do the same."

"She is good at it," Elizabeth confirmed. "Better than Jane, in some ways. Jane's instinct is to comfort. Kitty's instinct is to distract, which is more useful in company."

"Papa is the worst," Kitty said, and a ghost of her usual warmth crept back. "He forgets himself and makes remarks. He once told Mr Collins that Elizabeth had a particular talent for conversing with the unseen, and Mr Collins took it as a compliment to her prayer life and talked about it for half an hour."

Georgiana's mouth fell open. Then she laughed, a shaky, startled sound, and Kitty allowed herself a small smile.

The room was quiet for a moment. Nana, in her chair, was watching Kitty with an expression Elizabeth had not seen on her face before. It looked remarkably like respect.

Georgiana straightened, and for a moment Elizabeth saw the steel that ran through the Darcy line, the same steel she had seen in Darcy himself when he was certain of his course. "I will not let anyone hurt you," Georgiana said, with a ferocity that took Elizabeth by surprise. "You are my sister now. Your secrets are mine. And I will not tell my brother. I promise."

Kitty studied her for a moment, then nodded. "Good."

"Well," Nana observed from her chair, in a tone of grudging satisfaction. "The girl has spine after all."

Elizabeth did not relay this, but she smiled. Kitty caught the smile, raised an eyebrow; Elizabeth shook her head. The old language of glances that the Bennet sisters had spoken since childhood expanded, just slightly, to make room for one more.

Later, after Georgiana had gone to dress for dinner and Nana had drifted away to inspect something she considered substandard, Elizabeth sat alone in her parlour and felt the quiet settle around her like cooling water.

She had been happy. That was the unsettling thing. In these past days at Pemberley, learning the house, meeting its ghosts, finding her footing with Nana, she had begun to believe she could do this. That the secret could be carried here as it had been carried at Longbourn, with care and cleverness and the right people watching her back. She had begun, without quite realising it, to relax.

Kitty's face, white and fierce in front of Georgiana, had cured her of that.

They would call her mad. They would have her locked away. Kitty had not been exaggerating. Kitty, who knew better than anyone how close Elizabeth had come over the years; the near-misses, the moments where a wrong word or a stray glance might have unravelled everything. Kitty was afraid because Kitty understood exactly what was at stake, and hearing that fear spoken aloud, in this house, had stripped away the gentle illusion Elizabeth had been building for herself: that Pemberley might be different. That she might, here, be safe.

She was not safe. She had never been safe. She had simply been lucky, and luck was not a strategy, and the more people who knew her secret, the thinner the luck stretched.

Elizabeth pressed her hands flat on the desk and breathed, and the stone in her chest, which had lightened over these first weeks at Pemberley, settled back into its familiar weight.

Chapter Eight

From her parlour window, Elizabeth could see the rose garden, and in it, two girls on their knees in the October mud, careless of their gowns.

Georgiana had taken to the restoration project with an enthusiasm that bordered on ferocity. She had commandeered a pair of old gloves from the garden shed, tied back her hair with a ribbon that was already coming loose, and was pulling bindweed from the base of a damask rose as though it had personally offended her. Kitty worked beside her, less methodical but equally determined, her bonnet abandoned on the stone bench where Lady Margaret sat smiling at roses that were, for the first time in years, being freed from the weeds that choked them.

It had been Nana's idea, or rather Nana's command, which amounted to the same thing. She had taken Elizabeth, Georgiana, and Kitty to the long gallery two mornings ago and pointed at the portrait of Lady Margaret Darcy. It was a fine painting, Elizabethan in style, formal and richly coloured, and behind the seated figure the artist had rendered the rose garden in careful detail: the beds laid out in a geometric pattern, the climbing roses trained along the south wall, the stone bench positioned beneath what appeared to be an especially magnificent specimen of old damask climbing a wrought-iron arch.

"That," Nana had said, "is how it should look. That is how it looked when Margaret planted it, and when my mother-by-law tended it, and when I kept it after her. The current state of affairs is a disgrace."

Elizabeth had relayed this to Georgiana, who had studied the portrait with the intensity she usually reserved for difficult pieces of music, and said, with quiet certainty, "My mother loved the rose garden. Mrs Reynolds told me once that she spent whole mornings there." She had looked at Elizabeth. "May I help?"

She had not needed to ask twice.

Now Elizabeth watched them from the window, Kitty laughing at something Georgiana had said, Georgiana brushing dirt from her cheek with the back of her wrist, Lady Margaret observing the proceedings from her bench serenely approving. The ghost had not spoken; she never did. But the smile had changed since the girls had begun their work, becoming something warmer, less distant, as though the living hands in her garden had reached some part of her that centuries of silence had not touched.

It was a good morning. A peaceful morning. The kind of morning Elizabeth had begun to believe Pemberley might offer more often, now that Georgiana knew, now that the household had settled into a rhythm that accommodated both the living and the dead without either colliding too violently with the other. Darcy had ridden out early to visit a tenant, Mrs Annesley was writing letters in the morning room, and Nana had not yet arrived for her daily inspection, which meant Elizabeth had the rare luxury of a quiet hour to herself.

She was reviewing the household accounts, or trying to. Mrs Reynolds had left them on her desk the previous evening with a tactful note suggesting that the new mistress might wish to familiarise herself with the quarterly expenditures, and Elizabeth was discovering that Pemberley's quarterly expenditures were significantly larger than Longbourn's annual ones, which required a certain adjustment of perspective. She had just identified what appeared to be an alarmingly large sum allocated to candles when she heard the door open behind her and saw, from the corner of her eye, a tall figure entering in a dark-blue riding coat.

"You are back early," she said. "I thought you meant to ride to the Hendersons' farm and would not return before noon. I am glad of it, though; I have a question about the candle budget which I suspect Mrs Reynolds would rather I put to you than to her."

The silence that answered her was wrong.

She knew it was wrong before she looked up. It was the quality of it, the weight. Darcy's silences had texture; they were warm, considered, the quiet of a man choosing his words before he spoke them. This silence was something else. It was dense, charged, and it pressed against her awareness the way no living person's presence ever had.

Elizabeth turned her head to look properly.

The man standing in the doorway of her parlour was not her husband.

He looked like her husband. That was the shock of it, the thing that made her breath catch and her hands go still on the ledger. He was tall, dark-haired, with the same strong jaw and the same grave set to his mouth. He stood the way Darcy stood, straight-backed and formal, his weight settled, his chin level. He was dressed in the fashion of perhaps fifteen years ago, well-cut, expensive, the kind of clothes a man of considerable fortune would wear without thinking about them. The coat was much like the one Darcy wore regularly; the same colour, though the cut was slightly different. He could have been Darcy. At first glance, in poor light, he was Darcy.

But he was not Darcy, and Elizabeth reeled with shock, because he was a ghost, and he was wrong.

He was too solid. That was the only way she could describe it. Every ghost she had ever known carried some mark of their nature: a faint translucence, a softness at the edges, a quality of light that was not quite right. Even Nana, who was among the most vivid ghosts Elizabeth had encountered, had a shimmer to her, a reminder that she existed between states. This man had none of that. He was dense with presence, heavy with it, as though the force that kept him here had compressed him into something almost more real than the living. The air around him felt tight, and the candle on Elizabeth's desk guttered and flattened as though pressed by an invisible hand. And the door; the door had been closed and now it was open. This ghost had more control over matter than any Elizabeth had ever encountered.

He was also, she realised as her vision adjusted and the first shock faded, older than Darcy. The lines around his eyes were deeper, the hair touched with grey at the temples. There was a heaviness about his face that went beyond age, a rawness, as though something had been stripped from him that ought to have been there and the absence of it had left the bone too close to the surface.

His eyes were the worst. They were Darcy's eyes, the same dark brown, the same intelligence, but where Darcy's held reserve, this man's held fury. Controlled, contained, banked like coals beneath ash, but fury nonetheless, and grief so deep it had become indistinguishable from rage.

Elizabeth's hand tightened on the edge of the desk.

"You are George Darcy," she said, as certain of it as she had ever been of anything in her life.

The ghost did not move. He stood in the doorway and looked at her, and the look was so like Darcy's most penetrating gaze that Elizabeth could hardly breathe.

"You can see me." His voice was Darcy's voice made rougher, the vowels the same but the control thinner, as though the effort of keeping his tone level was costing him something considerable. "They said you could. The servants, the children. Even my great-grandmother told me, though she also told me to wait, and I have been waiting, and I find I cannot wait any longer."

Nana. Of course. Nana had been deflecting about George Darcy for a reason, and the reason was standing in her doorway, radiating a grief so powerful it was making the candle smoke.

"She means well," George Darcy said, and the flicker of tenderness that crossed his face was so like Darcy's expression when he spoke of Georgiana that Elizabeth's throat constricted. "She has always meant well. She has been trying to manage me as she manages everything else, and I have let her, because she carried me in her arms when I was small and I have never been able to refuse her anything. But this cannot be managed. What I have to tell you cannot wait for her schedule or her approval or her sense of the proper order of things."

He stepped into the room, and the temperature dropped. Not the gentle chill of Pemberley's older ghosts, the faint coolness that brushed past when Sarah Dunn walked through a wall or the children ran through the gallery. This was a visceral cold, sharp and sudden, the kind that made Elizabeth's fingers ache and her breath mist in the air despite the crackling fire.

"Sit down, please," Elizabeth said, because she had been managing ghosts since she was old enough to speak to them, and the first thing she had ever learnt was that a seated ghost was calmer than a standing one. "There is a chair. Will you use it?"

His expression shifted. He looked at her. For an instant the rage and the grief receded, and she saw the man he must have been: courteous, careful, a little formal. A good man. A man much like his son.

He sat. The chair did not creak under his weight, because he had no weight, but the upholstery compressed slightly, which Elizabeth had never seen a ghost do before. His solidity was extraordinary.

"I am Elizabeth," she said. "Your son's wife."

"I know who you are. I have been watching you since you arrived." He paused, and when he spoke again his voice was quieter, though no less intent. "You are not what I expected. He did well. Better than I deserved, given what I failed to teach him about the world."

"Mr Darcy..."

"George. My son is Mr Darcy now, and I would not take it from him." He leaned forward, and the air between them tightened. "Mrs Darcy. Elizabeth. I need you to listen to me very carefully, because what I am about to tell you will change everything you think you know about this family, and about a man you believe you already understand."

Elizabeth gripped the edge of the desk. She had sat with grieving ghosts, confused ghosts, angry ghosts. She had held Nell Whitmore's sorrow in a coaching inn and let Aunt Irene scold her one last time on her wedding morning. She had spent a lifetime learning to be steady in the presence of the dead, to offer calm where they had none.

But the way George Darcy looked at her made every ghost she had ever known seem like a candle flame beside a bonfire.

"I was murdered," he said. "In my own house, by a man I loved as a son. A man I raised, educated, trusted, and defended against every warning, including those of my own boy, who tried to tell me the truth and whom I refused to hear." His voice cracked, just barely, on the word *refused*, and the crack was worse than shouting would have been. "George Wickham poisoned me. He put something in my brandy. I drank it. By morning I was dead, and everyone believed it was my heart, because why would they not? I was not old, but these things happen, do they not?

A sudden illness. A weak heart nobody knew about. A tragedy, but a natural one."

The room was freezing now. Elizabeth could not feel her fingers.

"It was not natural," George Darcy said. "It was murder. The man who did it is walking free. I have waited six years for someone who could hear me. Now, at last, you are here, and I am asking you for justice."

Elizabeth could hardly breathe. The ledger was forgotten, the candle account absurd, the peaceful morning with its rose garden and its laughing girls a world she had inhabited five minutes ago and could not return to. She looked at George Darcy, at his fury, his grief, his terrible, unshakeable solidity, and felt the ground shift beneath her.

Wickham.

Of course it was Wickham. Wickham, who had charm the way a knife had an edge, who wore his smiles like currency and spent them where they would buy the most. Who had tried to elope with Georgiana when she was fifteen, who had ruined Lydia and been bought into marrying her. Wickham, whom Elizabeth herself had once believed to be everything agreeable, before Darcy's letter had torn the veil from her eyes and shown her the man beneath.

A seducer. A fortune hunter. A liar. But a murderer?

She looked at George Darcy's face and saw the answer there. The rage was not madness. It was the fury of a man who had trusted absolutely and been betrayed absolutely, who had died for the sin of believing the best of someone who deserved the worst, and who had spent six years watching his killer walk free while his own son carried a guilt that was never his to bear.

"Tell me everything," Elizabeth said.

The story came out in pieces, not because George Darcy was incoherent but because he was trying to be fair, even now, even about the man who had killed him. He wanted Elizabeth to understand not just what Wickham had done but why, and to understand that, she needed to know the history: the godson raised alongside the heir, the faithful steward's son given every advantage, the slow divergence between the boy Wickham had been and the man he became.

Elizabeth listened, and while she listened, her mind was running ahead of his words, assembling a picture she did not want to see.

Wickham was married to Lydia. Wickham had eloped with her youngest sister and been bought into respectability by the very son of the man he had murdered. George Darcy did not know this. He had said "the man who did it is walking free", but he had not said "your sister's husband." He did not know. And Elizabeth, sitting behind her desk with her hands gripping the edge of it, was going to have to decide what to do with that.

Not now. She could not tell him now. The knowledge would be a grenade thrown into a conversation already charged with enough grief and fury to crack the walls, and she did not know what it would do to him, this ghost who was already more solid, more powerful, more volatile than any she had encountered. If he learnt that the woman he was asking for help was bound by family to the man who had killed him, would he trust her still? Or would the rage that was already pressing against the edges of his control burn through entirely?

She did not know. She did not want to find out. And so she layered another secret onto the ones she was already carrying, and listened.

And beneath all of it, sharp as a blade, one thought: *Thank God I did not tell Darcy.* Kitty had been right. If Elizabeth had followed her own instinct, if she had confessed her gift in some tender moment and Darcy had believed her, what then? She would now be standing before her husband, saying: *your father was murdered by the man I call brother. His ghost told me so.* His love, and her marriage, would not survive it. Not the revelation, not the source, not the impossible tangle of family and guilt and accusation that would follow. Kitty's fear, which had seemed so fierce and so final in the parlour, now looked like the clearest thinking anyone in Elizabeth's life had ever done.

"I did not see it," George Darcy said, and the self-accusation in his voice was raw. "My son saw it. Fitzwilliam tried to warn me, more than once, and I dismissed him. I told him he was jealous, that he could not bear to share his father's affection. I said things to my own boy that I…" He stopped. Controlled himself. Continued. "I was wrong. About all of it. Wickham was not what I believed, and Fitzwilliam was everything I should have trusted, and by the time I understood that, it was too late."

The breaking point had been a girl from the estate. Sally Wilson, the daughter of a tenant farmer. She had come to her father in distress, naming Wickham as the man who had sired the child growing in her belly. Her father had gone to George Darcy, who had believed him immediately, without question, because the scales had fallen from his eyes at last and he could see what his own son had been telling him for years.

Elizabeth thought of Lydia. Lydia, who was loud, careless, still so young, married to this same man, living with him in lodgings in Newcastle while he drank, ran up debts, his charm wearing thinner by the month. Lydia, who did not know she was married to a murderer. Lydia, who was Elizabeth's sister, for all her faults, and who was in danger she could not begin to comprehend.

The horror of it was building, layer upon layer, and she could not let any of it show on her face.

"I confronted Wickham that evening," George Darcy said. "I told him he must marry the girl. I told him that if he refused, I would cut him off entirely, revoke the promised living, and see to it that every door in society was closed to him. He stood in my study and looked at me for a moment with eyes that were just, flat. Like there was nothing behind them at all. And then he smiled, and agreed to everything. Said he was sorry. Said he would do right by her. I believed that too."

He paused. The candle on Elizabeth's desk had gone out. The room was cold.

"He brought me brandy that night. A gesture of goodwill, he said. A peace offering. I drank it. I went to bed, and never woke."

Elizabeth's hands were shaking. She pressed them flat against the desk and held them there until they stopped. *A gesture of goodwill. A peace offering.* Wickham had smiled, poured, watched his benefactor drink, and gone away knowing that by morning the only man who could ruin him would be dead. The calculation of it, the cold, smiling patience of it, was worse than violence would have been.

And this was the man who shared Lydia's bed.

"Nana knows all of this," she said, because she needed to say something, and the things she could not say were crowding so thick behind her teeth that she was afraid of what might escape if she did not choose her words with care.

George Darcy's composure fractured. It was a small fracture, controlled almost instantly, but Elizabeth saw it: the flash of anguish, the raw edge of a grief that six years had not blunted.

"She screamed at me not to drink," he said. "She could not make me hear. She watched me die and could do nothing. She will carry that until this house crumbles to dust, because she will never leave, and she will never forgive herself, and she will never forgive him."

"That is why she would not speak of you to Georgiana," Elizabeth realised.

"She is protecting the girl. Protecting all of them. In her way." He looked down at his hands, and for a moment he was simply a father, grieving, exhausted, held to the world by a thread of rage he could not release. "My son carries guilt that should never have been his. He believes I died still deceived about Wickham. He believes that if he had pushed harder, argued more, been less proud, I might have listened. He has carried that since the day I died, and it has damaged him in ways he does not let anyone see."

"I know," Elizabeth said quietly. "I have seen it."

George Darcy looked at her then, truly looked, and whatever he saw in her face made some of the tension leave his shoulders. "Yes," he said. "I think perhaps you have." He was quiet for a little while. "I loved my son, Mrs Darcy. I loved him badly, inadequately, with all the blindness of a man who thought he knew better than a boy of twenty. But I loved him, I love him. And I need him to know that I saw the truth, in the end. That I heard everything he had tried to tell me. That I was the one who failed, not him."

Elizabeth thought of Darcy. Of the way he carried himself, that careful, guarded reserve that she had once mistaken for pride and now understood as something far more painful. Of the guilt he wore so quietly that most people never saw it at all. She thought of what it would mean to him to hear his father's words, and what it would cost to explain how she had come by them, and the distance between those two things yawned like a chasm she could not yet see the bottom of.

"I will help you," she said. "I do not yet know how, but I will help you."

She meant it. She also knew, with a clarity that was almost painful, that she had no idea what helping would look like. Every ghost she had ever tended had needed something she could give: acknowledgement, kindness, a willing ear, the gentle encouragement to let go. George Darcy did not need any of those things. He needed justice, and justice meant evidence, and evidence meant proving a murder that had been designed to look natural, committed six years ago by a man who was now embedded in her own family. She could not go to a magistrate with a ghost's testimony. She could not tell Darcy without revealing her gift. She could not act against Wickham without destroying Lydia, disgracing the Bennets, and handing Lady Catherine the ammunition to have her committed as a madwoman.

The walls of the trap closed around her as she sat there, and she could see no door.

George Darcy closed his eyes. When he opened them again, the fury was still there, and the grief, and the unshakeable purpose that had kept him tethered to this house for six years. But there was something else now. It looked, tentatively, like hope.

"Thank you," he said. "That is more than anyone has given me since the night I died."

Nana swept in at that moment, took one look at George Darcy sitting in the chair opposite Elizabeth, and said, in a voice that chilled the room even further, "I told you to wait."

"I have waited long enough, Nana."

"You have waited six years. Another week would not have killed you." She paused, heard what she had said, and added, with magnificent dignity, "Again."

Elizabeth, who had just been told that her sister's husband was a murderer, felt an entirely inappropriate urge to laugh, and bit the inside of her cheek, hard.

Nana and George Darcy regarded each other the way they always did: as two people who loved each other deeply and disagreed about everything. Nana was half his height and had been dead since he was a toddler, but she had been winning arguments since before the Glorious Revolution, and she was not about to stop now.

"You have upset her," Nana said, with a sharp glance at Elizabeth.

"I have told her the truth. If the truth is upsetting, that is not my doing."

"It is entirely your doing. You could have let me prepare her. I had a plan."

"Your plan involved six more weeks of household introductions and a gradual escalation of hints. I do not have six weeks' worth of patience left in me, and I never did."

"You never had any patience at all. You were an impatient child and you are an impatient ghost, and I told your father the same thing when you were two years old."

"My father agreed with you. He agreed with everyone. It was his chief failing."

"His chief failing," Nana said, drawing herself up, "was dying before I could finish teaching him sense. A failing you have inherited."

They were, Elizabeth realised, arguing exactly the way Darcy and Lady Catherine argued: with absolute conviction on both sides and no possibility of resolution. The resemblance was so striking, and so absurd given that both participants were dead, that the urge to laugh returned with redoubled force.

She did not laugh. She sat at her desk in the cold room with the dead candle, the forgotten ledger. She looked at these two ghosts, great-grandmother and great-grandson, bound by love, loss, a fury that had nowhere to go, and she thought: *I am not equal to this.*

She had managed Longbourn's ghosts since childhood, navigated Netherfield's with grace, handled a chaotic coaching inn full of confused spirits with nothing but composure and common sense. She had met Nana and held her own. She had been doing this her entire life, and she had always, always been enough.

This was different. This was murder, and family, and a web of secrets so tangled that pulling any single thread would unravel everything. She was one-and-twenty years old. She had been married for less than a month. A dead man was asking her to bring his killer to justice; his killer was her youngest sister's husband, and she could not tell anyone, because every truth she might speak would detonate in a different direction. She could not yet see which explosion would be the least destructive.

George Darcy and Nana were still arguing. Elizabeth let them. She sat with her hands flat on the desk and stared at the window where, an hour ago, she had watched two girls pulling weeds in the sunshine, and she let herself feel, just for a moment, the full weight of what had landed on her.

Then she straightened her shoulders, because she was Elizabeth Bennet: a woman who had stared down Lady Catherine de Bourgh and won, who had told Nana to stay out of her bedroom and meant it, who had carried a secret her whole life without once letting it break her. She was afraid, and she was overwhelmed, and she did not have the faintest idea what to do next.

But she would find one. She didn't see that she had any other choice.

Chapter Nine

Elizabeth did not sleep well that night.

She lay beside Darcy in the darkness of the master bedroom, the one room in Pemberley where no ghost was permitted to enter. She stared at the canopy above their bed, turning the word *murder* over in her mind until it lost all shape, became merely a sound, ugly, blunt, impossible to let go of.

Darcy slept the way he did everything, with quiet self-containment, his breathing steady, one arm flung across the pillow between them. In sleep, the careful reserve that governed his waking hours dissolved, and his face became younger, softer, more like the boy he must have been before grief and responsibility had set his features into their habitual gravity. Elizabeth watched him and thought about his father, sitting in her parlour, wearing the same face with anguish scored into it, and she pressed her knuckles against her mouth to keep from making a sound.

She could not tell him. Not yet, not like this, not with nothing but a ghost's testimony and her own impossible gift as evidence. Darcy was a man who dealt in facts, in ledgers and stewards' reports and the tangible weight of responsibility. If she spoke to him now and said, "Your father was murdered by Wickham, and I know this because his ghost told me," the best outcome would be bewilderment. The worst did not bear thinking about.

And beneath that, coiled like a snake at the bottom of a well, was the other thing. The thing she had not told George Darcy.

Wickham was Lydia's husband. Wickham was family. Everything Elizabeth did from this moment forward would be a choice between justice for the dead and safety for the living. She could not yet see a path that offered both.

She slept eventually, fitfully, and dreamt of brandy glasses, smiling men, an old woman screaming warnings that nobody could hear.

Morning brought grey skies and a thin, persistent drizzle that turned the grounds to mud and kept the household indoors. Elizabeth came down to breakfast later than usual, having taken longer than she liked over her hair and dress, though the truth was that she had been standing at her bedroom window watching the rain and trying to arrange her face into something that would not alarm her husband.

She had not entirely succeeded.

Darcy looked up when she entered the breakfast room, and his gaze lingered on her face a beat longer than it might have done on an ordinary morning. He did not say anything immediately; that was his way, to observe before he spoke, to gather his evidence before reaching a conclusion. Elizabeth sat, accepted chocolate, and applied herself to a piece of toast she did not want with a concentration it did not deserve.

"You did not sleep well," he said. It was not a question, rather an observation, carefully neutral. She thought he did not wish to press, but he had clearly noticed.

"It was rather windy last night," Elizabeth said. There had been wind, which made it technically true and therefore worse than a lie, because it was not the wind that had kept her awake. "I am not yet accustomed to the sounds of the house at night. At Longbourn one knew every creak and groan; here, there are rather more of them."

Kitty, who had attempted a walk before breakfast only to be defeated by the weather, was already seated beside Georgiana, slightly windswept, buttering a roll with the air of a girl who had earned her breakfast the hard way.

"The west wing is the worst," Georgiana offered from across the table, where she was eating an egg with conspicuous slowness, her attention plainly more on the conversation than on her breakfast. "The timbers shift in the wind. When I was small, I used to think it was, well." She caught Elizabeth's eye, and colour rose in her cheeks. There was a small thud beneath the table. "Mice," Georgiana finished, with the desperate conviction of a girl who has just discovered she is a dreadful liar. "Large mice. In the walls." She returned to her egg with an intensity it had done nothing to deserve.

Ghosts. Georgiana had been about to say she used to think it was ghosts, and had remembered, a fraction too late, that she was now in possession of a secret that made such casual remarks rather more loaded than they had been a week ago. Elizabeth did not dare look at Kitty.

"Is there an indoor occupation that does not involve needlework?" Kitty said, with admirable lightness and no sign whatsoever that her foot had just made contact with Georgiana's shin. "I have never been able to set a straight stitch, and I refuse to pretend otherwise."

"The library," Darcy said. "You are welcome to anything on the shelves."

"Georgiana and I might play," Kitty suggested, turning to Georgiana with an eagerness that was only partly manufactured. "You promised to teach me that piece by Clementi, though I warn you, I am a dreadful student."

Georgiana brightened. "You are not dreadful. You only think you are because your previous teacher was not very good."

"My previous teacher was Mary, who plays as though the pianoforte has personally offended her and must be punished for it."

Even Darcy smiled at that, and the moment passed, and Elizabeth felt a rush of gratitude toward both girls so fierce it bordered on pain. They were covering for her, each in their own way, Kitty from long practice and Georgiana from new, fervent loyalty; trusted with something precious, and determined to guard it.

But Darcy was watching. Elizabeth could feel his attention even when she was not looking at him, that quiet, steady attention of his. He knew something was wrong. He was waiting for her to tell him what.

After breakfast, he found her in the corridor outside the morning room. Mrs Annesley had taken Georgiana and Kitty to the music room. The house was momentarily, blessedly quiet of both the living and the dead.

"Elizabeth."

She turned. He was standing close, close enough that she could see the small crease between his brows that appeared when he was concerned, and his eyes were searching her face with an intensity that made her want to tell him everything and made it absolutely impossible to do so, both at once.

"You have been quiet this morning," he said. "Not yourself. If something is troubling you, I hope you know that you may tell me."

"I am adjusting," Elizabeth said, and heard how thin the words sounded, how inadequate. "There is a great deal to learn, and I, it is simply that the household accounts are more, and the rose garden requires, and I..." She trailed off, hearing herself stumble, watching his expression shift from concern to something more guarded, more careful. He knew she was holding something back. He could hear it in the spaces between her words, in the sentences she started and could not finish. She could see him choosing not to press. The restraint was costing him something, and that cost was worse than any accusation would have been.

"I am well," she said, more firmly. "Truly. I simply need time."

He looked at her for a long moment. Then he nodded, and raised her hand to his lips, and the gentleness of the gesture tore at her heart.

"I shall be in my study if you need me," he said, and left her standing in the corridor. Elizabeth pressed her back against the wall, closed her eyes, and thought: *I cannot do this for very long.*

The concealment she had practised all her life, the careful hiding of her gift, had always been a burden she carried lightly because the alternative was unthinkable. But this was different. This was not hiding what she could see; this was hiding what she knew. What she knew was this: her husband's father had been murdered. The murderer was her own brother-in-law. The man standing in the corridor offering her his love and his trust deserved the truth, and could not have it. Not yet. Not until she had something more than a dead man's fury and her own impossible testimony.

She needed to talk to someone who was not a ghost about what she knew, which meant she needed Kitty.

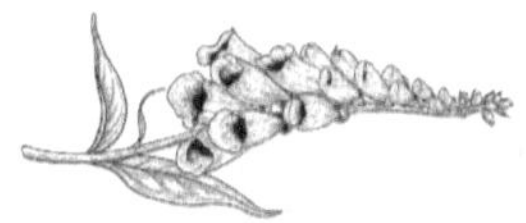

The drizzle had not let up by midday, but Elizabeth found she did not care. She needed to be outside, away from the house and its listening walls and its otherworldly residents who might drift through a closed door at any moment. She needed to speak aloud the weight of what she had learned yesterday, and she needed to speak it to the one person who could hear it without flinching.

"Walk with me," she said to Kitty, appearing in the music room doorway with her pelisse already buttoned and her bonnet in her hand.

Kitty took one look at her face, set down the sheet music, and stood. "I will fetch my cloak."

They went out through the side door, the one that led past the rose garden and down toward the lime walk. The rain was fine and grey, more mist than shower, the kind that soaked through fabric slowly, thoroughly, turning the paths to soft mud. The grounds were deserted; no gardeners, no grooms, nobody to overhear them except the spectral gardener who was pruning a hedge that no longer existed. He paused as they passed, squinted at the lime walk, and muttered, "Too close to the trunk. I said so in 'sixty-three,'" before returning to his phantom shrubbery.

Kitty walked beside her in silence for several minutes, waiting. She had always known when to wait. It was one of her greatest qualities, this patience that people who thought they knew Kitty Bennet would never have credited her with.

"George Darcy came to see me yesterday," Elizabeth said. "Darcy's father. He is a ghost. The most solid ghost I have ever encountered."

Kitty nodded. Her face was calm, attentive.

"He told me he was murdered," Elizabeth said. "Poisoned. Here in his own house, six years ago."

Kitty stopped walking. She turned to face Elizabeth. The rain beaded on her cloak, ran down in thin rivulets. Her expression did not change except for a tightening around her mouth that Elizabeth recognised as Kitty controlling a strong reaction.

"Who?" Kitty said.

Elizabeth looked at her sister, at this girl she had once underestimated, and said, "Wickham."

Elizabeth watched Kitty's face as the word landed, as the implications unfolded one by one: Wickham. Their sister's husband. The man who had eloped with Lydia. The man Darcy had paid to marry, to save the Bennet family from disgrace. The man who sat at their table, called their father "sir", kissed their mother's cheek, complained about his commission, drank too much claret, and was, apparently, a murderer.

"Lydia," Kitty said. One word. Everything that mattered.

"Yes."

Kitty turned away and walked three steps along the path, stopped, came back. The rain had darkened her hair; her cloak was spotted with mud. She looked, in that moment, not like the silly girl she had been and not like the sharp young woman she was becoming, but like someone caught between those two selves, trying to find the one that could bear what she had just been told.

"Does he know?" she asked. "The ghost. Does he know Wickham married Lydia?"

"No. He knows Wickham is walking free. He does not know Wickham married into my family. I did not tell him. We cannot tell Darcy either," Elizabeth said. "Not yet."

"No," Kitty agreed, and her voice was steady even though her hands, Elizabeth noticed, were clenched inside her cloak. "If you tell Darcy that Wickham murdered his father, he will act. Immediately, and probably violently, and certainly without waiting for evidence that anyone else would accept. And if you tell him how you know..." She did not finish the sentence.

She did not need to. They both knew what happened to women who claimed to see ghosts. The word *Bedlam* hung between them, unspoken, as present as the rain.

"We cannot tell Georgiana either," Elizabeth said. "She knows about my gift now, but this, the murder, Wickham. She has her own history with Wickham, from Ramsgate; has she told you of it? Yes, I thought she would have by now," when Kitty nodded. "Learning that the man who tried to seduce her when she was fifteen also murdered her father would be too much for her to bear, I cannot put that on her. Not yet. She is too young, and the knowledge is too dangerous, and while she will keep my secret from her brother until I give the word, this is not my secret. We cannot ask that of her."

"Agreed." Kitty was nodding, her expression settling into something Elizabeth recognised: the look she wore when she was working through a problem, sorting the pieces, finding the edges. "So. You know. I know. The ghosts all know, but they can't tell anyone. Who else?"

"No one living. I need to write to Jane."

"Yes. In code."

"Obviously in code."

They walked on. The lime walk stretched ahead of them, the trees bare in their autumn undress, the drizzle blurring the view of the grounds beyond. A spectral groom led a spectral horse along the path ahead of them and vanished around the corner of the stable block. Elizabeth barely registered him; her mind was too full.

"There is another thing," she said. "A thing I have been turning over since yesterday, and I cannot see a way around it."

Kitty waited.

"Even if we could prove it, even if we found evidence a court would accept, what then? Wickham hangs. Lydia is a murderer's widow at sixteen. The Bennet name will be in every scandal sheet in England, ruining your and

Mary's prospects of ever making a good match, dragging the Bingley and Darcy names into the mud as well. And the question everyone will ask is: how did Mrs Darcy know? How did the new mistress of Pemberley, married less than a month, come to accuse her own brother-in-law of a murder that happened six years before she arrived?"

"You would have to reveal your gift."

"Which I cannot do. Not publicly. Not in a way that anyone outside our family would hear. Because if I do, I am not a woman seeking justice. I am a madwoman. And a husband, in law, can do what he likes with a madwoman."

Kitty flinched. It was a small flinch, quickly controlled, but Elizabeth saw it. She hated herself for putting it there, but she had to say it anyway, because this was the shape of the trap and Kitty needed to see every wall of it.

"So," Kitty said, after a long pause, in a voice that was carefully level. "We need evidence that does not depend on ghosts. Real evidence. The kind a living person could have found through ordinary means."

"Yes."

"Then we must investigate. Quietly. The way we have always done things: you listen to the dead, and I watch the living, and between us we find out what really happened."

Elizabeth looked at her sister, standing in the rain in her muddied cloak, only seventeen years old, fierce and frightened and refusing to be anything less than equal to this. "Kitty. This is not covering for me at breakfast. This is not knocking over a glass when I look at something I should not. This is dangerous."

"I know," Kitty said. "Everything about your gift has always been dangerous. We have simply been fortunate, until now, that the danger was small."

They stood on the path, the rain falling around them, the great house behind them looming against the grey sky. Somewhere inside it, Darcy was in his study, wondering what was wrong with his wife. Georgiana was at the pianoforte. Mrs Reynolds was directing the household. And somewhere in the unseen corridors of Pemberley, George

Darcy was waiting, with a patience that was not patience at all but rage held in check by the thinnest thread of hope, for Elizabeth to find a way to keep the promise she had made.

"We should go in," Kitty said. "We are both soaked, and if we catch cold, Mrs Reynolds will dose us with something medicinal and we will lose a week."

Elizabeth almost smiled. "One moment."

She looked back at the house. From here, she could see the parlour window, the window where she had stood watching Georgiana and Kitty in the rose garden, the morning sunlight, Lady Margaret's smile, in the last moments before everything changed. The window was dark now, streaked with rain.

"I am going to write to Jane tonight," she said. "And tomorrow, I am going to begin asking discreet questions. About Mr Darcy's father, about his last days, about Wickham. The sort of questions a new bride might naturally ask."

"And I will be beside you," Kitty said. "Making sure nobody wonders why."

They walked back to the house together, arm in arm, their hems heavy with rain. Elizabeth held on to her sister and felt the fear settle into something she could carry, if not comfortably, then at least without breaking.

Chapter Ten

The coded letter to Jane took Elizabeth three attempts.

The first was too transparent. Anyone who intercepted the post would have understood she was implying Wickham murdered Mr George Darcy, and Elizabeth could not afford that. The second was too opaque; she read it back and could not understand it herself. The third struck the balance she needed, woven into a chatty account of the household and the rose garden restoration and Kitty's music lessons with Georgiana.

"The house continues to reveal its character in the most unexpected ways. I have learnt a great deal about the family history, some of it difficult to hear. One particular chapter concerns the passing of my husband's father in the presence of person we both know, whose conduct, I am coming to believe, was far worse than any of us imagined. I need your counsel, Jane. Not your comfort, though I will take that too. Your judgement. I find I do not trust my own."

Jane would understand. Jane always understood. She would read "a person we both know" and her mind would run through the possibilities, and she would arrive at the right answer, because Jane, for all her sweetness, was far from being a fool.

Elizabeth sealed the letter, set it on the tray for the morning post, and sat for a moment in the candlelight, trying not to think about how long it would take to reach Netherfield.

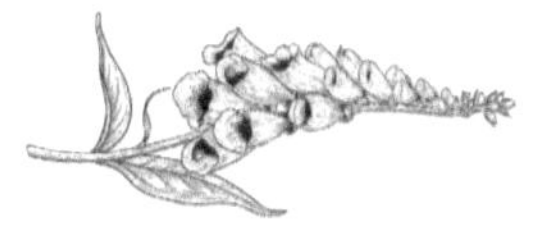

She began the necessary investigation with Mrs Reynolds the following morning, over the menus.

This was the natural order of things: the mistress of the house consulting the housekeeper about meals, about provisions, about the running of the household. Elizabeth had been doing it since her arrival, learning the rhythms of Pemberley with dutiful attention, because she understood that a great estate ran on a thousand small decisions, each one apparently trivial and each one essential. Mrs Reynolds had been patient with her, gently guiding her through the complexities of a household that numbered, between family, guests, and servants, upward of fifty souls. And that was just the ones that were alive and needed feeding.

Today, however, Elizabeth had a different purpose. She needed Mrs Reynolds to talk about the past, and she needed it to sound like nothing more than a new wife's curiosity.

"I have been looking at the family portraits in the gallery," Elizabeth said, as Mrs Reynolds poured her tea in the housekeeper's sitting room. It was a warm, cluttered space, fragrant with dried lavender and the particular beeswax polish that Mrs Reynolds favoured. "Georgiana has told me a little about her mother, and I should like to know more. I feel I ought to understand the family I have married into, and there is a great deal of it."

Mrs Reynolds's face softened, the way it always did when Lady Anne was mentioned. "Lady Anne was the finest woman I ever knew, ma'am. I came to Pemberley the year she married Mr Darcy, and she was kindness itself from the first day. She knew every servant by name within a fortnight, and she never forgot a birthday or a sick child. When she died, this house lost its heart."

"And Mr Darcy? The late Mr George Darcy, I mean."

"A good man, ma'am. A very good man." Mrs Reynolds set down the teapot. "He was not easy to know, not at first. Reserved, like his son. But fair, always fair, and generous with it. He loved his children fiercely, though he did not always show it in ways they could see. After Lady Anne died, he closed in on himself. The house felt it."

"The house felt it?" Elizabeth looked at the housekeeper with interest.

Mrs Reynolds paused, and something moved behind her expression, a hesitation that was not reluctance but something more careful, as though she were choosing how much of herself to reveal. "Pemberley is an old house, Mrs Darcy. Very old. I have been here a long time, and I have learnt, well. I have learnt to feel when things are right and when they are not. After Lady Anne died, the house was not right. I cannot explain it better than that. There was a heaviness, a coldness in certain rooms. The master felt it too, I think, though he would never have said so. He spent more time in his study, alone."

Elizabeth realised Mrs Reynolds was describing an awareness of the house's unseen residents that went beyond intuition. Lady Anne had not lingered as a ghost, but the ghosts would have grieved her passing.

"Did Mr Darcy have many visitors in his last months?" Elizabeth asked, keeping her voice light, curious. "I know so little about that time."

"Not many, ma'am. He had withdrawn from society after Lady Anne. Lord and Lady Matlock visited several times; Lady Matlock was worried about Miss Georgiana having no mother, of course, and Colonel Fitzwilliam came regularly; the master was very fond of his nephew. And Mr Wickham, of course."

The name landed in Elizabeth's chest like a stone.

"Mr Wickham visited often?"

"Indeed, ma'am. The master had been very good to him, educated him alongside Master Fitzwilliam, treated him almost as a second son. Mr Wickham had a way about him, very easy, very charming. The master enjoyed his company." Mrs Reynolds's mouth tightened, barely perceptibly. "He visited rather unexpectedly, just before the master's death. I remember it particularly because the master had seemed, well, not distressed exactly, but unsettled. As though something weighed on his mind. And then Mr Wickham arrived, quite unannounced. Though Mr Darcy did not seem surprised, as I recall. Perhaps he had written to summon Wickham for something or other."

Kitty, who had accompanied Elizabeth on the pretext of discussing the linen cupboards, was examining a shelf of preserves with studious concentration. She did not look up, but Elizabeth saw her shoulders tighten.

"And Mr Darcy's death," Elizabeth said carefully. "Was it sudden?"

Mrs Reynolds was quiet for a moment. The lavender-scented room felt close, the ticking of the mantel clock unnaturally loud.

"It was, ma'am. Very sudden. He had been quite well, or so it seemed. He dined as usual that evening, retired early, and in the morning he was gone." She pressed her lips together. "The physician said it was his heart. A sudden failure, he called it. These things happen, he said, in men of a certain age, though the master was not old. Not old at all."

"It must have been a terrible shock."

"For the whole house, ma'am." Mrs Reynolds stopped, and when she spoke again her voice had changed, dropping into something lower, more private, as though she were sharing something she had never quite put into words before. "I had thought the house heavy when Lady Anne passed. But after Mr Darcy died, it was nothing like that. It was as though the very stones cried out against the master's passing."

Not the stones, Elizabeth thought. *The ghosts.* George Darcy's rage, reverberating through every corridor, felt by a woman who could not see its source but whose instincts were sharp enough to register its presence.

She looked at Mrs Reynolds more closely, at this practical, warm, thoroughly sensible woman, and saw something she had not noticed before: a faint awareness behind the eyes, a quality of attention that went beyond the ordinary. Mrs Reynolds did not have Elizabeth's gift. She did not see the dead or hear them. But she was sensitive to them, she felt them, the way some people felt a coming storm in their bones, and she had been feeling them for thirty years without ever understanding what it was she felt.

"And Master Fitzwilliam," Mrs Reynolds continued, her voice thick now. "He was away, in London. He rode day and night when the express reached him, though his father was long gone. I have never seen a young man look as he looked when he came home and took Miss Darcy in his arms. He has carried it ever since, though he would never say so."

Elizabeth set down her teacup and found that her hand was steady, though the rest of her was not. "Thank you, Mrs Reynolds. I know this cannot be easy to speak of."

"It is not, ma'am. But I am glad you asked, because you deserve to know, and it would be more painful for either Mr or Miss Darcy to tell you about it." Mrs Reynolds hesitated, then added, carefully, as though she had been turning something over for quite some time and had never found anyone to say it to, "I was fond of the late master. Very fond. And I have always thought, though it is not my place to say so, that his death did not sit right. Nothing I could put my finger on. Just a feeling. The house has never been the same since, and I do not mean only the grief. Something is unsettled. Something has been unsettled for six years, and I have never spoken of it to anyone, because what would I say? That the house feels wrong?"

"Feelings," Elizabeth said quietly, "are not nothing, Mrs Reynolds."

The housekeeper looked at her with an expression that was almost startled, as though she had expected to be dismissed and found instead that she had been heard. "No, ma'am," she said, finally. "I do not believe they are."

They parted at the door of the housekeeper's room, and Kitty fell into step beside Elizabeth as they walked back through the ground floor. She was quiet until they were out of earshot, and then she said, low, "You cannot tell him, Lizzy."

Elizabeth did not pretend to misunderstand. "I know."

"I mean it. I watched your face in there. You were thinking about it. You were thinking: if only Darcy knew what Mrs Reynolds feels, if only I could explain it to him, he would understand." Kitty caught her arm and stopped her in the corridor. "He would not understand. He would think you had gone mad, or that you were cruel, raking over his father's death for some reason he could not fathom."

"Mrs Reynolds feels it too, Kitty. She has felt it for six years. I am not the only one who knows something is wrong."

"Mrs Reynolds feels uneasy in old rooms. That is a long way from 'your father's ghost told my wife he was poisoned.'" Kitty's grip on her arm was tight. "Promise me. Promise me you will not tell him until we have real evidence. Something that does not begin and end with you seeing things nobody else can see."

Elizabeth looked at her sister's face, fierce and frightened. She thought of Darcy, patient, genuinely concerned, waiting for a truth she could not give him.

"I promise," she said.

Nana was waiting in the parlour when Elizabeth returned.

She was in her chair, naturally, her small frame rigid with contained impatience. She had something to say and had been waiting to say it for longer than she considered acceptable. Elizabeth checked that the corridor was empty of the living, closed the door, and sat.

"You spoke to Mrs Reynolds," Nana said.

"I did. She told me a great deal. More, I think, than she intended to."

"Good. She is a sensible woman. I have been working on her for years."

Elizabeth looked at Nana sharply. "Working on her?"

"She feels things," Nana said, with the matter-of-fact air of someone describing a useful household tool rather than a human being. "She always has. Not seeing, not hearing, nothing so definite as that. But she is aware of us, in her way. When I stand near her, she shivers. When I am displeased about something, she becomes uneasy until it is put right. I learnt early on that I could direct her attention to things that needed fixing, matters the living staff had overlooked. A cold draught near a neglected window. An unsettled feeling in a room where the furniture had been wrongly placed. She does not know why she notices these things. She believes it is instinct, or experience, or simply the accumulated wisdom of twenty years in an old house."

"You have been using her."

"I have been guiding her," Nana corrected crisply. A hundred and fifty years of getting what she wanted without anyone realising she was doing it had given her a fine sense of the distinction. "There is a difference. I have never made her do anything she would not have done herself, given sufficient information. I have merely ensured she had the information, delivered in the only way available to me. A chill in the right corridor. An unease near a stain that needed scrubbing. I once stood beside the curtains in the blue bedroom for three consecutive mornings until she felt so uncomfortable she sent for the seamstress." A flicker of satisfaction crossed Nana's face. "They were rehung within the week. A persistent discomfort in the room where my great-grandson was poisoned, which she has felt every day for six years, because I have stood in that room every day for six years and made certain she would feel it."

Elizabeth absorbed this. It was manipulative, and it was also, in its way, extraordinary: a ghost who could not speak to the living, who could not write or touch or move objects with anything like the force George Darcy commanded, finding a way to communicate through the only channel available to her, the sensitivity of a woman who did not even know she was listening.

"You kept the memory alive," Elizabeth said. "You made sure Mrs Reynolds never quite forgot that something was wrong."

"Someone had to. Nobody else could hear me." Nana's voice was steady, but something flickered behind her eyes, the same guarded look Elizabeth had seen when George Darcy's name was first raised with Georgiana. "I could not solve it. I could not tell anyone the truth. But I could keep the wound from closing over, so that when someone finally came who could hear me, the evidence would not have been entirely buried."

There was a silence. Then Nana said, more quietly, "I owe you an apology."

Elizabeth nearly dropped her teacup. She had not expected to hear those words from Nana in this lifetime, or any other.

"George should not have come to you the way he did. I told him to wait. I wanted to prepare you, to give you time to settle into the house, to build trust between us, before all of that was laid on you. He is impatient. He was always impatient, even as a child, and death has not improved him in that regard." She paused, and her mouth compressed. "But he is also right that it could not wait forever. I have been holding him back since you first arrived, and his patience was at its end. If I had not let him come to you soon, he would have done something reckless, and a reckless ghost of his particular strength is not something this household needs."

"What would he have done?"

"Shown himself to Fitzwilliam. Moved furniture. Broken something valuable." Nana's tone suggested that the damage to Pemberley's furnishings concerned her at least as much as the damage to Fitzwilliam's composure. "He has the power for it, as you have seen; he opened your door, he compressed the chair. He is the most solid ghost at Pemberley. His rage feeds that solidity, and I have spent six years making sure he directs it inward rather than outward, because the alternative would have terrified this household and possibly damaged the house itself."

Elizabeth thought of the candle guttering, the temperature dropping, the misted breath in a room with a fire burning. "You have been managing him."

"I have been managing everything," Nana said, and for a moment the weariness in her voice was so vast, so old, that Elizabeth felt the weight of it like something physical. "For almost a hundred and thirty years, I have been managing this house, everyone in it, living and dead. I am tired, Mrs Darcy. I am very tired. And now you are here, and you can hear me, and I do not have to do it alone."

She stopped, as though surprised by what she had said, and drew herself up, and the sharpness returned to her face like a visor snapping shut.

"That is not an invitation to sentimentality," she added crisply. "I expect you to be practical about this. George requires justice. Mrs Reynolds has given you a beginning. What you do with it is your concern, but I suggest you do it quickly, before my grandson loses what remains of his patience and does something we will all regret."

"Understood," Elizabeth said.

"Good. Now. The drawing room curtains. I have been meaning to speak to you about them, and I will not be put off any longer."

Elizabeth, who had just been given an apology, a confession, and an ultimatum by a woman who had been dead for half a century, found that she was grateful for the curtains. The curtains were manageable. The curtains she could do something about.

She found Darcy in the library that afternoon.

He was standing by the window, a book open in his hands, though Elizabeth suspected he had not been reading. He turned when she entered, and his expression was the one she had come to dread: attentive, careful, watchful. He was studying her the way he might study a difficult passage of Latin, looking for the meaning beneath the words.

"I have been talking to Mrs Reynolds," Elizabeth said, sitting in the chair by the fire and picking up the book she had left there the previous day, a poor attempt at normality. "About the house, the family. She has been very helpful."

"She is fond of you," Darcy said. "She told me so yesterday. She said you remind her of my mother."

The words should have been a gift. They felt like a knife. "That is a great compliment," Elizabeth managed.

Darcy closed his book and came to sit across from her. The distance between them, the distance Elizabeth had put there with her secrets and her silences, felt as solid as the table that separated them. The ghostly governess,

Miss Pardoe, glanced up at him, registered that domestic tension was afoot, and returned to her book with the deliberate focus of a woman who had survived decades in other people's households by knowing precisely when not to involve herself.

"Elizabeth," he said. "You have been different these last two days. You smile, but it does not reach your eyes. You are present at meals but your thoughts are elsewhere. You and Kitty whisper together and grow quiet when I approach." He paused, and what followed was not an accusation but something worse: an appeal. "I do not ask you to tell me everything. I know there are things a wife keeps to herself, adjustments that must be made, and I have no wish to crowd you. But I need to know that you are not unhappy. That you are not regretting..."

"I am not regretting anything," Elizabeth said, and this, at least, was the truth, complete and unqualified. "I do not regret marrying you. I could not regret it. You must not think that."

"Then what is it?"

She looked at him across the table, at this man she loved, who was offering her an opening she could not walk through, and felt the impossibility of her position with a sharpness that took her breath. She could not tell him about his father. She could not tell him about Wickham. She could not tell him about any of it, because the moment she did, one of two things would happen: he would believe her, act, and the consequences would be catastrophic. Or he would not believe her, and the marriage she was desperately trying to protect would crack along lines she could never repair.

"I am learning," she said. "About the house, about the family, about all the things a new wife must understand. And some of what I am learning is, it is a great deal to take in. The history of this place, the people who have lived here, the weight of it all. I am not unhappy. I am simply, adjusting."

It was the same word she had used the day before, a vastly inadequate one, and they both knew it.

Darcy sighed, audibly, but he did not seem exasperated or angry. Just weary. "When you are ready to tell me what it is that is troubling you, I will be here."

He rose, crossed to her chair, and kissed the top of her head, and left the library. Elizabeth sat listening to his footsteps retreat down the corridor. She pressed her hands over her face. She did not cry, because crying would not help and Mrs Reynolds might come in.

She sat there for a long time. The fire shifted and settled. Miss Pardoe turned a page of her eternal book and did not look up.

Eventually Elizabeth took her hands from her face, straightened her back, and reached for the notebook she had begun keeping, the one disguised as household observations. She wrote:

Mrs R confirms: late Mr GD well before death. W present in the house, unexpected visit, summoned? Mr GD unsettled in days prior. Physician attributed death to heart. Mrs R has always felt something was wrong. House itself unsettled since. Mrs R sensitive; more so than she knows.

She looked at what she had written. Circumstantial. All of it circumstantial. A sudden death, a house guest, a housekeeper's unease. Nothing a magistrate would consider for a moment.

But it was a beginning. Tomorrow she would ask more questions, gently, carefully, wearing the mask of a bride who simply wanted to understand the family she had joined. Kitty would be beside her, watching, covering. Between them they would somehow build a case out of whispers, memories, the unshakeable testimony of a dead man who could not rest.

Through the library window, the late afternoon sun broke through the clouds for the first time that day. The grounds of Pemberley spread out in their autumn beauty. Elizabeth looked at them, thought of Darcy's face as he had left the room, patient, hurt, trusting, and added one more line to her notebook:

I must find a way. I must find it soon.

She closed the notebook and put it in the drawer of her writing desk, beneath the household accounts, where nobody would think to look.

Chapter Eleven

THE PHYSIC GARDEN WAS behind the kitchen wing, tucked into a south-facing corner where the old stone walls held the warmth of the sun even in late October. Elizabeth found it by accident, or rather the way one does when looking for something without knowing what it is.

She had been walking the grounds with Kitty, ostensibly to learn the paths and outbuildings that a mistress ought to know. In truth she was restless, her mind turning over Mrs Reynolds's words from the day before, the unsettled feeling in the house, the housekeeper's conviction that something was wrong. She needed to move, and she needed to think, and she found she could do both better outside than in, where every room held either a ghost or a husband or both.

They had passed the kitchen garden, where the last of the autumn cabbages sat in stolid rows, and the herb beds, where the lavender had gone grey, woody, the rosemary putting out its final pale flowers. Beyond these, half hidden by a yew hedge, was a smaller garden Elizabeth had not seen before.

"What is this?" she asked Kitty, stepping through the narrow gap in the hedge.

It was a proper physic garden, the kind that great houses had maintained for centuries before physicians became fashionable and apothecaries took over the business of healing. The beds were laid out in the old formal style, each one bordered with low box hedging, and though the plantings had gone wild in places, Elizabeth could see the logic of the original design: herbs grouped by use, medicinal plants separated from culinary ones, the dangerous specimens given their own bed near the far wall.

She knew what she was looking at before her mind caught up with her eyes. The tall spires, their flowers long since faded to brown seed heads, standing in a dense clump against the south wall where they would have caught the best of the summer sun. Foxglove. *Digitalis purpurea.* She had grown up in the country and knew every hedgerow plant by name, and her father's library had contained Withering's treatise on the foxglove, which she had read at fourteen with the same indiscriminate appetite she applied to every book in the house.

Foxglove, which in careful doses could steady a failing heart. Which in larger doses could stop one entirely.

Which produced symptoms, in excess, that would look to any physician like a sudden and natural failure of that organ.

Elizabeth stood and stared. The autumn sun was warm on her shoulders. A blackbird sang from the top of the yew hedge. The kitchen garden was full of ordinary sounds, a door opening, a maid's voice calling to someone about turnips, the scrape of a wheelbarrow on gravel. Everything was normal. Everything was exactly as it should be, except that Elizabeth was standing in front of the plant that had killed her husband's father, and it was growing twenty yards from the kitchen door.

Kitty had come through the hedge behind her. She looked at the garden, then at Elizabeth, then at the foxglove.

"Oh," she said. Quietly.

Kitty had read Withering too. Or if she had not read the whole of it, she had read enough, because Elizabeth had told her about it at fourteen, breathless with the thrill of a new discovery and desperate to share it with someone. That was the year they had walked every hedgerow around Meryton identifying plants, Elizabeth reciting their properties while Kitty collected specimens and pressed them in a book they kept hidden from their mother, who would have found the whole enterprise unwholesome.

"It has been here for years," Kitty said, looking at the established roots, the self-seeded plants that had spread beyond their original bed. "Long before Mr Darcy died."

"Anyone in the household could have picked it. Anyone who knew what it was."

"And Wickham was educated here. Alongside Darcy. He would have known this garden."

They stood together in the autumn sunshine. The blackbird went on singing. The foxglove stood in its bed against the wall, tall, brown, entirely innocent, entirely damning.

George Darcy was in the parlour when Elizabeth returned.

She had not summoned him; she did not know how to, or where he spent his time usually. He simply appeared, the way he had the first time, filling the doorway with his too-solid presence, and the temperature of the room dropped several degrees in the time it took Elizabeth to close the door behind her. Kitty, who could not see him but could feel the sudden chill and see from the expression on Elizabeth's face that they were not alone, wrapped her arms around herself and sat in the chair nearest the fire.

"I need to ask you something difficult," Elizabeth said, without preamble.

George Darcy sat. The chair did not creak, but the cushion compressed. "Ask."

"The night you died. I need you to tell me exactly what happened. Not the confrontation with Wickham, not what led to it. The evening itself. What you ate, what you drank, when you began to feel unwell. Everything you can remember."

He had told her the broad truth of it, the poisoning, the brandy, the morning when he did not wake. But she was asking for the details now, the specific, granular memory of his own death, and she could see what it cost him to go back to it.

"We dined at seven," he said. "The household dined together that evening. Wickham was there. He was, he was very easy. Very pleasant. As though the conversation that afternoon, the confrontation about Sally Wilson, had not happened at all. I remember thinking that either he had taken it better than I expected, or he was playing a deeper game than I had credited him with."

He paused, shaking his head slowly. Elizabeth could clearly see the regret on his face, the self-blame.

"After dinner, I went to my study. Wickham came to me there. He poured brandy. I have thought back on this a hundred thousand times. I remember that he stood at the sideboard with his back to me while he poured it, then brought over two glasses and put one into my hand. He said he wished to apologise properly, man to man, and to discuss the arrangements for the marriage. He was, I cannot describe it. He was the boy I remembered. The boy

I had loved. Open, earnest, sorry for his mistakes. I wanted to believe it. God help me, after everything, I still wanted to believe it."

Kitty, who could hear only Elizabeth's half of the conversation, sat with her hands folded in her lap and her face turned toward the fire and did not move.

"I drank the brandy," George Darcy said. "He stayed for perhaps half an hour. We talked. He agreed to everything I asked, the marriage to Sally, the terms, the living at Kympton still agreed upon when its current incumbent passed, and a smaller degree of support in the meantime while he completed his studies and made his living as a curate. He was reasonable. He was contrite. He was everything I wanted him to be, and I was a fool, because I had spent twenty years believing in a version of George Wickham that never existed, and I could not stop believing it even when my own son told me the truth."

His voice had dropped. The room was bitterly cold now. Elizabeth could see her breath, and Kitty's, hanging in the air between them.

"I retired at ten. My heart began to trouble me on the stairs. A flutter, nothing more, the kind of thing one notices and dismisses. By the time I reached my bedroom, it had become something else. Not a flutter. A stutter. My heart was stuttering, slowing, beating in a rhythm that was wrong, that I could feel was wrong, though I had never in my life had cause to think about the beating of my own heart."

He looked at Elizabeth, and the rawness in his face was terrible.

"I called for no one. I thought it would pass. I lay down on my bed. I waited. The stuttering grew worse. The room grew cold, or I grew cold; I could not tell which. The last thing I remember is the ceiling above my bed, then nothing, then waking to find that I was still in the room but the body on the bed was no longer mine."

The silence that followed was absolute. Even the fire seemed to have stopped moving.

"Foxglove," Elizabeth said.

George Darcy looked at her.

"Digitalis," she said. "Derived from foxglove. In small doses it is used to treat conditions of the heart. In large doses it causes exactly what you have described: an irregular heartbeat, a slowing, a failure that looks entirely natural. Any physician examining you afterward would have concluded that your heart simply stopped. Because it did. It was made to stop."

"You know this how?"

"I grew up in a country house, where there was an old physic garden. Not on the scale of Pemberley's, of course, but I recognise every plant in it and know what they are used for. And I read a great deal," Elizabeth said. "There is a bed of foxglove in the physic garden, not twenty yards from the kitchen door."

George Darcy was silent. Then he said, in a voice that was barely a voice at all, "I showed him every corner of Pemberley, inside and out. Every garden, every path, every room. I showed him the physic garden when he was a boy. I do not recall telling him exactly what each plant was for, but I do remember warning him that while they could be of great medicinal benefit, some of the plants were dangerous in the wrong quantities, or given for the wrong reasons. And certainly, there are books in the library which could have given him the information that foxglove is one of them, and why."

"You could not have known."

"No. But I showed him the weapon he used to kill me, and that is something I must live with. Or not live with. Whichever term you prefer." The ghost's attempt at dark humour was so like something Darcy would have said that Elizabeth felt her chest tighten.

Nana arrived ten minutes later, which was ten minutes longer than Elizabeth had expected her to wait.

She came in briskly; she had been listening at the door, if ghosts could be said to listen at doors. She looked at

George Darcy with fierce love and exasperation in equal measure.

"You told her about the brandy," Nana said.

"She asked."

"She would have. She is thorough." Nana turned to Elizabeth. "You found the foxglove."

"I did. And I have a question for you, Nana. You said you saw him die. You said you screamed at him not to drink. Did you see Wickham prepare the brandy?"

Nana's face changed. The usual briskness fell away. What was left was old, tired, furious.

"I saw him put something in the glass as he poured. I watched him hand the glass to George. I watched his face as George drank. I have seen many faces in a hundred and thirty years, Mrs Darcy. I know what a man looks like when he is watching something he has planned come to pass. He was not anxious. He was not hopeful. He was satisfied. He looked like a man watching a trap close. I screamed and I tried everything I could to make George spill his glass, but I could not."

"Unfortunately," Elizabeth said gently, "your testimony is not the kind anyone living would accept."

"No," Nana agreed. "It is not."

George Darcy stood. He did not pace; he was not a man who paced, any more than his son was. He walked to the window, stared out over Pemberley's grounds. His posture was so like her husband's that Elizabeth's heart wrenched.

"I had two children," he said, and the anger in his voice was not directed at Elizabeth but at something larger, encompassing the whole wretched scope of what Wickham had done and what his death had left behind. "Two children and no wife and a house full of responsibility. Now my son bears it all. My daughter barely knew me. And this, this is what I have. A ghost's fury and a garden full of foxglove and no way to prove any of it."

"You could have married again," Nana said, and her voice was gentler than Elizabeth had ever heard it. "You should have. You were young enough."

"I could not." He looked away from the window, back at them. "Annie was... she was everything. I could not put another woman in her place."

"I know. You loved your Annie too much." Nana paused. Something crossed her face that Elizabeth had never seen there before: a tenderness so old, so deep, it seemed to come from somewhere beyond the woman herself. From the girl who had been widowed at twenty, who had raised a son alone, who had lived almost eighty years more. "It is all right, boy. You did your best."

George Darcy looked at his great-grandmother. For a moment the rage left him, and he was simply a man who missed his wife, who had failed his children, who wanted someone to tell him it was all right. Nana had told him. It was enough.

Then the moment passed. The anger returned. The room was cold again.

Elizabeth looked at the two of them, the matriarch and the great-grandson, bound by blood, grief, the walls of a house they could not leave. She understood something she had not understood before.

This was not a haunting. This was a family. Her family, now.

And families, living or dead, deserved the truth.

"I need to tell you both something," she said. "There is a complication I have not mentioned, because I was not sure how to say it, and because I was afraid of what it might mean. But you deserve to know, and I cannot keep it from you any longer."

Nana's eyes narrowed. George Darcy turned to her with the full force of his attention, and the pressure of it was considerable.

"Wickham is married," Elizabeth said. "To my youngest sister. Lydia."

The silence that followed was of a different kind than the one that had come after George Darcy's account of his death. That had been the silence of grief revisited. This was the silence of something fundamental shifting, of two ghosts recalculating everything they had asked of her in light of a fact that changed the shape of every possible outcome.

George Darcy spoke first. "Your sister." He looked at Kitty, sitting by the fire, watching the flames silently. "Not this one?"

"No, that is my sister Kitty. Lydia is the youngest of us; only sixteen. She eloped with him in the early summer. My family was saved from disgrace only because your son, my husband, paid Wickham's debts and bought him a commission in the regulars and made certain they married. Darcy did it for my sake, though I did not know it at the time. He has never spoken of it as anything but a duty, but it was more than that, and we both know it."

"And you did not tell me this," George Darcy said slowly, "because?"

"Because if Wickham is brought to justice for your murder, my sister is a murderer's widow at sixteen, and the Bennet name, and the Darcy name, are dragged through every scandal sheet in England." She nodded at Kitty, who had looked up, realising she had become part of the discussion. "I have two sisters yet unmarried who cannot afford such a scandal to tarnish their prospects. I was afraid that if you knew, you would not care about the consequences to my family. I would not blame you for that. Your claim to justice is real and righteous, and it does not become less so because the man who killed you had the poor taste to marry my sister first."

Nana was watching her with an expression Elizabeth could not read.

George Darcy sat down again. Slowly. The cushion compressed beneath him, and he put his hands together, and he sat silently for several minutes.

"I would not have demanded that your sister suffer," he said, at last. "I am angry. I am, I think, angrier than any man has a right to be, living or dead. But I am not cruel, and I was not cruel when I was alive, whatever else I was. Your sister is little more than a child when he married her, taken in by him as more than one innocent young woman has been. She is not my enemy."

"No," Elizabeth said. "She is not. But she is part of the problem, and I needed you to understand why this cannot be solved with a magistrate and a courtroom. Even if we had evidence, which we do not, the cost of using it would be catastrophic."

"Then what do you propose?"

Elizabeth looked at him. She looked at Nana. She thought of the foxglove in the garden, the brandy six years gone, the death certificate that said heart failure, the physician who had seen nothing amiss, the household that had grieved and moved on, the world that had forgotten George Darcy's death as anything other than a sad but unremarkable loss.

"I do not know yet," she said. "But I am not going to stop trying to find proof."

It was not enough. She could see that it was not enough, in the set of George Darcy's jaw and the tightness around Nana's mouth. But it was honest, and honesty was the only currency she had left that was worth anything.

Nana spoke into the silence. "The girl. Your sister. Is she safe?"

The question surprised Elizabeth. She had expected re-crimination, or at least frustration. She hadn't expected Nana to ask about Lydia.

"I don't know," Elizabeth said. "His debts were paid, but I don't doubt they are mounting again. His temper will be worsening, constrained as he is by a wife to fetter his pursuit of his pleasures. And now I know what he is capable of when he feels cornered."

"Then you had better find your answers quickly," Nana said. "For her sake as much as ours."

It was, Elizabeth reflected afterward, the most unsettling thing Nana had ever said to her. Not because of the words themselves, but because of what they implied: that the danger was not only in the past but in the present, not only to the dead but to the living, and that the longer she took to find a solution, the more people stood to be hurt by a man who had already proved that he would kill to protect himself.

Somewhere in the house, Darcy was waiting for his wife to come down to dinner. She would go. She would smile. She would sit across from him, be charming, warm, present, and she would not tell him that she had spent the afternoon with his dead father and his dead great-great-grandmother, discussing the plant that had been used to murder one of them, the man who had done it, the sister who had married him, the impossibility of bringing any of it to light.

Chapter Twelve

MRS ANNESLEY LEFT THE following Tuesday, for an extended visit to her sister in Nottingham. It had been planned for some time; with a new mistress in residence at Pemberley, and Kitty for company, Darcy had agreed that Georgiana could well do without her companion for a month or two.

Elizabeth had not given much thought to Mrs Annesley's role in the household until she was gone. She was a quiet, steady woman who made everything run smoothly by the simple expedient of always being in the right place, saying the right thing, ensuring that Georgiana's days had shape and purpose without ever seeming to impose either. She had been Georgiana's companion since Ramsgate, hired by Darcy in the aftermath of that near-disaster, and she had done her job so well that her presence had become essentially invisible, the way all truly competent people eventually become.

Her absence was not invisible at all.

Georgiana found Elizabeth in the library on the first morning, hovering in the way she did when she wanted something but was not quite sure she was allowed to ask for it. She was dressed for the day, but she looked slightly unmoored, as though she had gone to the breakfast room and found that the person who usually anchored her morning was not there.

"May I sit with you?" she asked.

"Of course," Elizabeth said. "Always."

Georgiana sat, looked at her hands, then looked at Elizabeth. "Are any of them here now?" she said, carefully casual, as though she had been rehearsing the question.

Elizabeth glanced around the library. Miss Pardoe was in her usual chair, reading. "Miss Pardoe," she said. "The governess; she always sits in that chair half-hidden between the shelves. She is reading, as she always is. I don't think she has turned a page in sixty years, but she seems content."

Miss Pardoe looked up at the sound of her name, regarded Elizabeth with the mild displeasure of a woman who had been discussed as though she were a fixture, and returned to her book.

Georgiana's eyes went to the chair where Miss Pardoe sat, and her expression was a complicated mixture of fascination and unease. She could see nothing, of course. The chair was empty to her, as it was to everyone except Elizabeth. But knowing that someone was sitting in it, someone who had been dead for decades, someone who had lived and breathed and read books in this room, changed the way Georgiana looked at the space around her.

"Does she know I am here?" Georgiana asked.

"She is aware of you, yes. But she is not much interested in the living, I'm afraid. When she discovered I could see her, she spoke to me briefly, which is how I know her name and that she was a governess here sixty years ago, to your grandfather's sisters, I think, but she has not spoken to me since. She is quite absorbed in her book."

"What is she reading?"

"I've never been able to see the title. I have tried, but it seems to be part of her, if that makes sense. The book she was reading when she died, or perhaps the book she most loved. It does not change."

Georgiana absorbed this. She had a hundred questions; Elizabeth could see them queuing behind her eyes, and over the course of that morning she asked most of them. How did Elizabeth's gift work? Had she always been able to see ghosts, or had it come upon her at a certain age? Was she the only one in her family who could see them? Could she see every ghost, or only some? Did they know they were dead? Could they touch things? Could they leave the house?

Elizabeth answered as honestly as she could. She had been seeing ghosts since before she could remember; her mother said she had talked to empty rooms as a baby, and the family had assumed it was the babbling of infancy until it became clear that Elizabeth was holding conversations with people nobody else could see. So far as she knew, nobody else in her family could see them, though her father had speculated once that her grandfather on her mother's side, old Mr Gardiner, had seemed to have knowledge he should not have at times, which made him an uncommonly successful businessman. But he had died before Elizabeth was born, so there was no asking him now. Not every ghost was visible to her, she thought; she suspected there were spirits so faint, so far gone, that even her gift could not reach them. Every ghost she had encountered knew they were dead, though some took longer to accept it than others. They could not leave the places they were bound to, which was why Pemberley's ghosts were all connected to the house or its grounds. And they could not, as a rule, touch things.

"As a rule?" Georgiana said.

"Some ghosts are more solid than others. It depends on, I'm not entirely sure what it depends on. How long they have been here, how strong their connection to the place, how much unfinished business holds them. Nana is remarkably vivid, wholly present, but she cannot move objects or open doors. Others are fainter, barely there, more like impressions than people."

She was walking a line and she knew it. Every answer she gave led Georgiana closer to the question Elizabeth could not answer, the question that was sitting in the room as surely as Miss Pardoe was sitting in her chair: *what about my father?*

It came after luncheon.

They were in the music room, Georgiana at the pianoforte, Kitty turning pages. Elizabeth was pretending to read. The music was Handel, something stately and formal that Georgiana played with a fluency that made it sound effortless, though Elizabeth could see the concentration it took.

Georgiana finished the piece, rested her hands in her lap, and said, without looking up, "Nana said my mother moved on. That she was at peace. She did not linger."

"Yes," Elizabeth said. "That is what Nana told me."

"But my father." Georgiana's voice was steady, and she looked up, directly at Elizabeth. "Nana would not speak of him. She changed the subject."

Kitty, who had been sorting through the sheet music, stopped moving.

"Georgiana," Elizabeth said.

"I'm not a child, Elizabeth. I know when I am being managed, and Nana was managing me, as you are managing me now. Which means there is something about my father that she did not want me to know, and I have been thinking about it ever since, and I cannot think of a reason for the silence unless..." She stopped, drew a breath. "Unless he is here. Unless my father is a ghost at Pemberley, and Nana did not want to tell me."

The room was quiet. Kitty was looking at Elizabeth with an expression that said: *this is yours to handle, and I am sorry.*

Elizabeth set down her book.

"Your father is here," she said. "Yes."

Georgiana's composure held, but only just. Elizabeth could see the effort it took, the straightening of the spine, the deliberate steadying of the hands in her lap. The Darcy backbone, Elizabeth was learning, was hereditary.

"Why did Nana not tell me?"

"Because your father is not at peace, Georgiana. He is angry, grieving, bound here by unfinished business. Nana was trying to protect you from the force of that. She has been managing him for six years, keeping him contained, keeping the household from feeling the full extent of his presence. She didn't want you burdened with it until she was sure you could bear it."

"And can I bear it?"

"I think you can bear a great deal more than most people give you credit for."

The gratitude in Georgiana's expression was so raw that Elizabeth had to look away.

"Can I see him? Can you, can you arrange for me to be in the room when he is there, the way you did before, with Nana? You could tell me what he says."

"I can. But not yet. There are things I need to, there are aspects of his situation that I am still working through, and I need to do that before I bring you into it. I'm asking you to trust me. Can you do that?"

Georgiana studied her face in silence. "You are protecting me from something," she said finally. "The way Nana was."

"Yes."

"And you will tell me what it is. When you are ready."

"Yes. I promise."

Georgiana nodded. She turned back to the pianoforte, opened a new piece of music, and began to play. It was something quick, bright, demanding; a piece that required every particle of attention and left no room for the thoughts that crowded in when the hands were idle.

Kitty caught Elizabeth's eye over Georgiana's bent head. The look said: *how long can you hold this?*

Elizabeth did not have an answer.

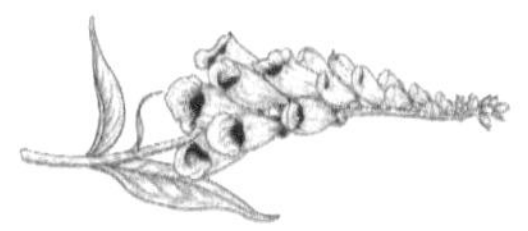

The letter from Lydia arrived the next morning, and it changed everything.

Elizabeth opened it at breakfast, expecting the usual litany of complaints and gossip. Lydia's letters were predictable: the dullness of Newcastle, the inadequate entertainment to be found among the other officers' wives, the injustice of being so far from Brighton and London and everywhere that mattered. Elizabeth had learnt to read them with affectionate impatience, scanning for anything that required a response and setting the rest aside.

This letter was different.

My dearest Lizzy, Lydia wrote, in the large, looping hand that used three sheets where one would do.

You cannot imagine how dull Newcastle has become. There is nothing to do and nobody worth knowing and Wickham is out most evenings and when he IS home he is not good company at all. He lost a great deal at cards last week and has been in a BLACK temper about it. I know I should not complain for he is my husband and I am sure it is very hard for him but Lizzy, he frightens me sometimes.

Elizabeth's hands went still on the paper.

He does not shout. He never shouts. But when I said something about the butcher's bill he went very quiet and looked at me and his eyes went FLAT, like there was nothing behind them at all, and I thought for just a moment that I did not know him. Only a moment. Then he smiled and said he was sorry and kissed my cheek and was all kindness again. But I did not sleep well that night and I have not slept well since.

I do not mean to worry you. I am sure it is nothing. He is under a great deal of strain with the money and everything. I should be more patient. Please do not tell Mama. And please do not tell Darcy.

Elizabeth read it through twice. She folded it, put it in her pocket, turned to Darcy, who was watching her across the table. "Lydia sends her love."

After breakfast, she gave the letter to Kitty without a word. Kitty read it in the morning room, standing by the window where the light was good, and when she finished she looked up and her face was white.

"His eyes went flat," Kitty said. "Like there was nothing behind them. And then it all passed over."

"Yes."

"That is how George Darcy described him. When Wickham agreed to everything and smiled and was the boy he remembered. The charm that switches on and off."

"Yes."

Kitty folded the letter along its creases, slowly, carefully, as though it were something fragile. "She says she is sure it is nothing."

"She is sixteen and she doesn't know what she is looking at."

"No. But we do." Kitty handed the letter back. "What are you going to do?"

Elizabeth put the letter in her pocket, beside the notebook she kept there now, the one filling up with evidence that proved nothing and meant everything.

"I'm going to talk to Darcy," she said. "About Lydia. Not about the rest of it. Just about Lydia."

"She said not to tell him."

"I know what she said. But I'm already keeping too many secrets from my husband, and this one is better not kept. He needs to know what Wickham is doing to her. If there is anything to be done about the money, Darcy is the one who can do it."

"That is managing a murderer's comfort."

"Yes. Until I can think of something better, that is exactly what it is."

She found him in his study after luncheon. He was at his desk, going through the estate ledgers. When she came in he set down his pen and looked at her. "It was the letter, was it not?"

Elizabeth stopped in the doorway. "How did you know?"

"Because you read it at breakfast, your face changed, you have been somewhere else ever since. Kitty has been watching you the way she does when something is wrong. You have come to find me in my study in the middle of the day, which you do when you have something to say and are not sure how to say it." He paused. "I am not as unobservant as you seem to think, Elizabeth."

"I have never thought you unobservant. That is rather the problem."

His mouth twitched at the corners. Not quite a smile, but the beginnings of one, the first easing she had seen in his face in days. The strain of keeping George Darcy's secret, on top of her own secrets, was putting a pressure on their marriage that was rapidly becoming unbearable. She could not wait much longer, but first; first she had to try to secure her sister's safety.

"Lydia asked me not to show you this," Elizabeth said, taking the letter from her pocket. "But I think you should read it."

She handed it to him and sat in the chair across from his desk and waited. She watched his face as he reached the passage about the card game, the debts, the temper. She saw the moment he read the words *his eyes went flat,* because his jaw tightened and something cold and hard settled behind his own eyes, something that was not surprise.

He set the letter down.

"She is afraid of him," he said.

"Yes. Though she doesn't yet know she is."

"She says *please do not tell Darcy.*" He looked at the letter, then at Elizabeth. "And yet you are showing me."

"Because I am your wife, she is my sister, and I won't keep this from you. I have too much on my mind already, and this is something you need to see."

She had almost said it. *I am keeping too many secrets.* She had caught herself, barely. She saw from the flicker in Darcy's expression that he had heard the stumble, registered the sentence she had started but not finished, chosen not to press. The restraint was becoming its own kind of language between them, a grammar of silences and near-misses that said more than the words themselves.

"His debts," Darcy said, after a moment. "If I were to settle them again. Quietly. Through a solicitor, so that Wickham did not know the source. It would ease the pressure, at least for a time."

"For a time. He will accumulate more."

"He will. He always does." Darcy was quiet, looking at the letter on his desk. Elizabeth could see him turning something over; the same deliberate process she had watched him apply to estate problems, tenant disputes, every difficulty that came before him. "I could arrange a quarterly allowance, paid through the solicitor. Enough to keep him afloat. Not enough to fund his worst habits, but enough that the debts do not become desperate. It would be a leash, not a cure, but it would keep him manageable."

"You would do that. For Wickham."

"I would do it for Lydia. And for you." He looked at her steadily. "I know what he is, Elizabeth. I have known since we were boys. He is a man who takes what he wants and discards what he does not need, and he has never once, in all the years I have known him, shown remorse for anything he has done. I do not say this to frighten you. I say it because I need you to understand that whatever you are working through, whatever it is you are not yet ready to tell me, I am not coming to it blind. I know what Wickham is."

The words hung between them. Elizabeth looked at her husband, at this man who was offering her exactly what she needed: money for Lydia, patience for herself, the unspoken assurance that when the truth came he would not be as shocked as she feared. She wanted to tell him everything. The pull of it was so strong that she could feel the words forming, the whole of it; ghosts, murder, foxglove, his father's ghost sitting in her parlour with rage burning behind his eyes.

She did not say it. Not yet. But she leaned forward, took his hand across the desk, held it. "Thank you."

Darcy lifted her hand to his lips and lightly kissed her knuckles, and for a moment the distance between them was not a wall but a window, something she could almost see through to the other side.

"When you are ready," he said.

"Soon," Elizabeth said, promising herself just as much as him.

Kitty was waiting in the morning room. She looked up when Elizabeth came in, read her face. "He is going to help."

"He is going to settle the debts and arrange a quarterly allowance. Enough to keep Wickham afloat."

"Good." Kitty paused. "And the rest?"

"Not yet. But soon. I told him soon, and I meant it, Kitty. I can't keep this up much longer. He knows something is wrong and he is being so patient about it that it is worse than if he demanded answers."

Kitty's expression changed. She crossed the room and closed the door.

"Elizabeth. You almost told him. Just now. I can see it on your face."

"I didn't tell him."

"But you wanted to. You were sitting across from him. He was being kind, steady, offering to help with Lydia, and you wanted to tell him everything." Kitty's voice was low, urgent. "You can't. You want to tell Darcy, who will go after him the moment he knows, and what do you think Wickham will do then? What do you think he will do to Lydia?"

The words hit Elizabeth like cold water.

"He killed a man who threatened to cut him off," Kitty continued. "A man he supposedly loved. Lydia is a six-teen-year-old girl he married because he was paid to. If Darcy confronts him, if Wickham feels the trap closing, do you truly believe Lydia is safe?"

Elizabeth sat down. She had not thought of it that way. She had been so focused on the impossibility of telling Darcy about the ghosts that she had not considered what Darcy would do with the information, what Wickham would do in return, who stood closest to the blast.

"I need to get her out first," Elizabeth said slowly. "Before anything else. Lydia has to be safe before we move against him."

"Yes." Kitty's voice was fierce. "You need to get our sister away from a murderer before you hand your husband a reason to go to war with one."

They were both quiet for a moment. Then Kitty said, more gently, "Georgiana asked me this morning if her father's ghost wants to see her."

Elizabeth closed her eyes.

"I told her I couldn't see him, so I didn't know. She accepted it. But she is going to keep asking, Elizabeth. She is patient, she is clever, she has nothing else to think about now that Mrs Annesley is gone. She is going to work it out."

"I know."

"So whatever you are going to do," Kitty said, "you need to do it before Georgiana gets there on her own. And before you crack and tell your husband. Because once you tell Darcy, everything moves, and it will move faster than any of us can control, and Lydia isn't safe, Lizzy. She is married to a murderer."

Elizabeth could see the fear on Kitty's face; the fear for the sister who Kitty had, after all, always loved best because she and Lydia were so close in age. Elizabeth was afraid for Lydia too, but not in the way Kitty was. She thought how she would feel if it was Jane in such a position, and nodded.

"I'll figure it out, Kitty. In a way that protects Lydia first and foremost. I promise."

Chapter Thirteen

Darcy told her at breakfast, looking up from a letter he had just opened.

"My uncle and aunt Matlock propose to come to us on Thursday for a visit of some few weeks, if it is convenient."

"Of course," Elizabeth said, because what else could she say? The Matlocks were Darcy's closest family. Lord Matlock was his mother's brother, Lady Matlock the woman who had tried to be a mother to Georgiana after Lady Anne died. They had every right to visit. Darcy clearly wanted them here. Elizabeth could not explain that the prospect of houseguests filled her with a dread that had nothing to do with the housekeeping and everything to do with the fact that two more sharp-eyed observers in the house meant two more people she would have to hide from.

Georgiana brightened visibly. "Aunt Margaret! Oh, I am so glad. She will want to hear about the renovations of the rose garden, and my music studies, and... everything." She looked at Elizabeth, looked away again quickly.

"She will want to hear about everything regardless of whether we wish to tell her," Darcy said, but he was smiling.

Kitty caught Elizabeth's eye across the table. The look was brief, but it said everything: *more people, less room.*

Elizabeth spent the three days before their arrival with Mrs Reynolds, going through the household preparations with the thoroughness that Pemberley expected and that Elizabeth was learning to provide.

It had become the best part of her day, these morning sessions in the housekeeper's sitting room. Mrs Reynolds had a way of making the vast machinery of Pemberley's household seem manageable, breaking it down into decisions that Elizabeth could weigh and approve and, increasingly, make on her own. The menus for the week had been planned already, but Mrs Reynolds walked her through the adjustments that must be made because of the expected visitors: Lord Matlock preferred his beef underdone and could not abide turnips; Lady Matlock drank only bohea tea and took it without sugar; both were accustomed to a fire in their dressing room regardless of the season.

"You know them well," Elizabeth said.

"They have been visiting Pemberley since Lady Anne married the old master, ma'am. Lord Matlock came for the shooting every autumn, and Lady Matlock came whenever Lady Anne needed her, which was often. They were as close as sisters." Mrs Reynolds paused in her counting of the silver, and her face softened in the way it often did when she spoke of the past. "It will be good to have them here again. The house is better when the family gathers."

Elizabeth thought about what that phrase meant in a house where half the family was dead, and said nothing.

The truth was that she had come to rely on Mrs Reynolds in ways she had not anticipated. Not merely for the practical running of the household, though that would have been enough, but for the steadiness the woman offered, the unflappable competence that was slowly turning Elizabeth from an imposter playing at being mistress of a great estate into a woman who might, in time, actually become one. Mrs Reynolds never patronised her. She never implied that Elizabeth was out of her depth, even when Elizabeth clearly was. She simply presented the information, offered her opinion when asked, and trusted Elizabeth to make the right decision.

What Mrs Reynolds did not know, and what Elizabeth could never tell her, was that she had a silent partner in the business of running Pemberley. Nana had opinions about everything from the rotation of bed linens to the arrangement of flowers in the front hall, and she communicated them to Elizabeth with a directness that Mrs Reynolds's sensitivity could only approximate. The result was that Elizabeth often arrived at her morning meetings already knowing which rooms needed attention, which servants were unhappy, and which supplier was overcharging for candles, information she presented as her own observations and which Mrs Reynolds received with quiet, growing respect.

It was dishonest, in its way. Another deception layered onto the ones Elizabeth was already maintaining. But it was also, she had to admit, remarkably effective. Between Nana's centuries of household management and Mrs Reynolds's thirty years of practical experience, Pemberley ran like a clock, and Elizabeth was learning to read its workings faster than anyone could reasonably have expected of a country gentleman's daughter married barely a month.

"I believe we are ready, ma'am," Mrs Reynolds said, tucking her lists away with a satisfied smile.

"Thank you, Mrs Reynolds. I could not manage any of this without you."

"You could, ma'am. You would simply manage it differently." Mrs Reynolds hesitated, then added, carefully, as she always was with personal observations, "Lady Anne used to say that a house does not need a perfect mistress. It needs one who pays attention. You pay attention, Mrs Darcy. The house knows it."

Elizabeth thanked her for the immense compliment, went upstairs to change, found Nana already stationed at her parlour window. The Matlocks' carriage had been spotted on the Lambton road, and Nana had no intention of missing the arrival.

"Half past three," Nana said, checking the mantel clock. "She is punctual, I will give her that." This was, according to Nana, exactly the time Lady Matlock preferred to arrive anywhere, because it allowed her to assess the household's afternoon arrangements, pass judgement on the state of the tea, and still have time to dress for dinner.

"She has been doing it for thirty years," Nana said, watching from the parlour window. She had been watching arrivals at Pemberley for considerably longer than that. "The first time she visited, she was newly married and trying desperately to be impressive. She wore a silk gown entirely unsuitable for the country and spent the first evening picking burrs from her hem. I liked her immediately. Anyone who tries that hard and fails that thoroughly has character."

Elizabeth said, "You will behave while they are here."

"I always behave."

"You will not stand behind Lady Matlock making faces. You will not rearrange things in their bedroom. You will not do whatever it is you did to the dining-room curtains, which Mrs Reynolds has now rehung twice."

Nana drew herself up. "The curtains were wrong. They are still wrong. I've been trying to communicate this to Mrs Reynolds for a fortnight, and the woman is being uncharacteristically obtuse about it."

"The curtains are fine."

"The curtains are an affront to the memory of everyone who has ever lived in this house, and I include the ones who are still living in it. But very well. I shall restrain myself. For the duration of the visit." She paused. "The curtains, however, will be addressed afterward."

Elizabeth left Nana to her grievances and went down to the front hall, where Darcy was already waiting, Georgiana beside him looking excited, Kitty a step behind them in her best afternoon dress, standing rigidly straight. Mr Graves had also positioned himself near the door, Elizabeth noticed; he stood at attention with the solemn dignity of a butler who had never quite accepted that the household could receive visitors without his supervision.

The carriage drew up. A footman opened the door. And Lady Matlock descended as though Pemberley had been built specifically to receive her.

She was tall, fair-haired, handsome in a way that owed more to the force of her personality than to the arrangement of her features. She wore a travelling dress of deep blue that managed to look elegant despite the dust of the road, and she took in the front of Pemberley with one swift, comprehensive glance. It appeared to pass.

"Fitzwilliam," she said, kissing Darcy on both cheeks with brisk affection. "You look well. Marriage agrees with you; I said it would, and I was right, as I invariably am. Georgiana, my darling girl, you have grown again; I shall have to speak to someone about it." She turned to Elizabeth, and the assessment in her eyes was thorough but not unkind. "Mrs Darcy. How good it is to see you again." She stepped forward, took Elizabeth's hand in hers, squeezed gently, a slight smile curving her lips. "You look well. I think Pemberley agrees with you."

"How could anyone not be happy at Pemberley?" Elizabeth said, quite earnestly, earning a wider smile from Lady Matlock.

Lord Matlock emerged from the carriage behind his wife, unhurried. He had long since accepted that his entrances would be overshadowed by hers, and seemed perfectly content with the arrangement. His face was pleasant and shrewd. He listened more than he spoke, and he remembered everything he heard.

"Darcy," he said, shaking his nephew's hand with genuine warmth. "The place looks well. Better than well, in fact. What have you done to the grounds?"

"Elizabeth has been working with the gardeners on the south border," Darcy said, and the pride in his voice was quiet but unmistakable.

"Has she? Good. It needed doing." Lord Matlock turned to Elizabeth and bowed, and his eyes were kind. "Mrs Darcy. A pleasure to see you again. I hope we do not alarm you by descending on you with little notice. We can, I fear, appear quite alarming, but I promise we are not."

"I heard that," Lady Matlock said, already walking toward the house with Georgiana's arm through hers. "And I absolutely contradict it. We are exactly as alarming as we appear. It is one of our better qualities."

Elizabeth liked them at once. She had expected to; Darcy spoke of his aunt and uncle with a respect that bordered on tenderness, Colonel Fitzwilliam was one of the most agreeable men she had ever met, and such a man had to come from somewhere. She had little chance to become acquainted with them before the wedding, but she found that she was looking forward to getting to know both of them better. After weeks of secrets, their directness felt like fresh air after a closed room.

The household rearranged itself around the Matlocks with the easy smoothness of a house that had been entertaining senior family for generations. The rhythms of

Elizabeth's days, which she had only just begun to feel were her own, shifted to accommodate the visit: morning calls with local gentry, afternoon tea in company, the yellow drawing room full every evening, conversation expected and silence conspicuous.

It was the silence that worried her. Or rather, the lack of it. For the past several weeks, Elizabeth had been able to slip away to her private parlour, to walk the grounds with Kitty, to have the conversations that mattered in the gaps between the ones that were merely expected. With the Matlocks in residence, those gaps closed. Lady Matlock expected Elizabeth's company and was perceptive enough to notice if it were withheld. Lord Matlock was observant in his quiet way, registering absences and irregularities even when he did not remark on them. The house was fuller, louder, more watched, and Elizabeth's double life was being pressed into a space that grew smaller by the day.

Nana was not helping.

"Margaret has rearranged the flowers in the blue sitting room," she reported to Elizabeth on the second morning, appearing in the dressing room while Elizabeth was pinning her hair. "She does this every time she visits. She believes the flowers should complement the wallpaper, which is nonsense; the flowers should complement the season. I've been fighting this battle for thirty years and I haven't yet won it, but I am patient."

"You are the least patient person I have ever known, living or dead."

"Patience and persistence are not the same thing, Mrs Darcy. I am abundantly supplied with the latter." Nana leaned on the edge of the dressing table. "Margaret has also been asking Mrs Reynolds about the household accounts. She does this too. She considers it her right, as the senior female relative, to ensure the house is being properly managed. Since Annie died she has appointed herself inspector-general of Pemberley's domestic arrangements. It is insufferable and it is also, I must admit, occasionally useful. She spotted a discrepancy in the wine accounts three years ago that would have gone unnoticed. An under-butler had to be dismissed."

"Do you like her?" Elizabeth asked.

Nana considered this. "I like her better than I liked her when she was twenty, which is not saying a great deal, as she was thoroughly silly at twenty. She has improved with age, which is more than can be said for most people. She is loyal, she is shrewd when she chooses to be, and she loves this family with a fierceness that I respect, even when it manifests as rearranging my flowers. She is also," Nana added, with the air of someone delivering a final verdict, "the only woman of her generation who has never once complained about the temperature in the east corridor, which tells me she has more fortitude than she lets on."

Or less sensitivity, Elizabeth thought, but did not say.

Lady Matlock, meanwhile, occupied Pemberley as though it was one of her own homes. She claimed the end of the sofa nearest the fire in the yellow drawing room, commandeered Georgiana for a full accounting of her musical progress, interrogated Kitty about her preparations for the upcoming season in London with a directness that would have been rude from anyone less charming and was instead oddly flattering, and surveyed the household.

Kitty acquitted herself beautifully. Elizabeth watched her sister navigate Lady Matlock's rapid-fire questions with a composure that would have been impossible a year ago, when Kitty would have been tongue-tied or giggling or both. She spoke about Longbourn with affection but without apology, about her music lessons with Georgiana with genuine enthusiasm, and about her sisters with a frankness that made Lady Matlock laugh and say, "Five girls! Your poor mother. I had three boys and nearly lost my mind."

"My mother's mind is entirely intact," Kitty said, "though she has put it to some unusual uses."

Lady Matlock laughed again, and Darcy, sitting nearby with his uncle, allowed himself a small smile that was mostly directed at Elizabeth, as if to say: *your sister is a credit to you, and I am glad she is here.*

Lord Matlock, meanwhile, was quieter but no less observant. He sat with Darcy after dinner, port in hand. The two of them talked about the estate, about politics, about the progress of the war, the price of wool, the particular challenges of managing tenants through a wet autumn. Elizabeth, watching from across the yellow drawing room, saw something in Darcy she had not seen before: an ease, a loosening. With his uncle, the careful reserve that governed his public manner softened into something closer to the boy he must once have been, the nephew who had looked up to this man and learnt from him and trusted him.

Darcy laughed at something Lord Matlock said, a real laugh, unguarded, and Elizabeth felt a pang that was not jealousy but something adjacent to it: the recognition that there were parts of her husband she had not yet reached, parts that belonged to older relationships, deeper history. She would have to earn her way into them rather than expect them as a right.

Lord Matlock asked questions that sounded casual and were not, listened to the answers carefully, and offered his own views measuredly; he was accustomed to being heard. He never raised his voice. He did not need to.

Elizabeth, watching from across the yellow drawing room where she was pretending to listen to Lady Matlock's account of a disastrous dinner party in London, found herself studying Lord Matlock with fresh attention. He was a man of influence, with connections in the government, in the law, in quiet circles where things could be done without fanfare and without scandal. If he believed something needed to be investigated, he could set that investigation in motion through channels that would never touch a public courtroom.

The thought formed slowly, taking shape the way a figure emerges from fog: not all at once but piece by piece, until the outline was clear. If she could find evidence, real evidence, the kind that did not depend on the testimony of the dead, Lord Matlock was the man who could act on it. Not with the blunt force of a magistrate and a trial, but with the careful, private authority of a family protecting its own. Wickham could be dealt with discreetly. The scandal could be contained. Lydia could be shielded.

If. The word sat in the centre of everything, small and immovable.

George Darcy was waiting for her in her parlour when she went up after the household had retired. He was standing at the window again, looking out over the darkened grounds, and his posture was so like Darcy's evening stillness that Elizabeth had to remind herself, again, that this was not her husband.

"I heard Margaret," he said, without turning. "She sounds exactly the same. Exactly."

"You are fond of her."

He turned then, and his expression was complicated, layers of feeling shifting beneath the surface the way they always did with him, never quite settling into anything as simple as one emotion. "She was Anne's closest friend. They were debutantes in London together, before Anne married me, then Margaret married Anne's brother." He paused. "Margaret held my children together when I died. She came within the week, stayed for a month, did everything I should have arranged for but did not, because I was too proud and too foolish to admit I would not live forever."

"She offered to take Georgiana after Anne died, she said today."

"More than once. I refused because I could not bear to lose my daughter as well as my wife, even to someone who would have cared for her well." His mouth tightened. "I was not a good father, I fear. I was grieving, blind. I let Wickham into my home while pushing my own son away. Margaret saw it, said nothing, because she was too kind to tell a mourning man that he was making a mess of everything."

"She was not too kind," Elizabeth said. "She was too tactful. There is a difference."

George Darcy looked at her, and the ghost of a smile crossed his face. "You sound like her when you say things like that."

"I'll take that as a compliment."

"It was intended as one."

They were quiet for a moment. Then George said, "Her husband. Matlock. He was here often in those last years too. He and I were not close, not in the way Margaret and Anne were close, but I respected him. He is a man who sees things clearly and acts on what he sees. If there had been anything to notice about my death, he would have noticed it."

"But there was nothing to notice."

"No. That is the genius of what Wickham did, is it not? There was nothing to see. A sudden death, a grieving household, a physician's verdict, and the world moved on. The only witnesses were the dead, and the dead cannot speak to anyone except you."

The candle on the mantelpiece flickered. The room was cold, but not with the sharp, aggressive cold that signalled George Darcy's anger. This was quieter, sadder.

"Matlock could help," Elizabeth said. "If I had evidence. He has the connections, the authority, the discretion."

"He does. He is also Fitzwilliam's uncle and Georgiana's guardian in all but name, and if he believed for one moment that their father had been murdered, he would not rest until the man responsible was destroyed. He would do it quietly, because that is his way, but he would do it thoroughly."

"That is what I need."

"Then find him something to act on, Mrs Darcy. Because I can tell you what happened, and Nana can tell you what she saw, but neither of us can lay evidence before Matlock. Only you can do that."

From somewhere down the corridor came the sound of a door closing, footsteps, Lady Matlock's voice saying something to her maid that Elizabeth could not quite catch. George Darcy looked toward the sound, and his face was naked with longing. She was going about the ordinary business of living in a house where he could no longer do the same.

"She visits Anne's grave every time she comes to Pemberley," he said. "In the family graveyard. She goes alone, first thing in the morning, before anyone else is awake. She has done it every visit for sixteen years."

Elizabeth said nothing. Some things did not require a response.

"I cannot visit it," George Darcy said. "I am bound to the house. The graveyard is beyond my reach. I have not been to my wife's grave since the day I was buried beside her, and I do not remember that, because I was already dead."

He turned back to the window, and the candle guttered, and the cold in the room deepened.

"Find the evidence, Elizabeth. Give Matlock something real. And when this is over, when Wickham has been dealt with and I can finally rest, perhaps Margaret will come to the grave one last time, and I will be there to meet her."

"Tomorrow," she said. "Lady Matlock will want to walk the grounds, and I intend to walk with her. I intend to listen carefully to everything she says."

George Darcy nodded once. Then he was gone, not fading the way the gentler ghosts did, but simply absent, as though the force that held him had released its grip for the night.

The parlour was warm again. The candle burned steady. Elizabeth went to bed, where her husband was already sleeping. She lay beside him in the dark, trying not to think

about evidence, or the lack of it, or the visit to the church-
yard that Lady Matlock would make in the morning.

Chapter Fourteen

Lady Matlock proposed the walk herself, on the third morning of the visit, and Elizabeth did not have to manufacture a reason or steer the conversation toward it. She simply appeared at breakfast in a walking dress and sensible boots, announced that she intended to see the grounds properly, that Elizabeth would accompany her, that everyone else could amuse themselves for the morning.

"I have been cooped up in a carriage for two days, a drawing room for two more, and I require air, exercise, and intelligent conversation, preferably in that order," she said. "Elizabeth, you will oblige me."

It was not a question. Lady Matlock did not ask questions when she already knew the answer.

They set out through the garden door, past the rose garden where Georgiana and Kitty's restoration work was beginning to show results, the bindweed cleared, the beds edged, the first signs of order emerging from what had been years of neglect. Lady Margaret Darcy was sitting on her bench beneath the old climbing rose, smiling at the newly tended beds with the same serene contentment she always wore; if a ghost could look pleased, Lady Margaret looked pleased. Lady Matlock paused to look.

"This was Anne's," she said. "She spent whole mornings here. She said it was the only place at Pemberley where she could hear herself think, which I took to be a comment on her husband rather than the house, though I never said so to her face." She touched one of the bare rose stems, gently. "Who has been working on it?"

"Georgiana and Kitty. They found a portrait in the gallery that shows how it looked in the last century, and they are trying to restore it."

"Good." Lady Matlock withdrew her hand and walked on. "Anne would have liked that. She would have liked your sister too. Kitty has something of Anne's quality about her, that quiet attention to things other people overlook."

Elizabeth filed that away. It was not the first time someone had compared Kitty to Lady Anne; Mrs Reynolds and Nana had both made remarks to that effect, and the comparison was becoming more interesting each time.

They walked in silence for several paces, along the path that led toward the south border and the lime walk beyond it. The morning was cold and bright, the kind of late October day where the sky was high, brilliantly blue, the light making everything sharp. Lady Matlock walked briskly, her stride long and sure. The spectral gardener was on the lime walk as they approached, inspecting the trees with an expression of deep personal betrayal, but he withdrew to the hedge as Lady Matlock bore down on the path, and Elizabeth could hardly blame him.

"Now then," she said, when they were well clear of the house. "I have several things to say to you, and I prefer to say them where we will not be overheard, because some of them concern your husband and I find it easier to speak frankly about family when the family in question is not listening."

Elizabeth braced herself.

"First. You are doing well. Better than well. The household is in excellent order, Mrs Reynolds adores you, and Georgiana is happier than I have seen her in years. Whatever you are doing, continue."

"Thank you."

"I am not finished. Second. You must give a ball."

Elizabeth had been expecting an interrogation. She had not been expecting this. She stopped mid-stride, stared.

"A ball?"

"A ball. A proper one. You are the new mistress of Pemberley, and the neighbourhood expects to be entertained. It is not optional, Elizabeth; it is part of the position. Every new bride at a great house gives a ball within the first few months of her marriage. It announces her, it establishes her, it tells the county that Pemberley is open and thriving and that the Darcy family is moving forward. If you do not do it, people will talk, and they will draw precisely the wrong conclusions about why."

"I hadn't thought about it," Elizabeth said, which was true. A ball had been the furthest thing from her mind, wedged as it was between a murder investigation, a ghostly household, a sister married to a killer, and a husband she was lying to.

"Of course you had not. You have been busy learning the house, adjusting to your new life. I respect that, but the adjustment period has a limit, and society is less patient than you might wish. I suggest early November. Lord Matlock and I will still be here, which gives you the weight of the family behind you. I shall help with the arrangements, naturally."

"Naturally," Elizabeth said, hearing the word come out rather faintly.

"Three hundred guests, I should think. The principal families of Derbyshire, certainly, and the nearer families from the neighbouring counties. The Matlocks will write to our connections. Darcy will invite the local gentry. And you," Lady Matlock looked at her with an expression at once commanding and kind, "will invite your family. Your mother and father, if they will come. Your other sisters. The Bingleys."

The Bingleys.

Jane.

Elizabeth's breath caught, and for the first time since Lady Matlock had said the word *ball*, she felt something other than dread. Jane could come to Pemberley. Jane, who had read the coded letter, who understood what Elizabeth was facing, who could not see the dead but had always known, always been the steady ground beneath Elizabeth's feet. Jane, whom she needed with an urgency that was becoming harder to conceal.

"The Bingleys, yes," Elizabeth said. "I should like that. Jane, my eldest sister, Mrs Bingley; she would come early, I think. To help with the preparations."

"An excellent idea. I remember Jane from the wedding; she is a lovely girl, and a sensible one. She will be a great help to you."

They had reached the lime walk. The trees were bare now, their leaves stripped by the October winds, and the path stretched ahead of them long and straight, the view of the grounds beyond blurred by a faint mist that clung to the lower ground.

Lady Matlock was quiet for several paces. When she spoke again, her voice had changed. The briskness was still there, but beneath it was a note Elizabeth had not heard before, careful and private.

"I have another matter," she said. "Less pleasant than the ball, though that is perhaps not saying much, since the ball appears to have alarmed you considerably."

"I'm not alarmed. I am merely... recalibrating."

"A good word." Lady Matlock glanced at her. "Mrs Reynolds tells me you have been asking about the family. About the history of the house, the Darcy line. She mentioned it to me because she was glad of it; she thinks it shows you care about the family you have married into, and she is right. But she also mentioned that you have been asking specifically about George. About his last days."

Elizabeth kept walking. She kept her gaze fixed ahead, her expression serene, and did not let her step falter.

"I have," she said. "It seemed right to understand what happened. Darcy does not speak of it easily, and I did not want to press him. Mrs Reynolds was kind enough to share what she remembered."

"Yes. She remembers a great deal, Mrs Reynolds." Lady Matlock paused, and when she continued, the performance had fallen away entirely. What was left was a woman who had lost her closest friend to illness and her friend's husband to sudden death, and who had been carrying her doubt alone for six years. "George was not an old man, Elizabeth. He was two-and-fifty. He was not ill. He rode every day, he managed the estate himself, he was vigorous and sharp and in full command of himself. Then one evening he went to bed and did not wake up. We were told it was his heart. We accepted it, because what else could we do?"

"What else indeed?" Elizabeth said, carefully.

"I had been visiting for a few weeks, before he died. Did you know that?"

Elizabeth shook her head, a little surprised. Nobody had mentioned that, not George or Nana or even Mrs Reynolds.

"I left, oh, three days or so before his passing. He had become quite agitated, which was unlike him. George was always the calm one, the steady one; it was Anne who felt things keenly, and George who held everything together. But that visit, something was wrong. He was distracted. Short with the servants, which he never was. He said something to me about his godson, Wickham." Lady Matlock frowned, reaching for the memory. "I cannot recall the exact words. Something about being disappointed, about discovering something, I do not know. I did not press him. I assumed it was the old business, the tension between Wickham and Fitzwilliam. I knew George favoured Wickham too much and that it caused friction. I thought he was simply coming to terms with what everyone else could already see."

"That Wickham was not worthy of his favour?"

"That is an interesting way to put it." Lady Matlock eyed her curiously. Elizabeth wondered if she knew about Wickham's marriage to Lydia, how that had come about, or even about Ramsgate and Georgiana. "I meant, that it was unwise and unkind to favour his godson over his son. Whatever George thought about Wickham, it was Fitzwilliam who was his son, and his heir."

"Of course," Elizabeth murmured.

Lady Matlock stopped walking and turned to face Elizabeth. "And then George died. Wickham was at Pemberley when it happened, which I did not think anything of at the time, because Wickham was always at Pemberley, in and out as though he owned the place. The physician said it was his heart. Lord Matlock arranged everything. Fitzwilliam came home. We buried George beside Anne, the world continued, and I never said a word to anyone about the feeling I had that something was not right."

"Why not?" Elizabeth asked.

"Because what would I have said? A feeling? A sense that things did not sit well? That is not evidence, Elizabeth. That is a woman's intuition, and I learnt a long time ago that a woman's intuition, however accurate, carries no weight in a man's world unless she can back it with facts. I had no facts. I had only a dead friend's husband, a physician's verdict, and a feeling that I had buried because feelings were not enough."

"Feelings are not nothing," Elizabeth said. She heard the echo of what she had said to Mrs Reynolds, knew that she was not the first woman in this house to feel the truth and be told it did not count.

Lady Matlock looked at her thoughtfully. "No," she said. "They are not. Which is why I am telling you now, because you have been asking the same questions I never dared to ask, and I think you deserve to know that you are not alone in finding the answers uncomfortable."

They stood facing each other on the path, and the mist moved between the trees, and Elizabeth thought about what it would mean to bring Lady Matlock into the full truth. Not yet. Not without more tangible evidence than she currently had. But the door was open, and Lady Matlock had opened it herself, and that mattered more than Elizabeth could say.

"Thank you," Elizabeth said. "For telling me."

"Do not thank me. I should have said something six years ago. I should have asked the questions and demanded the answers and not let the world tell me that a feeling was not enough." Lady Matlock's voice was steady, but her eyes were bright. "If you find something, Elizabeth, if your questions lead somewhere, promise me you will not make the same mistake I did. Promise me you will not stay silent."

"I promise."

Lady Matlock nodded once. Then the performance returned, the armour she had worn for thirty years, bright and impenetrable, and she said, briskly, "Good. Now. The ball. The ballroom must have new candles in the chandelier, which will need a good cleaning. The floor must be polished, then chalked. We shall need to discuss the supper menu with Mrs Reynolds, and I have strong opinions about the music, which you will hear whether you wish to or not."

"I would expect nothing less."

"Excellent. Then we understand each other." Lady Matlock took Elizabeth's arm, and they walked back toward the house together as the morning sun broke through the mist, and Pemberley gleamed ahead of them in the sharp autumnal light.

Elizabeth wrote to Jane that afternoon.

She did not use the code. She did not need to, because this letter was simple and true and contained nothing that needed hiding: *come to Pemberley. Come early, before the ball. Come as soon as you can. I need you here.*

She sealed it and gave it to the footman for the afternoon post, and felt, for the first time in weeks, that the ground beneath her had firmed. Lady Matlock's doubt was not evidence. Her memories were not proof. But they were confirmation, from a living woman, that the unease Elizabeth felt was not hers alone, that the questions she was asking were the right ones, that when the time came to act she would not be acting alone.

She had thought, walking back to the house with Lady Matlock's arm through hers, about what else the Matlocks might do. Lady Matlock had influence. She had connections, social authority, the kind of power that opened doors and rearranged lives without anyone quite noticing it had happened. Could she be persuaded to take an interest in Lydia? To invite her for a long visit, perhaps, or to find some pretext for separating her from Wickham for a time?

But every version of the plan collapsed under its own weight. Lydia would not leave Wickham willingly; she was sixteen, married, still half in love with the idea of being in love. She would resist any interference. Wickham would see through any pretext in an instant and charm his way around it, or simply refuse, and a refused invitation from Lady Matlock would raise exactly the kind of questions Elizabeth could not afford to answer. To explain why Lydia needed rescuing meant explaining what Wickham was, what he had done. Elizabeth had promised Kitty she would not do that until Lydia was safe. The logic was circular and merciless: she could not save Lydia without revealing the truth, and she could not reveal the truth without endangering Lydia.

So. The money, for now. Darcy's quiet allowance, keeping Wickham comfortable, keeping Lydia fed and housed and out of the worst of it. It was not enough, but it was what she had.

The ball she could manage. She had Nana, Mrs Reynolds, now Lady Matlock. Between them Pemberley would be ready. And Jane was coming.

Jane was coming. Everything would be easier after that, and somehow she would find the courage, the words, to tell her husband the truth.

Chapter Fifteen

Elizabeth had rehearsed the exact words she would say twice that morning: once in the bath, once walking the length of the portrait gallery after breakfast while Edmund and Charlotte chased each other from end to end and Kitty watched her while making a thoroughly poor job of pretending to examine a painting.

The argument with Kitty had taken most of the previous evening.

"You can't tell him about his father," Kitty had said, flat and certain, the moment Elizabeth raised it. They were in Elizabeth's parlour, the door locked, speaking low.

"You can't tell Darcy that his father was murdered. You promised me, Elizabeth."

"I know. I'm not going to tell him about the murder. Just about the ghosts. About my gift, about what I am."

"And not George."

"And not George." But even as she said it, the problem took shape. "Except I have to. Kitty, I told Georgiana. She knows her father is here. The moment Darcy knows about my gift, Georgiana will know he is in on the secret, and she will talk to him about it. About their father. I can't ask her to lie to her brother, and I can't stop her from speaking to him. So I either tell Darcy about George myself, or he hears it from Georgiana and knows I kept it from him deliberately."

Kitty stared at her. "Then you can't tell him at all."

"I must. Darcy knows I am hiding something, and his patience will not last forever, and I would rather tell him a partial truth than have him discover the whole of it by accident." She paused. "And Lydia. The money will help, but money is not enough. I need my husband beside me in this, not watching me across the breakfast table wondering what I am hiding. I need to be able to ask him for help, real help, for Lydia, without having to weigh every word for what it might reveal. I can't do that while he thinks his wife is an ordinary woman."

"So you tell him about George. And when he asks why his father is still here?"

"I say... I don't know. That some spirits are bound to the places they loved, and I don't fully understand why some linger and others move on. It is not even entirely a lie."

"That is a lie, Elizabeth."

"Yes. It is the best I have."

Kitty had not argued further. She had not agreed, exactly, but she had stopped objecting, which amounted to the same thing. What she had said, this morning, looking almost as strained as Elizabeth felt, was: "Just go. Before you lose your nerve again."

Elizabeth had not lost her nerve. She had simply, on all the previous occasions when she might have spoken, found a reason not to.

But Jane was coming, and Jane would ask whether Elizabeth had told her husband, and Elizabeth could not face that conversation without an honest answer.

She found him in his study, as she had expected to at this hour. He was reading correspondence, but he set it aside when she came in, because he always did, and the gladness in his face made what she was about to do both easier and more terrible.

"I need to tell you something," she said.

Darcy looked at her. His expression did not change, but his gaze sharpened.

"Will you not sit down?" he said, his tone gentle. As though perhaps he thought she might flee if he sounded formal, or stern.

She sat. She folded her hands in her lap and unfolded them again. "There is something about me that I should have told you before we married. Something I have carried my whole life, that my family knows, and I have been trying to find the right moment to tell you, and there is no right moment, so I am choosing this one."

Darcy had gone a little stiff, his posture rigid, almost as though awaiting a blow. She could see him preparing for something, though she could not tell what he expected. An unhappiness. Some grief she had been hiding.

He was not wrong, exactly.

"Darcy, I..."

A knock at the study door cut her off before she could begin to say it. The knock was sharp, urgent. Darcy shot

Elizabeth an apologetic look before rising and going to the door.

Elizabeth twisted her hands together, made herself breathe slowly. *Whoever it is will go away in a moment,* she thought, *and then I will say it.*

But the voice at the door was Mrs Reynolds, who would never interrupt them lightly, and she sounded carefully composed but not quite calm as she said, "I beg your pardon, sir, but a carriage has just been sighted on the drive. It is Lady Catherine de Bourgh's carriage."

The silence lasted perhaps two seconds. It felt considerably longer.

"She has not written," Darcy said.

"No, sir."

Darcy turned from the door and looked at Elizabeth. Elizabeth looked at Darcy. The truth she had spent days gathering the courage to deliver sat between them, stranded.

"We will continue this conversation," Darcy said. It was not a question.

"Yes," Elizabeth said. "We will."

But the moment had passed. They both knew it. Elizabeth stood, smoothed her dress, went to meet the carriage with her husband beside her and the words still locked behind her teeth.

Lady Catherine descended from her carriage as though conferring a favour upon the ground.

She was dressed in black bombazine, worn less for mourning than for authority, and she surveyed Pemberley's front entrance in a single sweeping glance and an expression that clearly indicated she found the sight before her entirely inadequate. Behind her, Anne de Bourgh was helped down by her companion, pale and thin and blinking in the October sun like a creature emerging from long captivity. Which, in some respects, Elizabeth supposed, she was. She had truly never expected to see Anne de Bourgh at Pemberley, so far from the safety of Rosings.

"Fitzwilliam," Lady Catherine said. "I have come."

"So I see," Darcy said. His voice was perfectly civil and perfectly cold, and Elizabeth could hear the effort required to be both.

"I am not staying long. A week, perhaps two. I wish to see how the house is being kept. Anne needs the air; she has been unwell, and Mrs Jenkinson insists upon the country. I have matters to discuss with my brother Lord Matlock. And I wish," she turned her gaze upon Elizabeth, and the force of it was considerable, "to see how you are getting on, Mrs Darcy."

"Very well, I thank you," Elizabeth said, and smiled, because the best defence against Lady Catherine had always been courtesy delivered with an impeccable straight face.

From somewhere behind her, she heard George Darcy say, "Oh, God. Not Catherine."

Elizabeth did not flinch. She kept her eyes on Lady Catherine, her smile in place, and did not, by any visible sign, acknowledge the ghost of her father-in-law, who had materialised just inside the front door, staring at his sister-in-law with undisguised horror.

"She is wearing the black again," George said. "She has been wearing it for seventeen years. Lewis has been dead for seventeen years and she is still punishing everyone with it. He would not have wanted this. Lewis wanted to be cremated on a Viking pyre, which Catherine refused to consider, so I hardly think she is wearing it for his sake."

Elizabeth had to bite down on the inside of her cheek to keep the laughter from erupting as she envisioned Lady Catherine's expression upon being told that her husband had wished to be cremated on a Viking pyre. It was one of the most difficult things she had ever done. She tasted blood.

Lady Catherine swept into the entrance hall, cataloguing deficiencies. "The floors need polishing. The flowers are wrong. Why are the curtains different in the yellow drawing room? They were blue when I was last here."

"Because they were faded," Nana said, materialising at Elizabeth's shoulder with a loud sniff. "They had been faded for years, and she did not notice when she last visited. On the last three occasions she visited."

Elizabeth now had two ghosts providing commentary, and Lady Catherine had only reached the yellow drawing room.

George and Nana followed Lady Catherine, and Elizabeth trailed behind them all, receiving commentary from two directions at once. Catherine examined the furniture, ran a finger along the mantelpiece, checked it for dust, and found none, which appeared to disappoint her. She examined the arrangement of chairs and declared them wrong. She looked at the pianoforte and said it needed tuning, though how she could possibly tell without playing a single note, Elizabeth could not imagine.

"She can't play," George confided to Elizabeth. "She never could. She has strong opinions about everyone else's music, and she can't manage a scale herself. Annie used to say it was Catherine's greatest sorrow, though she never would have admitted it."

Catherine paused before the portrait of Lady Anne that hung above the fireplace. She was quiet for a moment, and George was quiet too. Then Catherine said, "The frame wants cleaning," and walked on.

"She cannot say she misses her," George said. "Sixteen years, and she still cannot simply say she misses her sister."

"The servants look well enough," Lady Catherine continued, turning her attention to the two maids and two footmen who were lined up against the wall awaiting instruction. "Though the footmen could use better posture. In my household, I insist upon it. Good posture is the foundation of domestic order."

"She said exactly the same thing in 1796," George observed. "And in 1802. And on every visit in between. I believe she considers it a philosophy."

Georgiana, who had come down to greet her aunt, caught Elizabeth's eye at the precise moment George delivered this. She could not see her father; she could not hear him. But she could read Elizabeth's face, and whatever she found there was too much; she made a sound that was nearly a laugh, turned it into a cough, said, "Excuse me, I think I left something in the music room," and fled.

Lady Catherine watched her go. "The girl is still nervous. You must do something about that, Fitzwilliam."

"Georgiana is well," Darcy said, in a tone that did not invite further comment.

Lord Matlock appeared in the doorway, unhurried, because he had survived decades of his sister's arrivals and had learnt the value of a late entrance. "Catherine. What a pleasant surprise."

"It is not a surprise, Matlock. I wrote to you."

"You did not."

"I intended to. The effect is the same."

"It is not remotely the same," Lady Matlock said, entering behind her husband, "but we shall manage. Mrs Reynolds says you will have the blue rooms, Catherine; they face east, and I know you prefer the morning light. Mrs Darcy, shall I see to the arrangements?"

"Thank you," Elizabeth said, and meant it with her whole heart, because Lady Matlock was already steering Lady Catherine out of the yellow drawing room and in the direction of the staircase. Elizabeth was quite desperate for a few moments alone before she disgraced herself entirely.

"I like Margaret," George said, watching the two women disappear up the stairs. "I have always liked Margaret. She is the only person alive who can make Catherine do anything without Catherine noticing she is being made to do it."

Elizabeth allowed herself, for one brief moment, to close her eyes.

Anne de Bourgh had not followed her mother upstairs. She stood in the entrance hall, small and quiet and looking around at Pemberley as though seeing it clearly for the first time. When she caught Elizabeth watching her, she smiled; a tentative thing, uncertain. Elizabeth smiled back, and thought: *here is a girl who has been told all her life what to think, and is beginning to wonder whether any of it was true.*

"Miss de Bourgh," Elizabeth said. "Welcome to Pemberley. I hope you will be comfortable here."

"Thank you, Mrs Darcy," Anne said. "I believe I shall be."

It was such a simple sentence, and Anne delivered it so quietly, but it sounded remarkably like relief.

"We've the yellow rooms ready for you, Miss de Bourgh," Mrs Reynolds said warmly. "If you'll allow me to escort you upstairs?"

"Thank you, Mrs Reynolds," Elizabeth said, deeply grateful for the housekeeper's efficiency. How Mrs Reynolds had two of the best guest suites prepared on ten minutes' notice was a mystery, but Elizabeth had no doubt that Pemberley would not be disgraced by the efforts.

By the second evening, Elizabeth understood that Lady Catherine was going to be a problem of an entirely different order to the Matlocks.

She had expected the disapproval. She had expected the comments about the furniture, the menus, the household management, the fact that Elizabeth had been born a mere country gentleman's daughter rather than into the peerage. She had weathered Lady Catherine's opposition before, and she was not afraid of the woman's opinions.

What she had not expected was the watching.

Lady Catherine watched everything. She watched Elizabeth at meals, during walks, in the yellow drawing room. She noted who Elizabeth spoke to and how long the conversations lasted. She tracked Elizabeth's exits and entrances: when she left a room, how long she was gone, whether she returned looking different than when she had left.

Kitty, alert to the danger from the first moment, adjusted accordingly. In the yellow drawing room after tea, when George Darcy appeared beside Elizabeth, talking about Lady Catherine's petty cruelties toward her sister when they were young, Kitty launched into a long, animated account of a novel she was reading, directing it at Elizabeth in a way that required nothing but the occasional nod and murmur of agreement. Elizabeth could listen to George while appearing to listen to Kitty, and Lady Catherine, watching from her chair by the fire, saw only a young woman being bored by her sister's literary enthusiasm. It was seamless, the product of years of practice, and Elizabeth was grateful for it in a way she could not express.

But Kitty could not be in every room.

The following morning, Elizabeth paused in the corridor to listen to Nana, who wanted to tell her about an under-housemaid who was making eyes at one of the footmen, and when she turned, Lady Catherine was standing at the far end of the corridor, watching.

"Were you speaking to someone, Mrs Darcy?"

"I was counting the candle sconces," Elizabeth said. "Mrs Reynolds asked me to check whether they all had fresh candles before the ball."

"You were standing quite still. And your lips were moving."

"I was counting," Elizabeth said again, and smiled, and walked past Lady Catherine with her heart hammering.

"Witch," Nana said, and for a moment Elizabeth thought it was Lady Catherine who had spoken, directing the remark at her, and the terror that washed over her almost stopped her breath.

At dinner that evening, Lady Catherine held forth on the management of great estates, a subject upon which she considered herself the foremost authority in England. She addressed most of her remarks to Darcy and Lord Matlock, though she directed the occasional observation at Elizabeth that carried the sting of a test.

"I trust you have not been making changes to the household, Mrs Darcy. A new wife ought to observe for at least a year before she presumes to alter anything."

"I have made few changes," Elizabeth said. "Mrs Reynolds and I consult daily, and she guides me admirably."

"Mrs Reynolds." Lady Catherine's tone suggested that relying on a housekeeper was a confession of inadequacy. "When I took charge of Rosings, I did not require guidance. I knew at once what was needed."

"How fortunate for Rosings," Lady Matlock murmured, and Lord Matlock became intensely interested in his wine.

But then, as the dessert was cleared, Lady Catherine turned her attention to Elizabeth again, and this time there was nothing casual about it. "You look tired, Mrs Darcy. Are you sleeping well? I have always believed that women of a nervous disposition require more rest than others. It is a failing of the constitution, not a moral deficiency, and there is no shame in admitting it."

The table went quiet. Darcy set down his glass.

"Elizabeth is in excellent health," he said.

"I did not say she was not. I said she looked tired. There is a difference, Fitzwilliam, and a husband ought to attend to these things."

Elizabeth smiled and said, "I am perfectly well, Lady Catherine. I thank you for your concern." Beneath the table, she gripped her hands tightly together, because Lady Catherine had just played her first card. *Nervous disposition. A failing of the constitution.* The language of physicians, of commitments, of women put away. And one which was easy to target at Elizabeth, the daughter of a woman who complained constantly about her nerves.

After dinner, she found Kitty in the library, reading quietly in the company of Miss Pardoe, though Kitty of course thought she was reading alone.

"She is watching me," Elizabeth said, flopping rather ungracefully into a chair. "Not casually. She is looking for something."

"She has always wanted this marriage to fail," Kitty pointed out. "If she can find evidence that something is wrong with you, she will use it."

"I know."

"Then you must be more careful. No more conversations in corridors where anyone might see. No pausing. No looking at things that aren't there."

"George Darcy has information I need. I can't stop speaking to him because Lady Catherine is in the house. And Nana will certainly not be quiet, not ever."

"Then find somewhere to speak to them that doesn't involve standing in hallways moving your lips."

Elizabeth sat, considering the shape of the problem. Thus far Pemberley had been a sympathetic household, where Mrs Reynolds was kind, Darcy patient, the Matlocks fond. Lady Catherine was none of those things. She was hostile and perceptive, and she had the weapons society gave women who wished to destroy other women: gossip, insinuation, the suggestion of madness. In 1812, a husband could commit an inconvenient wife on nothing more than a physician's word. And Elizabeth had still not told Darcy the truth, for which she was now berating herself even more thoroughly.

"Catherine knew this house well," George Darcy said from behind Elizabeth, startling her. He seemed to have been more present this evening, as though his sister-in-law's arrival had stirred something restless in him. "She visited often when Anne was alive. She and my wife argued about everything, from carpets to child-rearing, but they were family, and family came when it was needed. Catherine was here when Fitzwilliam was born. She was here when Georgiana was born too, and Anne died in her arms."

"Was she here when you died?"

"No. We had quarrelled. Catherine thought me foolish for the favour I showed Wickham. A steward's son, she called him, as though that settled the matter. She told me I was being sentimental, that I was elevating a boy with no claim on the family above my own son and heir." He paused. "She was right, though not for the reasons she imagined. She saw the problem of rank. She did not see the problem of character. Nobody did, except Fitzwilliam."

"And you quarrelled over this?"

"Bitterly. The last time she visited, she told me I would live to regret my blindness where Wickham was concerned. I told her that the management of my household was not her affair. She left the following morning and did not return." His voice went flat. "I did not live to regret it, as it happened. I simply died of it."

Elizabeth was quiet. Lady Catherine, who was wrong about so many things, had been right about Wickham. Not about his character; she had objected to his station, not his soul. But the conclusion had been correct even so, and George had dismissed it because it came wrapped in Catherine's particular brand of snobbish condescension. Just as he had dismissed Fitzwilliam. Just as he had dismissed everyone who tried to tell him what he did not wish to hear.

"She won't make this easy for you," George said. "Catherine does not forgive, she does not forget, and she has never once in her life let a matter rest when she believed herself to be in the right. She came here to find fault with you, Elizabeth. She will find it, if you give her the smallest opportunity."

"Kitty," Elizabeth said. "We need Jane."

"Jane is coming."

"Jane needs to come faster."

She went to the writing desk, drew out a fresh sheet of paper, and began a second letter to Jane. This one was not about the ball. Kitty left her alone, and so did George, both perhaps sensing that she needed to concentrate. To focus on expressing her urgency in words that would not convey it to anyone but her intended target.

She had barely sealed it when there was a knock at the door. It was her husband. He stood in the doorway, still dressed for dinner, and looked at her for a moment before he spoke.

"You were going to tell me something, when you came to my study yesterday morning."

"Yes."

"My aunt's arrival does not change that. Whatever it is, Elizabeth, I would rather hear it from you than discover it some other way."

She looked at him. He was not demanding. He was not angry. He was simply standing in her doorway, asking her to trust him, and the worst of it was that she wanted to.

"You will," she said. "Soon."

"You said that before."

"I know. And I mean it more each time, which ought to count for something."

He studied her face. Then he crossed the room, kissed her forehead, and said, "Goodnight, Elizabeth."

"Goodnight."

He left. Elizabeth listened to his footsteps retreat down the corridor, then turned back to her letter, and added a single postscript on the back: *Come quickly.*

Chapter Sixteen

Lady Catherine did not come down to breakfast the following morning. She had sent word through Mrs Jenkinson that she would take a tray in her rooms, as the night had been disturbed by unaccountable restlessness and she had a headache.

It occurred to Elizabeth then that the blue rooms bordered the east corridor, which a few of Pemberley's older and more melancholic ghosts happened to frequent. Ghosts who were unlikely to have much tolerance for Lady Catherine de Bourgh's haughty ways and dislike of Pemberley's new mistress. Elizabeth caught Nana's eye across the breakfast table. Nana looked innocent, which was always a warning sign.

"I did nothing," Nana said. "It is not my fault that Catherine chose the blue rooms."

"You suggested the blue rooms to Mrs Reynolds," Elizabeth murmured, under cover of accepting more chocolate from the footman.

"How could I possibly, when Mrs Reynolds cannot see or hear me?" Nana looked piously indignant.

Elizabeth let it go, because Lady Catherine's absence had produced a transformation at the breakfast table that was worth any amount of ghostly mischief.

Anne de Bourgh was eating.

Not merely accepting toast and pushing it around her plate, as she had done the previous morning under her mother's watchful eye, but actually eating: two slices of bread with butter and honey, a boiled egg with a thick slice of ham, a cup of tea that she drank to the bottom, then refilled. She sat beside Georgiana, listened to Kitty's account of the book she was reading, offered an observation of her own about the author that was so dry, so precisely aimed, that Kitty laughed aloud. Georgiana looked at her cousin as though seeing her for the first time.

"She has Annie's eyes," George Darcy said.

He was standing by the window, watching his niece. Elizabeth had grown accustomed to the angles of his face when he was angry, the rigid set of his jaw when he spoke of Wickham, the cold fury that radiated from him when his murder was discussed. This was none of those things. He looked, for the first time since Elizabeth had known him, simply sad.

"Catherine named her for my wife," he said. "It was the only generous thing Catherine ever did, and she has been punishing the girl for the resemblance ever since. Annie was everything Catherine wanted to be and could not. Beautiful. Beloved. Married to a man who adored her rather than merely tolerated her. And now Annie's namesake sits at my table, thin, pale, half the woman she might have been, because Catherine could not bear to raise a daughter who reminded her of what her sister had."

"The child needs feeding up," Nana said from her station near the sideboard. "She needs sunlight, air, conversation that does not begin and end with what her mother permits. Look at her, George. She is three-and-twenty and she has never been allowed to take up the space she deserves."

"I see it," George said. "I have been seeing it for years."

"Then stop looking mournful about it and let Elizabeth do something."

Elizabeth, who could not respond to either of them without alarming the living members of the table, took a careful sip of her chocolate and said, to the room at large, "It is a beautiful morning for the time of year. Anne, would you care to walk in the gardens after breakfast? Georgiana and Kitty can show you what they have been doing with the rose garden."

Anne looked up, and the cautious pleasure on her face was almost worse than misery. She looked like a girl who had learnt not to want things, and who was now being offered something she was not at all sure she was allowed to accept.

"I should like that," she said. "If you are certain I will not be in the way."

"You will not be in the way," Georgiana said firmly. "You will be in exactly the right place."

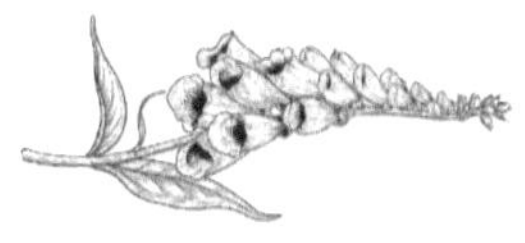

The four of them spent the morning in the rose garden, and by luncheon Anne de Bourgh had dirt under her fingernails for what Elizabeth suspected was the first time in her life.

Georgiana and Kitty had been working on the restoration for weeks now, guided by the portrait in the gallery and by Nana's exacting memories of how the garden had looked in its prime. They had cleared the worst of the bindweed, edged the beds, and begun coaxing the established roses back into order, though winter was coming and there was a limit to what could be done before spring. They showed Anne Lady Margaret's portrait, explained their plans, and put a pair of secateurs in her hand, and Anne, who had probably never held a gardening tool in her life, took to it with a quiet concentration that reminded Elizabeth, with a sharp pang, of what George had said about his wife. Annie's quality. That careful attention to living things.

Lady Margaret's smile was wider, Elizabeth thought, and she was directing it at the girls just as much as the roses.

Well, at least one of Pemberley's ghosts was content. Elizabeth wondered if Lady Margaret would move on, or simply fade in place, happy so long as her roses were tended and loved.

The garden was also, Elizabeth had to admit, the safest place in Pemberley for her to be while Lady Catherine was in residence. Catherine did not garden. Catherine did not walk in the cold if she could avoid it. Out here, among the bare rose stems, the turned earth, Elizabeth could speak to Nana without fear of being observed by anyone who might draw conclusions about her sanity.

George did not come to the garden. His restlessness kept him in the house, pacing the corridors he could not leave, and the grounds beyond the terrace seemed to hold no pull for him. But Nana came, drifting near the old sundial that marked the garden's centre, watching the four young women work.

"She is better out here," Nana said. "She has colour. She looks almost alive."

"She is alive, Nana."

"I meant that she looks as though she knows it, which is more than could be said for her yesterday."

After luncheon, with Lady Catherine still mercifully absent, Georgiana suggested going for a ride. She had been wanting to show Kitty the view from the ridge above the south meadow. The afternoon was bright and cold; the horses needed exercise.

"Anne," Georgiana said, turning to her cousin as though it were the most natural thing in the world, "will you come?"

Anne's face went through several expressions in quick succession: surprise, longing, and then a shadow that was unmistakably fear. "I don't have a riding habit with me," she said. "Mother did not think I should ride."

"I have three," Georgiana said. "We are near enough in size that one of them will fit you, I am sure. And Elizabeth, you must come too."

"I'm not much of a horsewoman," Elizabeth said, which was true, but Kitty gave her a look that brooked no argument, and so Elizabeth went.

Darcy himself, when he heard their plans, came out to the stable and selected horses for them all. He put Elizabeth up on a bay gelding he promised was calm and exceptionally steady, but with a turn of speed if she wished to prompt it. As Darcy moved on to choose a mount for Anne, one of the spectral groom brothers drifted closer to the gelding's head. He leaned in and murmured something Elizabeth could not quite catch, and the horse's ears pricked forward, its neck arching as though acknowledging a familiar hand. The gelding could feel him, Elizabeth realised. Animals, it seemed, had their own awareness of the dead. The groom caught her eye, touched his cap respectfully. "You'll be safe with Jasper, ma'am. He knows to look after you."

She had been confident Darcy would put her up on a horse he trusted with her, but it was nice to know the spectral grooms were looking out for their new mistress as well. She wondered if the horse actually understood what the groom had whispered.

For Anne, Darcy told the grooms to bring out a gentle mare, a placid creature with soft eyes and an easy gait. Anne mounted stiffly, as though the muscles had forgotten what to do, but her hands found their memory within the first few minutes, and by the time they reached the south meadow she was sitting tall and easy in the saddle, her face turned into the wind.

"Mother stopped allowing it when I was twelve," Anne said. They were riding abreast along the wide path that led toward the ridge, the October sun casting long shadows across the parkland. "She said I was too fragile. Dr Harris agreed, though Dr Harris agrees with everything Mother says, because she pays him handsomely to confirm her opinions."

"That is a remarkably clear-eyed observation," Elizabeth said.

"I have had a great deal of time to make it. There is not much else to do at Rosings." Anne's hands were steady on the reins now, her posture improving with every stride. She had been well taught, Elizabeth could see; the skill was buried under years of disuse, not absent. "I used to ride with my father when I was small. He had a grey hunter called Atlas, and he would put me in front of him and we would go out before breakfast. I remember the smell of the horse and the cold air and his arm around my waist. Being entirely, perfectly happy."

"How old were you when Sir Lewis died?"

"Six. Everything changed after that. Mother had always been, well, Mother, but Father balanced her. He could make her laugh, which nobody else has ever managed, and he could make her listen, which is harder still. After he died, there was nobody to balance anything, and she took charge of everything instead."

They reached the ridge, stopped their horses, and looked out over the valley. Pemberley spread below them in the autumn light: the house, the grounds, the lake, the dark line of woods beyond. Anne was quiet for a long time, looking at the view.

"I came here as a child," she said finally. "With my mother, before Aunt Anne died. She passed only a year after Papa, so I suppose I would have been seven then. I remember the lake, the gardens, Fitzwilliam trying to teach me to skip stones. Quite badly. And I remember Mrs Reynolds, who gave me gingerbread and called me Miss Annie."

"Mrs Reynolds mentioned that," Elizabeth said. "She was rather fond of you."

"She was kind." Anne looked at the view a moment longer, and when she spoke again her voice was different. Quieter. More careful. "Mother talked about Pemberley, you know. Constantly. About Aunt Anne, about Uncle George, about how things should have been managed."

Elizabeth paused a moment, then asked delicately, "Did she ever say anything about your uncle's death?"

Anne looked at her, and Elizabeth saw those eyes sharpen, the eyes George had said were his Annie's. Not suspicion, but attention. The quiet, careful attention of a woman who had spent her life listening from the edges of rooms where nobody thought she mattered.

"She said he died because he would not listen," Anne said. "I remember that quite clearly, because it struck me as a strange thing to say about a man who had died in his sleep. But Mother says strange things often enough, and I learned young not to ask what she meant by them."

Kitty caught Elizabeth's eye, and there was surprise in the glance. Elizabeth was becoming less surprised every time someone said they had the feeling something was not quite right about George Darcy's death, but it was interesting to hear that Lady Catherine might have a more solid theory about it. Not that Elizabeth could exactly ask her.

"Shall we ride back?" Georgiana said. "The light is going."

They turned their horses toward home. Anne rode beside Georgiana, the two of them talking about music, about London, about things that young women talk about when nobody is telling them to be quiet. Kitty fell back to ride beside Elizabeth.

"He died because he would not listen," Kitty said, low.

"Lady Catherine meant he would not listen to her," Elizabeth agreed. "About Wickham."

"Yes. But it is a strange way to put it."

"Everything Lady Catherine says is a strange way to put things. That doesn't make it less true. Even if Lady Catherine has her suspicions of Wickham, what then? I can't ask her about it, and suspicions aren't proof."

Kitty grimaced, because she knew what Elizabeth was saying was the truth. Anne called to her then, and Kitty urged her horse forward, pasting a smile back on her face. Elizabeth was left to follow them back, musing on what Lady Catherine had meant by *he would not listen.*

That evening, while the household was dressing for dinner, Nana found Elizabeth in her parlour.

"You need to take that girl to London," Nana said, without preamble.

Elizabeth had been thinking the same thing since the ride, watching Anne come alive in the saddle, watching the colour return to her face, the stiffness leave her spine, watching her talk and laugh and be, for a few hours, something closer to the woman she might have become if Lady Catherine had let her.

"With Georgiana and Kitty, for the Season," Elizabeth clarified.

"Yes. She needs it. She needs concerts, exhibitions, assemblies. She needs to discover that she has opinions of her own and that people will listen to them. And she needs," Nana said, with the particular vehemence she reserved for matters she considered urgent, "to be away from that woman long enough to remember who she is."

"Lady Catherine will never agree."

"Lady Catherine's agreement is not required. Anne is a grown woman. She is three-and-twenty, which is older than you are, and she has a right to her own life. What is needed is someone brave enough to offer it to her."

"And someone to stand between her and her mother when Catherine objects."

"You have Darcy. Darcy has Lord Matlock. Between the two of them, Catherine can be managed. She will rage, she will threaten, she will make everyone's life a misery for a fortnight. Then she will sulk. Then she will claim it was her idea all along. I have watched her do it a hundred times. It is her way."

Elizabeth found Darcy after dinner, in the library. Lord Matlock was with him, and she decided that fate had done her a favour, because she could make the case to both of them at once.

"I would like to invite Anne to London for the Season," she said. "With Georgiana and Kitty. All three of them, together."

Lord Matlock set down his glass. Darcy looked at Elizabeth, and his face opened. Not surprise; recognition. As though he had been waiting for someone to say what he had been thinking for years.

"Anne has never had a Season," Lord Matlock said. "Catherine would not permit it. She said Anne's health would not stand it, which was nonsense then and is nonsense now. The girl is not robust, but she is not dying, whatever Catherine may have convinced herself."

"She rode this afternoon," Elizabeth said. "For the first time in years. She was magnificent."

"Was she?" Lord Matlock looked pleased. "She was a good little rider as a child. Lewis taught her. He would have been glad to hear it."

"Then you support the idea?"

"Wholeheartedly. Darcy?"

"I think it an excellent idea. Anne is not a child, and she has been kept in that house long enough."

"Catherine will rage," Lord Matlock observed, without particular concern.

"Aunt Catherine will rage," Darcy agreed. "But Anne deserves a life, Uncle. She has waited long enough for one. Elizabeth and I have the opportunity to give her this; if she agrees, we must not let Aunt Catherine stop her."

They told Anne the following morning, before breakfast, in the small parlour where the early sun came through the east windows and made the room bright. Elizabeth had asked Georgiana and Kitty to be there too, because she wanted Anne to see the welcome waiting for her, and because Georgiana had rehearsed a small speech about how much she wanted her cousin's company that Elizabeth did not have the heart to prevent.

Georgiana did not get through the speech. She managed, "Anne, we would like you to come to London with us for the Season, if you would..." before Anne put her hand over her mouth and her eyes filled, and the speech became unnecessary.

"Yes," Anne said. "Yes. If you are sure. If it is truly..."

"It is truly," Kitty said, taking Anne's hand, which was clearly far too inadequate a gesture, because Anne threw her arms around Kitty instead, then turned to Georgiana and repeated the embrace.

"Mother will not allow it," Anne said, after a moment, when she could speak again.

"Your mother's permission will be obtained," Elizabeth said. "Darcy and Lord Matlock have already agreed to manage her."

Anne looked at Elizabeth with an expression that was gratitude, terror, hope, all mixed together, and Elizabeth thought of what Nana had said: *she needs to remember who she is.* Perhaps this was the beginning of that remembering.

From the doorway, unseen by anyone but Elizabeth, Nana watched the scene with her arms folded and her chin lifted and an expression that was, for once, entirely without complaint.

"Good," she said. "That is one thing done properly in this house."

And from the far corner of the room, George Darcy stood motionless, watching his niece cry for joy over a thing her namesake would have taken for granted, and said nothing at all. He did not need to. His face said everything.

Elizabeth looked away before her own expression could betray her, and said, briskly, "Now then. Breakfast. And we had better eat quickly, because Lady Catherine will be down by nine, and I should like to enjoy the morning while it lasts."

Chapter Seventeen

It was the name that kept coming back to her mind, niggling at the edges of her thoughts. As though it was important somehow, a thread she had not yet pulled on.

Sally Wilson. George Darcy had spoken of her, the night he told Elizabeth about the confrontation with Wickham. The girl Wickham had got with child. The girl whose father had come to George in desperation. George had believed him, confronted Wickham that same evening. By morning George was dead. That was where the story ended, for George. He had died not knowing what became of Sally Wilson, or her child, or whether Wickham had ever faced any consequence at all.

Elizabeth had asked Nana. Nana had heard the name, yes, she remembered the Wilsons, a respectable tenant family who had been at Pemberley as long as she had, but she had no way of knowing what had happened after George died. She was bound to the house and the close gardens. The lives of tenants beyond Pemberley's walls were beyond her reach. "You will have to ask the living," Nana had said, and left it at that, as though the living were a resource Elizabeth had not thought to consult.

The living.

Elizabeth did not want to ask her husband. But there was one other person who might have the information she needed; might have more than Darcy, in fact, because she had been here when George Darcy died.

Mrs Reynolds.

Mrs Reynolds knew the tenants. If Sally Wilson had been helped, Mrs Reynolds would know. She might know when exactly Mr Wilson had spoken to George Darcy too. And if she did, it was evidence. Real evidence, from a living witness, that did not depend on ghosts, and that Elizabeth might finally be able to take to her husband. But asking meant drawing Mrs Reynolds further in, and Mrs Reynolds was already closer to the truth than anyone except Kitty and Georgiana. Elizabeth was running out of patience for doing nothing, but she was not yet out of reasons to be careful.

She was thinking about this in her parlour, late in the afternoon, while the rest of the household was occupied. Lady Catherine had commandeered the yellow drawing room for a lecture on the management of servants that Lady Matlock was silently suffering through. Lord Matlock had retreated to the library. Darcy was out with his steward. Kitty had taken Georgiana and Anne to the music room, and the three of them were working through a piece that required two players at a time, which meant the third needed to turn pages for them, which lot fell to Anne since she could not play, though Georgiana had begun to teach her a little, without letting Lady Catherine know about it.

Elizabeth's parlour was the one place in Pemberley where she could think without performance. It was a small room, warm and private, with a writing desk, a chair by the fire, bookshelves lining the far wall. The bookshelves had been there for as long as anyone could remember, but did not have many books on them, more trinkets and knick-knacks. Elizabeth had added more books and was slowly removing the less aesthetically pleasing trinkets, though each change was criticised by Nana.

Nana appeared beside the writing desk, drifting through the bookcase as she always did, as though the wall behind it were no more substantial than air.

"You are brooding," Nana said.

"I'm thinking," Elizabeth denied the charge.

"There is a difference?"

"Yes. Brooding is unproductive, and I'm being exceedingly productive, or I will be when I have resolved this conundrum." Elizabeth sighed. "If you must know, I am thinking about how to ask Mrs Reynolds about Sally Wilson without revealing why I need to know."

"You do not need a reason. You are mistress of this house. The tenants are your concern. Ask about the families, the farms, the welfare of the women and children. It is your right and your duty, and Mrs Reynolds will think nothing of it."

Elizabeth considered this. It was true. She had been making a study of the tenants since her arrival; Darcy had encouraged it, and Mrs Reynolds had been walking her through the families, their histories, their needs. Asking about the Wilsons could be part of that. A natural question in a natural conversation.

A knock at the door heralded Mrs Reynolds herself, looking apologetic.

"I am sorry to disturb you, ma'am, but Lady Catherine has advised me that there is a draught in Miss de Bourgh's rooms and the fire is smoking, and the curtains are not to her liking. She wishes it attended to immediately."

Elizabeth suppressed a sigh. Mrs Reynolds had probably already inspected the rooms herself before making the long walk down one staircase and up another, to deliver Lady Catherine's complaints in person. A waste of the house-keeper's time, and all for a fire that was almost certain-ly fine and curtains that were certainly not going to be changed on Lady Catherine's whim. At least Elizabeth did not have to take that route; there was a hidden door from her parlour directly to the east wing.

"Very well," she said, and marched across the room to press the catch beneath the second shelf of the bookcase. The left side swung inward on old hinges, revealing the narrow passage behind. She was two steps in before she realised Mrs Reynolds was not following.

Elizabeth stopped. Turned.

Mrs Reynolds was standing exactly where she had been, her hands folded, her face perfectly composed. But her eyes were wide.

Behind her, Nana said something that would not have been considered ladylike in any century.

Elizabeth looked at the passage. Looked at Mrs Reynolds. And understood, with a cold drop in her stom-ach, what she had just done. Nana had shown her this door weeks ago, after Elizabeth had watched her drift through the bookcase one too many times and asked what was on the other side. A servants' passage, long forgotten, con-necting to the east wing corridor behind a floor-length painting. Elizabeth had used it half a dozen times since, always alone. She had stopped thinking of it as a secret. It was simply the quick way to get to the east wing.

Mrs Reynolds obviously had not known it existed.

"I," Elizabeth said. And could not think of a single thing to follow it with.

"I did not know that was there, ma'am," Mrs Reynolds said.

"I found it by accident," Elizabeth said. "The catch is behind the shelf. I was reaching for a book and the panel shifted."

It was a poor lie and they both knew it. Elizabeth could see Mrs Reynolds weighing the explanation against everything else she had observed in the weeks since Elizabeth's arrival, and finding it wanting.

"Shall we?" Elizabeth said, gesturing toward the passage, because she could not undo what Mrs Reynolds had just seen, and she might as well make use of the shortcut.

Mrs Reynolds hesitated only a moment. Then she stepped through the bookcase after Elizabeth. They walked the narrow passage together in silence, emerged through the painting into the east wing corridor, went to inspect Anne's rooms as though nothing unusual had happened at all.

The fire was fine, the curtains were fine, and Lady Catherine's complaints were satisfied, or at least exhausted, which amounted to the same thing.

They took the long way back. The main staircase, the gallery, the proper route. Neither of them suggested the passage.

It was not until they had reached the housekeeper's sitting room, and Mrs Reynolds had poured tea for both of them, and the door was closed, that Mrs Reynolds spoke.

"You did not find that door by accident, Mrs Darcy."

Elizabeth set down her cup.

"I have been housekeeper of this house for thirty years," Mrs Reynolds said. "I did not know that passage existed. Lady Anne never mentioned it, nor the old master, nor anyone. And you have been here two months and you use it as though you have known about it your whole life."

Elizabeth said nothing, because there was nothing she could say that would make sense.

"I do not understand how you know what you know," Mrs Reynolds said. "I am not asking you to explain it. Not today. But I want you to know that I see it, ma'am. I have seen it since your first week here. You know things about this house that you should not know, and the hidden door is only the latest." She paused. "I have my own sense of this house. I have had it for thirty years. Feelings. Impressions. The east corridor makes my skin prickle when I walk through it after dark, and I could no more tell you why than I could explain any of it. I do not understand what you are doing. But I believe your reasons are good ones, that you love the master and Miss Darcy, that you have their best interests, and Pemberley's, at heart. And I should like to help you, if I can."

"There is something you could help me with," Elizabeth said, after a careful pause. "I should like to continue learning about the tenant families. Specifically, the Wilsons, who have the large farm by the mill."

Mrs Reynolds did not hesitate. "Thomas Wilson is a good man. Hardworking, honest. His wife is the same. They had some trouble, years ago. Their eldest daughter, Sally, was got with child when she was seventeen. The father could not be made to answer for it."

Elizabeth waited.

"Mr Darcy handled it," Mrs Reynolds said. "Our Mr Darcy. He gave the Wilsons a better farm, found a decent young man willing to marry Sally and raise the child as his own. A farrier's son from Lambton, Joseph Cooper, who had always been sweet on Sally and did not hold another man's actions against her. Mr Darcy settled money on the child, and Sally married Cooper within the month, and the child was born respectable." She paused. "Mr Darcy had been master of Pemberley only a few months then."

"The father of Sally's child," Elizabeth said. "It was George Wickham." She did not phrase it as a question, and Mrs Reynolds did not ask how she knew.

"Yes. It was George Wickham." Mrs Reynolds said the name flatly. "He was the old pmaster's godson, and he had been given every advantage a young man could ask for, and he repaid it by preying on a girl who could not defend herself."

"Did the old Mr Darcy know? Before he died?"

Mrs Reynolds was quiet for a moment. Then she said, "Mr Wilson told me something once, years after. He said he had gone to the old master about Sally. That he had spoken to him directly, told him everything. Just before he died."

Elizabeth's hands were still in her lap. She made them stay that way.

"Mr Wilson said the master believed him at once. Said he went white as chalk, asked Mr Wilson to tell him everything, every detail. When Mr Wilson had finished, the master thanked him and said it would be dealt with. He summoned Mr Wickham home, spoke to him privately in his study, dined with him. They were all smiles and I thought, Wickham must have agreed to do the right thing. But then the next morning, the master was dead, and Wickham went away without marrying Sally. The physician said it was Mr Darcy's heart, and Mr Wilson said to me once that he felt guilt, that perhaps the strain of learning his godson would behave so badly brought it on."

Elizabeth sat with this. She had the thread now. It was real, it was solid, it connected to a living man who could confirm it.

"I should like to visit the Wilsons," she said. "With Mr Darcy. I should like to meet them."

Mrs Reynolds nodded. Then she said, quietly, "I have been carrying this feeling for six years, Mrs Darcy. That something was not right about the master's death. If you find what you are looking for, I hope you will tell me. I should dearly like to set it down."

"When I can," Elizabeth said. "I promise. When I can."

She told Kitty that evening, in her parlour, with the door locked.

"Sally Wilson had a child," Elizabeth said. "Wickham's child. Darcy handled it after his father died. Found her a husband, settled money, gave the family a better farm. But the important thing is this: Mr Wilson went to George Darcy and told him about Wickham and Sally. George summoned Wickham to Pemberley, spoke to him. Mrs Reynolds thought that because they were smiling, seemed amiable, Wickham must have agreed to do the right thing. But by morning, George was dead."

Kitty was staring at her. "You have this from Mrs Reynolds."

"From Mrs Reynolds, who had it from Mr Wilson himself. A living witness, Kitty. Not a ghost. A man who went to the old master and told him the truth, and who has spent six years wondering whether it killed him."

"It did kill him. Just not the way Mr Wilson thinks."

"No. But the point is that Mr Wilson can testify that George Darcy knew about Wickham's character while he was still alive. That George was angry enough to confront him. That is motive, Kitty. Wickham had every reason to want George dead before he could act on what he knew. Mr Wilson can say all of this to Lord Matlock, or to a magistrate, or to anyone who asks, because he was there. Mrs Reynolds can corroborate it."

Kitty drew a breath. "This is the first real evidence you've had, that doesn't come from a ghost."

"Yes."

Kitty looked at her, and Elizabeth could see the calculations running behind her eyes: the same fierce, practical intelligence that had been holding Elizabeth back for weeks, now turning toward a different question. Not whether to act, but how.

"You're going to visit the Wilsons."

"Tomorrow. With Darcy. I shall ask him to take me, and see if I can lead the conversation to what I want him to know. He has spent six years believing his father died blind to Wickham's true nature. Learning that George saw the truth at the end, that he tried to act on it; that will shift how Darcy understands his own father."

"And it will make him ask questions."

"Yes."

"The right questions."

"I hope so."

Kitty was quiet. Then she said, "You're not going to tell him about the murder."

"No. I'm going to provide the facts and let him reach his own conclusions. If Darcy looks at the timing, if he sees that his father confronted Wickham the evening before he died, he may begin to wonder whether his father's death was what the physician said it was. And if he reaches that conclusion himself, from evidence, from the living world, then I haven't revealed the ghosts, and the suspicion comes from a place that can be acted on."

"That is a fine line, Lizzy."

She knew it. But it was the first thread she had pulled on that might lead to something tangible, so it was a line she must walk nevertheless.

She found Darcy after the household had retired, in the sitting room they shared. He was by the fire, not reading, simply sitting. He looked up when she came in, and some of the tension in his face eased at the sight of her.

"You have been quiet today," he said.

"I have been thinking."

"That is usually my failing, not yours."

She sat in the chair opposite him, drew her feet up beneath her skirt, because it was late, they were alone, and she was tired of sitting like a portrait.

"Mrs Reynolds finally told me what she meant, that day I first toured Pemberley with my aunt and uncle, when she said Wickham had turned out very wild." She watched his face. "A girl named Sally Wilson?"

Darcy set down his glass. "Sally Wilson," he said. "Yes."

"Tell me."

"Wickham." He said it without inflection. "The child is Wickham's. Sally was seventeen. Her father came to me after mine died. He was wretched about it, ashamed, as though it were his fault his daughter had been preyed upon."

"What did you do?"

"What I could. I gave the Wilsons a larger farm, one that had come vacant that autumn. I found a young man willing to marry Sally and raise the child as his own. Joseph Cooper, a farrier's son from Lambton. I settled an income on the child. Sally married Cooper within the month, and he works with Joseph Wilson on the farm; they do well."

"And you did all of this at two-and-twenty."

"Who else was there? My father was dead. Georgiana was ten. I handled it because it needed handling, and because Wickham was, in some wretched sense, still my responsibility." He paused. "I've never told anyone about Sally. Mrs Reynolds knows because she was here and because nothing escapes her. But I have never spoken of it."

"You are speaking of it now."

"Because you asked. And because I'm tired of carrying things alone, Elizabeth. I've been carrying things alone since I was two-and-twenty, and I find that I no longer wish to."

Elizabeth felt the weight of that, and the ache of knowing she was still keeping from him the thing that mattered most.

"I should like to visit the Wilsons," she said. "With you. I am mistress of Pemberley now. Sally is one of our tenants, and I should like to meet her, see that she and the child are well."

"We can go tomorrow, if you wish."

"I wish."

He was quiet for a moment. Then he said, "You are still building something, Elizabeth. I can feel it. Every question you ask, every conversation with Mrs Reynolds, with my aunt. You are gathering threads, and I cannot yet see the pattern, but I know it has to do with my father."

"Yes," she said. "It does."

"Will you tell me?"

"Soon. I promise you. Soon."

He studied her face in the firelight. Then he stood, crossed the room, held out his hand.

"Come to bed," he said. Not a demand. Something gentler.

Elizabeth took his hand and let him draw her to her feet. He did not release her. His thumb moved across her knuckles, and he was looking at her with an expression that had nothing to do with Wickham or secrets. He was looking at her as though she were the only real thing in the room.

"Darcy," she said, and he kissed her. She kissed him back, and for a few minutes the weight of everything she carried lifted and there was nothing but this.

He led her through the connecting door to their bedroom, and closed it behind them, and the rest of the evening belonged to no one but themselves.

Chapter Eighteen

They rode out after breakfast, just the two of them.

The morning was bright and cold, the kind of November day that made the Derbyshire hills look sharp-edged against the sky. Elizabeth rode Jasper, the bay gelding Darcy had chosen for her, and he rode beside her on his tall grey, and they did not speak much on the way. She could feel him thinking. He had that particular stillness about him that meant something was turning over behind his eyes, being examined from every angle before he committed to a response.

The Wilson farm was north of the river, perhaps three miles from Pemberley, set in a shallow valley with good pasture on either side and a mill stream running through the lower field. It was well kept. The fences were sound, the yard was clean, smoke rose from the chimney in a steady line that spoke of a household that was up and working. A good farm. Better than the one the Wilsons had held before, Mrs Reynolds had said. Good enough to support a daughter, her husband, their child, and any others who might have come along since.

Darcy had sent word ahead, and Thomas Wilson came out to meet them. He was a broad, weathered man in his fifties, hat in hand, visibly honoured by the visit and slightly nervous about it. His wife appeared behind him, wiping her hands on her apron, and behind her a young woman with fair hair and a careful face, who could only be Sally.

"Mr Darcy, sir. Mrs Darcy. You are very welcome."

Darcy dismounted, helped Elizabeth down. The introductions were made with the easy formality of a landlord who knew his tenants well and respected them. Mrs Wilson invited them inside. The farmhouse kitchen was warm and scrubbed clean, and there was tea on the table before Elizabeth had finished removing her gloves.

Sally Cooper sat at the edge of the group, quiet, her hands folded in her lap. She would be about three-and-twenty now, pretty in a subdued way, and she watched Elizabeth warily, as though the interest of her betters had not always been kind to her. Elizabeth smiled at her and asked about the farm, about the dairy, about the preserves that Mrs Wilson was evidently proud of, and slowly, carefully, Sally's shoulders began to come down from around her ears.

A boy appeared in the doorway. He was about six, sturdy and fair-haired, with a gap-toothed grin and mud on his knees. He looked nothing like Wickham, which Elizabeth noted with a relief so sharp it surprised her. He had Sally's colouring, Sally's wide-set eyes, and none of the easy charm that would have marked him out as his father's son.

"William," Sally said. "Come and make your bow to Mr and Mrs Darcy."

William made his bow with an expression of solemn concentration. Darcy looked at the boy, and Elizabeth saw something cross his face that was too quick to name but too painful to miss.

"What a fine boy," Darcy said. "He looks well."

"He is a terror," Mr Wilson said, with undisguised pride. "Runs the dogs ragged. Joseph cannot keep up with him."

"Joseph is Sally's husband?" Elizabeth asked, though she knew.

"Aye, ma'am. Joseph Cooper. He is out with the sheep this morning, or he would be here to pay his respects. A good lad. The best thing that ever happened to our Sally, begging your pardon." Mr Wilson glanced at Darcy, and Elizabeth caught something in the look: gratitude so deep it had become part of the man's bearing, woven into the way he stood and spoke in Darcy's presence.

William, having completed his social obligations, escaped back to the yard. They could hear him through the open door, talking to the dogs in the earnest, commanding way of small boys who believe themselves in charge.

"He wants a pony," Sally said, quietly. It was the first thing she had volunteered, and she said it with a small, surprised smile, as though her son's ambitions still had the power to astonish her. "Joseph says he is too young. I say he will simply get on one without permission if we do not provide one soon."

"I suspect you were much like him at that age," Elizabeth said, glancing at Darcy, and was rewarded with a look from her husband that was equal parts denial and amusement.

"I was an excellent rider from the age of four," Darcy said, with just a touch of pomposity. "My father put me on a horse before I could properly walk. It is the Darcy way."

"It is the way of every boy who grows up in the country, sir," Mr Wilson said, and the ease between them was real, built on years of quiet respect.

"I do know of a good little riding pony who might be coming available," Darcy noted. "The Cookson boys are rather too large for it now. I shall tell Mr Cookson to bring it by, see if William might like it?"

"That'd be right kind of you, sir," Sally said gratefully.

Mrs Wilson refreshed the tea, and Elizabeth let the conversation settle into the comfortable talk of farming families: the autumn ploughing, the state of the winter stores, whether the mill would need its wheel repaired before spring. Darcy talked to Mr Wilson about the fencing on the upper pasture. Elizabeth sat with Sally and Mrs Wilson, listened to them talk about William's schooling, conducted at the village school in Kympton three mornings a week by the vicar, and about Sally's second child, a girl of two who was sleeping upstairs and who was, Mrs Wilson declared, even more of a terror than her brother.

"Two children," Elizabeth said to Sally. "You are fortunate."

"I am," Sally said, and the simplicity of it carried more weight than any elaboration could have. She looked out at the yard, where William was now attempting to climb a gate while the collie watched with patient resignation. "Joseph is a good father. William does not know that he is not... that Joseph is not his..." She stopped, and colour rose in her face.

"William is loved," Elizabeth said kindly. "That is what matters."

Sally nodded. She did not say anything else about it, and Elizabeth did not press. But she filed it away: a boy who did not know who his real father was, raised by a man who loved him anyway, in a home that existed because Darcy had built it for them out of the wreckage Wickham left behind. Wickham, who had left Sally without a backward glance. Who had moved on to Georgiana, then to Lydia, who knows how many other young women in between, stopping only at Lydia because Darcy had caught up and forced him to marry her.

Elizabeth turned the conversation gently. "Mr Wilson, I have been learning the history of Pemberley's families since my marriage. Mrs Reynolds has been most helpful, but there is still a great deal I do not know. You have been tenants here a long time."

"All my life, ma'am. My father before me, and his father before him."

"Then you knew the old Mr Darcy well."

The kitchen went quiet. Sally looked down at her hands. Mrs Wilson became absorbed in the tea things. Mr Wilson's expression shifted, and the ease of the last few minutes gave way to something more guarded.

"I did, ma'am. He was a good master. The best I have known, saving Mr Darcy here."

"I understand you spoke to him," Elizabeth said. "Before he died. About the matter of William's parentage."

Mr Wilson looked at Darcy. Darcy looked at Elizabeth. She could feel his attention sharpen, but he said nothing, and she was grateful for it.

"I did, ma'am." Mr Wilson's voice had dropped. Sally was staring at the floor, her face flushed. "I went to the old master about... about the trouble. About Sally. I told him what had happened, and who was responsible. I was ashamed to go, but Sally was starting to show, and I could not leave it any longer."

"And the old Mr Darcy believed you?"

"At once, ma'am. He did not question it, did not doubt us for a moment. He went white when I told him. White as the wall behind you. He asked me to tell him everything. I did. When I had finished, he thanked me and said it would be dealt with. Those were his words. *It will be dealt with.*"

"When was this, Mr Wilson? How long before he died?"

Mr Wilson rubbed his jaw. "It was... I went to him on the Tuesday. He died on the Saturday, I believe."

Elizabeth did not look at Darcy. She did not need to. She could feel the stillness beside her, the held breath, the sound of a man hearing his own history rewritten.

"I have always wondered," Mr Wilson said, and his voice was rough now, "whether it was the shock that killed him. Whether learning what his godson had done to my girl put a strain on his heart that it could not bear. The physician said it was his heart, and I have told myself for six years that it was not my fault for telling him, that he had a right to know, but I have never been easy about it. If I had gone to him sooner, or if I had waited... but Sally was showing, and I could not wait."

"You did the right thing," Elizabeth said. "You must not blame yourself for what happened after."

"That is what Mrs Reynolds says too, ma'am. She has said the same to me more than once."

Darcy spoke for the first time in several minutes. His voice was steady, but Elizabeth could hear the effort it cost him. "Mr Wilson. Did my father say anything else to you? About what he intended to do?"

"Only that it would be dealt with, sir. And that he was grateful I had come to him. He shook my hand when I left. I remember that. He was not a man who shook hands with his tenants as a rule, but he shook mine that day, and his grip was fierce."

Darcy nodded. He stood, thanked the Wilsons for their hospitality, admired the farm once more, and said something kind to Sally about William that made her eyes fill. Then they were outside in the cold air watching William throwing a stick for the collie as Mr Wilson fetched their horses from the barn.

They mounted in silence. The horses walked steadily, their breath clouding in the cold air, and Elizabeth let the silence hold. This was Darcy's way. He did not think aloud. He took things in and turned them over and came back with something considered.

"I asked you last night whether you would tell me what you have been building," he said at last. "This is it, is it not? This is what you wanted me to hear."

"Part of it. I wanted you to hear it from Mr Wilson, not from me."

"Why?"

"Because it is his story. And because I thought it would mean more to you, coming from a man who was there, who has carried it for six years."

Darcy looked ahead at the path. "My father shook his hand. He was not a man who shook hands with tenants. He shook Mr Wilson's hand because he was grateful, and because he was ashamed that his blindness about Wickham had cost that family their daughter's honour. And then he sent for Wickham."

"Yes."

"And just days later he was dead."

Pemberley came into view ahead of them, pale stone against the dark November woods. Darcy pulled his horse up and sat looking at it.

"I have spent six years believing my father died without ever seeing the truth about Wickham," he said. "That he went to his grave blinded by affection. And now I learn he did see it. At the very end, he saw it, and he tried to act on it, and he did not have time."

"He did not have time," Elizabeth agreed, and felt the weight of what she was not saying.

They rode on. As they came down the slope toward the house, Elizabeth glanced up at the windows and saw George Darcy standing at the one he always stood at, watching them return. He could not know what had just happened. He could not know that his son, riding beside her in silence, was turning over the same questions that had kept his father's ghost pacing these corridors for six years. Elizabeth looked away before Darcy could follow her gaze, and the window, when she glanced back, was empty.

At Pemberley, Darcy gave the horses to the groom and went directly to find Mrs Reynolds. Elizabeth followed. She had intended to engineer this conversation herself, but Darcy was ahead of her now, moving with the quiet purposefulness she had seen in him when a problem presented itself and he intended to solve it.

He found Mrs Reynolds in her sitting room, waited for Elizabeth to enter behind him, and closed the door behind them.

"Mrs Reynolds. When my father died. Was Wickham at Pemberley?"

Mrs Reynolds looked at Darcy, then at Elizabeth. Whatever she saw in Elizabeth's face must have told her that the time for caution had passed.

"Yes, sir. Mr Wickham came in answer to your father's summons over the Sally Wilson business. Your father spoke with him privately in his study. They dined together that night, and seemed amiable enough. I remember thinking that the trouble must have been resolved, to Mr Darcy's satisfaction." She paused. "Your father died sometime that night."

"Wickham was in this house the night my father died."

"Yes, sir. He did not spend the night, riding back to Lambton late in the evening to stay with friends there, and he did not return to Pemberley. I did not think anything of it at the time. Mr Wickham was always coming and going."

Darcy did not move. Elizabeth watched him absorb it: the final piece, the one that turned a sequence of events into a pattern. His father had learnt the truth about Wickham. His father had summoned Wickham. They had dined together. By morning his father was dead. Wickham had gone. The physician had said it was his heart, and nobody had questioned it for six years.

"Thank you, Mrs Reynolds," Darcy said. His voice was perfectly controlled. "That is all I needed to know."

He left the room. Elizabeth stayed.

"You told him," Mrs Reynolds said.

"He heard it from Mr Wilson. About Sally, and about his father knowing."

Mrs Reynolds sat down. She looked older suddenly, and weary. "I should have said something. Years ago. I should have gone to him and told him what I felt, what I suspected."

"You had nothing to go on but a feeling."

"A feeling is not nothing, Mrs Darcy. You taught me that."

Elizabeth touched the older woman's hand, briefly. Then she went to find Kitty.

Kitty was in the library reading, alone except for the ghostly Miss Pardoe. She looked up when Elizabeth came in and read her face at once.

"He knows?" Kitty said.

"He knows his father confronted Wickham. He knows Wickham was here when his father died. He hasn't said the word murder, but I believe he is thinking it." Elizabeth closed the door behind her and leaned against it. She felt suddenly drained. The morning had required a kind of performance she was not accustomed to: not lying, exactly, but steering, guiding her husband toward a conclusion she already held while pretending to be discovering it alongside him. It had worked. She was not proud of it.

Kitty closed her book. "Then it begins."

Elizabeth sat down in the chair beside her sister, allowing herself to slouch, though Miss Pardoe glanced over the top of her book and gave her a disapproving little frown for it. "Yes. It begins. And I still haven't told him about the ghosts, Kitty."

"I know."

"He thinks this is it. He thinks Sally Wilson and the timing and his aunt's doubts are what I've been hiding from him. He thinks this is the secret. He looked at me with such... he was grateful, Kitty. Grateful that I had found this for him, and led him to it carefully, so that he can corroborate it for himself with the people who were there. And all I could think was that it is only a small part of the truth, and when he discovers the rest he will wonder why I didn't trust him with it."

"You are protecting him."

"I am lying to him. There is a difference, whatever we tell ourselves."

Kitty did not argue. "How long can the ghost secret hold? Now that he is pulling on the thread himself?"

"I don't know," Elizabeth said. "He will go to Lord Matlock, I think, and they will investigate. They will look into the physician's verdict, into Wickham's movements. None of that requires ghosts."

"And Lydia?" Kitty's face was tight. That was always what it came back to: Lydia, married to the man they were building a case against, sixteen years old and bound to a murderer.

"One thing at a time," Kitty said. "Darcy and Lord Matlock will investigate. We deal with Lydia when we must, and not before, because we don't yet know what shape this will take."

She thought about Sally's quiet pride in a son who wanted a pony. About Darcy's face when he looked at William and saw a boy who existed because Wickham had taken what he wanted and walked away. She thought about George Darcy, somewhere in the corridors of this house, pacing as he always paced, not yet knowing that the son he had failed was fighting for him at last.

"You are doing the right thing, Lizzy," Kitty said. "I know it doesn't feel like it. But you are."

Elizabeth was not sure she believed that. But she was sure of this: it had begun, and there was no stopping it now.

She tried not to think about what Darcy's face would look like when he finally learnt the whole truth.

Chapter Nineteen

Darcy spoke to Lord Matlock that evening, after dinner.

Elizabeth did not know what passed between them, because she was not invited to hear it. Darcy had kissed her forehead before they went down to the yellow drawing room. "I am going to tell my uncle what we learned today," he said quietly. Elizabeth had nodded, and that had been the end of her involvement. The men withdrew to the study.

It was a long evening. Lady Catherine held forth on the inadequacies of modern education, a subject that required no audience participation and received none. Lady

Matlock worked at her embroidery, serenely immune to the monologue. Georgiana played softly. Anne sat beside her, turning pages. Kitty read. Elizabeth sat with her hands folded and her mind entirely elsewhere, wondering what Darcy was saying and how Lord Matlock was receiving it.

She excused herself as early as she reasonably could, pleading a headache that was not entirely invented, and went to her parlour.

George Darcy was waiting for her.

He was pacing. She had never seen him pace in so confined a space; he usually haunted the gallery or the long corridor of the east wing, where his restlessness had room to stretch. In the parlour he was like a caged thing, turning at the bookcase, turning at the window, his agitation so palpable that the candle flames bent as he passed them.

"They are talking," he said, before she had closed the door. "Fitzwilliam told Matlock everything. Mr Wilson's testimony. What Mrs Reynolds confirmed. The timing."

"And?"

"Matlock listened. He did not interrupt. He sat, let Fitzwilliam speak. When Fitzwilliam had finished, Matlock said, 'I have wondered about this for six years, and I am ashamed that I did nothing.'"

Elizabeth sat down. "He believed him?"

"At once. He said your aunt had spoken to him too, years ago, about a feeling she had. He dismissed it then. He is not dismissing it now." George stopped pacing and faced her. His expression was fierce, intent, the rigid composure he usually maintained entirely gone. "Elizabeth. They are planning what to do next. They are talking about the physician who signed the death certificate, about Wickham's movements that week. But they are missing something important. Margaret was here. She was at Pemberley in the days before I died. She saw me agitated. She heard me speak of Wickham. She left before Wickham arrived, but she can place the timeline. She can say that I was disturbed, that I had learned something that changed how I spoke of my godson. And she is Lord Matlock's wife. Her word carries weight that a tenant farmer's cannot, however honest Mr Wilson may be."

"I see."

"Then tell Darcy. Tell him to bring Margaret into this. She has been waiting six years to be asked, and she will not forgive being excluded now."

Elizabeth pressed her fingers against her temples. The headache she had claimed was becoming real. "I will speak to him in the morning. I can't go to the study now; it would look as though I had been listening at doors."

"You have not been listening at doors. I have been listening at doors, or rather, I was listening in the room. There is a meaningful distinction."

Despite everything, Elizabeth almost laughed. "I'm not certain that distinction would comfort my husband."

George resumed his pacing. "There is one other thing. They spoke of writing to the physician, a Dr Grieve in Bakewell. Matlock said he could make enquiries through the College of Physicians. That is sensible, but it will take time, and the longer this takes, the more danger there is that Wickham will hear of it. He has friends. He has contacts. He has always had a talent for discovering things he should not know."

"Wickham is in Newcastle with Lydia. He has no friends here."

"Wickham has friends everywhere. That was always his gift. He could walk into a room of strangers and leave with allies." George's voice was flat. "I gave him that. I taught him how to be charming, how to speak to people above his station, how to make himself indispensable. Every weapon he has, I put in his hand."

Elizabeth did not argue with him. It was true, and he knew it, and pity would not help either of them.

"I will speak to Darcy in the morning," she said again. "About Lady Matlock. And about... there may be another source of information, though I am not yet sure how to approach it."

"Who?"

"Lady Catherine."

George went still, staring at her. "Catherine?"

"Anne told me something. On the ride, last week. She said her mother once said that your death happened because you would not listen. It struck Anne as odd, and she remembered it. If Catherine believed you died because you would not take her warnings about Wickham seriously, she may know more than she has ever said. She was angry with you about Wickham, was she not? Before you died?"

"Furious. She told me I was a fool for favouring a steward's son over my own blood. I told her to mind her own affairs. We quarrelled badly. She left Pemberley and did not return before I died. It was before Wilson came to me, but…" He paused. "Catherine is many things, but she is not stupid. If she suspected Wickham, she would not have forgotten it."

"Then I need to find out what she knows."

"Be careful. Catherine does not give up information. She uses it."

Elizabeth blew out her candle and went to bed. Darcy had not yet come up. She lay in the dark, listened to the house settle around her, thought about what she would say to Darcy in the morning, how she would approach Lady Catherine.

She caught Darcy before breakfast, in his dressing room, while he was pulling on his boots.

"You should speak to Lady Matlock," she said. "About your father."

He looked up. "Aunt Margaret?"

"She was at Pemberley before your father died. She told me so herself, not long after she first arrived, on a walk. She said your father was agitated, distracted. He spoke to her about Wickham, and I think that means it was after Wilson had come to him. She left a few days before his death, and she has carried a feeling ever since that something was not right about it." Elizabeth sat on the arm of his chair, close enough to touch him but not touching. "She has been waiting six years for someone to ask her, Darcy. Do not leave her out of this."

He was quiet for a moment. Then he said, "You have been thorough."

"I have been paying attention. Several people have been thinking something was not quite right for six years, and nobody quite had the words to tell you, and you were too busy carrying everything alone to hear them anyway."

He caught her hand. Held it. "I will speak to her today."

"Good. There is one other thing. Lady Catherine."

His expression shifted, became somewhat resigned. "What about her?"

"Anne mentioned it to me. Her mother said once that your father died because he would not listen. Catherine quarrelled with your father about Wickham before he died. She thought him foolish for the favour he showed Wickham. If she believed your father's death was connected to that quarrel, to Wickham, she may have information."

"You want to speak to Aunt Catherine about my father's death." Darcy looked as though he did not quite know what to make of that. Perhaps he had expected her to say something else; some grievance about his aunt's behaviour, though Elizabeth was determined never to bother him with that. She could handle Lady Catherine.

"I want to find out what she knows. If there is even the smallest chance that she has a piece of this, I would rather ask and be rebuffed than leave it unasked."

Darcy studied her face. "Be careful with her, Elizabeth. My aunt does not respond well to questions she has not invited."

"I know. But I would rather have her angry than silent."

He kissed her hand, let it go, went to find Lord Matlock. Elizabeth went down to breakfast, sat through Lady Catherine's opinions on the proper temperature of toast, waited for the right moment.

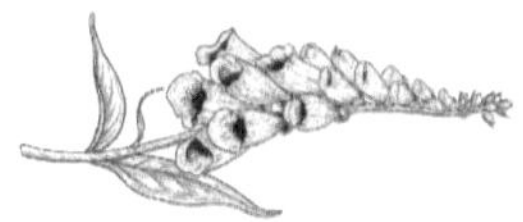

She approached Lady Catherine in the yellow drawing room after luncheon, alone. Lady Matlock had gone to walk with Anne and Georgiana. Kitty was reading in the library. The house was quiet. Catherine sat by the fire looking dissatisfied at being without companionship. Elizabeth came in and closed the door behind her, and did not look at Sir Roderick, sleeping in his chair in the corner.

"Lady Catherine. May I speak with you?"

Catherine looked up. Her expression was the one she reserved for Elizabeth: civil tolerance layered over deep disapproval. "You may."

Elizabeth sat. She had thought carefully about how to approach this, and had decided that indirection would not work. Lady Catherine despised indirection. She respected boldness, even when she punished it.

"I have been learning a great deal about my home and my new family since my marriage," Elizabeth said. "About the history of the house, the tenants, the people who have served Pemberley over the years. And about the late Mr Darcy."

Catherine's eyes sharpened. "What about him?"

"You knew him well. Better than most, I think. And you were not afraid to tell him when you thought he was wrong."

"I was not. George was a good man but a stubborn one, and he did not always see clearly where his affections were engaged."

"You mean Wickham."

The name landed in the room like a stone dropped into still water. Catherine's face was rigidly controlled, utterly still, and Elizabeth could see the calculation behind her eyes: what did Elizabeth know, and what was the purpose of this conversation.

"I mean Mr Wickham, yes. I told George repeatedly that his attachment to that boy was misguided and would end badly. He refused to hear me. He said I was jealous of a motherless child, which was offensive, and that I did not understand the bond between them, which was patronising. We quarrelled. I told him he would live to regret it." She paused. "He did not live to anything, as it happened."

"Anne told me you once said he died because he would not listen."

Catherine's eyes narrowed. "I shall have to speak to my daughter about discretion. I do not care to have my words repeated to all and sundry."

"She did not repeat them indiscreetly to all and sundry. She repeated an observation her mother made, because I asked her about her uncle, and she answered honestly. As I am asking you now."

"And what exactly are you asking, Mrs Darcy?"

"Whether you believe your brother-in-law's death had anything to do with George Wickham."

The silence that followed was long. Catherine looked at Elizabeth with an expression that was not anger, not quite. It was closer to appraisal. She was weighing Elizabeth, measuring her, deciding what she was worth.

Then the calculation gave way to a harder look, one that Elizabeth recognised a moment too late as the coldness of a woman who has decided to attack rather than answer.

"I think," Lady Catherine said, "that you are remarkably skilled at asking questions and singularly poor at attending to what is happening under your own roof."

"I beg your pardon?"

"You ask me about George's death. You ask about Wickham. You busy yourself with history, tenants, matters that are not, frankly, your concern, while your husband conducts his affairs beneath your nose and you do nothing about it."

Elizabeth felt the ground shift under her feet. "I do not know what you mean."

"I mean the Wilson family, Mrs Darcy. I mean the farm your husband gave them, the money he settled on the child, the visits he has been making to that household for six years. I mean the boy they named William, after him, because Fitzwilliam was too grand for a tenant farmer's bastard."

Elizabeth stared at her.

"My dear Mrs Darcy." Catherine's voice was soft now, soft and terrible, dripping with a sympathy so false it curdled in the air between them. "I feel it is my duty to tell you, since nobody else appears willing to do so. That child is your husband's. Darcy has been supporting him since birth, visiting the family, ensuring they want for nothing. He took you there yesterday, I am told. Introduced you to the child. You sat in that kitchen, drank their tea, and did not see what was right in front of you. The boy is fair-haired, I understand. As Darcy was, as a child."

The fury came so fast it blinded her.

It was not the cold, controlled anger Elizabeth had felt before, the careful strategic fury she had used against Lady Catherine at Longbourn. This was something hotter, something that rose from her chest and flooded her face and made her hands shake. Not because she believed a word of it. Not because there was the smallest doubt in her mind about her husband, or who the real father of Sally Wilson's child was, or the real reason that child had been named William. Her rage rose because this woman, this poisonous, spiteful, meddling woman, had taken Darcy's kindness, his quiet, years-long care of a family who were his responsibility and a girl who had been wronged, and twisted it into something foul. Had taken the best thing about him and made it ugly.

"How *dare* you."

Her voice did not sound like her own. It was low and shaking, and Lady Catherine blinked at it.

"How dare you speak of my husband in that way. You know nothing of what you are saying. Nothing."

"I am trying to help you, Mrs Darcy. A wife ought to know…"

"You are not trying to help me. You are trying to wound me, because you have never forgiven Darcy for marrying me, and because you cannot bear that he is happy, and because you would rather believe your own nephew capable of fathering a child on a seventeen-year-old girl than admit that you do not know what you are talking about."

Catherine's face went white. "You are hysterical."

"I am furious. There is a considerable difference."

Elizabeth was on her feet. She did not remember standing. Nana was in the room too, she realised, standing beside the mantelpiece with an expression of such concentrated outrage that the air around her seemed to crackle.

"The viper," Nana said. Her voice was low, almost a hiss. "The absolute viper. She dares…"

Elizabeth could not respond to Nana. She could not look at her. She kept her eyes on Lady Catherine, who was looking at Elizabeth with an expression of cold satisfaction. Catherine was not dismayed by Elizabeth's anger. She was pleased by it. She had wanted a reaction, and she had received one, and she was filing it away.

Emotional. Unstable. Unable to govern herself.

Elizabeth saw it, saw exactly what Catherine was doing. She could not stop herself, because the anger was real, it was righteous, and she could not tamp it down without pretending that Catherine's accusation did not matter, which it did, because it was a slander against the man she loved.

"I will not discuss this further," Elizabeth said. Her voice was steadier now, though her hands were not. "You are wrong. You are profoundly, viciously wrong, and if you repeat this accusation to anyone, I will make certain that Darcy and Lord Matlock know exactly what you have said."

She left the room before Catherine could reply. She walked quickly down the corridor, through the entrance hall, past a startled footman. She ran up the stairs, into her parlour, closed the door, pressed her back against it, stood there breathing until the shaking stopped.

Nana came through the bookcase. Her face was terrible.

"That woman," Nana said. "That poisonous, connivi ng..."

"Nana."

"She has a spy in this house. A traitor. Someone told her about the visit. Someone told her about the child. Someone is feeding her information, and she is using it to..."

"I know."

"I will find out who it is. I will haunt every servant in this house until I discover which of them has been carrying tales to that woman, and when I find them..."

"Nana. *Stop.*" Elizabeth pressed her hands flat against the door behind her. "I need to think about what just happened, what it means, what Catherine will do next. I can't do that if you are listing the people you intend to haunt."

Nana stopped. But the fury did not leave her face. It settled there, hardened, became fixed.

"She slandered this family," Nana said. "She slandered my boy. She sat in his house, accused him of fathering a child on a tenant's daughter, and she did it to hurt you. I will not let it stand."

Elizabeth looked at her. "What do you mean, you will not let it stand?"

Nana did not answer. She turned and walked through the bookcase, and was gone.

That night, Lady Catherine had a terrible time of it.

Elizabeth heard about it the following morning, from Mrs Reynolds, who had been roused twice in the night by Mrs Jenkinson, Lady Catherine's companion, who reported that her ladyship's rooms were intolerably cold, that the fire would not stay lit, that the doors would not remain closed no matter how firmly they were latched, and that Lady Catherine was certain she had seen a portrait on the wall move.

"I checked the rooms myself, ma'am," Mrs Reynolds said. "The fire was drawing perfectly well. The doors were sound. I could find nothing amiss."

"And the portrait?"

"It is a landscape, ma'am. A view of the south meadow. It has hung in that room for forty years and has never, to my knowledge, moved."

Elizabeth allowed the slightest hint of exasperation to enter her tolerant expression. "I am sure Lady Catherine was simply overtired. She has been keeping later hours than she is accustomed to at Rosings, I think."

"Yes, ma'am." Mrs Reynolds paused. The pause itself suggested she had her own theories about the blue rooms and their nighttime disturbances, and that she was keeping them to herself.

Elizabeth found Nana in the portrait gallery after breakfast. Nana was standing before Lady Anne's portrait, arms folded, looking extremely pleased with herself.

"You can't terrorise the guests," Elizabeth said.

Nana turned to her with an expression that could have curdled milk. "She is not a guest. She is an invader. And I did not terrorise her. I merely ensured that the blue rooms were somewhat less comfortable than usual."

"Nana."

"She accused my grandson of debauchery in his own house! To his wife! She deserves far worse than a cold room and a creaky door." Nana sniffed magnificently.

"She deserves to be dealt with carefully, not frightened into leaving before I have got what I need from her. She knows something about George's death, Nana. She all but admitted it yesterday, before she changed the subject. If you drive her out of Pemberley with your haunting, I lose the chance to find out what it is."

Nana's expression shifted slightly. Not chastened, exactly. Nana did not do chastened. But the strategic argument had landed where the moral one had not.

"One night," Elizabeth said. "You have had your one night. Now let her sleep, and let me work."

"I make no promises," Nana said. But she unfolded her arms, which was as close to agreement as Elizabeth was likely to get.

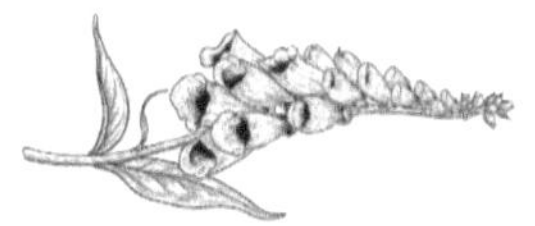

George Darcy found her in her parlour that afternoon. He had been quiet all morning, absent from the rooms Elizabeth moved through, and when he appeared he did not pace. He stood by the window, looking out at the November grey, and his face was grave.

"I heard what Catherine said to you," he said. "About Fitzwilliam and the Wilson child."

"Everyone dead in this house has heard by now, I suspect." Elizabeth smiled wearily. "I'm only glad that there is no one among the living who can hear Nana apart from me."

"She is still furious. She has recruited the maids from the east corridor and Miss Pardoe, and they are debating whether to extend their campaign to Catherine's dressing room." He paused. "Miss Pardoe's contribution, as I understand it, is to sit in Catherine's room and stare at her. She has not closed her book for anything in sixty years, so the fact that she is willing to put it down for this should tell you the depth of feeling involved."

"I told her to stop."

"She will not stop. You know that. Nana does not stop when she is angry. She redirects." George turned from the window. "But that is not what concerns me, Elizabeth. Catherine is not merely annoying. She is dangerous."

"I know."

"I'm not sure you do. Catherine has always believed that she should have had charge of this family after I died. She expected Fitzwilliam to marry Anne, and she expected to control Pemberley through her daughter. Your marriage ended that possibility, and she has never forgiven it, and she will not rest until she has found a way to undo it or to punish you for it."

"She can't undo my marriage."

"She can make your life difficult. She has connections, influence, the ear of people who matter. And she now believes, wrongly, that Fitzwilliam has a bastard child, which she will use against him if it suits her purpose. The accusation does not need to be true to do damage. It only needs to be repeated in the right drawing rooms."

Elizabeth felt cold. She had been so focused on her anger, on the injustice of Catherine's accusation, that she had not thought clearly about the practical danger. Catherine was not merely spiteful. She was strategic.

"What do I do?"

"Tell Darcy. Tell him what Catherine said, and let him deal with his aunt. He will be angry, and his anger will be useful, because it will force Catherine to defend herself rather than attack you. And while she is defending herself, you may find an opening to ask your questions again."

Elizabeth nodded. She would tell Darcy tonight. She would tell him what Catherine had accused, and watch his face, and let his anger do its work. And somewhere in the chaos that followed, she would find out what Lady Catherine knew about the death of George Darcy.

But first, she had to make sure Nana and her minions did not burn down the blue rooms.

Chapter Twenty

SHE TOLD DARCY THAT evening, after the household had retired.

They were in their sitting room, the fire burning low. Elizabeth sat in the chair opposite him and said, without preamble, "Your aunt came to me yesterday with information she believed I ought to have. She told me that William Cooper is your child."

Darcy set down his glass. Carefully, as though he did not trust what his hand might do if he were not precise about it. "She said what?"

"She said the boy is yours. That you fathered him on Sally Wilson, that you have been supporting the family to conceal it, that you took me to visit them without telling me the truth. She said it with great sympathy. She felt it was her duty."

The colour left his face first, then returned, darker. He did not speak for several seconds.

"How did she know about the boy?"

"I don't know. But she knew about the farm, the financial support, even our visit today. She knew the boy's name, knew he is fair-haired. Someone told her, Darcy. Someone in this house has been reporting to her." Nana had said it, and Elizabeth had known at once that she was correct.

He stood. He walked to the fireplace and stood with his back to her, one hand on the mantelpiece. She watched the tension move through his shoulders.

"She accused me," he said, "of fathering a child on a seventeen-year-old girl. A girl whose family has depended on me for their livelihood."

"Yes."

"She said this to you. To my wife."

"Yes."

He turned around. His face was rigidly controlled, but his eyes were not. "She insulted you. She insulted Sally. She insulted Mr Wilson, his family, the man who married Sally and raised that boy as his own. She took every decent thing I have done for that family and made it filthy."

"Yes," Elizabeth said, for the third time, because there was nothing else to say. She had never seen Darcy angry, not like this. The rage burning in his eyes reminded her uncomfortably of George Darcy's, whenever he spoke of Wickham.

"And she has a spy in my household."

"She must. There is no other way she could have known."

Darcy left the room. Elizabeth heard his footsteps on the stairs, quick and hard, then silence.

Mrs Reynolds came to Elizabeth's parlour the following morning, before breakfast.

"Mr Darcy has asked me to determine how Lady Catherine obtained her information," she said. She looked as though she had not slept. "I have been thinking about it most of the night, ma'am, and I believe I know."

"Who?"

"Thomas Hawkins. He has been a footman here for seventeen years, by my records. Competent enough at his duties, though not exceptional. Reliable, I should have said, until now." Mrs Reynolds paused, ordering her thoughts carefully; she did not make accusations lightly. "He applied for the under-butler's position more than once when vacancies arose, but both Mr George Darcy and the current Mr Darcy passed over him in favour of other candidates who were better suited to the role, though sometimes younger men."

"And you believe he has been writing to Lady Catherine?"

"I believe Lady Catherine offered him what Pemberley did not: recognition, remuneration. She would have approached it carefully, expressing concern for her nephew and niece. Flattery, which Lady Catherine dispenses when it serves her. Hawkins would have seen no harm in it at first. A few details about the running of the house, the comings and goings. Then, gradually, more." Mrs Reynolds folded her hands. "He was on duty when you rode out to the Wilsons with Mr Darcy. I checked; he was the one sent to the stables to order the horses made ready, would have been told your destination so he could pass it to the stable-master. He served tea to Lady Catherine that afternoon, alone in the yellow drawing room with her for several minutes. He was in the entrance hall when you came back through after she spoke to you, walking quickly past him."

Elizabeth remembered. The startled footman she had passed on her way to her parlour after the confrontation with Catherine. She had not looked at his face. She had been too angry to look at anything.

"I cannot prove it," Mrs Reynolds said. "Not without searching his room or confronting him directly."

"Tell Mr Darcy what you have told me. He will decide what to do."

Darcy did not hesitate. Elizabeth was not present when Hawkins was called to the study, but Mrs Reynolds told her afterwards that it had been brief. Darcy asked the man directly whether he had been corresponding with Lady Catherine. Hawkins denied it, poorly. Darcy asked Mrs Reynolds to search the man's room. In a drawer beneath his spare livery they found three letters from Lady Catherine, the most recent dated just weeks ago, requesting specific information about Mrs Darcy's movements, her habits, stating that Lady Catherine herself would be arriving soon. Mention of payment being enclosed was made, though no money was found with the letters.

Hawkins was dismissed within the hour. He was given his wages and nothing else. No reference, no letter of character. He left Pemberley in a cart with his trunk while the rest of the household watched from the kitchen windows in shocked silence.

Mrs Reynolds told Elizabeth afterwards that the man had looked more relieved than ashamed, which she found the most damning thing of all.

"He was never loyal," Mrs Reynolds said. "Some are not. You can train a man's hands and not his heart. Hawkins always felt he deserved more than he was given. Lady Catherine saw that, used it. I should have seen it sooner, ma'am. I pride myself on knowing this household, and I did not see it."

"You are not responsible for Lady Catherine's scheming, Mrs Reynolds."

"No. But I am responsible for this household, and a spy operated under my roof for years without my knowledge. That is a failure I do not take lightly."

"She can't blame herself," Nana said, from her usual chair. "Even I didn't know."

"You can't watch everyone all of the time," Elizabeth said, to both of them. Neither of them looked satisfied by this response, but it was true whether they liked it or not, so there was nothing more to say.

The confrontation with Lady Catherine took place in the study, after luncheon.

Darcy arranged it precisely. He asked Lord Matlock and Lady Matlock to be present. He asked Elizabeth to be there. He sent word to Lady Catherine that he wished to speak with her on a matter of family business. Catherine arrived expecting, Elizabeth suspected, to find herself in a position of strength. She swept in looking armoured and righteous, faltered only slightly when she saw the audience assembled.

"Fitzwilliam. What is this about?"

"Sit down, Aunt Catherine."

She sat, because Darcy's tone left no room for refusal. He stood behind his desk. Elizabeth sat in the chair by the window. Lord Matlock stood at the fireplace, his face unreadable. Lady Matlock sat beside Elizabeth with her hands folded in her lap and said nothing.

"Yesterday," Darcy said, "you told my wife that I had fathered an illegitimate child on a tenant's daughter. That the boy currently being raised by Sally and Joseph Cooper on the Wilson farm is my son."

Catherine's chin lifted. "I felt it was my duty to inform Mrs Darcy of what the household clearly knows and she apparently did not."

"The household does not know it, because it is not true. The child is not mine. He is George Wickham's."

The name did what Elizabeth had known it would do. Catherine's face changed. Not shock, exactly. Recognition.

"Wickham seduced Sally Wilson when she was seventeen years old," Darcy continued. His voice was level, measured, perfectly controlled, but Elizabeth could see the rage still burning behind it and was glad it was not directed at her. "He left her with child and departed without a backward glance. My father learned of it days before he died. He summoned Wickham to Pemberley and confronted him about it, but was not able to set the matter right in the little time remaining to him. After my father's death, I discovered the matter. I gave the Wilson family a better farm. I found a good man willing to marry Sally, to raise the child as his own. I settled money on the boy to ensure he would not suffer for his father's sins. I have visited the family regularly for six years, because they are my tenants, my responsibility, because Wickham's wreckage does not repair itself."

The room was silent. Catherine sat rigid in her chair. Nobody moved.

"You came into my house." Darcy's voice had an edge to it now, thin, cold. "You recruited a spy among my servants. A footman named Hawkins, who has been corresponding with you for years, since before my father's death, reporting on the household, my movements, my wife. You paid him for information. You used that information to construct a lie. You delivered that lie to Elizabeth with the intention of causing her pain, undermining our marriage."

"I was protecting this family," Catherine said. Her voice was steady, but her colour was high. "If there was a child, your wife had a right to know."

"There is a child. He is not mine. You did not come here to protect anyone. You came here because you have never accepted my marriage, and you seized on the first piece of gossip your spy could provide to attack Elizabeth where you thought she was most vulnerable."

"I will not be spoken to in this manner."

"You will be spoken to exactly in this manner, Aunt Catherine, because what you have done is unforgivable. You slandered me to my wife. You slandered an innocent woman and her family. You corrupted a member of my household. You did it for spite."

Catherine's face was white, her jaw set. But Elizabeth was watching her eyes, and what she saw there was not merely the rigidity of a woman under siege. It was the look of a woman whose ground had shifted. The bastard child she had been so certain of had dissolved, and in its place was Wickham, whose name she had been saying for years, whose character she had warned George about long before anyone else in this family had been willing to see it.

The ghosts arrived then. Elizabeth felt them: Nana first, crackling with vindicated fury; then George, drawn perhaps by the sound of his own name in his sister's mouth.

"You are not surprised," Elizabeth said. It came out before she could stop it. "You heard the name Wickham and you were not surprised."

Catherine looked at her. For a moment the mask slipped, and what was underneath was older, rawer, more complicated than spite.

"I told George," Catherine said. Her voice was different now. Quieter. "I told him that boy would be his ruin. He would not listen. He said I did not understand. He said I was jealous of a motherless child, as though I could not recognise a predator when I saw one."

George, by the window, closed his eyes.

Catherine drew a breath. "Then George died. Hawkins told me Wickham was at Pemberley when it happened. I have thought about that for six years, Fitzwilliam. Six years."

The room went absolutely silent. Lord Matlock straightened at the fireplace. Darcy's hands, flat on the desk, did not move.

"What exactly are you saying, Catherine?" Lord Matlock asked finally.

"I am saying I warned George. He did not listen, and he died. I am saying that Wickham was there. That I have never been easy about it."

"Do you have evidence?" Darcy said. "Anything beyond a feeling?"

"If I had evidence, do you think I would have kept it to myself for six years?" Catherine's voice rose. "No, Hawkins knew no more than that Wickham was here. But I have a feeling. I have always had a feeling. I told George he would live to regret his blind spot when it came to Wickham, and he died instead. I cannot prove that Wickham is anything worse than a seducer, a fortune hunter, a man with no honour. But I know what I know."

Elizabeth watched the frustration move through the room. Catherine had given them exactly what Anne had hinted at: a suspicion, a conviction, a lifetime of being right about Wickham's character. None of it was evidence they did not already have; that Wickham had been at Pemberley the day George died. None of it could be acted on. It was Lady Catherine's certainty, which was as boundless as it was useless, because Lady Catherine was certain about everything, and being right this once did not make her word proof.

"You should have come to me," Darcy said. "Years ago. You should have told me what you suspected, instead of nursing it in silence and continuing to spy on my household."

"I was protecting this family. I went about it badly, I will grant you that." It was as close to an apology as Catherine was capable of, and it cost her visibly. She stood. "I will not apologise for the instinct. Only for the method."

"The method," Lord Matlock said, his voice heavy with weariness, "was to plant a spy in your nephew's house and deliver a poisoned accusation to his wife. That is not instinct, Catherine. That is malice dressed up as duty."

Catherine turned on her heel and swept toward the door.

"We were not finished, sister!" Lord Matlock said crossly, and followed her out. Lady Matlock sighed, looked at Elizabeth with an expression that managed to convey both sympathy and resignation, went after them.

The door closed.

The study was quiet. Darcy stood behind his desk, both hands flat on its surface, his head bowed slightly. Elizabeth sat in her chair by the window and did not speak, because she could see that he was not finished thinking.

George stood at the window still, his back to the room. He had not moved since Catherine spoke his name. Nana watched him from the corner with an expression Elizabeth had never seen on her face: something almost gentle.

"She should tell him," Nana said. "About the murder. He is ready."

"Not yet." George's voice was rough. "Let him come to it himself."

"He is coming to it. Look at him. He is thinking about the timing. About Wickham being here the night you died. He is almost there."

"Then let him arrive."

Darcy spoke. His voice was quiet, the anger spent, what remained something more careful.

"Elizabeth."

"Yes?"

"My father learned about Wickham and Sally Wilson. He summoned Wickham to Pemberley. They dined together. By morning my father was dead, and Wickham rode away." He lifted his head and looked at her. "I am beginning to wonder whether my father's death was what the physician said it was."

The ghosts fell silent.

Elizabeth held perfectly still. This was the moment she had been steering toward for weeks, the conclusion she had wanted him to reach on his own, from the evidence, from the living world. He had reached it. She had to decide what to say.

"I believe you are right to wonder," she said. "But how could anything be proved, after six years?"

He sat down. He sat in his father's chair, behind his father's desk, and said nothing. The fire shifted. Nana opened her mouth; George shook his head, once. She closed it again.

"And even if we could," Darcy said at last. "Then what? Wickham is married to your sister."

The impossibility of it filled the room. Lydia, sixteen years old, married to a man who may have murdered his own benefactor. Lydia, whose reputation and future were bound to a man whose exposure would destroy her along with him.

"I know," Elizabeth said.

Darcy looked at her across the desk. "You have known this was coming. You have been leading me here, carefully, one piece at a time, because you knew that once I saw it I could not unsee it. You wanted me to be ready."

"Yes."

"Lydia is why you hesitated. Why you did not simply tell me what you suspected, weeks ago."

"Yes."

He was quiet again. Then he said, "Thank you. For not telling me. For letting me find it myself. I would not have believed it, Elizabeth, if you had simply said it. I would have thought you were letting your dislike of Wickham colour your judgement, because even though I despise him myself, I did not think him capable of this. But the evidence..." He stopped. "The evidence does not lie."

"No," Elizabeth said. "It does not."

George Darcy turned from the window and walked through the wall without a word. Nana watched him go. For the first time in Elizabeth's memory, she looked uncertain. She glanced at Elizabeth with an expression that was almost a question. Then she too faded, leaving Elizabeth and Darcy alone in the study, the fire burning low, the weight of what they now both knew pressing down on them.

"What do we do?" Elizabeth asked.

Darcy considered. She could see him turning it over, examining it from every angle, the way he always did. The fire crackled. Outside, the November wind pressed against the windows.

"If we pursue this," he said, "and if we find proof, then Wickham hangs. Lydia is a murderer's widow at sixteen. Your family will be ruined. Kitty and Mary will never make good marriages. The scandal will touch Bingley, Jane, Georgiana, ourselves. All of it, ruined."

"I know."

"If we do nothing, then we live with it. We live knowing that my father was murdered, that the man who did it is married to your sister and walking free."

"I know that too."

He looked at her. Elizabeth's heart ached, because she had wanted to relieve his burdens, to help him carry the weight he had been carrying alone for six years. She could see in his face that he had now realised the weight was twice what he thought it was.

"We will not do nothing," he said. "But we must be exceedingly careful about what we do, how we proceed, who knows. Lord Matlock and I will continue the enquiry into my father's death. Quietly. If there is evidence to be found, we will find it. When we know what we are dealing with, we will decide together what comes next."

"Together," Elizabeth said.

"Together. I am done carrying things alone."

He held out his hand across the desk. She took it. They sat together in the quiet while the November dark came down around Pemberley, the ghosts keeping their own counsel in the corridors beyond.

Chapter Twenty-One

A LETTER ARRIVED FROM Longbourn the next morning. Mrs Bennet wrote with her usual breathless urgency to say that she was prostrate with a cold, that Mr Bennet refused to travel anywhere in November, that Mary had no interest in balls and would not be persuaded, and that they would all three stay at home, though Mrs Bennet wished it known that her nerves were greatly affected by missing the event and she hoped Elizabeth would write her a full account of every gown, every dance, and every eligible young man in attendance who might potentially show interest in Kitty.

Mr Bennet had added a postscript in his own hand: *Your mother's cold is a sniffle. My refusal to travel in the winter is genuine. Enjoy your ball, Lizzy; we shall perhaps come in the summer, for I am truly eager to see Pemberley's library.*

Elizabeth read this in her parlour and felt a complicated mixture of disappointment and relief. She missed her father. She did not, at this particular moment, need her mother in the house, and the guilt of that thought sat uncomfortably alongside the truth of it.

"One fewer problem," Kitty said, reading the letter over her shoulder. "Mama in the same house as Lady Catherine would have been a disaster."

"Mama in the same house as Lady Catherine would have been entertaining," Elizabeth corrected. "For about ten minutes. After which it would have been a disaster."

The Bingleys arrived three days before the ball.

Elizabeth had been watching for the carriage on the drive all morning and was at the front door before the footman could announce them, which was not dignified and she did not care. The carriage drew up. Bingley descended first, beaming, ruddy-cheeked from the cold, radiating goodwill like a man who had never once in his life walked into a room and made it worse. Behind him, Jane.

Elizabeth rushed down the steps, across the gravel. Jane was already coming toward her. They met in the middle and held on. Elizabeth pressed her face into her sister's shoulder and breathed, and for the first time in weeks, the knot beneath her ribs loosened.

"You came," Elizabeth said, stupidly, because of course she had come, she had been invited, she had written to say she was coming.

"Of course I came," Jane said, held her tighter, did not let go until Elizabeth was ready, which took rather longer than was strictly appropriate for a greeting conducted in full view of the household.

Bingley, bless him, filled the silence with cheerful noise. He shook Darcy's hand vigorously, admired the house, admired the November sky, admired the horses being led away, complimented Mrs Reynolds, greeted Kitty and Georgiana with genuine warmth, and generally made himself the centre of uncomplicated pleasure that the household had been sorely lacking. The tension of the past week did not evaporate, but it receded, as tension always did in Bingley's presence. He was sunshine in human form, and Pemberley needed sunshine.

Darcy, who loved Bingley in the quiet, unexpressive way of a man who does not make friends easily and knows the value of the ones he has, looked genuinely glad to see him. Elizabeth watched them together, Darcy's reserve softening by degrees, Bingley's hand on his friend's arm, and thought: this is what he needs. Someone who asks nothing of him but friendship.

Behind the Bingleys, a second carriage produced Caroline Bingley, Louisa Hurst, and Mr Hurst.

Caroline descended with more flamboyance than grace, glancing over the assembled household with the rapid, assessing eye of a woman who was cataloguing what had changed. Her gaze lingered on Elizabeth just a moment too long.

"Mrs Darcy," she said, with a smile that was warm on the surface and calculating underneath. "What a pleasure. You are looking very well. Pemberley agrees with you."

"Thank you, Miss Bingley. You are very welcome."

Mrs Hurst followed her sister with less theatre and more genuine fatigue from the journey. Mr Hurst made brief greetings and marched straight to the front door, clearly confident that somewhere inside there would be a comfortable chair and a glass of port. He found both within ten minutes and was not heard from again for some time.

"Nana is going to have opinions about Miss Bingley," Kitty murmured to Elizabeth as they went inside.

"Nana has opinions about everyone."

"Yes, but she is going to have *particular* opinions about Miss Bingley. I rather wish I could hear them. You must relay some of the highlights to me later."

Kitty was not wrong. Nana appeared in the entrance hall as the guests were being shown to their rooms, watched Caroline Bingley ascending the staircase, and said, "Oh, she is back. Thank the Good Lord, Fitzwilliam had the sense not to marry that one."

Elizabeth could not reply. She pressed her lips together and kept walking.

"The dress is too fine for the country, and too thin for the weather," Nana continued, keeping pace beside her. "The bonnet is London, the pelisse is London, and the expression is pure ambition. She cannot have Fitzwilliam now, so she will settle for the most eligible bachelor she can find in his circle, and she is already measuring everyone to see who stands in her way."

This was, Elizabeth had to admit, entirely accurate. But she could not say so. Jane was beside her, Bingley behind them, Caroline just ahead on the stairs. The entrance hall of Pemberley was not the place for a conversation with thin air.

"I shall enjoy this visit," Nana said, with relish. "Miss Bingley always did keep me entertained."

Mrs Reynolds had the Bingleys in the Chinese rooms, which were the best guest rooms after the blue rooms currently occupied by Lady Catherine, and which Jane declared lovely. Caroline and the Hursts were placed in the west wing, which was comfortable, well-appointed, and as far from the family rooms as could be managed without actually putting them in a separate building. Elizabeth suspected Mrs Reynolds had her own opinions about Caroline Bingley. Mrs Reynolds's opinions about people were rarely wrong, and she expressed them entirely through room assignments.

Elizabeth and Jane found each other alone that afternoon, in Elizabeth's parlour, with the door locked.

Jane sat in the chair by the fire and Elizabeth sat on the floor at her feet, because Jane was the one person in the world with whom she did not have to perform in any way. Jane ran her fingers through Elizabeth's hair, the way she had when they were children. Elizabeth closed her eyes, rested her head against Jane's knee, let the sheer relief of it wash through her.

"Tell me," Jane said.

Elizabeth told her everything. All of it, from the beginning. Nana, running Pemberley for a hundred and thirty years. George Darcy's ghost, growing more insistent as the investigation advanced, pressing her to steer Darcy toward conclusions. The Sally Wilson thread, the visit, Mr Wilson's testimony, Mrs Reynolds's corroboration. The timeline: George learning the truth, summoning Wickham, dining with him, dying that night. Lady Matlock's six years of unease. Catherine's spy, her vile accusation, the confrontation that followed. Catherine's own suspicion of Wickham, which turned out to be just a feeling, just certainty without evidence, useless precisely because Lady Catherine was certain about everything, and being right this once did not make her word proof. Darcy reaching the conclusion himself, sitting in his father's chair in the study, saying *Wickham is married to your sister.*

Jane listened. She did not interrupt. She held Elizabeth's hand and let her talk.

"You have been carrying this for weeks," Jane said, when Elizabeth had finished.

"Almost since I arrived at Pemberley."

"And Darcy still does not know about the ghosts."

"No. He knows about Sally Wilson, about the timeline, about Lady Catherine's suspicions. He does not know that his father's ghost told me most of it, or that Nana has been helping me since my first week here. He thinks I have been painstakingly thorough, impossibly clever. He does not know I have had help from the dead."

Jane was quiet for a moment. Her fingers had not stopped moving through Elizabeth's hair. "Lizzy. You cannot keep this from him much longer."

"I know."

"The longer you wait, the more it will hurt. Not because the secret is terrible, though it is strange, and he will need time to accept it. But because he will wonder why you did not trust him. He will look back at every conversation, wonder what was real, what was managed. That will wound him more than the ghosts themselves."

Elizabeth pressed her forehead harder against Jane's knee. "I know. I know you are right. I'm not ready."

"I didn't say you had to do it today. I said you cannot wait much longer." Jane's voice was gentle, implacable, the voice of a woman who had spent her whole life being kind and had learnt that kindness sometimes meant saying the hard thing. "He loves you, Lizzy. He married you knowing you were not ordinary. He may be readier than you think."

"Or he may think me mad."

"He will not think you mad. He will think you extraordinary, which you are."

Elizabeth almost smiled. "You are biased."

"I am your sister. Of course I'm biased. I am also correct." Jane paused. "And what of Lydia? Have you heard from her?"

"Yes." Elizabeth told Jane about Lydia's letter, about Lydia's description of Wickham's eyes going flat. About Darcy having agreed to make Wickham a small allowance, to make Lydia's life a little more comfortable, even before he suspected that Wickham may have been involved in his father's death. "She does not know her husband has killed a man," Elizabeth finished, "but I think she has learned to fear him."

"She is sixteen," Jane said, and there was pain in it. "She is sixteen and married to him and there is nothing we can do about it until we know for certain."

"Darcy said the same thing. He said if it comes to proof, Wickham hangs, and Lydia is destroyed. If we do nothing, we live with it."

"There must be a middle course. There must be some way to protect her, even if Wickham is guilty."

"If you find one, I should very much like to hear it. I have been looking for weeks."

Jane did not answer, because there was no answer, not yet. But Elizabeth could see her turning it over, examining it with the sensible practicality that people mistook for sweetness, and she thought: Jane will think of something. She always does. It may take her time, and it may not be what any of us expect, but Jane will find a way through.

They sat together in the quiet, and the fire burned, and for a little while Elizabeth did not have to be brave or strategic or careful. She simply had to be Jane's sister, which was the easiest thing in the world.

At dinner that evening, Caroline Bingley began her campaign.

She seated herself near Darcy, which required some manoeuvring since the seating had already been arranged, and addressed him with particular warmth. She complimented the wine, the table arrangements, the paintings in the dining room. She asked after Georgiana's playing, as though she and Georgiana were intimate friends, and was met with Georgiana's polite, slightly bewildered acknowledgment.

"What a full house you have, Mr Darcy," Caroline said, surveying the table. "Lady Catherine, Lord and Lady Matlock, all of us. Pemberley is quite transformed."

"We are glad of the company," Darcy said, in a tone that did not invite elaboration.

Caroline was not deterred. She turned her attention to the younger women, assessing Anne with a quick, dismissive glance, Kitty with a longer, more calculating one, and Georgiana with careful courtesy, because Darcy's sister was a strategic asset and Caroline never forgot it.

"Miss Bennet, you are looking very well," Caroline said to Kitty, with the kind of compliment that was really a measurement. "Country life suits you. Though I suppose you must be longing for the company of officers by now."

"Not at all," Kitty said pleasantly. "Pemberley has been wonderful. We ride, we read, we have been restoring the rose garden. I haven't wished for other company once."

This was not the answer Caroline had expected, and Elizabeth watched her recalibrate. Kitty was not the silly girl Caroline remembered from Hertfordshire. Pemberley had changed her, or perhaps had simply given her room to be who she had always been underneath Lydia's shadow.

"That shade of orange is really quite dreadful on her," Nana observed from the sideboard. "And the feathers in her hair are peacock, which is vulgar at a family dinner. Peacock feathers are for a ball, and even then, only if one has the neck for them. She does not."

Elizabeth hid the smirk she could not quite suppress in a careful sip of wine.

"She sat herself next to Fitzwilliam like a chess piece moving into position," Nana continued, warming to her theme. "She did the same thing every time she visited before, but it is even sillier now, trying it with a married man. I watched her try every trick in the book: the concerned friend, the devoted sister, the woman who understood Pemberley better than anyone. She even tried befriending Georgiana, which was the closest she came to being clever about it. Fitzwilliam never noticed, because Fitzwilliam does not notice women who are trying to catch his attention. He noticed you, Elizabeth, because you were not trying at all. That is what Miss Bingley has never understood, and she never will."

Across the table, Jane caught Elizabeth's eye and smiled, and Elizabeth felt the warmth of it like sunlight. She smiled back and laughed because Lord Matlock had just laughed, and whatever had amused him was excellent cover for the laughter she could no longer suppress at Nana's caustic wit.

After dinner, in the yellow drawing room, Caroline attempted to establish herself as the natural leader of the younger, single women. She proposed music, which was clearly an excuse to display her own accomplishments at the instrument, and she addressed Georgiana and Anne with the condescending warmth of an older sister who expected to be deferred to.

Jane intercepted her without appearing to do anything at all.

"What a lovely idea, Caroline. Miss Darcy, will you play for us? I was utterly enchanted on the one occasion I was privileged to hear you play at Netherfield. Miss de Bourgh, will you turn pages?"

It was done so smoothly, so pleasantly, that Caroline could not object without appearing churlish. Georgiana sat at the instrument. Anne took her place beside her. Caroline was left standing by the pianoforte with her offer to play gently, immovably, redirected.

Elizabeth watched her sister with something close to awe. Jane had always been kind. She had always been good. But somehow since her marriage, Jane had acquired an additional quality that Elizabeth could only describe as steel wrapped in silk. She did not argue with Caroline. She did not confront her. She simply occupied the ground, pleasantly, refusing to move. Caroline could not work out how to get past her without appearing rude, which was the one thing Caroline could not afford to be in this company.

It was, Elizabeth realised, the same quality Lady Matlock possessed: the ability to manage people without them noticing they were being managed. Jane had been watching Lady Matlock since the Bingleys' arrival, and Lady Matlock had been watching Jane, and Elizabeth suspected they recognised each other. Two women who understood that real authority did not need to announce itself.

"Your sister," Nana said, appearing beside Elizabeth's chair, "is rather magnificent. I like her. And I quite see why you speak of her so fondly."

For once, Elizabeth agreed with Nana entirely.

Caroline tried once more, later in the evening, approaching Darcy by the fire to ask his opinion on some matter or other. Jane appeared at Darcy's other side, asked him whether he had written to Mr Gardiner about the fishing, and drew him into a conversation about trout that Caroline could not possibly contribute to without betraying her complete ignorance of country sport. Caroline retreated to the sofa, where Mrs Hurst was dozing. She sat with her back rigidly straight, her face perfectly composed, her eyes moving around the room, looking for another opening.

She did not find one. Jane had closed them all.

"Elizabeth," Georgiana said quietly, as they went up the stairs together a little later. "Your sister Jane is terrifying."

"Jane? Terrifying?"

"In the nicest possible way. Miss Bingley does not know what to do with her."

"No," Elizabeth said, and she smiled proudly. "She doesn't."

Chapter Twenty-Two

THE BALL CONSUMED EVERY moment of Elizabeth's time, as the day approached.

She spent the morning of the first day in the ballroom with Lady Matlock, who had produced a list of requirements so long it needed both sides of the paper. Lady Matlock read aloud while Elizabeth took notes, the notes multiplying: which families must be greeted first (the Ashbournes, because Lady Ashbourne was the county's oldest dragon and would take lasting offence if she were not); which local worthies required particular attention (Sir Edward Morris, deaf in one ear, who must be spoken to from the left; his wife, not deaf but pretending to be whenever the conversation bored her); where the carriages should queue so that guests arrived in the correct order of precedence; why the musicians must be fed before the dancing began, because musicians who thought about supper played badly.

Mrs Reynolds had the house in hand. The ballroom was opened and aired, the chandeliers taken down and cleaned crystal by crystal by a team of maids who had been at it since dawn. The floors were polished until they shone. The kitchens operated at full capacity. Mrs Reynolds moved between the cook, the housekeeper's pantry, the wine cellar, checking stocks, issuing instructions, maintaining the tireless calm of a woman who had overseen Pemberley's entertainments for thirty years. She was not about to let standards slip for the new mistress's first ball.

Jane appeared at Elizabeth's elbow whenever a decision was needed. Should the supper be served at half past ten or eleven? Eleven, Jane thought, because the receiving line would take a long time and the first set could not start until it had concluded, and they must have time for enough dances before supper. Should the card room be opened as well as the yellow drawing room for those who did not dance? Yes, because Mr Hurst would complain bitterly if it was not, and he was not the only gentleman who preferred cards to cotillions. Jane deflected the questions that could wait, escalated the ones that could not, and within a day the household had accepted her as Elizabeth's deputy without anyone formally naming her so.

Elizabeth, watching Jane direct a footman where to place the card tables in the yellow drawing room, thought: she was wasted at Longbourn. We were all wasted at Longbourn.

Nana, meanwhile, was everywhere. Elizabeth could not enter a room without finding her already in it, arms folded, inspecting. She had declared the flowers wrong before the vases were half filled, pronounced the candle arrangements inadequate before they were lit, and sent Elizabeth back to Mrs Reynolds three times about the musicians' gallery, which she insisted needed dusting despite the fact that Elizabeth had watched two maids dust it with painstaking care that morning.

The real difficulty was the curtains. Nana wanted the ballroom curtains drawn back to show the grounds by moonlight, which was a fine idea, but she wanted them drawn back to a precise degree that Elizabeth could not communicate to the footmen without revealing her source. Elizabeth spent twenty minutes adjusting the left curtain by inches while Nana stood behind her saying "More. More. No, that is too much. Back a little. There."

"She is enjoying herself," George observed, drifting through the ballroom on one of his restless circuits of the house. He paused to watch Nana direct Elizabeth's curtain adjustments, his mouth twitching, which was as close to a smile as George Darcy ever came. "She has not been this animated since the last ball, which was before Anne died. This is her natural element. Pemberley's reputation as host of the county's premier events was entirely built during her lifetime."

Elizabeth, who was balancing on a footstool adjusting the curtain tie while Lady Matlock waited patiently behind her with the seating plan, could not respond. She gave George a look that she hoped conveyed both acknowledgment and a strong desire for him to go away. He took the hint and drifted on.

Caroline Bingley, having been outmanoeuvred by Jane repeatedly, adjusted her strategy. She could not dominate the older women: Lady Matlock outranked her, Lady Catherine ignored her, Jane blocked her at every turn, and Elizabeth was mistress of the house. But the younger women, Caroline clearly reasoned, were another matter. Kitty was a country nobody. Georgiana was shy. Anne was sickly and sheltered and could not possibly have anything interesting to say.

She found the three of them in the music room after breakfast on the second day, where Georgiana was practising, Anne was reading, and Kitty was writing a letter. Caroline claimed the settee without hesitation, spreading her skirts as though the room had been arranged for her comfort.

"I do hope you are all looking forward to the ball," Caroline said. "It will be your first real introduction to society, for some of you. Georgiana, of course, has been to London, but Miss Bennet, Miss de Bourgh, you must be quite overwhelmed at the prospect."

"I am not overwhelmed," Kitty said, without looking up from her letter. "I have been to assemblies. And indeed, the ball your brother hosted at Netherfield, a year past."

"Assemblies in Hertfordshire," Caroline said, with a smile that made it clear what she thought of assemblies in Hertfordshire, and conveniently ignoring the latter part of Kitty's remarks. "This will be rather different. Three hundred guests, the principal families of Derbyshire. One must know who is who, of course. Lady Ashbourne will certainly come; she is the grande dame of the county set, terribly exacting, and one must be very careful not to offend her. And Lord and Lady Vernon, naturally, from Chatterton. And I understand Sir Peregrine Howe and his family are in the neighbourhood; I met them in London last Season, at Lady Jersey's. Delightful people. The second son is said to be looking for a wife."

She delivered this catalogue with evident authority and looked around for the expected admiration.

Anne turned a page of her book. "Lady Ashbourne is my great-aunt, on my father's side," she said mildly. "She and my mother have corresponded weekly for many years. I believe she is bringing her granddaughter Clara, who is about Georgiana's age; a very sweet girl who plays the harp. I think you and she might make a duet, Georgiana, which would be charming. The Vernons I have known since I was a child; they came to Rosings every autumn for the shooting until Papa died. As for Sir Peregrine, his father and mine were at school together. The second son, Frederick, has a stammer and is very shy, and he is not looking for a wife; he is looking for a living, which my cousin Fitzwilliam has promised to provide when the next one falls vacant."

Caroline stared at her. Her smile set like plaster.

"I see," she said.

"Mama keeps a very thorough correspondence," Anne added, returning to her book. "If there is anyone you wish to know about, I am sure I can help."

Kitty and Georgiana exchanged a look of pure, undisguised delight. Georgiana bit her lip. Kitty suddenly needed to attend with great concentration to her letter.

Caroline excused herself shortly after, and Anne watched her go with an expression that was not unkind but was certainly not sorry.

"Was that too much?" Anne asked Georgiana, when Caroline was safely out of earshot.

"It was perfect," Georgiana said. "Absolutely perfect."

"My mother would have been much worse," Anne said thoughtfully. "She would have told Miss Bingley exactly where she ranked in the social order, precisely why she would never rise above it. She would have done it in front of everyone. She would have enjoyed it. I merely stated facts. I did not even enjoy it." She paused. "Well. Perhaps a little."

"You are a dragon's daughter," Kitty said admiringly.

Anne considered this. "I suppose I am. Though I should like to think a rather more polite one."

Caroline retreated to the yellow drawing room, where Louisa Hurst was established on the sofa with a novel she was not reading and a cup of tea she had let go cold.

Elizabeth was not present for what followed. But Nana was. Bored with Elizabeth's insufficient attention to her opinions on the ball preparations, she had drifted off in search of better entertainment. She found it in the music room.

Caroline Bingley was, if nothing else, quite useful for keeping Nana amused.

Elizabeth was in her parlour going through the guest list one more time, marking the names she still did not recognise so that she could ask Mrs Reynolds about them before tomorrow, when Nana came through the bookcase looking as though Christmas had come early.

"You will not believe what I have just witnessed," Nana said.

Elizabeth set down her pen. Nana in this mood was not to be denied, and at least here there were no witnesses.

Nana settled in her chair, the smile on her face broader than Elizabeth had ever seen it, and related, at length, Anne's effortless set-down of Miss Bingley.

"And then," Nana said, with something that might almost have been a giggle, "Miss Bingley went to her sister in the yellow drawing room and complained, at length, about Miss de Bourgh. She called her sickly. She called her presumptuous. She said it was ridiculous that a girl who had never had a Season should pretend to know everyone worth knowing, and that Anne was putting on airs that her constitution could not support."

Nana looked far more gleeful than a mere witness had any right to be, much though Elizabeth wished she could have been there in person to see Caroline's face after Anne's puncturing of her presumptions.

"In the yellow drawing room," Elizabeth said thoughtfully. "Which is adjacent to..."

"To the eastern passage leading to the blue rooms. Yes. And Lady Catherine was in that passage, on her way to the yellow drawing room herself. She heard every word."

Elizabeth sucked in a breath. "What did she do?"

"She did not enter the room. She stood in the passage and listened, and she looked as though she was deciding where to place a knife. Not now. Later. When it would do the most damage."

"Catherine was considering Miss Bingley as a possible ally, before this," Elizabeth said slowly. "Another woman who resents me, who might be useful to her." It had been quite obvious the previous evening; Lady Catherine had been dismissive of Caroline up until the moment she heard Caroline aim a sly barb in Elizabeth's direction. Then she had turned to look at her, eyes narrowing thoughtfully, and begun to listen.

"If she was, she is not any longer," Nana said gleefully. "Nobody insults Anne except Catherine. That is Catherine's privilege, and she does not share it. Miss Bingley has managed to alienate every woman of consequence in this house, Elizabeth. Lady Matlock finds her tiresome. Jane has seen through her. Anne has humiliated her. Georgiana and Kitty are laughing at her. Now Lady Catherine, who looked down on her but might at least have become an ally through mutual dislike of you, despises her." Nana looked deeply satisfied. "She has no one left but her sister, who is useless, and her brother, who will never preference her over Jane. It is the most thorough social destruction I have witnessed in years, and the remarkable thing is that she did it entirely to herself."

Elizabeth ought to have felt sorry for Caroline. She did not, quite, but she did pity her: a woman so desperate to belong that she could not see she was pushing everyone away. There was a version of Caroline Bingley who might have been liked, if she had ever stopped performing long enough for anyone to see her. She was attractive, at least moderately clever, and rich. If she had just allowed herself to shine as the person she actually was, instead of letting her jealousy and insecurity get the better of her whenever she felt threatened, she could easily have been the toast of her social circle rather than the butt of its jokes. But Caroline could not seem to bring herself to stop the performance, and the performance was exhausting for everyone, including, Elizabeth suspected, Caroline herself.

But that was Caroline's problem, not hers. Elizabeth had enough problems of her own, and knowing that Lady Catherine de Bourgh was no longer considering making Caroline into her pawn actually removed at least one concern from the mountain of them Elizabeth had to deal with.

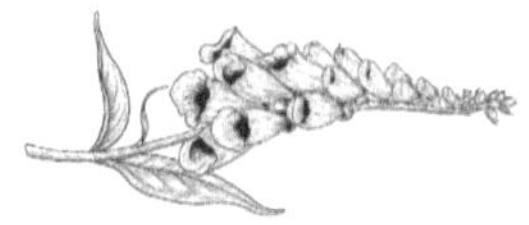

George Darcy was waiting in her parlour when she came back from dressing for dinner that evening. He was at the window, watching the last of the November light fade over the grounds, and he did not turn when she came in. Elizabeth closed the door, checked that her maid had gone, and sat down at her writing desk. She had fifteen minutes before she needed to go down.

"I do not care about Miss Bingley," George said, when Elizabeth tried to tell him about Caroline's destruction at Anne's hands. "She did not get what she wanted, and she is making a nuisance of herself about it but not so much as to cause any real trouble to anyone. She will leave Pemberley no better than she arrived. That is the whole of her story. Catherine is the one who matters."

"Catherine is subdued since the confrontation. She has not spoken to me directly in days."

"Catherine is never subdued. She is regrouping. There is a significant difference, and you would do well to remember it."

He was right, and she knew it. Catherine had been quiet at meals, civil when addressed, and had kept largely to her rooms. But quiet and civil were not Catherine's natural states, and their presence was more alarming than her usual fury.

"What can she do?" Elizabeth asked, rearranging the items on her desk because she needed to do something with her hands. "Darcy confronted her. Lord Matlock took his side. She has lost her spy, and she will lose Anne too."

"She can go back to Rosings and write letters to every connection she has, telling them whatever story serves her purpose. She can whisper about your marriage, about your family, about the Wilson child. The truth does not matter, Elizabeth. What matters is what people believe, and Catherine has the ear of people who will believe her because it is easier than questioning her."

"You are very cheerful this afternoon."

"I am dead. Cheer is not my forte."

Elizabeth smiled despite herself. George's humour was rare, dry, and always delivered as though it surprised him as much as anyone. He gave her that rare, brief twitch of his mouth that passed for a smile before sobering again.

"There is one more thing," George said. "Fitzwilliam has been in my study. Going through my papers."

"I know. He told me he intended to." She had looked in on him that morning, between consultations with Mrs Reynolds about the supper menu. He had been sitting on a footstool in the study, surrounded by stacks of journals and papers, his coat off and his shirtsleeves rolled up. He had looked up at her and she had seen the frustration in his face, the set of his jaw that meant he was not finding what he wanted but was not ready to stop. She had brought him tea and left him to it.

"He will not find anything. I did not write down what Wilson told me. I sent a rider to Wickham carrying a note, asking him to come to Pemberley. There is no memorandum, no record of any kind. I was going to deal with it in person, and then I was dead, and the evidence died with me." George paced to the window and back. "My son has been in there since this morning. He has been through the desk drawers, the correspondence files, the household accounts for that year. He found my will, which he has already seen. He found a letter from Wickham thanking me for a gift of fifty pounds on his birthday, which made him angry. He found some letters I wrote to Annie, after she had passed; they were just a way for me to order my thoughts, manage my grief, but I kept them. They made him sad. But he did not find what he was looking for, because it does not exist."

"He needs to look," Elizabeth said. "Even if there is nothing to find. He needs to feel that he has been thorough, and I can't tell him there is nothing to find, George, because there is no way I could know that. Only you could know that, and now is not the time for me to tell him about you."

"I know. But I am..." George stopped pacing. He stood at the window with his back to her, and when he spoke again his voice was rough. "I am proud of him for it. For looking. For caring. He came back to the study after luncheon and started on the bookshelves, checking for papers tucked inside the volumes. I watched him take down every book on the second shelf, shake it, check for loose pages, and replace it. He is methodical. He always was, even as a boy; he would not leave a puzzle until he had solved it." He turned from the window. "He is a better man than I was, Elizabeth. I favoured a charming boy over my own son, and my son grew up to be the man I should have been."

Elizabeth set down the pen she had been turning over in her fingers. George did not often say things like this. When he did, she could hear what it cost him, and she did not know where to look.

"He would be glad to know you think so," she said.

"Then perhaps you ought to tell him."

She met his eyes. George looked back at her, steady, waiting, and the challenge in his face was not unkind but it was real.

A month ago the idea of telling Darcy about the ghosts had felt impossible. Now, after everything he had absorbed without flinching, after Sally Wilson, Catherine's accusations, the slow, steady building of the case against Wickham, the idea of saying *your father is here, and he is proud of you* seemed less like madness, more like mercy. But the ball was in three days. The house was full of guests. If she told him now and it went badly, she would have to stand beside him and smile at three hundred people while her marriage fell apart. That was, of course, if she was not immediately locked up in a madhouse.

"It is not the time," she said again. "But... soon. After the ball, when the house is quiet again, I will tell him everything."

She had said *soon* so many times that the word had lost its meaning. But this time she meant it. She thought George could tell, because he nodded, once, then went back to his pacing. Elizabeth went downstairs to dinner.

Chapter Twenty-Three

THE DAY BEFORE THE ball, Elizabeth walked through Pemberley and found it ready. Or rather, the living half of Pemberley was ready. The dead half was in uproar.

The ballroom gleamed. The chandeliers had been cleaned until every crystal threw light. The chairs were arranged along the walls in neat rows, upholstered in pale gold silk that Nana had chosen forty years ago and that had so little wear they still looked almost new. The musicians' gallery had been swept and dusted, the music stands set out, the candles in their sconces trimmed and ready. The refreshment tables were placed at the far end, draped in white linen, bare now but waiting.

And on the ballroom floor, lined up alongside the living maids, Sarah Dunn was on her hands and knees, scrubbing away at floorboards she could not actually touch. Her cloth passed through the wood without friction, but her form was perfect, her elbows pumping, her face set in the grim concentration of a woman who had polished these floors throughout her life and was not about to stop simply because she was dead.

"She has been at it since dawn," Nana said, falling into step beside Elizabeth as she crossed the ballroom. "I told her it was unnecessary. She informed me that a ball at Pemberley required properly polished floors and she did not trust the new girls to get into the corners. She is not wrong about the corners."

"The new girls have been here for fifteen years, Nana," Elizabeth said, speaking under her breath. She had learned that Nana could hear her perfectly well at this volume, and it enabled Elizabeth to talk to her in public with nobody noticing. Most of the servants kept their gazes below her face, so they did not see her lips moving.

"As I said. New."

Nana walked beside her, inspecting. Not pacing, not restless; walking, the way she had walked these rooms when she was alive. She seemed particularly solid today, almost as solid as George Darcy appeared, and Elizabeth thought of what George had said about Pemberley's reputation for entertaining having been created during Nana's tenure. Did Nana seem so solid because she was interested in what was happening? Nana ran a critical eye over the flower arrangements, the candle placements, the supper tables, and Elizabeth braced herself.

"The lilies should be closer to the entrance," Nana said. "Guests should smell them as they arrive. It sets the tone."

"I will tell Mrs Reynolds."

"The roses are wrong. They are too dark for the room. We used pale roses, cream and blush, because they catch the candlelight. Dark roses absorb it. The room will look heavy."

"I believe the force-houses have already been stripped of blooms. We are too late to change them, I fear."

Nana sniffed, but did not attempt to argue the point. "And the curtains want tying back more firmly on the left. The right side is correct. The left is too far forward and it obscures the view of the lake, which is the whole point of the west windows."

Elizabeth forced herself not to snap that she had already spent far too much time tweaking the never-to-be-sufficiently-damned curtains. She adjusted the curtain herself. Nana watched, nodded, said nothing, which was approval.

Beyond the ballroom, the rest of the household was similarly engaged. Elizabeth passed through the entrance hall on her way to check the card room and found Mr Graves, the Georgian butler, stationed at the foot of the staircase in full livery, looking more harried than she had ever seen him. He was directing a procession of faint shades Elizabeth could barely make out: wispy figures in servants' dress from half a dozen different eras, filing through the hall and into the yellow drawing room and out again as though rehearsing a route. The shapes were so transparent she could see the wallpaper through them, but Graves was treating them as though they were solid footmen who required drilling.

"What on earth is he doing?" Elizabeth murmured to Nana, as they passed.

"He is marshalling the household for the ball," Nana said, as though this were perfectly obvious. "He did the same before every entertainment when he was alive, and he has not seen fit to retire from the practice. He has been at it since four o'clock this morning. Mrs Alcott is doing the same in the kitchens, I believe, though they are not speaking to each other at present because they disagree about whether the silver should be brought up before or after the candles are lit."

"They are not speaking to each other? They share a servants' hall."

"They have divided it with an invisible line. It is very dramatic. I have told them both to stop being ridiculous, but they take no notice of me, which is extremely vexing, because I am Mrs Darcy and my authority ought to be respected."

"I am Mrs Darcy," Elizabeth pointed out, and Nana shot her a glare, as though to say, *do not remind me.*

In the yellow drawing room, Sir Roderick Darcy still dozed in his chair, as he had for as long as any of Pemberley's ghosts could remember. He was still there, still apparently asleep, his wigged head tilted to one side. Elizabeth moved past him quietly.

"Do you think the ball will disturb him?" she asked Nana, once they were safely in the corridor.

Nana's face pinched. "I sincerely hope not. Sir Roderick has not stirred in my memory, and if the noise of three hundred people dancing and an orchestra playing until two in the morning does not wake him, we shall count ourselves fortunate. He was, by all accounts, a man of exceptionally foul temper. I have managed this house for a hundred and thirty years without Sir Roderick's input, and I intend to continue."

"What would happen if he did wake?"

"I do not know, and I do not wish to find out. Walk quietly past the yellow drawing room tomorrow evening and tell your guests to do the same."

"I am not going to tell three hundred guests to tiptoe past the yellow drawing room, Nana. It is being opened for their convenience and comfort."

"Then we must hope Sir Roderick sleeps through it. He has slept through everything else, including the time one of the chimneys caught fire in 1763, which was quite the commotion." Nana tutted and shook her head. "My fault, really. I was quite old then, had let a few things slip.

The newest Mrs Darcy was very young, and Pemberley was ill-served by its housekeeper. The chimneys were overdue for sweeping."

They stood together in the centre of the ballroom. The room was empty of living people now, the maids having finished their work, though Sarah Dunn was still working on the stairs that led up to the musicians' gallery with spectral determination. The space hummed with the anticipation of what it would become: three hundred people, music, dancing, candlelight. The first ball Elizabeth would host as Mrs Darcy. The first ball Pemberley had seen in over twenty years.

"You are ready," Nana said.

"I am terrified," Elizabeth admitted.

"That is the same thing. I was terrified before every ball. Forty-three of them, in this room. I counted them. Each one I thought would be the one where Pemberley failed, where the food was wrong or the music poor or the guests unhappy, and each one was better than the last. Yours will be no different."

"Forty-three balls," Elizabeth marvelled.

"Forty-three. The last was in 1785, for Fitzwilliam's christening. George wanted a small gathering. Annie told him that a Darcy heir deserved a proper celebration, and he gave in, because George always gave in when she insisted. Annie wore her blue silk and George could not take his eyes off her." Nana paused, and her voice softened in a way Elizabeth rarely heard. "It was the last time this room was truly alive. After Annie died, George could not bear it. He closed the ballroom and never opened it again."

Elizabeth realised that Nana was counting all the balls she had seen at Pemberley, even after her death. She did not ask how many of those forty-three had been during Nana's lifetime. She had slowly become aware that Nana was not always clear on what events had happened during her life, or after her death, the story about the chimney fire excepted.

They stood together a moment longer, and Elizabeth looked around the room that Nana had loved and tended for longer than anyone alive could remember. She was not Lady Anne. She was not Nana. She was only Elizabeth Bennet from Longbourn, but she would do Pemberley justice, or she would die trying, which Nana would probably consider acceptable.

"Thank you," Elizabeth said. "For all of it. For teaching me this house."

Nana looked at her. For a moment the sharpness left her face entirely. What remained was simply an old woman who loved Pemberley more than anything but the descendants who lived in it; who had found, at last, someone worthy of carrying her legacy forward.

"You were always going to be good at this," Nana said. "I knew it the moment you walked through the front door and did not exaggerate how impressed you were. You were impressed, but you did not perform it. That is the difference between a visitor and a mistress."

Elizabeth smiled. "I thought you disapproved of me."

"I did. Disapproval and approval are not mutually exclusive. I disapproved of your deplorably casual manners and approved of your character. Your manners are slowly improving under my tutelage, which is my favourite state of affairs."

Elizabeth found Darcy in the long gallery, late in the afternoon.

He was standing at the window that looked out over the south lawn and beyond, to where the lake lay dark and still beneath the grey sky. Simply standing, looking out, with an expression she could not quite read. Behind him, Edmund and Charlotte were running and playing, though of course he did not see them. They ran past Elizabeth with cheeky smiles, and she made a gentle shooing gesture, indicating that she wished to speak with her husband alone. They ran off without objection, leaving the long gallery empty of spectral company.

She went to him, stood beside him. He put his arm around her without speaking. They looked out at Pemberley together.

"It is strange," he said, after a while. "Standing here, the evening before the ball, looking out at this view. My mother used to stand at this window. I remember her doing it when I was very young, before a dinner or a party, just looking out, as though she needed to see the grounds one more time before she turned to face the guests."

"Perhaps she was gathering herself."

"Perhaps." He was quiet. Then: "I wish my father had lived to see this. To know you."

Elizabeth's throat tightened. She pressed her nails into her palms, hard, because George Darcy was here. He was in this house, in these corridors, watching his son. He did know Elizabeth. She thought he liked her, approved of her as Mrs Darcy, though he had not said it in exactly those words.

Darcy looked at her. He did not push. He waited, the way he always waited, with that patient, steady attention that was the best and most infuriating thing about him.

"I wish he could have known me too," Elizabeth said instead. "I think he would have liked me very much, eventually, once he had got over the shock."

Darcy smiled. The smile was real. The moment passed, and Elizabeth held on to him and did not let go.

Lady Catherine was watching her.

Elizabeth had noticed it three times that day. The first, coming out of the housekeeper's room after a consultation with Mrs Reynolds about the table linens. Catherine had been in the corridor, standing with her hands folded, in an attitude that suggested she might have been there for some time. She had said nothing. She had simply looked at Elizabeth with that sharp, assessing gaze, then walked away.

The second, in the entrance hall. Elizabeth had been telling Nana, in an undertone, that the front steps did not need sweeping again before tomorrow because they would be swept in the morning, and had turned to find Catherine by the grandfather clock. Not passing through. Not on her way somewhere. Standing still and watching. How long she had been there, Elizabeth could not tell. Again, she did not speak when Elizabeth caught her watching, only turned on her heel and left.

The third was after tea. Elizabeth had paused in the gallery to murmur a response to George, who had come to tell her that Darcy had finally given up his search of the study and gone to dress for dinner. She had spoken two words, barely moving her lips, and looked up to find Catherine at the far end of the gallery, motionless.

Each time, Catherine had said nothing and done nothing. She had simply been there, observing, and the silence was worse than any accusation. Elizabeth could defend herself against words. She could not defend herself against watching.

"She is doing it deliberately," Kitty said, when Elizabeth told her. They were in Elizabeth's dressing room, Elizabeth changing for dinner while Kitty sat on the bed. "She has lost her spy, so she is spying for herself. She is looking for proof that you are unwell, unstable, that you talk to yourself in corridors."

"I don't talk to myself in corridors. I talk to dead people in corridors."

"Which is precisely why you must stop doing it where she can see you."

Elizabeth thought about this while her maid dressed her hair. Catherine had been quiet, civil, contained since Lord Matlock and Darcy had reprimanded her. Catherine had been regrouping, as George had warned. Now Catherine was watching, calculating, collecting observations patiently and methodically, waiting for the moment that would make it all worthwhile.

She thought, too, about Caroline Bingley. Catherine had seemed to dismiss the idea of an alliance with Caroline after overhearing her insult Anne. But dismissing an alliance was not the same as dismissing a tool. Caroline was unhappy and eager for the attention of anyone who would take her seriously. If Catherine chose to whisper in her ear, to encourage Caroline's grievances and point them in a useful direction, Caroline would not even realise she was being used until it was too late. Though if the target was Elizabeth, Caroline would likely be more than happy to be used, Elizabeth thought.

Elizabeth resolved to warn Jane. Jane could manage Caroline. But nobody could manage Lady Catherine de Bourgh for long; she was the second most unmanageable person Elizabeth had ever met, after Nana.

Elizabeth wasn't sure whether Nana would be complimented or insulted by the comparison, so she resolved never to tell her.

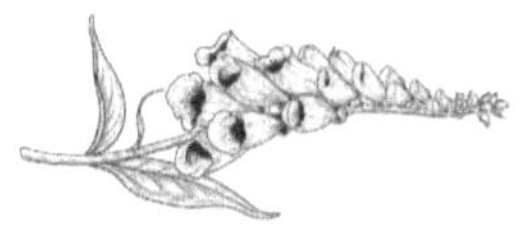

That evening, after dinner, Elizabeth excused herself from company after an hour and went to her parlour to review the final arrangements for the ball. The seating for supper, the order of dances, the small details that Lady Matlock had impressed upon her must be right: which dishes must be brought to the refreshment tables first, when to signal the musicians, where to stand when the guests arrived so that the receiving line flowed without awkwardness.

George Darcy was in the room when she entered. He was pacing, but not the way he usually paced. His circuits were short, tight, covering the same six feet of floor. He looked like a man trying to wear a hole through the carpet.

"George?"

He stopped. His face was drawn, his eyes dark.

"The house is wrong," he said. "I do not know how to explain it. The others feel it too."

"The others?"

"All of them. Miss Pardoe keeps putting down her book and staring at nothing. The footman in the west wing has been marching the same stretch of corridor since this morning, back and forth, as though on sentry duty. The housemaid who haunts the linen cupboard is crying, which she has not done in years. And the old butler..." He paused. "Graves is standing at the front door and will not move. He has abandoned his preparations for the ball entirely, which is unlike him. He takes his duties very seriously, as you know."

That stopped Elizabeth cold. She had walked past Graves that morning, drilling his ghostly footmen with the intensity of a man who considered a ball at Pemberley to be a matter of the highest importance. For him to abandon that and take up a post at the front door, unmoving, meant he felt his duty lay elsewhere. Graves had been a butler. A butler's first duty was the door.

"What does it mean?"

"I do not know. But the house feels different. Heavier." He resumed his pacing, shorter now, tighter. "I have been dead for six years, Elizabeth, and I have never felt the house like this. Not when Fitzwilliam brought Georgiana home after Ramsgate. Not when you arrived. Not even when Catherine came. This is different."

Elizabeth set down her notes and went to find Nana.

Nana was in the portrait gallery, standing before the painting of Lady Anne. Her arms were folded, her chin raised, and she was not looking at the painting. She was looking through it, past it, at something Elizabeth could not see.

"Nana. George says the house is unsettled."

"It is."

"He says the ghosts are restless. The footman is marching, Miss Pardoe will not leave the library, Graves has abandoned his ball preparations and is standing guard at the front door."

"Yes. Sarah Dunn is polishing the stairs to the musicians' gallery over and over again, starting at the top and working down to the bottom, and she will not stop."

"What is happening?"

Nana was quiet for a long moment. The gallery was dim around them, the portraits watching from their frames. The air felt thick. Not cold, not warm. Dense. Like the hours before a thunderstorm when the pressure drops and the birds fall silent.

"Be ready," Nana said.

"Ready for what?"

Nana turned to her. She was afraid. Elizabeth had not seen Nana afraid before, not once, not of Lady Catherine or of the murder investigation or of anything else. Nana did not do fear. She did authority, disapproval, caustic wit, on rare occasions tenderness. Not fear. Seeing it on her face now was worse than anything Catherine had done.

"I do not know," Nana said. "But something is coming. Whatever it is, it is coming, and I think the ball will bring it."

"That is not helpful, Nana."

"I am not trying to be helpful. I am trying to warn you. There is a difference, and you would do well to attend to it." She looked back at the portrait. "This house has stood for more than four hundred years. It has weathered grief, scandal, death, wars. It does not unsettle without reason, but even I cannot tell you what is coming."

Elizabeth hesitated, and then she reached out and placed her hand on the wall, wondering if she would feel anything other than wallpaper over plaster over cold stone.

She almost snatched her hand away, because the wall was vibrating. Faint, and she suspected no other living resident of the house would sense what she was feeling, but it felt almost like a heartbeat. Pemberley itself, the great house that had stood through four centuries of grief, scandal, death, wars, as Nana had said, was restless indeed. It was impossible to ascribe any human emotion to the feeling, but if Elizabeth had been pressed to name one, she would have said it was angry. It reminded her, unsettlingly, of the way George Darcy looked when he spoke of Wickham.

Elizabeth went to bed that night and lay beside Darcy, who was already sleeping, and stared at the canopy above them.

Tomorrow, three hundred guests would come to Pemberley to be entertained. There would be candlelight, music, the whole county watching the new Mrs Darcy, judging whether she was worthy of the name.

Beneath it all, the house was angry. The dead were restless. Nana was afraid.

Elizabeth closed her eyes, and did not sleep for a long time despite her exhaustion.

Chapter Twenty-Four

ELIZABETH WOKE ON THE morning of the ball feeling as though she had not slept at all.

She had, a little; Darcy was already up and gone when she opened her eyes, which meant she had slept through his rising. But her body felt heavy and wrong, as though something was sitting on her chest. She pressed her hand flat against her breastbone and breathed, and the pressure did not ease.

The house felt it too. She could tell the moment she put her feet on the cold floor and stood. The vibration from last night was still there, that faint hum in the stone and the wood, and it was stronger now. Her skin prickled as she crossed the room to ring for her maid. She told herself it was the ball. Three hundred guests, the first entertainment she had hosted as Mrs Darcy, the county watching and judging. Of course she was nervous. Of course her stomach was turning over. That was all it was.

She did not believe herself for a moment.

She was in the ballroom with Mrs Reynolds, reviewing the chalk pattern that had been painstakingly laid down in the design Nana had spent three days perfecting, when Jane appeared in the doorway.

"Lizzy. You need to come to the study."

"What has happened?"

"Lady Catherine has just gone in there with Darcy. Lord Matlock is there too. Georgiana heard raised voices and came to find me."

Elizabeth set down her list. Her hands were unsteady, which she told herself was the ball, and which she knew was not. She had been fighting nausea since breakfast and had eaten almost nothing, and the wrongness in the house was pressing on her like a headache.

She could hear Catherine before she reached the study door. She was not shouting. It was worse than shouting: she was speaking in the low, measured voice she used when she believed herself to be delivering an unassailable truth.

The study door was ajar. Elizabeth reached to push it open, but Nana was there, blocking the gap, shaking her head. She was tempted to walk straight through Nana, but instead she stood still and watched through the narrow space between the door and the jamb.

Darcy was standing behind his desk. Lord Matlock was by the fire. Lady Catherine stood in the centre of the room, her back straight, her chin raised, a piece of paper held in her hands.

"I have made enquiries," Catherine said. "I have observed. I have listened. And I tell you, Fitzwilliam, as your aunt and as someone who has the interests of this family at heart, that your wife is not well. She talks to empty rooms. She has been seen in the long gallery past midnight, speaking to no one. She pauses in corridors and moves her lips as though in conversation with a person who is not there. The servants have noticed, Fitzwilliam. They whisper about it. Mrs Reynolds protects her; loyalty misplaced. Your sister and Miss Bennet cover for her; youth and sentiment. The facts are the facts."

Catherine looked down at her paper. "On Tuesday she was observed speaking in the entrance hall with no one present. On Wednesday evening she paused in the portrait gallery and addressed the empty air. On Thursday she was seen emerging from a passage behind a bookcase that no living person in this house knew existed."

She turned to Lord Matlock. "Henry, you were there yesterday. We went to the ballroom looking for Margaret, and the maids were scrubbing the floor. Margaret and Elizabeth were there together. They saw us coming, walked towards us, stepped around the maids. Elizabeth stepped around nothing. She swerved to avoid a spot on the floor where nobody was kneeling, as though she could see someone there that the rest of us could not. Margaret noticed it too. I saw her face."

Lord Matlock said nothing, but Elizabeth, watching through the gap, saw his expression shift. He had noticed. He had put it aside, because he was a kind man and because he liked Elizabeth, but he had noticed. She had done it; she had stepped around Sarah Dunn without even thinking about it, because she had always felt that it was rude to just walk straight through ghosts, just as she had allowed Nana to block her path a moment ago. She had not even thought of how it might look to observers.

Catherine pressed on. "She has been asking about your father's death, about Wickham, about matters that are years buried and best left so. She has drawn your uncle and aunt into her obsession. She has acquired knowledge of this house that she could not have gained by any natural means. And I believe, Fitzwilliam, that she is suffering from a disorder of the mind that requires medical attention before it becomes a public scandal."

The room was deathly silent.

"You have the legal authority to act," Catherine said. "A husband may commit his wife on the recommendation of a physician. I know Dr Grieve in Bakewell personally, and I am certain he would..."

"You will stop speaking now, Aunt Catherine."

Darcy's voice cut through Catherine's speech like a blade. He came around the desk, and Elizabeth could see his face through the gap in the door. His jaw was set, his eyes flat and cold. "You have spent weeks in this house spying on Elizabeth, undermining her, telling her lies about my character in some dreadful attempt to drive a wedge between us, and now you stand in my study and tell me to lock her away. On the basis of what? That she talks to herself? That she asks questions you find inconvenient? That she discovered a passage in a house she is mistress of?"

"The pattern of behaviour is..."

"The pattern of behaviour is that of an intelligent woman exploring her new home and trying to understand the family she has married into. The questions she has asked about my father's death are questions that should have been asked six years ago, by anyone with eyes to see, and the fact that nobody asked them is to our collective shame, not hers."

"Fitzwilliam, I implore you..."

"My wife is not mad. She is not unwell. She is the finest person I have ever known, and I will not entertain this accusation for one moment, from you or from anyone else." He stepped closer to his aunt, looming over her, and Catherine flinched at the expression on his face. "After the ball, you will leave Pemberley. You will not return. Anne will remain here with us, and she will go to London for the Season with Georgiana and Kitty, as has already been arranged. You will not interfere with her plans. You will not write to her instructing her to return to Rosings. You will leave my wife and my household in peace from this moment forward, or I will see to it that you are the one committed to an asylum. This, I promise you."

Catherine's face had gone the colour of chalk. "You cannot bar me from this house. I am your aunt. I am…"

"You are a woman who has just asked me to imprison my wife." Darcy's voice was deadly quiet. "You have forfeited every claim you ever had on my loyalty or my patience, and you will leave this house the morning after the ball. I am only permitting you to stay that long because it is widely known you are here already, and I will not have Anne whispered about because her mother was publicly ejected from the house before the event."

"Brother," Catherine said, turning to Lord Matlock. "Surely you see…"

"I see a great deal, Catherine." Lord Matlock's voice was heavy. "I see a woman who has tried and failed to destroy her nephew's marriage by every means available to her, and who has now resorted to a weapon so contemptible even I am shocked you would stoop so low. I will not support you in this. I will not support you in anything, until you have made a full and sincere apology to Mrs Darcy, which I suspect will take you some considerable time. Even if she accepts your apology, I very much doubt your nephew ever will, and frankly, nor should he. I could not forgive you if you said something so terrible about Margaret."

Catherine was shaking, but Elizabeth could see from her expression that it was not with fear. She was shaking with utter fury.

"I am trying to protect this family," Catherine said. "I have always tried to protect this family, and I have been repaid with ingratitude and…"

"Mother, stop."

Elizabeth had not realised Anne was in the room. She stood up from a chair half-hidden behind Lord Matlock, pale, thin, her hands clasped in front of her. She had come to a decision, Elizabeth could see, and she would be as resolute in it as her mother had ever been about anything.

"Stop," Anne said again. "You must stop, now."

Catherine turned to her daughter. Her face crumbled. Not into tears; Lady Catherine de Bourgh did not crumble into tears. But the mask came off, and what was underneath was the bewilderment of a woman who has just been struck by the one person she never expected to oppose her.

"Anne..."

"You are wrong, Mother. You are wrong about Mrs Darcy. You are wrong about this family. You have been wrong for a very long time, and I cannot listen to it any more." Anne's voice was unsteady, but she did not look away. "Mrs Darcy has been kind to me. She and Darcy have offered me a life I did not think I would ever have. You are trying to destroy the woman who made that possible, because you cannot bear that she has what you wanted for me, and I will not be part of it."

Catherine stared at her daughter.

"We will discuss this privately," Catherine said. Her voice was barely audible.

"There is nothing to discuss. I love you, Mother. But you are wrong."

Catherine left the room without another word. She walked past Elizabeth as though she did not see her, her back rigid, her face a mask again, and the sound of her footsteps receding down the corridor was the loneliest sound Elizabeth had ever heard.

Nana laughed.

Anne came stumbling out of the study, trembling and white, walked right through Nana's spectral form and almost ran straight into Elizabeth. Elizabeth caught her by the elbows.

"That was the bravest thing I have ever seen," Elizabeth said.

"I think I am going to be sick," Anne said quietly. Elizabeth took her to the morning room, called a maid to bring tea, sat with Anne until the shaking stopped. She did not mention that her own hands were shaking too, that the nausea she had been fighting all morning had got worse, not better. The house pressed down on everyone in it, exacerbating every emotion, and only Elizabeth had the faintest inkling that it was even happening.

The ball was to start in six hours.

Elizabeth returned to the ballroom once Anne had settled, and found that Jane had taken charge. The chalk pattern on the floor was finished, crisp white curlicues and garlands that Nana would have been proud of. The flowers were arranged, the glasses being lined up on tables to be filled with the French champagne which would be brought up from the cellars later, the candles being placed. Kitty was directing the placement of additional chairs along the south wall. Lady Matlock was consulting with Mrs Reynolds about which wines to decant first. Even Caroline Bingley had been pressed into service, and was sorting place cards at a side table with an expression of surprised industry, as though she had not quite understood how Jane had managed to make her useful.

Jane looked at Elizabeth and crossed the room.

"You look terrible," Jane said, quietly enough that nobody else could hear. "What has happened?"

"Catherine tried to have me committed. Darcy stopped her. Anne sided against her mother. It is over." Elizabeth pressed her hand against her stomach, which was roiling. "Jane, I feel dreadful, and I don't think it is the ball."

Jane put her hand on Elizabeth's forehead. Cool, practical, the same gesture their mother had always used when checking for fever, though Mrs Bennet had always accompanied it with predictions of imminent death. "You are not feverish. Have you eaten?"

"I can't. My stomach won't allow it."

"Nerves."

"Perhaps." Elizabeth looked around the ballroom. Sarah Dunn was dusting a picture frame, the same one over and over, repeatedly. Graves had not moved from the front door. The pressure in the house was a constant weight behind Elizabeth's eyes, and she did not know how to explain to Jane that the building itself felt wrong without sounding exactly as mad as Lady Catherine had just claimed she was. "Jane, I need you to manage the preparations. I can't do this today. I am sorry."

"Don't apologise. Mrs Reynolds and Lady Matlock and I will take care of everything. Go and rest before tonight. You need to be well enough to stand in that receiving line."

"I won't rest. Darcy will come to talk to me. He has to. Lady Catherine said things that... he has questions, Jane. He has had questions for weeks, and I have been putting him off, and after what Lady Catherine just did, I can't put him off any longer."

Jane looked at her steadily. "Are you going to tell him?"

"I think I have to."

Jane took her hand and squeezed it, once, hard. "Then tell him. Come find me afterwards."

Elizabeth went to her parlour. She locked the door. She pressed her back against it and breathed. The house breathed with her, slow, heavy, wrong. Nana drifted through the bookcase, looked at her; Elizabeth shook her head. Nana drifted back out again without speaking. Elizabeth was grateful. If she was going to fall apart, she wanted to do it without an audience, living or dead.

She pressed both hands flat against the door behind her and tried to think. Her skin was clammy. Her stomach lurched constantly. The wrongness in the house was so strong now that the candle on her writing desk flickered without a draught, the temperature in the parlour shifting, warm then cold then warm again, as though the walls could not decide what season it was.

Three hundred people were coming to Pemberley in six hours. She had to be dressed, composed, standing beside Darcy in the receiving line, smiling, greeting the county, being Mrs Darcy. She would have to dance, and make conversation. She had to be well.

She did not feel well. She felt as though Pemberley itself was trying to tell her something, pressing against her with its four hundred years of stone and timber, and she could not hear what it was saying.

Darcy knocked on the parlour door ten minutes later, a distinct firm triple-tap she had quickly learned was his calling-card.

She opened it, and he came in. He closed it behind him and stood looking at her, and she could see in his face that he had come to ask the question he had been carrying for weeks.

"Elizabeth. I have told my aunt she is wrong. I have told Lord Matlock. I have told Anne. I do not believe you are unwell, and I will never believe it, and I will protect you from anyone who says otherwise." He paused. "But I am not blind. I have noticed things too, Elizabeth. The conversations with empty rooms. The way you know things about this house that you could not possibly know, like the passage from this room to the east wing, which not a soul in Pemberley knew existed, not even me. The questions about my father that you began asking before you had any reason to ask them." He looked at her steadily. "Tell me what is happening. I cannot protect you from what people are saying if I do not understand what they are seeing."

Elizabeth sat down. Her legs would not hold her. She sat in the chair by the fire and looked at her hands, which were shaking, and thought: this is it. This is the moment I have been dreading.

"Darcy," she said. "Sit down."

He sat. He sat in the chair opposite her, the way he had the night she talked to him about Sally Wilson, the night he told her he was tired of carrying things alone.

"I see dead people," she said.

The words came out flat, graceless, nothing like the careful speech she had rehearsed a hundred times. She had planned to lead with Longbourn, with Great-Aunt Irene, with the history of it, the gift perhaps passed down from her Gardiner grandfather who had been far more successful in business than he had any right to be. She had planned to be measured and clear and to present it in a way that made sense. Instead she said it baldly, bluntly, like a confession, because that was what it was.

"I see ghosts. I've seen them my whole life. Since I was a child. My family know, but we have kept it secret because the alternative is..." She gestured vaguely at the door, beyond which Lady Catherine had just tried to have her locked away, and could not finish the sentence.

Darcy did not say anything. He did not move. He just watched her, expressionless, just as he once had at Hunsford when she rejected him with a cruelty he had never deserved.

"There are ghosts everywhere, Darcy. Longbourn's are my family; my Great-Aunt Irene taught me how to manage my gift, how to live with it, how to keep it hidden. When I came to Pemberley, I walked through the front door and I saw them. Everywhere. The house is full of them. Servants, family, four hundred years of the dead, still here."

She was speaking too fast, the words coming out in the wrong order, but she could not slow down because if she slowed down she would stop, and if she stopped she would never start again.

"One of them, one of the strongest, is Nana. Her real name is Dorothea Darcy. She was your great-great-grandmother, who came here as a very young bride, had a son. Her husband died when she was only twenty and Pemberley became her charge, the Darcy family her responsibility, her legacy. She runs this house. She has run it for a hundred and thirty years. She decided I was acceptable, barely, mainly because I could carry out her orders I think. She's been teaching me Pemberley ever since. The passage behind the bookcase. The rose garden. She is the reason I know things I should not know."

She stopped. Drew breath. Made herself look at him and meet his eyes.

"And your father," she said. "Your father is here too."

For the first time, Darcy's expression changed, his jaw tightening. His eyes went bright. He gripped the arm of his chair hard enough that his knuckles whitened.

"My father." He did not sound incredulous. He sounded shocked, as though he believed her, and the belief had hit him like a fist.

"George Darcy. He died in this house and he has never left it. He is angry and grieving and desperate for justice, because he was murdered, Darcy. Wickham poisoned him. Foxglove in his evening brandy, the night they dined together, the night Mrs Reynolds said they seemed so amiable. Your father confronted Wickham about Sally Wilson, and Wickham killed him for it, and your father has been trapped in this house for six years, watching you, unable to tell you any of it."

She was crying. She did not know when she had started. The tears ran down her face and she did not wipe them away because her hands were gripping the arms of the chair as though she might fall out of it.

"Kitty has been helping me investigate because Kitty knows what I can do, so she covers for me. Georgiana knows about my gift because she was in the gallery when I was speaking to the ghost children who play there. She saw me talking to what she thought was empty air. I had to tell her. She's kept the secret. I know you will be hurt that she knew before you did, and I'm sorry for that, I'm so sorry, but I've been afraid, Darcy. I've been afraid my whole life. Because the world doesn't believe in ghosts, and a woman who sees things that are not there is a madwoman, and your aunt has just proved exactly how real that danger is."

She stopped. There was nothing left. She had given him everything: the gift, the ghosts, the murder, Kitty, Georgiana, the fear. The compact she had kept since childhood, broken open in a quiet parlour just hours before a ball, with her face wet and her hands shaking and the house pressing down on them both.

The clock on the mantelpiece ticked. From below came the distant sounds of the household preparing for the evening, making ready for three hundred guests who would arrive in a few hours to dance and eat and judge whether the new Mrs Darcy was worthy of the name, while the new Mrs Darcy sat in her parlour with tears on her face, waiting to find out whether her husband thought she was mad.

Darcy looked at her. His face was closed again, unreadable.

He did not speak.

Chapter Twenty-Five

Darcy was silent, looking at her, for what felt like forever.

Elizabeth sat in her chair and let him look. She had no more words. She had spent them all, every one, and what was left was just her: red-eyed, shaking, her hands gripping the chair arms, her face wet. From below, the faint sounds of the household preparing for the ball continued, indifferent to the fact that the world had just changed.

"You see ghosts," Darcy said at last. His voice was very level.

"Yes."

"You have seen them your whole life."

"Yes."

"My father is in this house."

"Yes."

He stood up. He crossed the room, not to the door, but to the window. He stood there with his back to her, looking out at the November grey. Elizabeth watched his shoulders, tried to read what was happening from the set of them. She could not. She gripped the chair arms harder. Her nails dug into the upholstery.

"Aunt Catherine's observations," Darcy said, still facing the window. "The conversations with empty rooms. The gallery at midnight. Stepping around something in the ballroom that she could not see."

"Sarah Dunn," Elizabeth said. "A former housemaid. She was scrubbing the floor. She has been dead for years, but she still does her job because she was a fiercely conscientious maid, and it was the maids' job to scrub the ballroom floor. I stepped around her because I have always thought it rude to walk through ghosts, and I did not think about how it would look to anyone watching."

Darcy turned around. His expression was not that of a man who thought his wife was mad. He looked like a man who was rebuilding his understanding of the world, piece by piece, and finding that the new structure held.

"I believe you," he said.

Elizabeth's hands unclenched. Her whole body unclenched, all at once, as though a fist that had been closed around her since childhood had simply opened. She bent forward in the chair, pressed her face into her hands, wept. Not the frightened tears of the confession but the sheer, overwhelming relief of a woman who has carried a secret for twenty years and set it down at last. Her shoulders shook. She could not stop, and she did not try.

Darcy crossed the room in three strides, knelt beside her chair, put his arms around her. She turned into him, pressed her face against his shoulder. He held her while she cried. He did not speak. He held her, his hand on the back of her head, his chin resting against her temple, and he let her cry until she was done. It took a long time; Elizabeth could not have said how long. When she finally pulled back, his waistcoat was soaked through, though he did not seem to care.

"I am sorry," she said. "For not telling you sooner. For telling Georgiana before I told you. For all the lies, Darcy, the half-truths, the things I led you to believe I had discovered through cleverness when really I had been told them by a dead woman standing beside me in a room you thought was empty."

"You were afraid," Darcy said. He was still kneeling beside her chair. He had not let go of her hands.

"I have been afraid my whole life. Nobody else in my family can see what I see, though they all know. My mother has always dealt with it by pretending it does not exist. My father protected me in his own way, by making sure nobody outside the family ever suspected. None of my sisters can see them, but they have spent their whole lives covering for me, learning to read the signs so they can distract people when my attention slips. I have been alone with this, Darcy. Completely alone. The rule, the only rule, has always been: do not tell, do not show, do not let anyone outside the family know, because the world will call you mad and the law will let them lock you away for it. Your aunt has just walked into your study and proved that the fear is justified."

"My aunt is a vindictive woman who has been looking for a weapon to use against you since the day she realised I intended to marry you. She would have seized on anything. If it had not been this, it would have been something else."

"But it was this. The observations she made were accurate, Darcy. Every one of them. I do talk to empty rooms. I do walk the gallery at midnight. I do step around people who are not there." She wiped her face with the back of her hand. "I am exactly what she described. The difference between her interpretation and the truth is a matter of faith, and I would not have blamed you if you had chosen hers."

"I chose you," Darcy said. "I chose you before I heard a word of explanation. I would have chosen you if you had told me nothing at all."

Elizabeth looked at him, kneeling before her with his warm hands wrapped around her shaking ones, his waistcoat ruined, and she thought: *I will remember this for the rest of my life. This room, this moment, this man on his knees choosing me when he knows what I am, all of what I am.*

"But Georgiana knew?" Darcy said. It was not an accusation, but the hurt was there, and Elizabeth knew it was justified.

"She walked in on me talking to Edmund and Charlotte. The ghost children who play in the long gallery, distant ancestors of yours. She was so quiet I did not hear her. She saw me speaking to what she thought was empty air. She asked me, and I couldn't lie to her. I tried. I could not." Elizabeth pressed her thumbs against his knuckles. "I should have told you first. I should have told you before we married. I meant to, more than once. There was an afternoon in your study when I started to. Lady Catherine's carriage pulled up the drive and interrupted me. After that I could never find the moment, or the courage. Every day that passed made it harder, because every day was another day I had not trusted you."

"You are trusting me now."

"I am, and if you want to ask me anything, anything at all, I will answer. No more lies. No more half-truths. Whatever you want to know."

Darcy was quiet for a few moments longer. Then he sat back down in the chair opposite her and said, "Tell me about my father."

Elizabeth went to the bookcase and pressed the catch, and the panel swung open into the passage. Nana was waiting on the other side. She looked at Elizabeth, looked past her at Darcy, and for once in her considerable existence said nothing at all.

"Is George near?" Elizabeth asked. "Will he come?"

"He is in the gallery," Nana said. "He has been pacing since this morning. He is worse than usual. Unsettled, like the house, but I still cannot tell you what is causing it."

"Please ask him to come here. Tell him, Darcy knows. Tell him everything."

Nana left. Elizabeth closed the panel and turned back to Darcy, who was watching her with as much shock on his face as she had ever seen from him. He had just watched his wife open a secret door and speak to the empty passage behind it. His face said he was still catching up to what he had insisted he did believe.

"Nana," Elizabeth said. "She was in the passage. She is going to find your father."

"You speak to them as though they are in the room."

"They are in the room. They are usually in the room. That is rather the difficulty."

Darcy almost smiled. Elizabeth loved him for it: for the fact that in the middle of learning his father had been murdered and his wife could see the dead, he could still almost smile at something she said.

They waited. Elizabeth sat. Darcy did not. He got up again, stood by the fireplace, his hands clasped behind his back. He looked as though he was waiting for an audience he could not see and did not know how to greet. Elizabeth understood. How did you prepare to hear your dead father speak through your wife's voice? There was no etiquette for this. Even Lady Matlock, who had etiquette for everything, could not have helped.

George came through the wall.

He came fast, not drifting, not pacing, but moving with a directness Elizabeth had never seen from him. He came through the wall beside the fireplace and stopped. He was standing three feet from his son. His son could not see him. The expression on George Darcy's face broke Elizabeth's heart.

"He is here," Elizabeth said. "He came through the wall beside you. He is standing very close to you, Darcy. On your left."

Darcy turned his head to the left. He could not see his father. He looked at the empty air where George stood, and George looked at his son's face, and neither of them could bridge the gap.

"Tell him," George said. His voice was rough. "Tell him I am here. I can see him. I..." He stopped. Started again. "Tell him I am proud of him. Tell him I have watched him carry this family for six years. He has done it better than I ever did. I am sorry. For Wickham. For not listening. For every time I chose that boy over my own son. I was wrong, and I knew it before I died, and I have not been able to say it until now."

Elizabeth repeated his words, exactly, changing nothing. She had learned from Nana that precision mattered: a ghost's words were their own, and she was the conduit, not the editor. She spoke George's sentences in George's cadence. Darcy stood and listened, his jaw clenching tighter with every phrase, his eyes growing brighter. He did not look away from the spot where his father stood.

When Elizabeth finished, the room was quiet.

"He knew," Darcy said, at last. "Before he died. He knew about Wickham."

"As Mr Wilson told us, he came to your father and told him what Wickham had done to Sally. Your father believed it at once, without question. He said the scales fell from his eyes. He saw what you had been trying to tell him for years, and he summoned Wickham home and confronted him."

"And Wickham killed him for it."

"Yes. Foxglove. Your father did not know it was coming. They dined together, talked afterwards in the library. Wickham brought him brandy to drink. George thought the matter was resolved. Then he went to bed and he did not wake."

Darcy pressed his hand over his eyes. He stood like that for a long moment, his hand covering his face, his shoulders rigid. Elizabeth sat and watched him, did not touch him, because she could see that he needed a moment where nobody could see his expression. She gave it to him.

George watched his son. His face was stripped of everything Elizabeth was accustomed to seeing there: the anger, the restlessness, the driving need for justice. What was left was simpler and more painful. A father looking at his son, knowing he had failed him, unable to do the one thing a father wants to do: reach out, put his hand on his child's shoulder, say *you did well. I am sorry. You did well.*

Darcy lowered his hand. His eyes were red, but he was composed.

"Ask him," Darcy said. "Ask him if he can hear me, when I speak."

"He can hear you. He has always been able to hear you. He simply cannot answer. That has been the worst of it for him, I think."

Darcy turned to the empty space where his father stood and said, "I forgive you, Father. For Wickham. For all of it. You were deceived, and you paid for it with your life, and I do not blame you. I have not blamed you for a long time."

George Darcy made a sound Elizabeth had never heard from him. It was not a word. It was not a cry. It was the sound of six years of grief breaking loose.

"He heard you," Elizabeth said. "He is..." She did not know how to describe what was on George's face, so she did not try. "He heard you, Darcy."

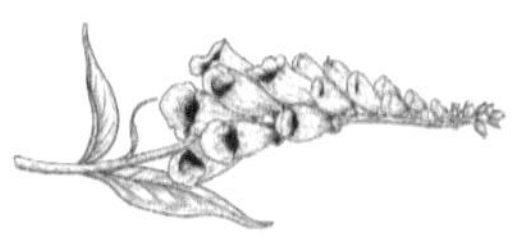

Georgiana came when Elizabeth sent for her.

She came quickly, because the note Elizabeth sent with a maid had said only *Come to my parlour at once, alone,* and Georgiana was not a girl who needed to be told twice. She knocked. Elizabeth opened the door. Georgiana came in, saw Darcy standing by the fire with his red-rimmed eyes and his ruined waistcoat, and stopped.

"What has happened?" she said. "Is it Lady Catherine? Anne told me what she..."

"Sit down, Georgiana," Darcy said.

She sat. She looked between them, her brother and his wife, and Elizabeth could see her reading the room: Darcy's face, Elizabeth's swollen eyes, the charged quiet of the parlour. Georgiana was good at reading rooms. She had been doing it since Ramsgate, watching for danger in the faces of the people around her.

"Elizabeth has told me," Darcy said. "About the ghosts."

Georgiana's eyes went wide. She looked at Elizabeth.

"I told him everything," Elizabeth said. "The gift. Nana. The household."

"You told him." Georgiana's voice was barely audible. "He knows?"

"He knows. He believes me."

Georgiana looked at her brother. Darcy met her eyes, and whatever she saw in his face made her exhale, a long, shaking breath. She had kept Elizabeth's secret for weeks, carrying it alongside her own fear of what would happen when her brother found out. Now it was out. He was not angry. The relief in her face was as naked as Elizabeth's had been.

"There is more," Elizabeth said. "Georgiana, I need to tell you something I have been keeping from you. I kept it from you because I was trying to protect you, but I cannot any longer."

Georgiana's hands tightened in her lap, and she looked nervous again.

"Your father is here," Elizabeth said. "His ghost. He has been at Pemberley since his death. He is in this room, right now, standing beside Darcy."

Georgiana did not cry. She went white, so white that Elizabeth reached for her hand, afraid she might faint, but Georgiana gripped Elizabeth's fingers hard and held on and did not faint. She stared at the spot beside Darcy where

Elizabeth had indicated, and her eyes moved as though searching for something she desperately wanted to see and could not.

"I can't see him," Georgiana whispered.

"No. Nobody else can. Not Kitty, not you, not anyone. Only me." She squeezed Georgiana's hand. "But he can see you, Georgiana. He is looking at you right now."

George was looking at his daughter. Elizabeth had seen many expressions on his face over these weeks: fury, grief, self-loathing, the bitter dry humour he used to keep the grief at bay. She had never seen this. He was looking at Georgiana with such naked tenderness that Elizabeth had to look away.

"Tell her," George said. His voice was barely audible. "Tell her I am sorry I was not there. After Ramsgate. She needed her father; he was dead. She had to face that man's treachery alone. I have never forgiven myself for it."

Elizabeth repeated his words. Georgiana's face crumpled.

"It was not his fault," Georgiana said. "He did not know what Wickham was. None of us did, until it was too late."

"He knows that now," Elizabeth said. "He learned the truth about Wickham just before he died. He confronted him. And Wickham..." She stopped. This was the part she had dreaded. "Georgiana, Wickham killed your father. He poisoned him. That is why your father has not been able to leave this house. He is trapped here because his murder has never been acknowledged, and he has been waiting for six years for someone who could hear him."

Georgiana's grip on Elizabeth's hand tightened until it hurt.

"Wickham," she said. The name came out flat, stripped of everything.

"Yes."

"The man who tried to seduce me at Ramsgate. The man who married Lydia. That man murdered my father."

"I am afraid so."

Georgiana looked at her brother. Darcy looked back at her. Something passed between them that did not need words: the shared knowledge of what Wickham had taken from them, the full accounting of it, laid out at last.

"I want to hear him," Georgiana said. "I cannot see him, but you can, Elizabeth. Will you... can you tell me what he says? Can we talk to him?"

"Of course," Elizabeth said.

What followed was the strangest conversation Elizabeth had ever been part of, and the most sacred. She sat between Darcy and Georgiana, relaying George's words as he spoke them, and George spoke to his children for the first time in six years. He told Georgiana about the roses: that seeing Georgiana restore the garden with Kitty had given him more joy than anything since his death. He told Darcy about the study, about watching him go through the papers, about the letters to Annie. He said he had watched Darcy shake every book on every shelf and had wanted to tell him there was nothing to find, and had not been able to.

He told them he was proud of them. He said it more than once, in different ways, as though he needed to be sure they heard it, as though six years of silence had dammed up so many words that they were all coming now, too many, too fast. Darcy listened with his jaw tight and his eyes bright. Georgiana wept quietly, wiping her face with the handkerchief Elizabeth gave her, and asked questions in a steady voice that belied the tears: was he in pain, could he sleep, did he like Mrs Annesley, had he seen Georgiana play the pianoforte? Yes, he said, to the last. He had stood in the music room more times than he could count and listened to her play, and she played like her mother, from the heart.

That was when Georgiana broke. She put her face in her hands and cried. Darcy put his arm around her. George Darcy stood in front of his children, unable to touch either of them, grieving as they were grieving for what had been stolen from them all when Wickham put foxglove in his brandy.

Elizabeth sat and said nothing, because there was nothing to say. She was the bridge between the living and the dead, and bridges do not speak. They hold.

After a long time, George said, quietly, "Thank you, Elizabeth."

She nodded. He turned and walked through the wall. He was gone. The room was warmer for his absence, and sadder.

The three of them sat in the parlour for a while after George left. Georgiana dried her eyes. Darcy sent a servant for brandy for himself and for Elizabeth, who drank it though it was barely four in the afternoon. She had not eaten since the previous evening. The brandy hit her empty stomach like fire.

"Wickham," Darcy said, after a long silence. He was standing at the window again, the glass in his hand, looking out at the grounds. "We have the truth of it all now from my father, but the testimony of a ghost cannot count for anything in the living world. We have Mr Wilson's account, and Mrs Reynolds' corroboration of those parts of it she knew of, which establish motive and timeline but not the act itself. We have a physician who signed a death certificate six years ago and may or may not remember the details." He turned from the window. "There is no legal path. Not one that would survive a magistrate's scrutiny, let alone a court."

"I know," Elizabeth said.

"If I could challenge him, I would. I would call Wickham out, put a bullet through him, hang for it if necessary, but that would destroy this family as surely as a trial would. It would not bring my father back." His voice was steady. The fury was there, banked, controlled, directed inward where it could be managed. "There must be another way. We cannot prove murder, but we can make it impossible for Wickham to harm anyone else. We can cut off his income, his connections, his ability to move through society as though he is an honourable man." He made a face. "Except we cannot do any of those things, because of Lydia."

"Lydia will not leave him willingly," Elizabeth said. "She is sixteen and married and she still thinks she loves him, even though she has begun to fear him."

"Then we make it possible for her to leave, and we wait until she is ready. Between us, Lord Matlock and I have resources that Wickham cannot match." Darcy set down his glass. "I will not let your sister remain in danger, Elizabeth. I promise you that. Whatever it takes, however long it takes, we will find a way to bring Lydia home."

Elizabeth looked at her husband. He was standing in the last of the November light, his face drawn with grief, anger, resolve. She thought: this is the man who proposed to me so badly at Hunsford. Who wrote me a letter so honest it changed my life. Who listened to his aunt call me a madwoman this afternoon and chose me before he knew the truth. Who is now promising to save my sister from a murderer because she is mine and therefore his responsibility. He has never once in his life walked away from a responsibility.

"I love you," she said. She had not planned to say it. It came out the way the ghost confession had come out: blunt, graceless, true.

Darcy looked at her. "I know," he said. "I have known for some time. You are not as subtle as you think you are, Elizabeth."

She laughed. It was a terrible laugh, half a sob, but it was a laugh. Darcy smiled. Georgiana, still red-eyed, smiled too. For a moment the three of them were just a family, sitting in a parlour, finding their way back to each other.

"The ball," Elizabeth said. She looked at the clock. Half past four. Three hundred people arriving in two and a half hours. She had not dressed. Her face was a disaster.

"The ball," Darcy agreed. "We will stand in the receiving line. We will dance. Pemberley will be as majestic as she has ever been, and the new Mrs Darcy will be praised as the finest hostess Pemberley could wish for. Tomorrow, when

Aunt Catherine has gone and the house is ours again, we will sit down together and decide what to do about George Wickham."

"Yes," Elizabeth said. "Tonight we will host the finest ball Pemberley has seen in twenty years, because Nana has been planning it for a hundred and thirty, and I'd rather face Wickham himself than tell her it's been cancelled."

Darcy held out his hand. Elizabeth took it. They went to dress for the ball, and Georgiana went to find Kitty, and the house hummed around them, waiting.

Chapter Twenty-Six

Pemberley blazed with light.

Every chandelier was lit, a white beeswax candle burned in every candlestick, and the ballroom threw back the light from a hundred surfaces: the crystals overhead, the gilt frames on the walls, the tall windows that showed nothing now but the reflection of the room itself, doubled and glittering, as though there were two ballrooms, two crowds, two orchestras playing the same music. The chalk pattern on the floor was crisp and white beneath the dancers' feet. The lilies by the entrance filled the air with scent, just as Nana had wanted. The curtains were drawn back to the precise degree Nana had specified, though there was no moonlight yet to show the grounds; the moon would rise later. When it did, the west windows would frame the lake and the parkland in silver. Pemberley would earn every compliment its guests could give it.

Elizabeth stood in the receiving line beside Darcy and smiled until her face ached. Three hundred guests filed past. She greeted each one, remembered their names, said the right things, because Lady Matlock had drilled her, Mrs Reynolds had briefed her, Nana had spent a hundred and thirty years preparing for this evening. Georgiana and Darcy stood on either side of her whispering occasional reminders. Lady Ashbourne came early, leaning on her granddaughter Clara's arm: a tiny, sharp-eyed woman who looked Elizabeth up and down and said, "So you are the one who tamed Fitzwilliam Darcy. I did not think it could be done." Elizabeth said she had not tamed him so much as reached an understanding that he was not allowed to bark or bite, and Lady Ashbourne laughed, a dry, crackling sound, and moved on.

Darcy stood beside her and greeted everyone with composed formality. He had been raised to this and while he would never delight in large social gatherings, at least this one was where he felt most comfortable, with the guests of his own choosing. His hand found the small of Elizabeth's back between greetings, a touch that said: I am here. She leaned into it and did not care who noticed.

Lord Matlock stood with Bingley, who was telling him a story that required extensive hand gestures and was making Lord Matlock laugh despite himself. Lady Matlock moved through the guests, steering conversations, making introductions, managing the evening as she had managed evenings for thirty years. She caught Elizabeth's eye across the room and gave her a small nod of approval.

Georgiana danced. She danced the first set with a young man from one of the Derbyshire families whom Lady Matlock had selected for the purpose, and she danced it beautifully, her face flushed, her shyness forgotten in the music. Kitty danced too, radiant in white muslin, pursued by two young men who were competing for her attention with a fervour that she was handling with a dignified grace that made Elizabeth fiercely proud of her little sister. Anne de Bourgh stood at the edge of the ballroom with Clara Ashbourne, the two of them talking quietly. Anne began laughing at something Clara said, her face open and unguarded in a way Elizabeth had never seen from her before.

Lady Catherine was there. She stood near the refreshment tables in her black bombazine, her back to the wall, her face set. She did not approach Darcy or Elizabeth. She spoke to those who spoke to her, and she was civil, because three hundred people were watching and Lady Catherine de Bourgh would not give Elizabeth Darcy the satisfaction of seeing her crumble in public. She was staying for Anne's sake, and everyone in the room knew it, and nobody mentioned it, because that was how these things were done.

Jane watched Elizabeth from across the room and Elizabeth felt the warmth of it. Jane had dressed her. Jane had done her hair, because Elizabeth's maid was competent but Jane was better. Jane had looked at her in the mirror and said, "You look like the mistress of Pemberley." Elizabeth had said, "I look like a woman who has been crying for three hours." Jane had said, "Both can be true," and handed her a cloth soaked in cold-cucumber-water for her eyes.

Bingley was everywhere, delighting everyone, because Bingley's good nature was so infectious. Caroline performed elegance near the pianoforte, her cream silk dress glowing in the candlelight. She had positioned herself where she could be seen to best advantage and was conversing with a knot of local gentlemen with determined charm. She intended to make the evening count, Elizabeth could see. She looked at Darcy several times with her head raised regally, as though willing him to look at her. *See what could have been,* Caroline obviously wanted to tell him. *See what you could have had. I could have been mistress of Pemberley, if only you had not been taken in by a country chit's fine eyes.*

But Darcy never so much as glanced in Caroline's direction.

And the ghosts were there.

Elizabeth saw them the moment she entered the ballroom. Every one of them. The gallery above was packed: spectral figures from every era of Pemberley's history, crowded together, watching. Sarah Dunn stood at attention near the entrance, her scrubbing forgotten, her face bright with excitement. Mr Graves had abandoned his post at the front door and taken up a position at the foot of the staircase to the musicians' gallery, in full livery, as though he were on duty for a ball that had happened several lifetimes ago. Mrs Alcott stood beside him, for once not bickering, the two of them united. The ghost children, Edmund and Charlotte, peered through the gallery railing, wide-eyed. Miss Pardoe had left her library. Elizabeth had not thought that possible. In all the weeks she had been at Pemberley, Miss Pardoe had never once ventured beyond the library door. But here she was, hovering near the entrance to the ballroom, her book still clutched to her chest, looking around at the crowd with a slight smile on her face, as though she was rather enjoying the spectacle.

George Darcy stood at the far end of the ballroom. He was not pacing. He was still, watching his son, his daughter, his house full of light and music. His face was so full of loving pride it hurt Elizabeth's heart that Darcy and Georgiana could not see it.

Nana was beside Elizabeth. She had been beside Elizabeth all evening, a constant presence, and for once she was not criticising. She watched the guests arrive, the dances begin, the supper tables fill. She said, several times, "This is what Pemberley is meant to be."

Elizabeth danced with Darcy. They opened the ball together, as was expected. The musicians played a minuet. Darcy led her through it with the same steady, careful attention he brought to everything. Elizabeth forgot, for the length of one dance, about ghosts, murder, Wickham, Catherine, the strange pressure that had been sitting on her chest all day. She forgot it all. She danced with her husband in a room full of candlelight. Three hundred people watched them and saw what Pemberley's new mistress was: a woman who belonged here, who was worthy of her place. Who loved the man beside her and was loved in return, whose ball was, by any measure, a triumph.

Nana, watching from beside the refreshment table, wiped her eyes with the back of her hand, and if Elizabeth noticed, she had the good grace not to mention it.

The terrace doors opened just as the first dance ended.

Elizabeth did not see them open. She felt them, the rush of cold November air into the warm ballroom, the murmur of the nearest guests as they turned toward the draught. She was standing with Darcy at the edge of the dance floor, still flushed from the minuet, her hand on his arm, and she turned with everyone else.

Wickham walked in.

He was in regimentals, because of course he was, the red coat that had charmed Meryton and dazzled Lydia and hidden the man beneath it from everyone who should have seen the truth. Lydia was on his arm, loud and overdressed in a gown too daring for her age, too bright for the occasion. She was beaming, thrilled with herself, thrilled with her entrance, thrilled to be at Pemberley.

"Surprise!" Lydia said, to nobody in particular and everybody at once. "We came! Wickham said we must come, that Darcy would want us here, and so here we are!"

Elizabeth's hand tightened on Darcy's arm. She felt him go rigid beside her. His jaw locked. His breathing changed.

Then the temperature dropped.

It dropped so fast that Elizabeth's skin prickled and her breath clouded, and the guests nearest the terrace doors shivered and pulled their wraps tighter. The candles nearest the doors guttered, flames bending sideways as though a wind had blown through the room, except there was no wind. The terrace doors were now closed behind Wickham. The cold was not coming from outside.

George Darcy was moving.

Elizabeth saw him cross the ballroom in three swooping, impossibly long strides, and he was behind Wickham, close behind him, so close that if Wickham had been able to feel the dead he would have felt George's breath on his neck. George's face was terrible. Elizabeth had seen his anger before, his grief, his bitter frustration. This was none of those things. This was the face of a man looking at his own murderer, and the hatred in it was so concentrated that the air around him warped, the candle flames nearest him bending away as though repelled.

"George," Elizabeth said. She said it under her breath, barely moving her lips. "George, wait."

He did not hear her. Or he heard her and did not care.

Wickham, oblivious, smiled his charming smile and looked around the ballroom as though it were his own. "Darcy! What a magnificent evening. Pemberley has never looked finer. Your father would have been so proud."

The words landed like a slap. Darcy's arm turned to stone under Elizabeth's hand.

"Such a good man, old Mr Darcy," Wickham continued, shaking hands with a local gentleman. "Practically a father to me. I spent some of the happiest days of my life in this house."

George Darcy was directly behind Wickham. Elizabeth could see his face over Wickham's shoulder. She gripped Darcy's arm harder because the expression on George's face was one she never wanted to see again. Wickham kept talking, kept smiling, kept praising the dead man he had murdered. Elizabeth's nausea surged so violently she nearly bent double.

Jane appeared at her side. Elizabeth did not know where Jane had come from, but she was there, her hand on Elizabeth's elbow, her eyes asking the question she could not ask aloud. Kitty was watching from across the dance floor, her face tight. Georgiana was nearby, staring at Elizabeth with an expression of pure alarm.

Darcy had not moved. He was looking at Wickham with an expression Elizabeth recognised, because she had seen it on his father's face: cold, focused fury, held in check by will alone. He was calculating. Elizabeth could see him doing it: weighing the options, measuring the consequences, deciding whether to throw Wickham out bodily in front of three hundred guests or to wait and deal with him after.

"Not here," Elizabeth said, pressing his arm. "Not in front of everyone."

Darcy looked down at her. His jaw unclenched by a fraction. He nodded.

Wickham, meanwhile, had taken a glass of champagne from a passing footman and was making his way through the room as though he were the guest of honour. Lydia trailed behind him, chattering to anyone who would listen about the regiment and Newcastle and a cottage on the estate where they had been staying with an old friend of Wickham's, and Elizabeth thought: he planned this. He planned to arrive through the terrace doors after the receiving line, so that Darcy could not turn him away at the front door. He came in the back way because he knew he was not welcome and he came anyway, because Wickham always did exactly as he pleased and counted on charm to smooth over the consequences.

"Lizzy," Jane said, very quietly. "What is happening?"

Jane was not asking about Wickham. She knew, already, that Wickham being here was not a good thing. She was talking about what everyone in the room who did not know Wickham was not what he appeared to be could sense. The candles were still guttering. The cold had not receded. Guests were commenting on it now, fanning themselves less and pulling shawls tighter, and the musicians had started the second set but the music sounded thin, the notes not carrying as they should, as though the air itself had thickened.

Every ghost in Pemberley was watching Wickham. Elizabeth could feel it. Sarah Dunn had pressed herself against the wall, her excitement gone, her face white. Graves stood at the foot of the musicians' gallery staircase, rigid, his hands clenched at his sides. Mrs Alcott had retreated to the far corner. Miss Pardoe had fled back to her library, clutching her book like a shield. The ghost children were gone from the gallery railing.

George Darcy followed Wickham through the room, step for step, never more than three feet behind him. The hatred radiating from him bent the candle flames, chilled the air, made Elizabeth's teeth ache.

"Trouble," Elizabeth said quietly to Jane. "I'll try to resolve it."

Jane did not question. She nodded, turned away, called to Bingley cheerfully, trying to break the tension everyone could feel.

"George," Elizabeth said again, under cover of accepting a glass of wine from a footman. "George, please. Let me find another way."

He did not answer. He did not look at her. He looked only at Wickham.

Nana was beside her, small hands clenched into fists.

"I can't hold this," Nana said. "I have been holding it since yesterday, Elizabeth. I have been holding the house, the household, managing George, trying to understand what was wrong. Now I know what was wrong, because that man is here, the man who killed George, standing in this ballroom drinking champagne and smiling. The house knew. Pemberley knew before any of us. The murderer is in the house and every ghost in Pemberley can feel it and I can't hold this much longer."

"You have to," Elizabeth said. "Nana, please. Not here. Not with three hundred people watching."

"I am trying," Nana said, and for the second time in Elizabeth's experience, she looked afraid. "But it is not only me, Elizabeth. It is the house. The house is angry. There are ghosts in this house older than me who do not take orders from anyone."

Of all people, it was Caroline Bingley who caused the tension to break.

She had been watching the evening curdle from her position by the pianoforte. She had been outshone by Elizabeth and ignored by Darcy. The ball was a triumph; none of the triumph was hers. Wickham and Lydia had walked in uninvited, loud, vulgar, impossible to ignore. Caroline saw an opening.

"How extraordinary," Caroline said, to Louisa Hurst, in a voice pitched to carry. "I had not realised the invitation extended to every connection of the Bennet family, however disreputable. One might as well have invited the militia regiment."

Several heads turned, and a few conversations close by quieted. Louisa looked uncomfortable. Caroline did not care. She was angry and humiliated and she wanted someone to bleed, and the Bennet connection to Wickham was the easiest wound available.

"I suppose when one's sister marries a man of no fortune and no character, one must expect him to appear at inconvenient moments," Caroline continued, speaking even more loudly as the silence around her spread. "It is the natural consequence of an imprudent alliance. Mrs Darcy must be mortified, though of course she is too well-bred to show it." The compliment was a knife wrapped in silk, and everyone within earshot knew it.

Nana looked at Caroline Bingley with an expression of such incandescent fury that the candles on the nearest candelabra guttered and went out, all six of them at once, and a footman nearly dropped his tray.

The footman did not drop his tray. But the tray tilted, just slightly, just enough, and a large glass of red wine slid from its surface and poured, in a single spectacular cascade, down the front of Caroline Bingley's cream silk dress.

Caroline screamed.

It was a magnificent scream, high and piercing. It cut through the music, the conversation, the oppressive cold, drew every eye in the ballroom. Louisa Hurst leapt to her feet. A nearby matron produced a handkerchief. Two footmen converged. Caroline stood in Pemberley's ballroom with claret running down her bodice and staining the chalk pattern beneath her feet, and for one glorious, terrible moment, every person in the room was looking at Caroline Bingley and not at the guttering candles or the unnatural cold or the man who had murdered the last master of Pemberley.

Nana, beside Elizabeth, folded her arms.

"She deserved that," Nana said.

Elizabeth could not disagree. It had been a reprieve, a momentary respite of the tension, though it was already fading. Louisa was bundling Caroline toward the door, the footmen were mopping the floor, the guests were turning back to the dancing. But the cold was still there, George Darcy was still following Wickham, the candles still guttering. Elizabeth knew it was only a matter of time.

Elizabeth looked at Darcy. Darcy looked at her. They both knew, though Darcy could not feel what she was feeling, he knew he was not the most furious person in this room at Wickham's presence. Whatever was building in this house, Caroline's scream had bought them minutes, not a solution.

The musicians played on. The guests danced. Pemberley blazed with fury as much as candlelight.

Chapter Twenty-Seven

Jane and Lady Matlock had handled the seating crisis between them by the time the supper room opened. Elizabeth saw the discreet consultation, the swift creation of two new place cards, the rearrangement of existing ones. The result: Wickham and Lydia were seated at the far end of the table, well away from family, bracketed by a local squire's wife on one side and a cheerful, slightly deaf colonel on the other. It was expertly done. Nobody who did not know would have guessed that the places had been created from nothing.

Wickham followed the crowd to supper from the card room, and the candles were finally burning steadily for the first time in an hour. George Darcy followed him, but at a greater distance now. Nana had been at him, Elizabeth suspected. She had seen Nana speaking urgently to George just before supper, and whatever she had said appeared to have had some effect, because George was no longer immediately behind Wickham's shoulder. He stood at the far end of the supper room instead, watching, his face rigid, his hands clenched at his sides. He had tried to harm Wickham, to throttle him or stop his heart from the inside. He had failed; ghosts could not touch the living. The failure had left him more furious than ever.

Elizabeth sat beside Darcy and ate nothing and smiled at everyone who spoke to her.

Lydia chattered happily to the squire's wife, who was too polite to excuse herself. She ate enormously and drank three glasses of wine. She complimented the food, the music, the house, the chalk pattern on the ballroom floor. At one point, between the fish and the meat, she leaned across the table toward Kitty and said, in the carrying voice that was so much like their mother's, "Kitty! Is it not the most wonderful ball? You must come and sit with me after supper, I have so much to tell you about Newcastle, you would not believe the officers..."

Kitty looked at Lydia. Her expression was neutral, polite as she said, "I cannot, Lydia. I am engaged to dance the next set."

"Oh, but after that! We have hardly spoken, Kitty, and I have missed you dreadfully, and there is so much..."

"I have promised all of my sets this evening, I am afraid. I shall have little time to sit and gossip." Kitty's voice was pleasant, firm. She turned back to her conversation with the gentleman beside her. Lydia's face fell for just a moment before the bubble closed over her again; she turned back to the squire's wife with renewed enthusiasm.

Elizabeth watched it happen. Kitty, who had spent her whole childhood in Lydia's orbit, who had been Lydia's shadow and Lydia's echo, had removed herself with quiet, deliberate finality. It was not cruelty. Kitty would not be cruel to Lydia. But she would not be pulled back in, either, and Lydia, for one brief instant, looked forlorn before she remembered that she was Mrs Wickham at a ball and there was no reason in the world to be forlorn.

Elizabeth looked at her youngest sister and thought: She is only sixteen. She is married to a murderer, and she does not know. Whatever happens tonight, I must get her out of this house before she learns it in the worst possible way.

"Jane," Elizabeth said, leaning toward her sister. "After supper, could I ask you to please take Lydia somewhere quiet? Keep her with you."

Jane did not ask why. She nodded.

After supper, the dancing resumed. The musicians struck up a country dance. Guests returned to the ballroom in high spirits, the claret and the conversation having done their work. Elizabeth stood with Darcy at the edge of the floor and watched the sets form, and for a few minutes the ball looked like what it was supposed to be: a celebration, a triumph, three hundred people enjoying the hospitality of Pemberley's new mistress.

Then Wickham came back.

He had been drinking steadily since his arrival, and the claret had done what it does to men who believe themselves charming: it had made him more so, in his own estimation, and less so in everyone else's. He walked through the ballroom loose-limbed, arrogant, as though Pemberley were his own. He stopped to admire the portraits. He paused at the refreshment table to take another glass.

Elizabeth followed him. She did not decide to follow him; her feet moved of their own accord, drawn by a dread she could not name, a certainty that wherever Wickham went in this house tonight, she needed to be near.

Darcy was beside her. He had not left her side since Wickham and Lydia walked through the terrace doors. He could not feel what she felt, could not see what she saw, but he could read her face, and her face was telling him that something was terribly, dreadfully wrong.

George Darcy was three steps behind Wickham. He had not left Wickham's side either. The cold moved with them, a pocket of chill air that trailed Wickham through the warm room. Guests stepped aside without knowing why, drawing their shawls tighter, blaming the draughts. The candles bent and guttered as George passed.

Wickham reached the staircase to the musicians' gallery. It was a narrow wooden stair, steep, curving upward to the balcony where the orchestra played. He stopped at the foot of it and looked up, and Elizabeth saw him smile, the easy, proprietary smile of a man remembering a happy childhood. He had played on these stairs as a boy, she realised. He had run up and down them when George Darcy was alive, the ballroom open, Wickham the favoured godson with the run of the house.

He put his foot on the first step.

"Wickham," Elizabeth said. "Please do not go up there."

He turned. The charming smile was still in place, but his eyes were flat, the way Lydia had described them in her letter. Dead eyes in a handsome face. "Mrs Darcy. Merely admiring the view. One can see the whole ballroom from the gallery. I used to sit up there as a boy and watch the guests below."

Behind Wickham, George Darcy's face was white with fury.

"The gallery is for the musicians," Elizabeth said. "It is not open to guests."

"Surely an exception can be made for an old friend of the family." He turned back to the stairs, climbed, glass in hand. Elizabeth could not stop him without making a scene; she could not make a scene with three hundred people watching, wondering why the mistress of Pemberley was chasing George Wickham up a staircase.

Graves was at the foot of the stairs. He had been there all evening, rigid, fists clenched. As Wickham climbed past him, Graves looked at Elizabeth, and his face held a question she did not know how to answer.

Wickham reached the top. He stood at the railing of the musicians' gallery, looking out over the ballroom, his glass raised, his red coat bright against the dark wood. The musicians had paused between sets. The gallery was empty except for Wickham and the music stands and the guttering candles in their sconces. He looked down at the crowd below and spread his arms, as though embracing the room, as though Pemberley itself had been waiting for him to return.

"Magnificent," he said, to nobody. To everybody. "Truly magnificent. Old Mr Darcy would have loved this."

Elizabeth gripped Darcy's arm. George was at the foot of the stairs, looking up at Wickham. Nana was beside Elizabeth. Every ghost in the ballroom had gone still. Sarah Dunn, Miss Pardoe, Graves, Mrs Alcott, the wispy shades in the gallery above. All of them watching Wickham lean against the railing of the musicians' gallery with his glass of claret and his charming smile.

Then Sir Roderick came through the wall.

He came *roaring*. There was no other word for it. Only one living soul in that room could hear it, but Elizabeth heard it in her bones, in her teeth, in the soles of her feet, and she flinched so hard that Darcy turned to her in alarm.

"Elizabeth? What is it?"

She could not answer. She was staring at the south wall of the ballroom, where Sir Roderick Darcy was emerging. He was enormous. Not tall, not physically large, but enormous in the way that George was solid and Nana was vivid: a presence that filled the space it occupied and pushed everything else aside. His face was a mask of absolute, ungovernable rage, his mouth wide open and the roar that emerged from it was so loud Elizabeth could hear nothing else. He had been asleep for as long as any ghost at Pemberley could remember. He was awake now.

He crossed the ballroom floor in strides that covered impossible distances. The candles did not gutter this time. They went out. Every candle on the south end of the ballroom, twenty or thirty of them, extinguished at once. Guests gasped. Someone dropped a glass. The musicians' gallery candles blew out too, plunging the upper level into shadow. Living guests stumbled aside without knowing why, clutching at their partners, their drinks, their composure. The cold hit like a wall. Elizabeth's teeth chattered. Darcy gripped her hand.

Sir Roderick did not look at Elizabeth. He did not look at Darcy. He did not look at Nana or George or Graves or any of the ghosts who pressed themselves against the walls as he passed. He looked only upward, at the musicians' gallery, at the man who stood at the railing in his red coat with his glass of claret and his dead eyes and his charming smile.

He went up the stairs. The wooden steps creaked under a weight that should not have been there. A living guest standing near the staircase looked down at the steps, frowning; the wood was groaning, yet nobody was on them.

Wickham was still at the railing. He had observed the extinguished candles, the rush of cold air, and his smile had faltered. Not because he could see Sir Roderick, but because the ballroom had gone suddenly cold, dark, and very wrong; even George Wickham, who had no gift, no sensitivity, no conscience, could feel it.

Sir Roderick reached the top of the stairs.

He crossed the gallery in two strides. He stood directly behind Wickham, and Wickham did not see him, but Wickham shivered, and his hand tightened on his glass.

"No," Elizabeth said. She said it aloud. She did not care who heard. "No, stop, please..."

Darcy looked at her. "Elizabeth?"

Sir Roderick put out his hands and *pushed*.

It should not have been possible. Ghosts could not touch the living. The rules were clear, had always been clear, and Elizabeth had understood them since childhood. But Sir Roderick Darcy had been sleeping for longer than anyone could remember. He had been reportedly been an exceptionally disagreeable man in life. He had woken to find his descendant's murderer standing in his ballroom drinking claret, and the rules, apparently, did not apply to him.

Wickham stumbled forward, his foot slipping on the top step which a ghostly maid had spent the whole day diligently polishing, and went over the railing.

He did not fall far. The musicians' gallery was one storey above the ballroom floor, perhaps twelve feet, but the staircase below was narrow and steep, all dark wood and sharp edges. Wickham hit the banister, twisted, fell the rest of the way. His glass shattered. The sound it made was slight, compared to the sound his body made when it hit the ballroom floor, head-first.

Someone screamed. Then someone else. Then the whole room was noise: shouting, chairs scraping, the crowd surging toward and away from the crumpled figure at the foot of the musicians' gallery staircase.

Graves drifted aside, his face blank. He had waited at the foot of those stairs all evening. Nana pressed her hands over her mouth; whether in horror or satisfaction, Elizabeth could not tell. George Darcy stood at the foot of the stairs, looking down at the body of the man who had murdered him. His expression was the same blank mask Darcy wore at Hunsford: processing something shocking, something he did not know how to answer.

Darcy was already moving. He pushed through the crowd, knelt beside Wickham's body. Elizabeth saw him press his fingers to Wickham's neck. She saw his face when he looked up. She knew before he spoke.

"Send for the physician," Darcy said. His voice carried across the silent ballroom. "And clear the room, please. My sincerest apologies, but the ball is over."

The guests left. They left in a confusion of carriages, cloaks, hushed voices: three hundred people who had come to dance, to eat, to judge the new Mrs Darcy, now going home with a different story entirely. A man had fallen from the musicians' gallery. *He had been drinking. The stairs were so steep. A terrible accident. What a dreadful end to such a lovely evening.*

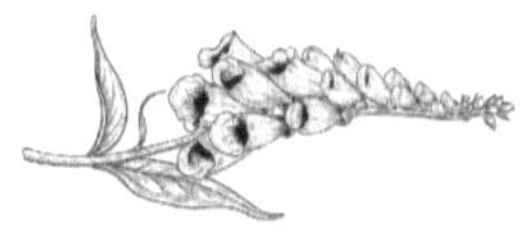

Elizabeth stood in the entrance hall and watched them go. She stood with her face composed, thanking each guest as they left, because she was the mistress of Pemberley; this was her duty. If her voice was steady, her eyes dry, it was because she had no tears left after the afternoon, no composure left to lose.

Jane was with Lydia. Elizabeth had heard the scream when Lydia was told, a raw, animal sound from somewhere deep in the house. Then Kitty's voice, low, steady. Jane's. Then quiet. Kitty had gone to Lydia because despite everything Lydia was still her sister and Kitty would not leave her alone in this. Bingley hovered nearby, trying to help and getting it slightly wrong but meaning every word of comfort he offered, which was Bingley's way and always had been.

Lord Matlock managed the physician when he arrived, and the removal of the body, and the dozen practical matters that attend a sudden death in a great house. Lady Matlock managed the guests who were staying overnight up to their rooms without delay. Mrs Reynolds managed the servants, who were deeply shaken.

The last carriage pulled away. The entrance hall emptied. The candles that had guttered, blown out, had been relit. The ballroom glowed again, warm, golden, as though nothing had happened. The chalk pattern on the floor was scuffed and stained, the white curlicues smudged by three hundred pairs of feet and one man's blood. The lilies by the entrance still smelled sweet.

Darcy found Elizabeth in the hallway outside the ballroom. She was leaning against the wall, her eyes closed, her ball gown creased and her hair coming down from the pins Jane had set so carefully. He stood before her, looking at her face. She opened her eyes. Looked back at him.

He knew, she could see it in his eyes. Not the details, of course. Not Sir Roderick, not the push, not the army of spectral Darcys and their loyal-even-after-death retainers who had watched their house deliver its own justice. But he knew that what had happened on that staircase was not an accident, that Elizabeth had seen it, and he knew that she would tell him, because she had promised that he could ask her anything and she would keep no more secrets from him.

"He fell," Elizabeth said.

"He fell," Darcy agreed.

"The physician will say he was drunk. The stairs are steep, and they had been well-polished, to look good for the ball. It will be ruled an accident."

"Yes."

"It wasn't an accident."

Darcy was quiet for a moment. The hallway was empty. The house was quiet, quieter than Elizabeth had ever known it. Even the ghosts were still. Graves had returned to the servants' hall. Mrs Alcott had gone with him. Sarah Dunn had vanished. The gallery above was empty.

"My father," Darcy said, and she heard something like fear in his voice. "Was it..."

"No. Your father was on the ballroom floor the whole time. He was standing beside me. He watched, but he did not act. It was Sir Roderick."

"Sir Roderick?" Darcy blinked, and she could see him searching his memory. "I know that name..."

Elizabeth pressed the back of her head against the wall. "He was Nana's husband's great-grandfather, or maybe one or two more greats than that, who was master of Pemberley in the time of Queen Elizabeth. He'd been asleep in the yellow drawing room for as long as anyone can remember. Nana was afraid of what would happen if he ever woke up."

"And he woke."

"He woke. He came into the ballroom, went up the stairs, pushed Wickham over the railing. I didn't think ghosts could touch the living. They can't, as a rule. Sir Roderick isn't a ghost who follows rules."

Darcy leaned against the wall beside her. They stood shoulder to shoulder, both of them exhausted, both of them in their ball clothes, both of them carrying a truth that would never be spoken aloud again after tonight.

"Wickham's death mirrors his crime," Elizabeth said, after a long silence. "It looks natural. Accidental. A man who had been drinking, slipping on a steep staircase. Only we know the truth."

"Only we will ever know."

"Can you live with that?"

Darcy opened his eyes. He looked at her. "Can you?"

Elizabeth thought about it. She had said *no, stop, please* and it had made no difference, because Sir Roderick did not take orders from anyone. She had watched a man die and she had not been able to prevent it and she was not entirely certain, in the darkest, most honest part of herself, that she had wanted to.

"I don't know," she said. "I think I can. I will have to, won't I?"

Darcy took her hand. He held it against the wall between them, his fingers laced through hers.

"Then we carry it together," he said. "The way we carry everything else." He leaned over and kissed her brow, tenderly. "Go to bed, Elizabeth. Sleep. I will stay up and wait for the doctor."

The house was quiet around them. Somewhere in Pemberley, Lydia was crying. In the yellow drawing room, Sir Roderick Darcy had gone back to his chair, closed his eyes, and slept.

Chapter Twenty-Eight

THE MORNING AFTER THE ball, Pemberley was quiet.

Elizabeth came down early, before anyone except the servants, and found the ballroom doors closed and a maid on her knees in the entrance hall, scrubbing the chalk dust that had been tracked across the marble floor. The house smelled of extinguished candles and lilies. The scuffed chalk pattern was still visible through the open ballroom door when Elizabeth pushed it ajar to look: white curlicues smudged and broken, the stain near the musicians' gallery staircase dark against the pale wood.

Mrs Reynolds was already up, because Mrs Reynolds was always up. She met Elizabeth with a look that asked several questions at once.

"How is Mrs Wickham?" Elizabeth asked a question of her own before Mrs Reynolds could begin.

"Sleeping, ma'am. Miss Bennet and Mrs Bingley are with her. She woke twice in the night and was distressed, but Miss Bennet settled her both times."

Kitty, who had spent her childhood being dismissed as the silly sister, the one who followed Lydia, the one nobody expected anything of. Kitty, sitting up all night with the sister she had quietly outgrown, holding her through a grief that was real even if the man Lydia was grieving for did not deserve it. Elizabeth's throat tightened.

"And the physician's report?"

"Dr Grieve attended and confirmed the death. He has recorded the cause as a fall, exacerbated by the consumption of alcohol. He noted the steepness of the staircase and the polish on the wood." Mrs Reynolds paused. "He did not indicate that he found anything unusual."

"Thank you, Mrs Reynolds."

Elizabeth went to the morning room, where she sat in the cold November light, drank the tea Mrs Reynolds brought her personally, tried to feel something other than exhausted. She had slept, a little, but not until Darcy finally came to bed. He had put his arms around her, held her in the dark. She had pressed her face against his chest and slept the way a person sleeps after a battle: deeply, dreamlessly, not nearly long enough.

Lady Catherine left Pemberley at ten o'clock.

Her carriage was brought to the front door. Her trunks were loaded. Mrs Jenkinson fluttered in attendance. Catherine descended the staircase in her black bombazine, her face a mask, her back rigid, and she spoke to no one on the way down except Lord Matlock, who was waiting in the entrance hall with the expression he always wore when dealing with his sister: patience stretched to its thinnest point.

"I shall write," Catherine said.

"I do not doubt it," Lord Matlock replied.

Anne stood at the foot of the stairs. She was pale. She had been crying, Elizabeth thought, though she had cleaned her face carefully and her composure was intact. She looked at her mother. Catherine looked at her daughter. The silence between them held years of love, of damage, a chasm that might or might not be bridgeable.

"Goodbye, Mother," Anne said.

Catherine opened her mouth. Closed it. She reached out, touched Anne's cheek briefly with the tips of her gloved fingers. Then she turned, walked out the front door, got into her carriage. She did not look back.

The carriage pulled away down the drive. Anne watched it go until it rounded the bend, disappeared behind the trees. Then she turned, walked past Elizabeth without a word, went up to her room. Elizabeth let her go. Some griefs required company. Others required solitude. Anne would know the difference for herself.

Caroline Bingley departed an hour later, subdued. Louisa Hurst accompanied her, and Mr Hurst followed, having been roused from a comfortable chair in the card room where he had apparently slept through Wickham's death, the evacuation of the ballroom, and the arrival of the physician. He looked bewildered. Nobody explained anything to him. He got in the carriage and went, destined for the inn at Lambton for a few days, because Pemberley did not need guests who required entertaining at this time.

Bingley stayed. Jane stayed. The Matlocks stayed. And Lydia slept, because Kitty had persuaded her to take laudanum in the small hours of the morning, and she would sleep until the afternoon.

Georgiana found Elizabeth in the parlour after luncheon. Elizabeth was at her writing desk, composing a letter to her father that she would have to write three times before it said what it needed to say without saying what it could not. She set down her pen when Georgiana came in and closed the door.

Georgiana sat in the chair by the fire. She looked composed, but her hands were folded in her lap the way they always were when she was controlling herself.

"I need to ask you something," she said. "About last night."

"It was not a natural fall," Elizabeth admitted, knowing what Georgiana meant.

"Was it my father?"

Elizabeth met her eyes. "No. Your father was on the ballroom floor the whole time. He was standing beside me. He watched, Georgiana, but he did not act."

Georgiana's breath came out in a rush. She had been holding it, Elizabeth realised. She had been carrying that question since last night, afraid of the answer, afraid that her father's ghost had killed a man in front of three hundred people and that the closure he had wanted for six years had come in a form that was vengeance rather than justice.

"Then who?"

"Sir Roderick Darcy. A distant ancestor of yours. He has been asleep in the yellow drawing room for as long as anyone can remember. Nana warned me that if he ever woke, she did not know what he would do. He woke. He did what he did. And then he went back to his chair and went back to sleep."

Georgiana stared at her. "He is asleep? After that?"

"He is asleep. I checked this morning. He is in his chair, exactly as he has always been, as though nothing happened."

"Can we... should we... is there anything to be done about him?"

"I don't think so. Nana has managed this house for a hundred and thirty years without Sir Roderick's involvement, and I intend to do the same. He sleeps. We let him sleep. And we hope nothing ever wakes him again."

Georgiana was quiet for a moment. Then she said, "Darcy told me that Wickham and Lydia had been staying on the estate since the day before the ball, with a friend of Wickham's who has one of the cottages near the north wood."

"That is why the house was unsettled," Elizabeth said. She had worked it out herself, lying in the dark waiting for Darcy, putting the pieces together. The vibration in the stone that had started two days ago. The ghosts growing agitated. Graves abandoning his ball preparations to stand guard at the front door. Nana's fear. The nausea Elizabeth had fought all day. Pemberley had *known*. The estate was more than the house. Wickham had been on Pemberley land, sleeping in a Pemberley cottage, and the house had felt the presence of the man who murdered its former master like a poison in the soil. The ghosts had not known what they were feeling. They had only known that their home was wrong.

"Pemberley knew before any of us did," Elizabeth said. "The house, the estate, felt him."

Georgiana took this in and considered it. She was Darcy's sister. She processed things the way Darcy did: carefully, thoroughly, turning them over before she committed to a response.

"Is my father at peace now?" she asked. "Now that Wickham is dead?"

"I don't know," Elizabeth said. "I haven't seen him this morning. But I will find him, Georgiana. And I will tell you."

Elizabeth found George in the long gallery, alone; Edmund and Charlotte tended to make themselves scarce when he was there, and today was no exception.

George was not pacing. He was standing at the window where Darcy had stood the evening before the ball, looking out at the south lawn and the lake beyond, and when Elizabeth came in he did not turn. She walked the length of the gallery and stood beside him, and for a while neither of them spoke.

"It is done," George said. His voice was quiet. Not the restless, driving voice she had come to know. Empty, almost.

"It is done," Elizabeth agreed.

"I have wanted to kill him for six years, and when I saw him walk into my house in that red coat, I wanted it so badly I could taste it. But I could not. I did not kill him."

"I know. I saw you. You were beside me the whole time."

"Sir Roderick." George shook his head, slowly. "I did not know he could do that. None of us knew. He has been asleep since he became a ghost, so far as any of us knows. Nana spoke of him sometimes, always with a note of caution. She said he had a reputation for being disagreeable. She did not say he was capable of..."

"Nana did not know either."

George was quiet again. The grey November light fell through the window and through his spectral form, casting no shadow.

"Elizabeth," he said. "I think I am ready."

She had been expecting it. She could feel it in the quality of his presence: a lightness, a thinning, as though the solidity that had kept him tethered to the house was dissolving. The rage that had held him here for six years was spent.

The justice he had demanded had been delivered, not by the law, not by his son, but by his ancestor, rising up to punish the man who had poisoned his descendant. It was not the justice George had imagined, she was sure. But it was enough.

"Not yet," Elizabeth said. "Please. Let me bring Darcy. Let me bring Georgiana. You can't go without saying goodbye."

George looked at her. His face was gentle in a way she had not seen before.

"Hurry," he said. "I do not think I have long."

Elizabeth ran. She ran through the gallery, down the corridor, found Darcy in the study. "Your father. Now. The gallery. He's going." Darcy stood up from his desk without a word and followed her. She sent a maid for Georgiana with a message that said only *Gallery, now, please hurry*, and by the time they reached the long gallery George was still there, still at the window, but fainter.

"He's here," Elizabeth said. "By the window. He is... he is fading, Darcy. He does not have much time."

Darcy turned to the window. Georgiana arrived, breathless. Elizabeth took her hand, positioned her beside her brother. The three of them stood before the window where George Darcy had spent so many hours watching the grounds he could not leave.

"Tell them," George said. His voice was fading too. "Tell Fitzwilliam that I am more proud of him than I ever managed to say in life. Tell him he was right about Wickham, and I was wrong, and the greatest regret of my death is that I did not listen to my own son when he tried to tell me the truth. Tell him that the way he has cared for this family, for Georgiana, for Pemberley, has been everything I could have hoped for and more than I deserved."

Elizabeth spoke his words. Darcy listened, his jaw tight, his eyes bright, and he did not look away from the place where his father stood.

"Tell Georgiana," George said, and his voice cracked, "that she has her mother's courage, her beauty, her heart.

That I have watched her grow into a woman Annie would have been proud of, and I am sorry, I am so sorry, that I was not there to see it in life."

Elizabeth repeated this too. Georgiana's face was wet, but she was smiling through it, a fierce, broken smile that was more Darcy than Darcy.

"And tell them both," George said, "that their mother is waiting for me. I can feel her. She has been waiting for six years, and I have kept her waiting long enough."

Elizabeth's voice broke on the last sentence. She got the words out, just. Darcy reached for Georgiana's hand. Georgiana gripped it. They stood together, brother and sister, facing the window where their father was fading into the November light.

George looked Elizabeth full in the face one last time, and he said one more thing, for her alone.

"Thank you, Mrs Darcy."

She could not speak, but she curtsied, deeply and respectfully, the way she would have curtsied to her husband's father if she had been presented to him while he was still alive.

George Darcy looked past Elizabeth. Past Darcy. Past Georgiana. Past the window and the grounds and the grey sky. He looked at something Elizabeth could not see, and his face changed. All of the grief, the rage, dissolved. What was left was pure, uncomplicated joy. He said, in a tone of utter delight:

"Annie?"

He was gone. The gallery was empty.

Nana stood in the doorway. Elizabeth did not know how long she had been there. She said nothing, her small hands clasped before her, looking at the place where George had been. After a moment she straightened her cap, turned, and left. There was a household to run, and Nana had kept herself busy doing it for a hundred and thirty years.

Elizabeth wept. Darcy put his arm around her, held her. Georgiana pressed against her brother's side. The three of them stood in the gallery, grieving together: for the man they had lost, the man they had found, the woman who had been waiting for him on the other side.

Anne de Bourgh found Elizabeth later that afternoon, in the rose garden.

Elizabeth had gone out because she needed air, needed sky, needed to be somewhere that was not inside Pemberley's walls. The rose garden was bare for winter, the beds turned and mulched, the stems cut back to dark stubs. Lady Margaret smiled from her bench, as she always did. The November cold bit through Elizabeth's pelisse, but she did not care. She sat on the stone bench opposite Lady Margaret, watching the lady in the Tudor gown with its stiff ruff, its panniered skirts. She wondered what Lady Margaret's life had been like, married to Sir Roderick.

Perhaps there were excellent reasons why Lady Margaret's ghost never went inside Pemberley.

Anne came down the path from the house, wrapped in a shawl, her thin face pinched by the cold. She sat beside Elizabeth without asking permission, which was new. The old Anne would have asked. The old Anne had asked permission for everything.

They sat in silence for a while. Then Anne said, quietly, "Elizabeth. May I ask you something? You need not answer if you would rather not."

"You may ask me anything."

"My mother said a great many things about you, these past weeks. Most of them were unkind, and wrong, and I did not believe them." Anne paused. "But some of what she described, the talking to empty rooms, the knowing things you should not know... they were not wrong. I have watched you too, Elizabeth. Not to gather evidence.

Because I was curious. And I have come to my own conclusion, which is quite different from my mother's."

Elizabeth waited.

"Did you chance to see my father at Rosings?" Anne asked. "When you visited with Mr and Mrs Collins?"

Elizabeth looked at her. Anne looked back, steady, unafraid, and Elizabeth saw Lady Catherine's intelligence in those eyes, stripped of Lady Catherine's malice.

"I did not," Elizabeth said. She could be honest about this, completely honest, and the relief of it was sweet. "Rosings, despite being old, is a quiet house. I believe your father moved on peacefully. George Darcy told me once that Sir Lewis was a good man, a happy one, and that he loved you very much. I think he had no reason to linger."

Anne's face did a complicated thing. Relief and grief and a small, private loss, all at once. She had hoped, perhaps, that her father was still there, still watching, the way George had watched over Darcy and Georgiana. And she had hoped, perhaps equally, that he was not: that he had been spared the long, trapped purgatory of Pemberley's ghosts, that he was at peace.

"Thank you," Anne said. "For telling me honestly."

"How did you know?"

Anne smiled. It was a small, careful smile, the smile of a dragon's daughter who had learned discretion from watching her mother fail at it. "My mother built her case from suspicion and spite. I built mine from observation and logic. You are not mad, Elizabeth. You are extraordinary. And I will keep your counsel as long as you need me to."

She stood, pulled her shawl tighter, walked back up the path to the house. Elizabeth sat in the rose garden with Lady Margaret's spectral smile for company and thought: *That girl is going to be far more formidable than her mother ever was.*

That evening, Elizabeth and Darcy sat together in their sitting room, the fire burning low. Georgiana and Anne had gone to bed. Kitty was with Lydia. Jane and Bingley had discreetly retired, and the Matlocks were in their rooms. The house was quiet, and for the first time in weeks, the quiet felt like rest rather than threat.

"Lydia will need care," Elizabeth said finally. "She is a widow at sixteen. She will need a home, at Longbourn or with us. She will need time, patience, people who love her despite everything."

"She will have it. I have already written to your father."

"You have?"

"This morning. I told him what happened, the public version. I said Lydia should return home to Longbourn as soon as she is well enough to travel, because I believe she needs her mother more than anything else at this time, and that I would provide whatever she needs."

Elizabeth looked at him. This man, who had spent the previous day learning his wife could see ghosts, that his father had been murdered, then watching the murderer killed by an ancestor who had been sleeping for centuries, had got up this morning and written a practical, kind letter to her father about looking after Lydia.

"I love you," she said, and it was not the awkward blurt of yesterday, but it was no less honest.

His eyes warmed, and he leaned down to kiss her. "I love you too, Mrs Darcy," he murmured against her lips.

"What do we do now?" she asked, after a few quite satisfactory moments had passed.

"We live our lives," Darcy said. "We take care of Georgiana, Anne, Kitty and Lydia. We let the world believe Wickham fell because he was drunk, and we carry the truth between us, and we do not let it poison what we have built."

Elizabeth leaned against his shoulder. The fire burned. The house settled around them, and for the first time since she had arrived at Pemberley, the settling felt like contentment.

"Your father is at peace," she said. "Lady Anne was waiting for him. He said her name, just before he went, and his face..." She stopped, because the memory of George's face in that last moment, the joy on it, was still too raw to describe without crying, and she had cried enough. "He is with her now. After sixteen years, he is with her."

Darcy was quiet for a few moments, grief and joy warring on his face as he absorbed what she had just said. Then he said, "Good," and kissed the top of her head. They sat together in the firelight. Pemberley held them. The dead rested. The living carried on.

Chapter
Twenty-Nine

THREE DAYS AFTER THE ball, the Bingleys left for Netherfield, taking Lydia with them.

It had been Jane's idea. Lydia would not go to Longbourn just yet; she was too fragile, and Jane and Elizabeth agreed that Mrs Bennet's particular brand of hysterical sympathy would do her more harm than good. Netherfield was quieter, Jane was steady, and Lydia needed steady more than she needed anything else. Kitty went with them. She hadn't left Lydia's side in three days, and she wouldn't leave her now. She would rejoin the Darcy party when they went to London for the Season, in the spring.

Elizabeth stood on the front steps of Pemberley and watched the carriage pull away until it finally vanished into the trees.

The Matlocks had left the previous day, Lord Matlock promising to make enquiries about the inquest, which would be a formality, and Lady Matlock promising to write. Anne remained. She would stay at Pemberley with Georgiana until they left for London, and she would have the life her mother had never permitted her to want. Elizabeth intended to make sure of it. Mrs Annesley was returning in a few days from her visit with her sister, and would have the two girls well in hand.

Pemberley was quiet. The house party was over. The ball gowns had been put away, the ballroom floor scrubbed clean of chalk, spilled wine, blood. The musicians' gallery staircase had been inspected by Mrs Reynolds and two carpenters, who pronounced the banister sound, the wood in good repair; they could not account for why a man should have fallen. They recommended a rail be added at the top of the stairs, and Darcy agreed, and that was the end of it.

Elizabeth walked through the house.

She walked slowly, the way she had walked on her first day as mistress of Pemberley, though everything was different now. The entrance hall was quiet, the marble floor clean. Graves was back at his station near the foot of the staircase, livery immaculate, his composure restored. He inclined his head as Elizabeth passed, and she inclined hers back, and neither of them mentioned the ball.

The library was warm. Miss Pardoe was in her chair, reading, as she had been reading for sixty years. She did not look up. Elizabeth had not expected her to. Miss Pardoe had ventured out of the library once, for the ball, and would probably not do so again for another sixty years, and that suited both of them.

The yellow drawing room was still. Sir Roderick slept in his chair, wigged head tilted to one side, exactly as he had been for as long as anyone could remember. Elizabeth paused in the doorway and looked at him. He did not stir. He would not stir, she hoped, ever again. She moved past quietly, and closed the door behind her, gently, and went on.

The long gallery was empty. The November light fell through the tall windows onto the floor where George Darcy had paced, raging, waiting for someone who could hear him. The air was still now. There was no cold spot, no pressure, no restless presence wearing a track in the floorboards. George was gone, and the gallery knew it, and the emptiness was not sad. It was peaceful. It was the peace of a room that has served its purpose and can rest.

Edmund and Charlotte were back. They ran past Elizabeth with cheerful waves, chasing each other through the gallery, their laughter bright and thin in the November air. The gallery was theirs again, and they were making the most of it.

The servants' hall was occupied. Mrs Alcott was berating Graves about the silver after the ball. The polishing had been inadequate, she said. The fish forks were a disgrace. Graves said the fish forks were perfectly acceptable; Mrs Alcott would not know a properly polished fish fork if it materialised in her spectral hand. Mrs Alcott said she had been polishing silver since before Graves was born, which was true, given that she had died during the reign of Queen Anne while he was merely Georgian. Graves said that was precisely the problem: standards had clearly been different in her day. Elizabeth walked past them, smiling. Neither of them noticed, because they were far too busy being furious with each other to pay attention to the living.

Sarah Dunn was dusting. She was on the upstairs landing, dusting behind the clock she insisted the new housemaid never dusted properly, and she looked up when Elizabeth passed and gave her a small, shy wave. Elizabeth waved back.

Elizabeth touched the wall as she walked. The stone was warm beneath her fingers, the warmth of a house at rest: four hundred years of stone, of timber, of the lives that had filled it, settled, content, holding the people within it safe and sound.

She reached her parlour and sat down at her writing desk. The parlour was quiet, and the candle did not flicker. The temperature did not shift. For the first time since she had walked through Pemberley's front door, the house was simply a house: beautiful, old, full of ghosts, and entirely at peace.

She sat for perhaps five minutes, enjoying the silence, before Nana cleared her throat.

Elizabeth looked up. Nana was in her chair. Arms folded. Chin raised. The expression on her face was the one she wore when she had decided it was time to discuss a matter of importance.

"You did quite well," Nana said. "All things considered."

"Thank you, Nana."

"The ball was excellent. The supper was adequate. The chalk pattern was, I will admit, rather fine. The wine incident with Miss Bingley was unfortunate, for her, though I do not regret it. And the business with Sir Roderick was... unforeseeable."

"That is one word for it."

"I have others, but they are not suitable for a lady's parlour." Nana unfolded her arms and folded them again, which meant she was working up to something. Elizabeth waited. Nana was not to be rushed.

"I am not going anywhere," Nana said. "In case you were wondering."

"I wasn't wondering. I know better than to expect you to leave."

"Good. Because my work is not finished." Nana looked at Elizabeth, and then she dropped her gaze deliberately to Elizabeth's stomach.

Elizabeth's hand went to her belly. She had not... she had not thought... but now that Nana had looked, now that the question was in the air, she counted back, and the counting took longer than it should have, and the answer at the end of it made her breath catch.

"Oh," she said.

"Indeed," Nana said. "Oh."

"How long have you known?"

"Since before you did, which is the natural order of things. I have seen a great many pregnancies in this house, Elizabeth, and the signs are quite unmistakable to a woman of my experience. You have been nauseous for days. You attributed it to the ball, to the house being unsettled, and you were not entirely wrong about the latter. But I have been watching you. The nausea preceded the unsettlement, and I know the difference between a woman who is anxious and a woman who is with child."

Elizabeth sat staring at Nana in shock, her hand on her stomach. She thought about the nausea she had blamed on Pemberley's restlessness, the food she had not been able to eat, the exhaustion that had pressed her down for days. She had thought it was the house. She had thought it was the ghosts, the investigation, the ball, the dread.

Some of it had been. But not all of it.

"I am going to be a great-great-great-grandmother," Nana said. She did not smile, because Nana did not smile when she could look satisfied instead, but her satisfaction was so complete it filled the room. "Which is the entire point. My mission, Elizabeth, such as it is, has always been to see enough of my descendants safely into the world that I need not worry about the line continuing. I have been here for a hundred and thirty years and none of my descendants have managed more than one child or at best two." Her expression grew, if anything, even more pointed.

"How many descendants, exactly, do you think would be a safe number?" Elizabeth asked. Her voice sounded strange to her own ears.

"I have really never considered that. I am not setting a number. I am merely saying that Pemberley needs its heirs, and I intend to be here to see that they are properly looked after."

Elizabeth looked at Nana. Nana looked back, implacable, eternal, a hundred and thirty years old and not one inch closer to moving on.

"You are going to haunt my children," Elizabeth said.

"I am going to ensure your children are raised correctly. There is a difference."

Elizabeth thought about arguing. She thought about pointing out that Nana had not, by her own frequent admission, always approved of how the intervening Darcys had been raised, and that her track record was therefore imperfect. She thought about reminding Nana that the living mistress of Pemberley was, in fact, Elizabeth, and that she and Darcy would raise their children as they saw fit.

She did not say any of these things. She would say them later. Nana would ignore them. They would argue about nursery arrangements, feeding schedules, whether the child should be taught to ride at three or four, and it would be exactly like every other argument Elizabeth had with Nana: fierce, exhausting, conducted with deep mutual affection that neither of them would ever admit to.

"I need to tell Darcy," Elizabeth said.

"Yes, you do. I shall leave you to it. Though I do think you ought to know that the east-wing nursery has the best light in the mornings and the warmest fires, and I have already put the thought into Mrs Reynolds' mind that she should start looking to the nursery linens."

"*Nana*. I've known for *two minutes*."

"And I have known for considerably longer, and I do not waste time. The linens are being aired. You may thank me later."

Nana rose from her chair, gave Elizabeth one last look of profound satisfaction, and drifted through the bookcase.

Elizabeth sat at her desk, with her hand on her stomach. She sat there for a long time, in the quiet parlour, wondering if the warmth in the walls was because Pemberley knew an heir was coming.

Then she went to find Darcy, because if Nana knew that meant all the other ghosts would know, and it was quite unfair that Darcy should be so far down the list of those who knew.

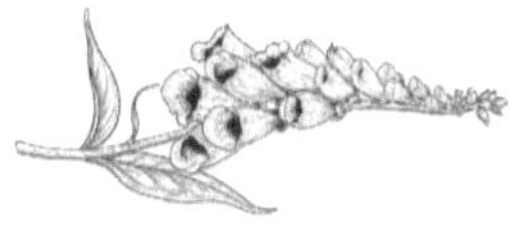

He was in the study, at his desk, dealing with some correspondence. He looked up when she came in. She closed the door behind her. He must have seen something in her face, because he set down his pen and rose to his feet.

"Elizabeth?"

"Nana has just informed me," Elizabeth said, "that she is not going anywhere. Her mission, as she describes it, is to see enough Darcy descendants safely into the world that she need not worry about the family line. She says she's been here for a hundred and thirty years; she intends to see our first child born and properly looked after. She will not set a number of Darcys who will be sufficient. I think it possible there will never be a sufficient number, and she will haunt Pemberley forever. But at least our child will have a most devoted guardian."

Darcy looked at her. His gaze dropped to where her hand rested on her waist, and she watched him draw the correct conclusion.

He let out a shout of laughter. It was the most startling sound Elizabeth had ever heard from Fitzwilliam Darcy: loud, unguarded, joyful, a sound that belonged to a man who had just survived the worst week of his life and then been handed the best news of it. He laughed, came around the desk, took her face in his hands and kissed her.

"We had better keep Nana happy," he said, against her mouth.

"She has already convinced Mrs Reynolds the nursery linens need to be aired; I had the sense not to inquire exactly how."

He laughed again. Then he took her hand and led her through the house to their bedroom, and Pemberley's ghosts, who had opinions about everything, kept their opinions to themselves for once.

Later, in the quiet of the afternoon, Elizabeth walked through the house again.

She walked slowly. She touched the walls as she passed, and the stone was warm, and the house hummed, very faintly, but not with dread or anger or the unsettled vibration of the days before the ball. It hummed the way a house hums when it is content: the creak of old timbers, the whisper of air through windows that had seen four centuries of weather, the distant sound of servants going about their work. There was a sense of anticipation, too, for the new heir. Life, continuing.

Graves was at his post in the hall. Mrs Alcott was in the kitchens, arguing with nobody about the proper storage of preserves. Sarah Dunn was dusting. Edmund and Charlotte were in the gallery, laughing. Miss Pardoe was reading. Lady Margaret was smiling in the rose garden. Sir Roderick slept.

Elizabeth paused in the entrance hall and looked up at the painted ceiling, the way she had on her first visit to Pemberley, that summer afternoon with the Gardiners when she had come as a tourist and tried not to think too hard about the man who owned it. She had looked up at the ceiling and she had been impressed, and Nana, watching from somewhere, had decided she would do.

She was still looking up when Nana's voice came from behind her.

"Mrs Reynolds wishes me to tell you," Nana said, "though of course she does not know I am telling you, that the kitchen maid, Ellen, has been making eyes at the under-gardener, Thomas. She does not approve. I do not approve either. The under-gardener is a perfectly decent young man, but the kitchen maid is needed in the kitchen. If she marries him she will leave service, and Mrs Reynolds has spent a year training her; she does not wish to start again. Ellen is too young to be making such momentous decisions. Another three years at least, Mrs Reynolds thinks."

"*Nana*. I have just received the most significant news of my life, and you wish to discuss the kitchen maid?"

"The kitchen maid is an immediate concern. The heir is not due for months." Nana folded her arms. "Priorities, Elizabeth."

Elizabeth looked at Nana. Nana looked at Elizabeth, and raised one imperious, ghostly eyebrow.

"I'll speak to Mrs Reynolds," Elizabeth said.

"See that you do. And while you are about it, the fire in the yellow drawing room is smoking again. Sir Roderick does not notice, because he is asleep, but the living guests will notice, and I will not have Pemberley's fireplaces smoking when there are people in the house."

"There are no guests in the house, Nana. They have all gone."

"Miss de Bourgh is still here. Standards do not slip because the audience is small."

Elizabeth took a breath. She let it out. She looked around the entrance hall of her home: the marble floor, the staircase, the portraits, the ghost of a mistress who wouldn't rest, the spectral servants who didn't know how to stop serving, the house that held them all, living and dead, in its ancient embrace.

Pemberley would never be silent. Elizabeth would never be alone in it. The dead would always be here, bickering, dusting, reading, sleeping, offering opinions she had not asked for about matters she was perfectly capable of handling herself.

She would not have it any other way.

"I'll see to the chimney, Nana, and about the kitchen-maid," Elizabeth said. She went to find Mrs Reynolds, and Pemberley hummed contentedly around her, warm and waiting for its new heir.

Also By Catherine Bilson

The Blushing Brides Series

An Earl For Ellen
A Marquis For Marianne
A Duke For Diana
A Captain For Clarissa

The Bookshop Belles series (co-written with Ebony Oaten)

Estelle's Ardent Admirer
Marie's Merry Gentleman
Louise's Christmas Champion
Bernadette's Dashing Doctor
Matthew's Willing Widow(exclusive gift for newsletter subscribers)

The Brides of Belle Haven series

A Bride For Belle Haven (prequel novella)
Good Golly, Miss Molly
Miss Clara and the Marquess
Miss Anna's Mistake
Miss Eliza Takes The Reins
Miss Charlotte Makes A Mess
Miss Laura In Love
Miss Louise Meddles

Regency Novels

His Darling Duchess

Phoebe And The Pea
Kidnapping Lord Blaymire
The Captain's Runaway Bride
The Wassail Wager
The Bride Said No
St. George and the River Horse (exclusive for newsletter subscribers)

Christmas Courting (collection of novellas)

American Pioneer Romance

Coming From California
Returning From Rhode Island

Pride & Prejudice Variations

The Best Of Relations
Infamous Relations
Mr Bingley's Bride
A Christmas Miracle At Longbourn
Grief and Grievances
The Second Mrs. Bennet
A Loss At Longbourn
The Meddling Matlocks
Possession and Prejudice
Lydia and the Colonel
The Ghosts of Pemberley
The Secret Diary of Anne de Bourgh (forthcoming)

The Crime & Consequences Trilogy

Malice and Misfortune
Rivalry and Ruination
Intrigue and Inheritance

Follow us on Facebook or Instagram, or

<u>sign up to the Shenanigans Press newsletter to find out about our latest new releases!</u>

www.ingramcontent.com/pod-product-compliance
Lightning Source LLC
Chambersburg PA
CBHW032044050726
47590CB00001B/130